DEATH
ON THE
LUSITANIA

DEATH
ON THE
LUSITANIA

R. L. Graham

MACMILLAN

First published 2024 by Macmillan
an imprint of Pan Macmillan
The Smithson, 6 Briset Street, London EC1M 5NR
EU representative: Macmillan Publishers Ireland Ltd, 1st Floor,
The Liffey Trust Centre, 117–126 Sheriff Street Upper,
Dublin 1, D01 YC43
Associated companies throughout the world
www.panmacmillan.com

ISBN 978-1-0350-2191-8 HB
ISBN 978-1-0350-3664-6 TPB

1 3 5 7 9 8 6 4 2

A CIP catalogue record for this book is available from the British Library.

Deck plan by Hemesh Alles

Typeset in Janson Text by Jouve (UK), Milton Keynes
Printed and bound by CPI Group (UK) Ltd, Croydon, CR0 4YY

Visit **www.panmacmillan.com** to read more about all our books
and to buy them. You will also find features, author interviews and
news of any author events, and you can sign up for e-newsletters
so that you're always first to hear about our new releases.

Dedicated to the memory of Dr Marilyn Livingstone, scholar, musician and writer, one half of R. L. Graham and co-author of this book, who died of cancer on 10 September 2023. Her memory will live on in her many books, her beautiful music, and her loving family and friends.

On 7 May 1915, the British liner RMS Lusitania was sunk by a German U-boat off the coast of Ireland. A single torpedo strike was followed by a mysterious second explosion, and the ship sank with the loss of nearly twelve hundred lives. This story is a re-imagining of that fateful journey. With the exception of Captain William Turner, all the characters who appear in this book are fictional.

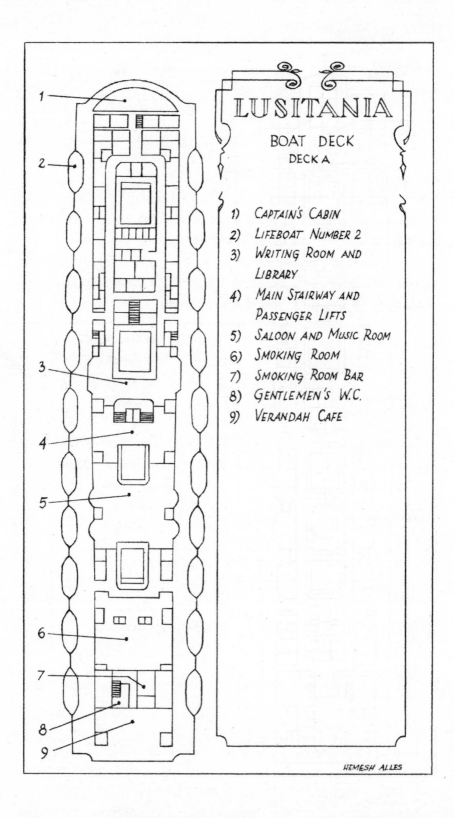

LUSITANIA

BOAT DECK
DECK A

1) Captain's Cabin
2) Lifeboat Number 2
3) Writing Room and Library
4) Main Stairway and Passenger Lifts
5) Saloon and Music Room
6) Smoking Room
7) Smoking Room Bar
8) Gentlemen's W.C.
9) Verandah Cafe

HEMESH ALLES

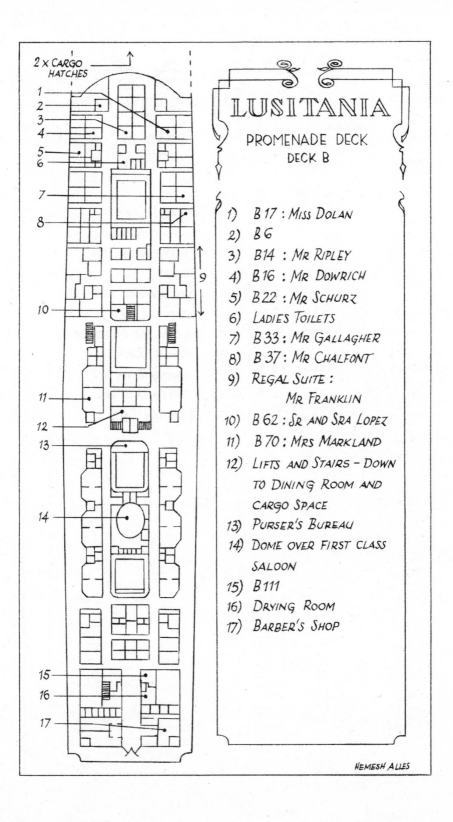

2 x CARGO HATCHES

LUSITANIA

PROMENADE DECK
DECK B

1) B 17 : MISS DOLAN
2) B 6
3) B 14 : MR RIPLEY
4) B 16 : MR DOWRICH
5) B 22 : MR SCHURZ
6) LADIES TOILETS
7) B 33 : MR GALLAGHER
8) B 37 : MR CHALFONT
9) REGAL SUITE :
    MR FRANKLIN
10) B 62 : SR AND SRA LOPEZ
11) B 70 : MRS MARKLAND
12) LIFTS AND STAIRS - DOWN
    TO DINING ROOM AND
    CARGO SPACE
13) PURSER'S BUREAU
14) DOME OVER FIRST CLASS
    SALOON
15) B 111
16) DRYING ROOM
17) BARBER'S SHOP

HEMESH ALLES

RMS Lusitania

DINING ROOM SEATING PLAN
Table 22

Mr Harry Chalfont, formerly British vice-consul in New York

Mrs Dolly Markland, wife of a Canadian army officer

Mr Charles Schurz, consulting engineer and efficiency expert

Mr William Coleman Ripley, theatrical impresario

Mr Edwin Peabody Franklin, industrialist

Señor Esteban López, pianist and conductor

Mr Patrick Gallagher, civil servant, Paymaster General's Office

Señora Corazón López, wife of Señor López

Mr James Dowrich, businessman and former Royal Navy officer

1

'Morning, Hammy. Still fiddling the ship's books, I see.'

The purser's bureau was on the promenade deck, a glass-fronted office facing onto a tiled foyer designed to look like the lobby of a hotel. The purser, a stocky, greying Glaswegian with a pair of steel-rimmed glasses perched on the end of his nose, looked up sharply, and then grinned when he recognized the speaker. 'Pat Gallagher. Now I know there's trouble on board.'

Gallagher smiled. 'I take it you are expecting me?'

'Aye, the captain passed the word.' Hamilton jerked his thumb upwards, towards the bridge. 'Have you seen Bowler Bill?'

'I've just come from him.' Gallagher picked up his travelling bag. 'Tell me where my cabin is and I'll get squared away.'

Hamilton reached under the counter for a key. 'You're in B33. I'll show you.'

Gallagher glanced at the queue of first-class passengers behind him; well-dressed, some of the younger ones excited, others looking apprehensive. 'How long must we stand here, Mummy?' a child's voice asked crossly. 'I want to go to my cabin *now*.' Another man's voice could be heard, demanding that he be seated at the captain's table at dinner.

'Aren't you busy, Hammy?' Gallagher asked.

'My assistants can handle them.' Hamilton motioned towards the forward part of the ship. 'We need a word.'

B33 was an outside cabin on the starboard side of the promenade deck, comfortable, light and airy. The washstand and
writing desk were both of finely carved mahogany; the wardrobe had inlaid mother of pearl. Two crystal decanters, one
full of whisky and one of brandy, stood on the sideboard. The
lamps had frosted glass shades etched in art nouveau style. 'I see
you've given me a decent cabin for a change,' Gallagher said.

'Plenty of room. We're barely more than half full. Quite a
few cancellations in the past few days.' Hamilton reached inside
his uniform jacket and pulled out a sheet of folded newspaper.
'I assume you'll have seen this.'

He pointed to two items in the right-hand column of the
page. The first was the official notice of sailings by Cunard
Lines – EUROPE VIA LIVERPOOL, LUSITANIA, FASTEST AND LARG-
EST STEAMER NOW IN ATLANTIC SERVICE, SATURDAY, MAY 1,
10 A.M. Below this, outlined in black like a death notice, was a
short proclamation.

N O T I C E !

Travellers intending to embark on the Atlantic voyage are
reminded that a state of war exists between Germany and
her allies and Great Britain and her allies; that the zone of
war includes the waters adjacent to the British Isles; that, in
accordance with formal notice given by the Imperial German
Government, vessels flying the flag of Great Britain, or any
of her allies, are liable to destruction in those waters and that
travellers sailing in the war zone on the ships of Great Britain
or her allies do so at their own risk.

IMPERIAL GERMAN EMBASSY
WASHINGTON, D.C., 22 APRIL 1915.

Gallagher nodded. 'Captain Turner told me. He said some of the passengers are receiving telegrams too, warning them not to sail. What's Bowler Bill doing here, anyway? I thought Dow was captain, and Turner had the *Transylvania*.'

'Didn't you hear? On the last voyage eastbound we had a warning there were U-boats operating in the war zone. Dow decided to fly the Stars and Stripes, to pass us off as a neutral. We got through safely, but the American embassy raised merry hell about it. The Foreign Office leaned on the directors at Cunard, and they fired Dow and put Bowler Bill Turner in command.' Hamilton paused for a moment. 'You'll see a lot of changes on Big Lucy,' he said. 'Not all of them good.'

'What do you mean?'

'The crew, for a start. The best seamen have all gone to the Royal Navy, and the replacements we've had so far are pretty green. Dow tried to train them up, but he didn't get very far, and Turner has only been on board for a couple of weeks. Doc Rawlings has been called up, too.'

'Sorry to hear it.' Rawlings had been the *Lusitania*'s doctor when Gallagher had served on board the ship; he was competent and clever.

'We have Doc Whiting now, but it isn't the same,' Hamilton said. 'We've also shut down one boiler room to conserve coal, so our top speed isn't much above twenty knots. And we've taken out some of the third-class accommodation on the lower deck and turned it into cargo space. There's plenty of empty cabins, but at least the hold is full.'

'Oh? What are we carrying?'

'Foodstuffs, mostly. Cheese, bacon, lard, tinned meat. They're running short of food at home.'

Gallagher nodded. 'There were queues outside the shops when I left London. What about the passengers?'

'A cut below the usual. There's a few rotten apples, I'll be bound.'

'I suspect you may be right. Where is Harry Chalfont's cabin?'

The purser's eyebrows rose. 'I was told you were travelling together, so I've put him in B37. That's directly across from you. Am I allowed to ask what's going on?'

Gallagher smiled a little. Hamilton was an old friend and they had been through a great deal together. 'I'm under orders to bring him home,' Gallagher said.

'Aye, you're his escort. I thought as much. What is he supposed to have done?'

'We don't know. Yet.'

'Fair enough.' Hamilton looked at him closely. 'And how are you doing, son?'

'About the same as usual. No better, no worse.'

'If you say so. There's some lines on your face that weren't there before.'

Gallagher smiled again. 'I could say the same for you.'

'It's the times we live in. All right. Let me know if there's anything you need.'

AFTER THE PURSER departed, Gallagher opened his bag and began to unpack. It did not take long. Years of service, first with the Royal Marines and then with the Special Branch of the Metropolitan Police, had taught him to travel light. A few suits of clothes; a travel kit with razor, soap, hairbrush and other necessities; a Webley Mark IV service revolver and a waxed paper box of cartridges bearing the broad arrow mark of the Royal Arsenal; a dog-eared copy of Baudelaire's *Les Fleurs du Mal* with an inscription inside the front cover, *With love from R.F.*; and at the bottom of the bag a rough cloth bundle streaked with paint, containing a folding easel, a roll of art canvas, a much-used palette board, tubes of paint, a tin of turpentine and a handful of brushes.

The bundle had been his constant companion for nearly twenty years, from the Red Sea and the China Station to Ireland and the North Atlantic. He no longer knew why he carried it with him; he had not painted, or even opened the bundle since Roxanne died. Inside, he knew, the turpentine would long since have evaporated, the brushes would have shed their fine hair, the coloured pigments in the tubes gone hard as rock. Yet he could not bear to throw it away.

A silver-framed mirror hung on the bulkhead across from the porthole. Gallagher studied his reflection for a moment, hearing the faint hum of machinery and fans in the distance. The deck under his feet trembled a little. Hamilton was right; there were more lines on his face, and a tinge of ash in his hair at the temples too, even though he had just turned forty. The scar on his temple, just behind his left eye, had faded a little with time, but it was still there, a reminder of a past he had never entirely left behind.

His eyes met those of his reflection in the mirror. It's not the years that age you, he thought. It is other people, their hopes and dreams and nightmares and deaths, that suck the marrow out of your soul.

And yet, would you have it any other way? Which is the greater tragedy: losing her, or never knowing her at all, never knowing what you missed?

And another voice said, *How can you speak of losing her? She was never yours to lose. She made that clear enough, although she never told you why.*

'Enough,' he said aloud to the mirror. 'Stop.'

The ship's siren gave several blasts, echoing long and

mournful along the Manhattan waterfront. Almost at once *Lusitania* began to move, sliding backwards away from Pier 54 out into the Hudson River. The vibration in the deck increased as the big engines began to beat harder. Turning away from the mirror, Gallagher placed the bundle carefully back into his travelling bag and put the bag in the bottom of the wardrobe. Then he went out, locking the cabin door behind him.

A voice in the corridor stopped him. 'Well, I'll be damned. Is that you, Gallagher?'

Gallagher turned. The man facing him was about his own age, square-built with a broad face and prominent chin. His eyes were wide with surprise, but he was smiling. 'Remember me?' he asked.

Memory came trickling back like water. He remembered the same face with a Royal Navy peaked cap and a lieutenant's stripe on his sleeve. 'Malta, '95,' he said. 'We were in the *Ramillies* together.'

'That's right. Worst battleship I ever sailed in. Even in calm seas she rolled like a hog.' The other man held out a hand. His accent was English with a tinge of the West Country and an overlay of American. 'Jimmy Dowrich.'

Gallagher smiled and shook his hand. 'What brings you on board?'

'Heading home to do my bit for the war effort. I'm still a reservist, and I expect I'll get the call any day now. I thought I'd save the Admiralty the trouble of finding me.'

'I'm surprised you haven't been called up already.'

'Oh, I've been out in America, on business. Say, do you have time for a drink? Now that we've met up, I'd really like to talk to you.'

Gallagher shook his head. 'Sorry, I'm already meeting someone. Later?'

'Sure. We'll take a rain check, as the Yanks say. Let's do it soon, though.' Dowrich smiled and leaned a little closer. 'I can tell you a few things about some of our fellow passengers. You'll be interested in this, old boy. That's a promise.'

Dowrich waved a hand in farewell and walked away. Quietly, Gallagher watched him go. *He pretended to be surprised to see me, but I reckon he was waiting for me. What is he doing here, and why?*

Gallagher stood for a moment longer, frowning, and then dismissed Dowrich from his mind and went in search of Harry Chalfont.

CHALFONT WAS IN the smoking room, an elegant wood-panelled room on the boat deck, high above the waterline. Men sat in leather chairs reading newspapers with an air of apparent unconcern. Cigar smoke curled blue in the light. Even though it was late morning the electric lamps were on, their mellow warmth clashing with the cold grey light coming through the windows and skylight. *Lusitania* was well through Upper Bay by now, Manhattan receding behind her, the Narrows coming up on the bow. Gulls wheeled over the river, white chevrons against dark clouds driven by a stiff north wind.

Chalfont was leaning on the bar, studying a glass of whisky. Grey hair hung down over his collar at the back. There were liver spots on the backs of his hands, which trembled a little as they curled around the glass. Ghosts of a former elegance looked out from his time-ravaged face. Gallagher knew from his record that his wife had died of cancer three years ago, and her loss had hit him hard.

He turned his head as Gallagher walked up beside him and raised his glass in salute. 'Care to join me?'

'Coffee,' Gallagher said to the barman. He looked at the whisky. 'Isn't it a little early?'

'Perhaps. But what does it matter? I have been relieved of my duties. I haven't a care in the world, at least until we reach Liverpool.'

The coffee came. Gallagher poured milk from a silver jug and stirred. Chalfont waited until the barman had moved away. 'Is a question permitted?' he asked.

'Of course.'

'Why do it this way? Why not arrest me and send me back to England in chains?'

Gallagher took a sip of his coffee. 'It's a fair point,' he said. 'Sir Courtenay Bennett wanted to do exactly that. But we refused.'

Bennett was the British consul in New York; until two days earlier, Chalfont had been his vice-consul. 'Why?' Chalfont asked.

'Because we don't yet know if you are guilty,' Gallagher said. 'Or indeed, what you might be guilty of.'

'But your chums from Special Branch will be waiting for me at the pierhead in Liverpool, won't they? And they almost certainly *will* arrest me, and take me away to a quiet place in the country where no one can hear me scream, and pull out my fingernails until I tell them what they want to hear. Correct?'

'Possibly.'

'You don't know?'

'My orders are to get you to Liverpool. What happens after that is none of my concern.'

That was not quite true; the orders in his coat pocket made it clear that he was to find out as much as possible about what Chalfont had done and why, but there was no point in showing

8

his hand just yet. Chalfont drank some of his whisky. 'Well, at least I have a week of freedom left to me. First-class accommodation with three square meals a day. Mustn't grumble.'

'Enjoy it while it lasts,' Gallagher agreed.

The big ship was passing through the Narrows now, her bow swinging towards the long bar of Sandy Hook in the distance, half obscured by sea spray. Lighthouses flashed, rays of light stabbing through the gloom. 'Will you miss New York?' Gallagher asked.

'No.'

'No? You were there for two years; you must have made some friends. Are you sorry you won't be seeing them again?'

'Dear boy,' said Chalfont, a hint of polite savagery in his voice, 'if the events of the past few months have taught us anything at all, it is precisely that I *have* no friends. In New York or anywhere else.'

Gallagher let a few seconds pass. 'Yes,' he said finally. 'So it would seem. Certainly no one was willing to come forward and vouch for your version of events, were they?'

'No, they were not. They were quite happy to throw me to the lions.'

'I find that surprising. What about Frederick Hansen, the arms merchant? You were close to him. Why wouldn't he speak up for you?'

'I don't know who you are talking about.'

'Ah. Perhaps you knew him better by his real name. Captain Franz von Rintelen of the Nachrichten-Abteilung, the German naval intelligence service. Does that ring a bell?'

'Go to hell,' said Chalfont, and he drained his glass and turned and walked out of the room. Unmoving, Gallagher watched him go. The *Lusitania* was a big ship, but there were only a limited number of places a man could hide and he knew them all. He could wait.

Sandy Hook was almost on the beam, the sheltered waters of Lower Bay sliding away astern, and *Lusitania*'s bow began to rise as she met the long rollers of the open Atlantic, slate grey and crested with gleaming ridges of foam. Gallagher signalled for another cup of coffee and the barman brought it, cup rattling a little in the saucer as he set it down. 'Is this your first time on the *Lusitania*, sir?' the barman asked.

'No,' Gallagher said, stirring his coffee. 'I've been here before.'

The barman nodded. 'Doesn't change much, sir, does it?'

Gallagher smiled a little. 'Yes and no. The faces change, the ship remains the same.'

'Yes, sir.' The barman, who had been hoping for a tip, moved away. Gallagher looked around the room. Most of the men were still reading newspapers; one, balding with a carefully trimmed black moustache, was reading what looked like some sort of technical document and making notes in the margin. Over by the windows four men had started playing cards, brandy glasses on the table before them; one had a loud waistcoat and an even louder voice. Already they are settling into their routines, Gallagher thought. The same men will come here every day to play poker, the others will come and read the same out-of-date newspapers. They will see the same faces in the same places, smoking room and saloon, dining room and library, a floating island of civilization in the midst of a hungry sea. Some will fall out with each other; some will conduct love affairs; some may die.

And then, waiting for us at the end, is the war zone.

No point in dwelling on that now, he told himself. But the

future could not be forgotten. The people around him knew it too; he could see it in the face of the barman, carefully polishing the counter, in the slightly unsteady hands of some of the newspaper readers, in the way one of the poker players gripped his cards tightly and kept glancing out of the window. Only the man reading the technical paper seemed unconcerned. Gallagher wondered how many of his fellow passengers really understood the risks they were facing, and whether they were regretting their decision to board the ship. As Hamilton had said, many others had chosen to stay behind.

Six days to the war zone, he thought again. Six days to wait.

2

'MONSIEUR GALLAGHER!' SAID the maître d', smiling and bowing. 'What a pleasure it is to see you again!'

'You too, Maurice. How have you been?'

Around them the first-class dining room glowed with light. Big portholes looked out over the darkening sea. The domed ceiling arched overhead, plastered in white and gold after the style of Louis Seize, glistening with painted panels set in ormolu frames. People came and went, women in brilliant gowns shimmering with jewels, men in black evening dress, waiters in white jackets carrying silver serving trays.

Maurice gestured at the scene. 'I am most distressed, my friend. This abominable war has quite upset trade. Nothing is what it used to be. The passengers are a rabble, and the tips!' Maurice's eyes rolled back in his head. 'You can only imagine what has happened to the tips. How is a man supposed to live?'

'I am sorry to hear it,' Gallagher said.

'Why are you sorry? It is not your fault. Come, I will show you to your table. As requested, I have placed Monsieur Chalfont at the same table. I am already under instruction from Monsieur Hamilton not to ask why.'

'Good.'

'Nevertheless, if you wish to tell me anyway, I am more than happy to listen. I am all ears, as you English say.'

'Sorry, old friend. I am not at liberty to say.'

'That is another thing I hate about this war. Too many secrets.' Maurice halted beside a big round table, covered in white linen and laid with crystal and silver. 'I believe you sat here on your very first time with us. Big Lucy's maiden voyage, all those years ago.'

'So I did,' Gallagher said quietly.

He took his seat and Maurice bowed. 'I shall bring you a glass of champagne. On the house.'

'I would prefer a glass of water.'

Maurice stared at him. 'Do not tell me you have stopped drinking. Mon Dieu, the world really is coming to an end.'

He departed. Gallagher sat for a moment, smiling a little. He had not stopped drinking, but he drank much less than he had in former days, especially during the time after Roxanne's death when drinking had seemed like the only way to deal with life. He had realized in time that it was not, but it had taken quite a lot of pain and effort to get back on an even keel.

He looked at the table and chairs, fixed to the deck like all the furniture to prevent them from moving around in bad weather. He had seen Roxanne Felix on stage, many times, and like audiences all over Europe and America he had been captivated by her beauty and grace, her ability to inhabit characters naturally and make them come alive. And then on the first night out of Liverpool, on *Lusitania*'s maiden voyage, he had heard her voice again, not on stage but right next to him, *Is this seat taken?* as she pointed to the chair beside him. In his memory he could still hear the tinkle of glasses, the conversation, the musical sound of her laugh. That evening he had stopped worshipping her as an actress and goddess of the stage, and started to see her as a woman; human, frail, fallible, very much like himself.

If I had known how things would end, would I still have fallen in love with her?

And another voice said, *Would you have had a choice?*

Someone sat down opposite him. Rousing, he looked up to see Chalfont, eyes hooded and the lines in his face deeper than usual. He had been drinking steadily, Gallagher guessed, but he sat upright with a posture that would have done credit to a guardsman, and his voice was steady. His evening dress was immaculate, white shirt freshly starched, an elegant flourish to the cut of his jacket and his white tie.

'Good evening, my dear fellow. I assume you have asked for my company at dinner so you can keep an eye on me. Don't want me down in the stokehold plotting sedition, that sort of thing.'

'That sort of thing,' Gallagher agreed.

The deck beneath their feet shuddered a little as *Lusitania*'s bow bit into a larger wave, and the cutlery rattled. 'I must apologize for my behaviour earlier,' Chalfont said. 'It was both rude and unnecessary. You have a job to do, of course.'

'Of course.'

'Allow me to make things easy for both of us. I give you my word as a gentleman that I will not make trouble or cause you any difficulty during the voyage. I am resigned to whatever fate awaits me in Liverpool.'

'Thank you.' Gallagher regarded him for a moment. 'Whatever happens, you will have a fair hearing.'

'I am very glad to hear it. Whether your superiors will allow you to keep that promise, of course, remains to be seen. But against you, dear boy, I have no animus.'

'Good evening,' said another voice; American this time, with a distinct midwestern accent. 'Are any of these seats taken?'

It was the balding man with the moustache, the one who had been in the smoking room that morning. He wore simple, sober evening dress with plain shirt and black tie, a sharp contrast to Chalfont's restrained flamboyance. Chalfont waved a hand. 'Please, join us. Sit wherever you wish.'

The man sat down, bracing himself against the roll of the ship. Around them the deck rose gently and fell, but the waiters hurrying past adjusted their step with an ease born of long practice, their silver trays always remaining level. 'My name is Schurz,' he said. 'I am a consulting engineer.'

Gallagher nodded. 'Gallagher,' he said. 'This is Mr Chalfont, the British vice-consul in New York.'

'The former British vice-consul,' Chalfont corrected, bowing in his seat. 'I have been recalled from my post.'

Another man might have offered condolences; Schurz simply looked blank. 'Why?' he asked.

'The bright lights of New York were becoming a little too bright for me. Your name is familiar, Mr Schurz. Are you a member of the Deutscher Bund?'

'I am,' Schurz said, a little stiffly. 'I do not recall hearing your name there, Mr Chalfont.'

'Oh, I used to drop in from time to time. The schnapps was always excellent, as you would expect. Which reminds me –' Chalfont looked around the dining room – 'I don't know about you chaps, but I could use a drink. Which waiter is ours, do you suppose?'

Schurz was still uncomfortable. 'And you, Mr Gallagher? What is your profession?'

Only an American would ask that question. 'I'm with the Treasury,' Gallagher said. 'The Paymaster General's Office, to be precise.'

It was a useful cover; no one, even in the rest of the British government, knew for certain what the Paymaster General and his staff did. Schurz made an attempt. 'Is the work interesting?'

'No,' Gallagher said. 'Quite the contrary, in fact.'

'Then why do you do it?' Schurz asked.

Gallagher smiled. 'That is a question I often ask myself.'

Chalfont had attracted the attention of a waiter and gave his drink order. 'Anyone else?'

'Scotch and soda,' Schurz said, and lapsed into silence. Gallagher watched him. Why had Chalfont mentioned the Deutscher Bund, the German-American social and educational club in New York? Gallagher knew the place; at night its members attended lectures on Goethe and talked knowingly about Sturm und Drang and the Nazarenes, but most of them had never seen Germany. By day it was mostly populated by businessmen looking to make deals. So why had the question got under Schurz's skin?

A man cleared his throat, and Gallagher turned to see James Dowrich looking down at them. 'I think this must be my table,' the latter said. 'Are any of these seats free?'

'Sit where you like, my dear fellow,' Chalfont said. 'We are just ordering drinks. What will you have?'

'Scotch, neat.' Dowrich sat down two seats away from Gallagher. 'I didn't realize we were at the same table, Pat. What a coincidence.'

Gallagher was fairly sure it was no such thing; Maurice was well known for taking bribes. Normally one would not be suspicious if a long-forgotten shipmate turned up out of the blue and introduced himself, but these were not normal times and it was Gallagher's job to be suspicious. He introduced Schurz and Chalfont; Schurz nodded stiffly and looked around the room. Chalfont took a silver case from his pocket and lit a cigarette, dropping the spent match into an ashtray. The drinks arrived a few moments later and Dowrich raised his glass. 'Good health,' he said. He smiled, his broad face full of good nature. 'I went looking for you this afternoon, Pat. I hoped we could have that little chat.'

'I'm afraid I was sequestered in my cabin,' Gallagher said. 'Sorry to be unsociable, but I had some work to do.' He had needed time to think about Chalfont and how to handle him, or so he told himself; in reality, he had just wanted to escape the oppressive atmosphere on board ship. 'What about this evening, after dinner?'

Dowrich shook his head. 'No can do, I'm afraid. I already have an engagement of my own. Shall we say tomorrow morning? We can find a quiet place after breakfast and talk.'

He looked meaningfully at Gallagher. 'This will be worth your while, Pat. I mean it.'

'Good evening, gentlemen.'

Another man sat down at the table. Unlike Schurz or Dowrich, he did not ask which seat might be free; he simply selected the one that suited him best, and appropriated it. He was tall, and in his younger days had probably been good-looking; his face had grown fleshy now, with the beginnings of jowls, but he was still handsome in an arrogant, self-regarding way. He looked, Gallagher thought, like a man who spent a lot of time gazing at his own reflection. His evening dress was even more expensively cut than Chalfont's, and the diamonds in his cufflinks must have been close to a carat each.

The man picked up the menu and began to study it. He did not introduce himself because he did not need to. Thanks to the papers, his face was as familiar as that of the president of the United States; indeed, his face and President Wilson's were both on the cover of the most recent edition of the *New York Illustrated Press*. His name was Edwin Peabody Franklin, and he was the most famous industrialist of his age; quite probably, of any age. Twenty years ago, he had founded a small company, Western Harvester, making tractors and agricultural equipment, and over the course of two decades he had turned it into a global behemoth with subsidiaries on every continent. His most famous design, the Sultan HC-40 tractor, could be seen in Canadian forests and Ukrainian wheat fields, French vineyards and Siamese rice paddies. He was the high priest of mass production; his plant at Evanston, Illinois, was a shrine, a place of pilgrimage for other captains of industry from around the world where they could learn from the works of the master, and his books on the philosophy of industry had sold millions. One reviewer had praised him as 'a new breed of industrial captain for a new age, ferocious in competition but compassionate to his people, an eagle-eyed servant of the public good.'

He was also, Gallagher realized, the man he had heard that morning demanding a place at the captain's table. Presumably, he regarded the others at Table 22 as not worthy of his company. In that case, why hadn't he bribed Maurice for a seat at a better table? Perhaps he had, but in terms that had offended the maître d'. Maurice was venal, but he also had his pride.

Schurz cleared his throat. To Gallagher's surprise, he rose and leaned across the table, extending a hand. 'It is a pleasure to meet you, Mr Franklin. I am Charles Schurz, consulting engineer.'

Franklin did not look up from his menu. 'Yes, I've heard of you. The time-and-motion fellow.'

The snub was calculated and painful. Schurz withdrew his hand slowly. 'My apologies, sir,' he said stiffly. 'I had no wish to intrude. I merely thought that—'

'Thought that I would be impressed by your reputation as an efficiency expert? No, Mr Schurz, I know your work, and I detest it. Your efficiency methods and your so-called scientific principles of management are a destructive force, and I will not have them in my factories or my workshops. Men like you, with your stopwatches and slide rules and Gantt charts, are destroying the very foundation of work itself.'

'And what might that be?' asked Harry Chalfont. His red-rimmed eyes were glittering with amusement.

A young woman walked past the table, body encased in a white silk gown, hips swaying a little. She was tall, with fair hair, and Gallagher had a brief impression of a sweet, almost child-like face. She did not look at them, but Franklin's eyes followed her as she crossed the room and sat down at a table on the far side, hidden from view by the crowd of diners between them.

'I speak of people, sir,' he said. 'Men and women, the backbone of industry. The toil of the people is the source of all our wealth, our personal and national prosperity. Their labour is a noble and honourable thing, and as industrialists we have a sacred trust to respect their dignity. But Mr Schurz and his time-and-motion men take away that dignity. If you let them into your workplace, you might as well turn your workers into machines, for they will have no more humanity.'

'That is untrue!' Schurz could contain himself no longer. 'Yes, we redesign tasks to make them more efficient, but we do so for the good of the workers! Thanks to our methods, work is carried out more quickly, the men are less fatigued, more productive and earn more money. That is to the benefit of the workers themselves!'

'And by standing over them, telling them what to do and how to do it, by turning their work into a series of monotonous tasks carried out by rote, you destroy their pride in their labour and rob them of their free will. No, Mr Schurz, I will not have it. I would sooner let Beelzebub and his devils into one of my factories than any of your efficiency experts.'

'Is this a private fight?' asked a woman's voice, dry and drawling. 'Or can anyone join in?'

The woman looking down at them appeared to be in her forties; only when Gallagher looked at her more closely did he realize that she was actually somewhat younger. She wore a gown of mint green silk from a not particularly fashionable dressmaker, and her only jewellery was a simple gold wedding ring and a rather austere necklace of glass beads. Straight dark hair was pulled up into a pompadour on top of her head. A slight smile played at the corners of her mouth.

Belatedly the men rose, Schurz placing a hand on the table to steady himself against the roll of the ship, Franklin sketching a languid bow. 'Forgive us, ma'am. Have we the honour of your company at dinner?'

'You do,' said the woman, taking her seat and folding the skirts of her gown. 'Permit me to introduce myself. I am Mrs Arthur Markland, from Toronto.'

The others made their introductions, Franklin this time condescending to identify himself. 'What takes you to England, ma'am?'

'My husband is a staff officer with the Canadian Expeditionary Force in France. It looks like he may be there for some time, so I am going to London to be nearer to him.'

'Very commendable, ma'am,' said Dowrich. 'And you must be very proud of your husband. The Canadians have performed prodigies of valour around Ypres, at Saint-Julien in particular. They have held the line despite all German attempts to break through, and I hear they have even mounted some counter-attacks.'

An expression of distaste crossed Franklin's face. A moment of silence passed before Mrs Markland spoke. 'Yes,' she said calmly. 'I have heard the same. However, my husband is the president of an insurance company, not a professional soldier. I would prefer he was doing something a little safer, and somewhat less valorous.'

'He might have a different opinion,' Dowrich ventured. 'It is natural for men to desire glory.'

'Is it?' asked Mrs Markland. 'You have never met my husband, Mr Dowrich. How would you know?'

Dowrich inclined his head. His face was a mask of contrition; behind it, Gallagher thought he seemed amused. 'You are right to rebuke me, Mrs Markland. Please accept my apologies.'

Mrs Markland looked like she wanted to throw his apologies back in his face. Still stiff with anger, she looked around the table. 'Is this a permanent arrangement? Are we shackled to each other at every meal?'

'That is standard practice at sea, ma'am,' said Gallagher. He considered recommending her to Maurice, but decided she was worldly enough to think of this herself. 'It goes back to the old days when every sailor had their own place in the mess. Or at least, that is what I have been told.'

'Are you also a seagoing man, Mr Gallagher?'

'I used to be,' Gallagher said.

Franklin looked around, discontent plain in his heavy face. 'I requested a seat at the captain's table, but it appears he does not dine with the passengers. It is very disrespectful of him, and I shall make my views known.'

'Captain Turner never dines with the passengers,' Gallagher said. 'He takes his meals alone in his cabin. He is, however, a very fine seaman.'

'He is still at the service of his passengers,' Franklin said sharply. 'He needs to remember that.'

Mrs Markland looked around the table again. She had calmed

a little. 'We are expecting three more?' she asked. 'Ah, here come two of them.'

The couple approaching the table, a little hesitantly, were probably in their sixties. The man was neatly dressed, and had greying hair and moustache; the woman was grey-haired as well, her face pale with dark eyes framed by long lashes, and she wore a black mantilla over the shoulders of her gown. She stumbled a little as the ship rolled, taking her husband's arm for support. 'Your pardon, señores, señora,' she said, gasping a little. 'I fear I am not used to travelling by sea.'

'You must not apologize,' said Gallagher, rising and helping her to the seat between himself and Dowrich. 'It will take you a few days to get your sea legs, but by the end of the voyage you will barely notice the motion of the ship.'

'Thank you, señor.' She gave him a shy, grateful smile. 'You are very kind.'

The newcomers introduced themselves as Señor and Señora López. 'We have been in Mexico for six years,' the woman said. 'Now we are returning home to Spain.'

'I hear things are bad in Mexico at the moment,' Chalfont said.

'Yes,' Señor López said quietly. 'They are very bad.'

'And what took you to Mexico in the first place?' Mrs Markland asked. Franklin sat looking faintly bored; unless the conversation concerned him, he was not interested. Dowrich was silent too; he had not looked at the newcomers or spoken a word since they arrived at the table. López glanced at him once, then looked quietly away.

'My husband was a professor of music at the Conservatorio Nacional in Mexico City,' said Señora López. She spoke hesitantly, her voice trembling a little. 'He also conducted the national orchestra. He is a fine pianist, and a very great musician.'

'Then we are honoured to have your company,' said Chalfont. 'I confess to being sadly ignorant of your work, señor, but the fault is entirely mine. Perhaps you would do us the honour of playing for us, after dinner?'

Mrs Markland was severe. 'Mr López is an esteemed professional musician, gentlemen, not a performing monkey. You must not expect him to play at your beck and call.'

López bowed in his seat. 'You are kind, señora, but playing the piano is my joy and my delight. I would be honoured to play for you.'

'You are generous, señor,' Mrs Markland said, and then she looked up and went very still.

'Evening, ladies and gents,' said a jovial voice behind Gallagher. 'Is there room for one more?'

The man who sat down on Gallagher's other side put all the rest of the party in the shade. He wore evening dress, but his black silk waistcoat had mother of pearl buttons and instead of a tie he wore a white lace cravat, like a seventeenth-century aristocrat. A black goatee beard and a moustache waxed to needle points completed the ensemble. He was, Gallagher remembered, one of the men who had been playing cards in the smoking room that morning.

'William Coleman Ripley, at your service,' he said, brandishing a small black cigar. 'I'm in the theatre trade, what they call an impresario. You'll have heard of my last production, *Hop-Scotch*? It was the toast of Broadway. People were queuing around the block to see it.'

'Were they?' asked Dowrich. 'That's not what I heard. There's a rumour going around that the show was a flop and you lost a lot of money.'

'Well, you heard wrong!' Ripley snapped.

They gazed at each other, Ripley red with sudden anger,

Dowrich's face hard-set. Gallagher studied Dowrich for a moment. Beneath that affable facade, there is something quite unpleasant about this man, he thought. Something was beginning to emerge in his memory, but he could not yet pin it down.

Chalfont intervened, an unlikely peacemaker. 'And what gives us the pleasure of your company, Mr Ripley?'

'I'm off to Europe to put on a few shows. Do my bit to help cheer up the folks, you know? War's a gloomy business, but I reckon my Roses will put a smile back on people's faces.'

Mrs Markland coughed behind her hand. The others ignored her, politely. 'Roses?' asked Chalfont.

'You never heard of Ripley's Roses? The most beautiful gals in America, and that of course means the world. My chorus girls, all-singing all-dancing. Ain't you seen any of my shows, Mr Chalfont?'

'Can't say as I have,' Chalfont admitted. 'American culture appears to have passed me by.'

'Well, you'll get your chance soon enough in London. We're gonna take the West End by storm.' Ripley blew out a cloud of smoke and looked at Mrs Markland. 'How're you doing, Dolly? It's been a while, hasn't it? What is it now, five years?'

'Is that all?' said Mrs Markland. She gripped the menu in her hands, her fingers white with pressure. 'It seems longer.'

'Well, perhaps I'm mistaken.' A note of caution had entered his voice. 'You're looking well, though. Did I hear you got married?'

'Yes, five years ago, as it happens. My name is Mrs Markland now.'

'You know each other?' Señor López asked politely.

Ripley blew out cigar smoke. 'Our paths have crossed once or twice,' he said, looking at the woman as if waiting for her reaction.

'I used to live in New York,' Mrs Markland said. 'I met Mr Ripley then. But it was a long time ago.'

'Sure,' Ripley said. 'Well, congratulations on your nuptials. Say, let's all have a drink to celebrate.'

'Certainly.' That was Franklin, asserting his authority once again. 'Waiter! Bring us a couple of bottles of champagne. The Ayala Grand Cuvée '05, and plenty of ice!'

3

THE CHAMPAGNE ARRIVED. Gallagher watched the bubbles rising fine as pinheads through the golden liquid and held the glass under his nose, inhaling its fragrance. Ayala had been Roxanne's favourite champagne; she had disdained the more fashionable labels, maintaining that one could taste the love and care with which this small estate made its wine. Somehow, in this company, he could not bear the memory. He set the glass down untasted.

The Royal Navy may have plundered *Lusitania* of her best seamen, but the quality of service in the first-class dining room had not changed. Waiters brought them trays of hors d'oeuvres and silver dishes of oysters on the half-shell resting on ice, each garnished with a slice of lemon. Ripley picked up an oyster and sucked it down, licking his lips in appreciation. Señora López watched him, dark eyes full of repugnance; not for the oysters, Gallagher realized, but for Ripley's manners. Bowls of consommé celestine followed, clear soup garnished with herbs and fine shredded crepes. 'This is passable,' said Franklin. 'My own chef, I daresay, might have added a touch more seasoning, but this is a creditable attempt.'

Chalfont's eyes glinted. 'You should have brought him with you, Mr Franklin. He could have fed us all.'

Franklin considered this for a moment, and decided to

regard it as a joke. He barked with laughter. 'I don't think Mrs Franklin would have forgiven me. Depriving her of both my company and our chef at the same time would have been too much for the poor woman to bear.'

That too was presumably meant to be a joke. 'Mrs Franklin chose not to accompany you?' said Schurz, his voice still tinged with resentment. 'I wonder why.'

'My dear Esmée has a delicate constitution,' Franklin said. 'She does not travel well. Never mind. My errand should not last long. A matter of a few months at most, and I will be home again.'

Dolly Markland laid down her spoon. 'No one is talking about the elephant,' she said.

They looked at her. 'I beg your pardon, señora?' López said politely.

'You have all seen the papers, I assume, so you know our situation. This ship is a target. We might well be attacked before we reach England. In other words, Mr Franklin, you might not be coming home.'

Schurz turned to her. 'I understand your fears, ma'am, but there really is no cause for alarm.'

'Thank you, Mr Schurz, I am very glad to hear it. May I ask why you are so certain?'

'German submarines operate under cruiser rules, ma'am. That means they are obliged to allow the passengers and crew of any unarmed ship to signal for help and evacuate before the ship is sunk. That's especially true when there are neutral citizens on board, like Mr Franklin, Mr Ripley and myself.'

Franklin looked briefly annoyed at being compared to either Ripley or Schurz. 'At the very worst we might spend a few hours in the lifeboats before we are picked up,' the engineer said. 'But we shall be none the worse for wear.'

Dowrich shook his head. 'Haven't you heard, Schurz? The Germans have abandoned cruiser rules. The Admiralty started putting weapons aboard British merchant ships. When the U-boats surfaced and ordered them to surrender, they opened fire. In the interests of self-preservation, the U-boats are now launching torpedoes first and asking questions later.'

'But that is against the rules of war,' objected Schurz. 'Arming merchant vessels in this way, I mean. It is completely contrary to the London Declaration on the Laws of Naval Warfare.'

Schurz, as was fast becoming clear, was a pedant. Dowrich smiled. 'When you get to London, Mr Schurz, look up the Admiralty and tell them as much. I am sure they will give you a favourable hearing.'

Franklin held up a hand. 'Allow me to reassure you, Mrs Markland,' he said. 'I have already spoken to Cunard's manager in New York, and he has confirmed that a naval escort will be waiting for us as soon as we reach the war zone. On Friday morning we will rendezvous with the protected cruiser HMS *Juno* off Fastnet Rock. She will convoy us to our first port of call at Queenstown in Ireland on Friday afternoon, and then on to Liverpool on Saturday. If I may borrow an English proverb, we are as safe as the Bank of England.'

Ripley sucked down another oyster and took a drag on his cigar. 'What's this about Queenstown? I thought we sailed straight to Liverpool.'

'It's standard practice,' Gallagher said. 'We call briefly at Queenstown to drop off the mails and let a few passengers ashore. Then we continue to Liverpool.'

Dowrich lit a cigarette of his own and blew out smoke, looking at Franklin. 'A protected cruiser, you say? How is she going to stop a U-boat? We need a squadron of destroyers.'

Franklin looked annoyed. 'I do not concern myself with

naval technicalities, Mr Dowrich. Be assured that both Cunard and the Royal Navy know who I am and what my mission is. This ship will not come to harm, not while I am on board.'

Cod with lobster sauce was followed by a choice of saddle of lamb or sirloin of beef. Ripley ignored the others, wolfing down his food with a lack of grace that made Señora López shudder. He was also drinking heavily, and Gallagher thought he seemed ill at ease; apart from boasting about his theatre empire, he had said very little. Mrs Markland ate slowly and carefully. 'Good grub, this,' said Dowrich. 'Better than we had in the wardroom, Pat, wouldn't you say?'

'I think you're mistaken,' Gallagher said. 'I wasn't in the wardroom. We never messed together.'

'Funny, I was thinking we did. Memory can play tricks sometimes.'

Franklin called for the wine list, wrinkling his nose at the selection and finally picking out a 1900 Château Margaux. 'Not my preference, but hopefully it will complement the food.'

The 1900 Margaux was one of the finest wines in living memory. 'I daresay you wish you had brought your own sommelier as well,' Chalfont said.

Franklin frowned. Like many self-regarding men, he had a skin like a rhinoceros; he could feel the darts, but he was uncertain of their nature. López laid down his fork; neither he nor his wife seemed to have much appetite. 'Earlier you spoke of a mission, Señor Franklin. What is it that you do?'

Franklin looked around the table, brown eyes meeting each of theirs in turn and commanding their attention. He uses that trick often, Gallagher thought.

'This war has gone on long enough,' Franklin said. 'Like many others, I was foolish enough to believe that this was a local disagreement, and that it would be over by Christmas as we were promised. Instead, the scale and scope of the conflict are increasing. As a convinced and committed pacifist, I believe it is time to bring the war to an end.'

Gallagher stirred a little. 'And where do you fit in, Mr Franklin?'

Franklin gazed at him for a moment. Silence fell, broken only by Ripley striking a match to light another cigar.

'My position in life has given me certain advantages,' Franklin said. 'Before the war I visited Britain and the Continental Powers many times, partly for business reasons, partly to advise various governments on commercial and industrial policy. Statesmen and monarchs have honoured me with their friendship. I have met King George V several times, and I was Kaiser Wilhelm's guest at Potsdam only a year ago. I know these men well; and what is more, they know me. They trust me to be an honest broker.'

Chalfont's jaw dropped. His cigarette fell from his fingers, burning a hole in the tablecloth. Dolly Markland reached across and stubbed it out quickly. 'You're going to negotiate peace?' Chalfont asked. 'Between the Kaiser and King George?'

'Yes,' said Franklin.

'My dear fellow, how absolutely splendid. Do you know, I had feared this voyage would be dull. My word, how wrong I have been. This is droll, very droll indeed.'

Franklin's brow furrowed. 'I am not accustomed to being the butt of other people's jokes, Mr Chalfont.'

'Oh, my dear chap, please don't take offence. I am sure you are very genuine and sincere, and I respect your intentions. But you don't have a snowflake's chance in hell.'

'I rather tend to agree,' said Schurz.

Franklin lost his temper. 'Do you? Do you now? With the

greatest of respect, Mr Chalfont, I think I know rather more about high affairs of state than the . . . what did you say you were? The former vice-consul in New York? When I walk into offices in Whitehall or Königsplatz, I am greeted as a friend and listened to with respect. I doubt very much if those same gentlemen have ever heard your name.'

'You are quite correct,' said Chalfont. 'I withdraw my earlier remarks, and apologize unreservedly.' His lips were quivering with amusement.

Franklin turned on Schurz. 'As for you, Schurz, I said I knew you by reputation. Most of your work has been in the armaments industry. You advise arms makers on how to make weapons and munitions, in greater quantity, better, faster, so more people can be killed more quickly and the directors can make more money. The sooner this war ends, and the sooner the warmongers you work with can be put out of business, the better.'

Another man would have grown angry; Schurz merely looked baffled. 'Why point the finger at me? I am not a belligerent in this war, I am neutral. I am an engineer, and my job is to help companies become more efficient. That is all I do, nothing more, nothing less.'

'You do not care that these companies deal in death?' asked López.

'That is not my concern, señor. Like I said, I am neutral. My province is technology, the industrial and mechanical sciences, and I seek to improve them wherever I can. Whatever these companies make and to what use their products are put is nothing to do with me.'

'How can you sit here and say that?' Franklin demanded. 'How can you be so blind, Schurz? Thanks to the improvements made by men of science like you, war is consuming the entire world even as we speak. It is not just Europe that is suffering.

Those were Indian troops who died on the barbed wire at Neuve-Chapelle. Those are Canadians up at Ypres right now, covering their faces in handkerchiefs soaked in their own urine to ward off the chlorine gas!'

'Mr Franklin!' Dolly Markland said sharply.

Franklin held up a hand. 'Of course, these are your compatriots. I am sorry, ma'am. I apologize for my words.'

'No,' López said, and there was a sudden note of passion in his voice. 'No, Mr Franklin, you are right. Of all the evils that mankind endures, war is the greatest of all. Have you seen war with your own eyes, any of you? Do you know what it does to people? My wife and I were in Mexico City when Pancho Villa's rebels invaded us. If I told you of the chaos, the murders and summary executions, the robberies and rapes that we saw committed there before our very eyes; if I told you even a tenth of these things, I swear to you, you would not eat one more mouthful of your dinner, for you would be too sick to continue.'

López subsided. His wife was trembling a little. Agitated, she picked up Dowrich's wine glass and started to drink from it, realized what she was doing and set it down again. Murmuring an apology, she hesitated, fumbling with the glasses before finally picking up her own and moving it towards Dowrich. 'Oh, dear,' she said under her breath, and then sat back looking distressed and confused. Gallagher watched her with sympathy, remembering the corpses he had seen lying in the streets of Peking fifteen years ago.

Chalfont was the first to speak. 'Well said, señor. It is easy for us to sit here in luxury and pass judgement on events that are far away. We have not endured what you and your wife have suffered.'

'I too am sorry,' Schurz said stiffly. 'But no matter how

terrible it may be, war is also a natural part of human affairs. It always has been, and always will be.'

'And men like you will always profit from it,' said Franklin.

'Your cause is peace, Franklin. Mine is efficiency. I believe in my creed, the same way you believe in yours.'

Surprisingly, it was Dowrich who attempted to change the subject. 'I hear the Allies are planning to open another front against the Ottoman Empire. Some sort of landing on the Aegean coast, and then a march on Constantinople to try and knock the Turks out of the war. What do you say, Mr Franklin? That could put more pressure on Germany to make peace.'

Franklin looked disdainful. 'I don't speculate on the basis of idle rumours, Dowrich. I advise you not to do the same.'

'I'm not sure it's an idle rumour,' Dowrich said. He looked at Gallagher. 'I daresay you've heard something similar.'

Gallagher shook his head. 'I work for the Treasury, not the Foreign Office.'

'Ah, yes,' Dowrich said. 'I was forgetting.'

Chalfont raised his glass. 'Well, at least out here in the wide Atlantic we're away from it all, for a little while. A toast, ladies and gentlemen. To a calm sea and a prosperous voyage.'

SATURDAY, 1 MAY 1915
10.25 P.M.

APART FROM THE rising and falling of the deck, the saloon of the *Lusitania* might have been in any grand house in Europe or America. Mahogany-panelled walls, green marble fireplaces imitating the malachite rooms of Russian palaces, a barrel-vaulted skylight set amid a plaster ceiling that could have been designed by Robert Adam, an immense green and yellow floral-patterned carpet and plush upholstered furniture; a mishmash of styles and motifs and yet somehow it all worked, combining to form a picture of effortless luxury sealed off and insulated from the outside world, where submarines launched torpedoes from hidden depths and men died crucified on barbed wire or suffocated in the gas vapours filling their lungs.

In the far distance a lighthouse flashed, blurry through driving rain: Montauk Point at the eastern tip of Long Island, sliding away astern. Ahead lay 3,000 miles of open sea; and then, the war zone.

López sat at the piano, his wife standing beside him and turning the pages of sheet music. He was playing *Iberia*, Isaac Albéniz's vast, spell-binding evocation of his homeland, part-flamenco, part-sound picture calling up the dust and heat and vivid swirling life of southern Spain. Cascades of notes fell like waterfalls, gathering themselves and flying into the air again. Gallagher stood listening, watching the pictures the music painted in his mind, barely noticing Dolly Markland move up beside him.

López came to the end of the sixth movement, 'Triana', and raised his hands for a moment. Applause rippled around the room. Gallagher took a deep breath, returning to the real world. 'What do you think of the music?' Mrs Markland asked, fluttering her fan.

It took Gallagher a moment to respond. 'He plays every note like he feels it in his heart. Señora López is right. Her husband is a great musician.'

'Really? I wouldn't know. I haven't much taste for music.'

'I am sorry to hear it,' Gallagher said.

'Oh, don't get me wrong, I used to love music. But I lost my interest in it some years ago.'

It was an odd expression. 'May I ask what happened?'

'Nothing,' she said abruptly. 'I just lost it. You were very quiet during dinner.'

Gallagher smiled. 'I didn't feel I had much to contribute.'

'That doesn't stop some people. Have you no views on anything that was discussed? Whether Mr Franklin can single-handedly make peace between Britain and Germany? Whether war is indeed a natural state of affairs? What will happen to *Lusitania* when we reach the war zone?'

Gallagher smiled again. 'As to the first, the answer is no, but I applaud him for trying.'

'Really? You think he is genuinely trying to negotiate a peace? Or is this just another way of feeding his own ego? As if the latter were not already monstrous enough.'

Franklin was across the room, his back to the piano, brandy glass in hand as he talked to a group of men. They looked like they were being lectured to by the head prefect. 'He is rather fond of himself,' Gallagher agreed.

'He is the living embodiment of narcissism. A Viennese psychologist could study that fellow for a lifetime, and never run out of material. What about my other questions?'

'Is war a natural state of affairs? Yes, probably. So are alcoholism and tuberculosis, but that does not make them desirable. My sympathies are with the Lópezes and, by extension, with Franklin.'

'And the ship? Are we going to be safe? Are you as blasé as Mr Schurz and Mr Franklin?'

Schurz was an odd one, Gallagher thought. For a man who professed to be objective, a scientist, he seemed to know a lot about the war. But perhaps it was the science of war that fascinated him.

'I am sure Mr Franklin is right,' he said. 'If a naval escort has been arranged, then we should be safe enough.'

'Your sympathies are with Mr Franklin, Mr Franklin is right. Don't tell me you too have fallen under his influence.'

Gallagher smiled. 'Hardly that.'

The music resumed, but something had happened; the spell had been broken now and he could no longer enter the dream palace that López was creating. His eyes drifted back to Franklin and the group of men listening to him. Chalfont was one of them. Another was a big man, square-shouldered and fair-haired, his face burned red by sun and wind. It was not so much his clothes or his face that made him distinctive, as the way he stood; his posture, loose-limbed and relaxed at the moment, suggested that action was never far away. A man of his hands, Gallagher thought. You don't see one of those every day; at least, not in first class.

He looked around the room. Rotten apples, Hamilton had said of the passengers, and Gallagher studied them one by one, looking for anomalies. He found another quickly enough, an elegant man with black eyes and neatly trimmed moustache who was watching the Lópezes very intently. There was nothing unusual about that; apart from Franklin and his acolytes, everyone in the room was watching them. But this man, Gallagher was quite certain, was not listening to the music.

In the middle of the ninth movement, 'Málaga', the music suddenly faltered. Señora López had forgotten to turn the page. She apologized swiftly in a murmur and the music moved on, but Gallagher could see she was upset. He realized she had spotted the man with the moustache, and from under the lashes of her lowered eyes she was watching him in turn.

The music ended, to warm applause, and López rose and bowed. Gallagher looked around the room. Schurz had retired earlier; Dowrich was presumably at his engagement. 'I don't see Mr Ripley,' Gallagher said.

'He's playing poker in the smoking room,' Mrs Markland said. 'He's been there ever since dinner.'

She wore green silk slippers that matched her gown. The toe of one was dark with damp, Gallagher noticed. 'Should I assume that your earlier relationship with Mr Ripley was not entirely happy?'

She smiled at him, flicking her fan. 'Very diplomatically put, Mr Gallagher. Are you sure you're not with the Foreign Office? If so, it is their loss.'

'Very kind of you to say so. But they seem to get on without me pretty well.'

'I'm guessing you weren't always with the Paymaster General's Office, either. Come along now, 'fess up. You said you used to be a seagoing man. What were you, Royal Navy?'

'Royal Marines.'

Her carefully trimmed eyebrows rose. 'Close, then. And you were shipmates with your friend Mr Dowrich?'

'He wasn't really a friend.'

'Are you sure about that? He certainly seemed matey with you at dinner.'

She was prying, he knew. He decided to retaliate. 'And you were a bit sharp with him, don't you think?'

'I am very protective of my husband,' she said abruptly.

'Given the circumstances, that is hardly surprising.'

'Mr Dowrich seemed to think it was . . .' She shook her head. 'You're right, I was being overly sensitive. It is the atmosphere on this ship. You could cut the tension with a knife. It is affecting all of us, I'm sure.'

'It's only seven days to Liverpool,' Gallagher said gently.

'By which time, I am sure we will all know each other's secrets.' She gestured around the room with her fan. 'Look at this place, it's like a goldfish bowl. Everyone watches everyone, and knows everything. You can't hide on a ship, can you?'

'Not in my experience,' said Gallagher, watching her.

'Well, at least the voyage won't be dull.' She closed her fan with a click. 'Goodnight, Mr Gallagher. I look forward to getting better acquainted as the voyage progresses.'

He looked into her cool, arid face and wondered what she meant by that. He wondered too about her husband, far away in France. He bowed. 'Goodnight, ma'am. Pleasant dreams.'

'That is highly unlikely,' said Dolly Markland, and she turned and walked away, straight-backed, the green silk of her gown shimmering in the light as *Lusitania* rose and fell through the long, rolling waves.

Others were drifting away towards bed. Ripley stumbled past, face red and sweating. Chalfont rested a hand on Gallagher's shoulder, smiling. 'A fascinating evening, dear boy. Don't you think?'

'If you say so.'

'My dear fellow, that scene at dinner was something out of a Gothic novel. The atmosphere was positively seething with emotion. I'm trying to work out who hates whom the most. Franklin and Schurz? Mrs Markland and Dowrich? Dowrich and Ripley? Dowrich and you?'

Gallagher was startled. 'What makes you think I hate Dowrich? I have no cause to.'

'Well, he certainly isn't that fond of you. I've seen his face when you're not looking. Watch yourself, dear boy. He's the kind who will plant a dagger in your back.'

'You're drunk. Go to bed.'

'I am, and I shall.' Chalfont reeled away. Gallagher took a deep breath, watching rain lash the dark windows of the saloon. Mrs Markland had thought he and Dowrich were friends, but Chalfont had clearly seen something different. He had already learned that, even when drunk, Chalfont seldom missed anything.

All of this was irritating, and distracting him from his job. Tomorrow morning he would see Dowrich, find out what was going on and, hopefully, put it behind him.

Hamilton the purser came up alongside him. 'You need to come with me, Pat.'

'What is it, Hammy?'

'You'll see when we get there.'

Cabin B16 was an inside cabin at the forward end of the promenade deck, on the port side and nearly opposite the ladies' lavatories. A white-jacketed steward stood outside the door. At a nod from Hamilton, he produced a key from his pocket and unlocked the door, standing aside to allow them to enter.

All the lights were turned off and the room was inky black. The first sensation was the smell of blood, sharp and sour like an invisible fog in the air. 'Christ,' Gallagher said quietly, and reached for the light switch. The overhead lamp flickered and came on, glowing mellow through its art nouveau shade.

James Dowrich lay on his back on the carpeted floor, still in the same evening dress he had worn to dinner. The front of his white waistcoat was crimson with blood.

4

SATURDAY, 1 MAY 1915
11.16 P.M.

THE STEWARD CLOSED the door behind them to keep out any curious eyes. 'Who found him?' Gallagher asked.

'I did, sir,' said the steward. His face and voice were steady. 'I like to check on my passengers during heavy weather, to make sure they're well and see whether they need anything. I knocked, and when he didn't answer I let myself in with my pass key, just to see if everything was all right. That's when I found Mr Dowrich, sir, just as he is now.'

The ship rolled and something clinked; the cabin key, sliding across the polished top of the sideboard and bumping against the glass decanters. There were two glasses on the sideboard too, both empty; the stopper had been removed from the whisky decanter but no drinks had been poured. 'How long ago was this?'

'Not more than fifteen minutes ago, sir. I went immediately to the pantry, where I telephoned Mr Hamilton and asked him to come along at once.'

'I arrived a few minutes later,' Hamilton said. 'When I saw what had happened, I sent for Doc Whiting and then went looking for you.'

'Why me?'

'Two reasons. When I tell the captain what happened, the first thing Bowler Bill will say is, *put Gallagher in charge*. And second, you were on his table at dinner. I thought you might know something.'

Gallagher looked down at the body. Vacant eyes in a pale dead face stared back at him. The blood on the waistcoat was turning dark, and black stains of gunpowder residue were visible. He could see two bullet wounds in the chest, very close together and almost certainly inflicted at the same time. The bullets would have been large, he thought; .45 calibre, or perhaps .41.

'I know him,' he said. 'We served together, briefly, but it was a hell of a long time ago.'

Hamilton said nothing. Gallagher turned to the steward. 'When did you last see Mr Dowrich?'

'Before dinner, sir.'

'You didn't see him return to his cabin?'

'No, sir. After dinner service finished I went in to turn down the bed; that would have been a little after nine. After that I was washing up in the pantry.'

Gallagher glanced at him. 'You're taking this very calmly.'

'I was with the army in South Africa, sir. Muddy River, and Magersfontein. I've seen worse.'

'Did you see anyone else in the corridor when you came to do the turn-down? Anyone who might have entered the cabin after you left?'

'No, sir. And they couldn't have entered the cabin because I locked the door behind me.'

The cabin key still lay on the sideboard, bumping and clinking like it was trying to call attention to itself. Gallagher thought for a moment. 'And you said the cabin was locked again when you came to check?'

'Yes, sir. As I said, I had to use my pass key. I assume the gentleman locked the door behind him when he returned to the cabin.'

Gallagher nodded. 'Not a word about this to anyone,' he said to the steward. 'Very well. That's all for the moment.'

The steward saluted and went out. Hamilton shook his head. 'Poor devil,' he said, looking at the body. 'Locked himself in his room and shot himself. God knows it's happened before.'

Gallagher shook his head. 'There are two bullet holes. Suicides will shoot themselves once, but not twice. And also, where is the gun?'

Hamilton frowned, looking around the cabin. It was very similar to Gallagher's, with wood panelling and fine furniture and etched glass lampshades. But, as an inside cabin, there was no porthole; the door was the only entrance.

'Very well', the purser said. 'Someone else came in and shot him. But how did they manage to lock the door behind them?'

'They must have had a key,' Gallagher said. 'Where are the spare keys kept, Hammy?'

'In the purser's bureau, like always. I'll check and see if any are missing.'

'Thank you. And check the stewards' pass keys too, if you please.'

Someone knocked discreetly at the door. 'That will be the doctor,' Hamilton said.

Dr Whiting was a grey-haired man with a pronounced stoop, his shoulders on the same level as his ears. Hamilton introduced Gallagher and motioned to the body. 'What can you tell us, doc?'

Whiting bent over the body and grunted. 'Nothing you don't already know, not at this stage. He was shot twice at close range. You can see the powder stains, and there are some grains of unburned powder mixed in with the blood.'

'Any idea when it happened?' Gallagher asked.

Whiting hummed gently to himself, tapping one finger on his chin. 'At least an hour ago,' he said. 'The blood has started to dry. But there's no sign of rigor, so I'd say not more than two or three hours ago.'

'Later than that,' Gallagher said. 'The steward came in a little after nine, and he hadn't returned.' He checked his watch. 'For the sake of argument, let's say death occurred between nine fifteen and ten fifteen. Is there anything else you can tell us, doctor?'

'Not without a post-mortem. I can't do a full autopsy, but I can at least make a detailed examination. Do you want me to do it here, or take him down to the hospital?'

Gallagher looked around the cabin. 'You'd better take him away, before the other passengers notice what's going on. If anyone asks, he slipped in his cabin and hit his head, and is badly concussed. He will remain in hospital under observation until we reach port.'

Hamilton went to fetch the steward, and the two of them returned a few minutes later carrying a stretcher. Covering Dowrich with a blanket, they carried him out. The doctor followed them. Alone in the cabin, Gallagher stood for a few moments looking down at the blood on the carpet.

He remembered Dowrich a little more clearly now. It had been nearly twenty years since they served together on the *Ramillies*, and despite being on the same battleship their paths had rarely crossed; Gallagher had been a sergeant of marines, while Dowrich was a navy officer. There were rumours that Dowrich was not well liked by his fellow officers, and he was also said to be a bully, although that hardly made him special; there was a rich vein of sadism running through the Royal Navy's officer class, as Gallagher himself knew from experience. But he thought again about the look on Dowrich's face when he challenged Ripley at dinner, and thought perhaps the rumours were true.

43

None of which explained why Dowrich was on *Lusitania* now, all hail-fellow-and-well-met, pretending to a past friendship that did not exist. And why had he wanted to talk to Gallagher?

The ship rolled and swayed, and the key rattled again on the sideboard. Wrapping a handkerchief around his fingers, Gallagher searched the cabin. The washstand contained nothing but a few toiletries and a hairbrush. The drawer of the bedside table held half a dozen books; one title caught his eye immediately, a brand-new volume called *Shrapnel Shell Manufacture*. The rest were well-worn paperbacks; Mark Twain's *A Connecticut Yankee in King Arthur's Court*, Jack London's *The Call of the Wild*, a couple of more recent Zane Grey westerns, *Riders of the Purple Sage* and *The Lone Star Ranger*.

Half a dozen suits hung from the clothes rail in the wardrobe, with shirts and small clothes folded neatly on shelves beside them. A waxed paper box revealed a row of celluloid collars. The wooden trunk at the bottom of the wardrobe was empty. Frowning, Gallagher began going through the pockets of the suits. He found a couple of handkerchiefs, a loose button, about three dollars' worth of small American coins, a book of paper matches with the front panel advertising Shanley's Oyster House and Grill on 43rd Street and a couple of dog-eared business cards, one for the Knickerbocker Hotel in New York and the other bearing the name of Mr Jonathan Buckland, managing director of the Union Metallic Cartridge Company in Bridgeport, Connecticut. Gallagher turned the card over and saw a note scrawled in ink on the back. *Ask him about White Star.*

He frowned again. White Star was a shipping line, a longtime bitter rival of Cunard, the owners of *Lusitania*. That rivalry had continued even during wartime. It was possible to imagine a connection; the Union Metallic Cartridge Company might be sending munitions to Europe in White Star cargo ships, for example. But why would this interest Dowrich?

What had he said that afternoon? *I've been out in America, on business.* And he had intimated that this business concerned some of the other passengers.

Gallagher put the cards in his pocket, and laid the coins and the matchbook down on the sideboard beside the room key. The key was a standard design to fit a ward lock, with a silver tag attached by a snap ring. The words *RMS Lusitania B16* were engraved on the tag. He looked again at the matchbook and saw it had been used; there were scratch marks on the strike plate. He opened it and saw most of the matches were missing. He also saw another note written in the same hand on the inside of the cover: *Deutscher Bund, 10th February, 3 P.M.*

Three months was a long time to keep a paper matchbook, Gallagher thought. On the other hand, judging by the contents of his pockets, Dowrich was not the tidiest of men and he never threw anything away. The matchbook might have been resting in his pocket ever since February, forgotten.

Chalfont had occasionally called in at the Deutscher Bund. So had Schurz, and he had been uncomfortable when Gallagher mentioned it.

Suddenly, this was becoming interesting.

The only place he had not yet searched was the bed. There was nothing under the covers or the pillows, but when he lifted the mattress he found two things concealed beneath it. The first was a wad of glossy new hundred-dollar bills with the face of Benjamin Franklin staring out from their obverse side; there was, he calculated, about $5,000 here. The second was a revolver, an old Colt Single Action Army with scuff marks on the barrel and trigger guard and a couple of notches carved in the plain wooden grips. Wrapping the handkerchief around his fingers again, he picked up the gun and broke it open. There was a .45 cartridge in every cylinder but one, as usual, and no sign of powder residue; the weapon had not been fired recently.

'Yes,' Gallagher said aloud. 'Very interesting indeed.'

The steward was waiting in the corridor. 'Mr Hamilton sent me to lock up, sir, after you were done. Oh, and he says the captain wants to see you as well, sir.'

'Thank you.' Gallagher paused for a moment. 'You've done well tonight.'

'Thank you, sir.'

The steward locked the door with his pass key. 'Goodnight, sir,' he said, and walked away. Gallagher turned to find someone else in the corridor behind him; Charles Schurz.

'Has something happened?' the engineer asked, bracing himself against the roll of the ship. 'I looked out earlier and saw someone being taken away on a stretcher.'

'Mr Dowrich has taken a fall and banged his head. A steward found him unconscious in his cabin. The doctor says he has concussion.'

Compassion towards his fellow human beings clearly did not come naturally to Schurz. 'Oh,' he said. 'I wonder if that was the noise I heard earlier.'

'What do you mean?'

'I returned to my cabin after dinner, to catch up on my reading. I've taken on a new engagement in Britain, you see, and I have a mass of technical literature to get through before I arrive.'

'I see,' Gallagher said politely. 'What was this noise you heard?'

'It's hard to say exactly. The ship was rolling about a bit, and there were quite a lot of noises in the background. This was a sort of sharp thump, if you see what I mean. Actually, now I think of it, there were two of them, very close together.'

'Perhaps one of the stewards dropped something,' Gallagher suggested.

'That was my first assumption, yes, so I paid the noise no attention. But then everything went silent, which seemed rather odd, so after a bit I opened the door and looked into the corridor.'

'What did you see?'

'Nothing. There was nothing to see. So, it occurs to me that what I heard was Dowrich falling over.'

'Where is your cabin, Mr Schurz?'

'Just over there.' Schurz pointed to B22, on the far side of the corridor and diagonal to B16.

Gallagher nodded. 'Out of curiosity, what time was this?'

'It was four minutes before ten P.M. I made a note of the time.'

'You didn't think to inform anyone?'

'Well, no. Who would I inform, and what would I tell them?'

'The poor fellow lay there for well over an hour before he was found,' Gallagher said. 'Let's hope he makes a full recovery.'

'Yes,' Schurz said. 'Well, goodnight then.' He turned and walked back into his cabin.

CAPTAIN TURNER WAS on the bridge, despite the lateness of the hour. Gallagher, who had sailed with him before, knew that he seldom slept during bad weather. Abrupt and eccentric he might be, but Turner was also a master seaman and his duty to his ship and his passengers was an article of faith.

The bridge lights had been dimmed; the binnacle lamp was a soft glow reflecting off brass speaking tubes and repeaters and the glass face of the engine room telegraph. Outside all was black save for the eerie phosphorescent streaks of foam where the waves crested and broke.

'You wanted to see me, sir,' Gallagher said.

Turner grunted and turned away towards the chartroom. Gallagher followed him into the big room behind the bridge. Sea charts lay spread out on a table, callipers and a slide rule on top of them.

The captain tilted his bowler hat back on his head. The hat was nearly new, the felt still glossy; for reasons lost in the mists of time, the captain always bought a new bowler hat upon taking up command, and usually wore it in preference to his uniform peaked cap. 'What happened?' he asked.

'One of the passengers has been murdered, a man named James Dowrich.'

'It was definitely murder?'

'He was shot twice in the chest at close range.'

Turner stared down at the charts for a moment. 'Has this anything to do with the other business? Chalfont?'

Gallagher thought about the matchbook. 'Possibly.'

'What is Chalfont supposed to have done?'

His orders from the service were to tell no one about Chalfont, but Captain Turner was responsible for *Lusitania* and every living soul aboard her. 'The Americans suspect him of spying for Germany. I am taking him back to England for interrogation.'

Turner grunted. 'Very well, I want you to look into Dowrich's death. See that a full investigation is carried out and deliver a report to the police when we reach Liverpool, with a copy to me.'

'Yes, sir. I'll need to send some telegrams.'

'I will inform the Marconi room. I don't need to tell you how important it is to keep this quiet, Gallagher. The passengers are nervous enough already, the purser says, and things will only get worse as we draw closer to the war zone. I don't want anything adding to their fears.'

'I understand, sir.'

The captain nodded. 'Good. Make it so.'

AT THE PURSER'S bureau Gallagher wrote a telegram and handed it over to one of Hamilton's assistants, asking for it to be sent up to the Marconi room without delay. It was after midnight now, but the telegraph room at the service's London office was manned around the clock.

Feeling stale and tired, he stepped out onto the starboard promenade for some fresh air. He found plenty of it; the wind was coming from the port side and the roof kept out most of the rain, but cold air still swirled around him and the deck was greasy with spray. Air and sea roared, drowning the thunder of *Lusitania*'s mighty engines.

Gallagher stood for a moment, balancing against the roll of the ship. There was a time when he had called the sea his home, but he had quit the marines after Peking, and after that he had never settled anywhere for long. That was one of the things that had drawn him to Roxanne; she too was rootless. *We are like thistledown*, she had pronounced in one of her more whimsical moments. *We drift on the wind.*

In her case, that was almost literally true. As one of the country's most gifted actresses she was constantly on the move, travelling from theatre to theatre around Britain and, later, across Europe and North America. Home was a series of hotel rooms, rarely for more than a few weeks at a time, and thus it had been for all her adult life. At the age of sixteen her own parents, God-fearing, Bible-worshipping and intolerant, had denounced her for bringing shame upon the family and cast her out of their home. After that, the stage had been her entire world. The stage and, latterly, himself.

His own mother had not disowned him – not quite – but she had made it clear she found him embarrassing and his presence was an uncomfortable reminder of her past mistakes. She was the daughter of a minor noble family, his father a merchant navy officer, and he himself had been conceived after a hasty elopement to Gretna Green. Her family brought her home and rammed through a divorce and a few years later she married again, this time as she should have done, to a wealthy Conservative MP with an estate in Hampshire. Gallagher himself had been packed off to boarding school as soon as possible to get him out of the way.

He had hated school from the moment he arrived, and tried repeatedly to run away; each time he escaped he made a few more miles before he was caught, and each time he was brought back the headmaster added a few more strokes of the cane. Eventually he managed to reach Portsmouth, where he enlisted in the Royal Marines, first as a boy bugler and later as a light infantryman. He thought for a while that he had found a home in the marines, but it had ended in the blood and disaster of the Boxer Rebellion, and dead women in the streets of Peking. For a time it seemed things had worked out for the best. Leaving the marines had brought him to work for Cunard, and that fateful first voyage of the *Lusitania* when she had sat down beside him at dinner and changed his life for ever. The next few years had been bright with happiness, until that night on the promenade deck when he discovered her lifeless body and the roof of his world caved in.

He had tried to forget her over the years, and had half succeeded. But coming back to the *Lusitania* again had broken down the wall that surrounded his memories, because it was here on *Lusitania* that she had died. She was all around him now; he could almost feel her spirit hovering in the air.

And now he had another death on his hands, another murder to solve as well as dealing with Chalfont; unless, of course, as Captain Turner had suggested, the two problems were related. Whom had James Dowrich met at the Deutscher Bund?

As always, there were plenty of questions. He looked out over the dark sea for a moment, and then turned away and went back to his cabin, looking for bed and the sleep he suspected would elude him.

5

ON THE AFTER part of the promenade deck, two shapes stirred in the shadows. 'I have been studying the situation,' said one. 'It will not be easy.'

'I told you it wouldn't be. This is the middle of the Atlantic, remember. If we are spotted, there will be nowhere to run.'

'What do you suggest?'

'I don't know.' The other man paused. 'I don't like this business, you know. I never have. We have absolutely no proof, none whatsoever.'

'Blood demands blood,' the first voice said, almost fiercely. 'Thousands of our compañeros are dead, thousands! Butchered by the government artillery, while our own shells failed to explode. We cannot let them lie unavenged.'

'Oh, bullshit. What's done is done, we can't bring the dead back to life. All we're doing now is putting our necks on the line to save someone else's pride. I tell you, I don't like it.'

'Then what do you suggest we do?' demanded the first voice.

The other man pondered. 'For a start, let's find some evidence,' he said at last. 'If we can prove that they were involved in the sabotage of our artillery shells, I'm prepared to think again. But I want to be damned certain.'

There was a long silence. When the first voice spoke again

it was quieter, more reflective. 'Perhaps you are right. It would be a mortal sin to kill someone who is innocent.'

'It would. And your uncle is not always right about everything.'

'Do not say that to his face,' warned the first voice.

'Don't worry, I have a strong sense of self-preservation. Do you think you can get into the cabin?'

'I can try.'

'Do it, then. Look for anything that connects them with the shells. Let me know if you find anything.'

'I shall do so.' There was a long pause. 'What do you think happened this evening? To the other one?'

'I don't know. Leave it to me and I will try to find out. Now, we have spent too long together. We must go before we are seen.'

'Indeed. I bid you goodnight, compañero. And good luck.'

Sunday, 2 May 1915
8.16 a.m.

Morning found *Lusitania* battering her way through heavy seas south-east of Nova Scotia, her decks swept with rain and spray. Most of her passengers kept to their cabins, and only Schurz the engineer joined Gallagher for breakfast in the domed dining room. After scanning the vast menu offering an array of fruit, grilled mackerel, pickled fish, eggs, ham, bacon, sausages, devilled chicken, hashed beef, lamb chops, kidneys, kedgeree and rolled ox tongue, Schurz ordered a bowl of porridge. 'Where is everyone this morning?' he asked.

The bow rose and then slammed down into a trough, causing the hull to shudder. Spray flew in sheets against the windows.

'Still asleep, or suffering from seasickness,' said Maurice the maître d'. 'Or both. They will find their sea legs soon enough. They always do.'

He departed with the air of a man who has seen everything and is no longer surprised by anything. Gallagher stirred milk into his coffee. 'May I ask a question, Mr Schurz?'

'Of course.'

'Why did you allow Franklin to goad you last night?'

Schurz was silent for a moment. 'Yes, I let him get under my skin,' he said finally. 'I shouldn't have done, of course. I pride myself on being a man of science, above emotion. But there is one thing I cannot abide, Mr Gallagher, and that is hypocrisy.'

One of the stewards came around selling tickets on a sweep-stake, and Gallagher reached into his pocket. This was an old tradition; passengers were invited to guess how many miles the ship would travel from noon to noon, and the closest guess received half the money collected with the rest donated to charity. Famously, in all his crossings of the Atlantic, Gallagher had never once won.

'You think Franklin is a hypocrite?' he asked when the steward had gone.

'Of course he is. He wears his pacifism like Joseph's coat, strutting around and showing off how holier-than-thou he is. All this talk of peace is nonsense, we all know it, but it helps draw attention to himself and that is all that matters.'

There were times when Schurz was annoying, and times when he could be quite acute. Gallagher remembered what Mrs Markland had said. 'There is no denying that Franklin has been very successful. But perhaps he has let success go to his head.'

'His head, his heart, his liver and every other organ in his body,' Schurz said. 'There's another thing, too. He has a mistress on board ship.'

'He does?'

'Remember that girl in white who walked past our table? Her name is Billie Dolan. They pretended not to know each other at dinner, but I saw them talking late last night, after the music finished. After everyone else had gone to bed, he took her into his stateroom.'

'How do you know this?'

'Because I followed them,' Schurz said.

And why did you do that? Gallagher wondered, but the answer was plain to see. Franklin had insulted Schurz and his profession and Schurz was looking to get even, hoping to find something to Franklin's discredit. So much, indeed, for the emotionless man of science.

GALLAGHER WAS MIDWAY through his bacon and eggs when a messenger from the Marconi room arrived, bearing a telegram. Ignoring Schurz's curious eyes, he put the telegram in his pocket and finished his breakfast; then, rising, he took the lift up to the boat deck and walked aft to the verandah café. In fine weather, its sliding glass doors could be opened to allow passengers to sit out on deck and drink coffee. Today, they were firmly shut and misted with spray, blurring the long, foam-crested waves. Gallagher was the only customer; he ordered coffee, waited until the steward had served it, and opened the telegram.

His colleagues at the department must have worked all night. They would do, of course; anything that might involve Chalfont, however tangentially, was of first-water importance. He began to read, and his eyes opened a little wider. The telegram told the history of James Dowrich, and what an eventful history it was.

Born in Devon into a seagoing family, he had gone to the *Britannia* at Dartmouth as a cadet and six months later had been commissioned as a Royal Navy officer. His naval career had lasted ten years and involved six different ships, which suggested that his captains had wanted to get rid of him. He had been admonished on two occasions for striking another officer. Ten years ago he had been accused of plotting to steal a large sum of money from his ship's pay chest; facing court-martial, he had chosen to resign his commission instead. Fearing a scandal, the Admiralty decided to hush up the matter and take no further action.

After leaving the navy, Dowrich had made a living as confidence man, specializing in dodgy share promotion schemes and blackmailing wealthy women who had secrets to hide. He also developed connections with underworld figures including Ikey Bogard, leader of one of the most powerful London gangs. In 1911, he had been involved in a bungled post office raid in north London, during which a policeman was killed. Other members of the gang were caught and hanged, but Dowrich dropped out of sight. Special Branch concluded that he had probably fled the country.

Gallagher sat with the telegram in his hand, staring out over the grey sea. Dowrich had become a professional criminal, but he was no ordinary thug, no East End bully-boy; he came from a good family, who had enough money to send him to Dartmouth. What had gone wrong in his life? Or was he one of those people who was just bad from birth? They were rare, but they did exist; Gallagher had encountered one or two of them before.

Dowrich had made it sound like he had gone over to America for a business trip, but if Special Branch was right, he had been there for some time, possibly as long as four years. That explained the trace of American accent, Gallagher thought.

Rising, he went back down to the promenade deck and

walked along to the purser's bureau, where he obtained another telegram form from the assistant and wrote a message to Captain Steven Peters of the New York Police Department, who was among other things an expert on New York gangs. He had connections in other cities too, and might be able to find out what Dowrich had been doing during those four years. As an afterthought, he also asked for information about Jonathan Buckland, managing director of the Union Metallic Cartridge Company.

Of course, Dowrich might have gone straight during those years in America, in which case the police would have no record of him. But Gallagher remembered the revolver and the money under the mattress, and doubted this.

HE FINISHED THE telegram and handed it to the clerk behind the desk just as Hamilton came down the stair into the lobby. 'We have another problem,' the purser said.

Schurz was with him, and something about the sight of Schurz made Gallagher's heart sink a little.

'What is it now?'

'Mr Schurz here saw a man on deck behaving strangely, and reported it to me.'

'Did you inform the captain?' Gallagher asked.

'Yes. He said I was to tell you, and you would deal with it.'

Gallagher swore silently, and turned to Schurz. 'What did you see?'

'There was a man up near the bow, standing beside one of the cargo hatches. I was intrigued, because he clearly was not a sailor and I didn't think passengers were allowed so far forward.'

'Why do you say he wasn't a sailor?'

'He wasn't wearing a uniform. He had an overcoat and a derby hat.'

'What was he doing?'

'When I first saw him he was bent over, inspecting something on the deck. It looked like a coil of rope. After a moment he took a portable camera from his pocket and made a photograph. He did this several more times, moving around the rope to photograph it from different angles.'

Hamilton shifted a little and caught Gallagher's eye. 'Did he see you?' Gallagher asked.

'I don't think so. I was at a higher elevation, at the forward end of the boat deck. I did nothing to draw attention to myself.'

'How long ago was this?'

Schurz drew a watch from his waistcoat pocket. 'Eight minutes ago.'

Gallagher could not resist. 'Did you make a note of the time?'

'Of course,' Schurz said. He looked surprised by the question.

'He may still be there.' Gallagher looked at Hamilton. 'We'll go in through the forecastle. There's a companionway beside the forward cargo hatch.'

'Shall I call the master-at-arms?'

'No, let's keep this quiet.'

'Shall I come with you?' Schurz volunteered

'No, Mr Schurz. Remain here, if you please.'

Hurrying downstairs, Gallagher and Hamilton ran outside and forward along the deck. Passing the door to the third-class smoking room, they came to the forecastle hatch, a heavy metal door which Hamilton opened with a key. All was silent inside save for the deep vibration of water against the steel hull; the air smelled of tobacco and hypochlorite bleach. 'This way,' Hamilton said.

The companionway was a steel ladder leading up to a raised hatch on the deck above. Gallagher climbed the ladder and threw the hatch open, stepping quickly out on deck. The man was standing next to the foremast, camera in his hands, his overcoat wet with sea spray. His eyes widened when he saw Gallagher and he turned, but there was nowhere to run.

'What are you doing?' Gallagher asked.

The man held up the camera. 'I was taking some photographs of the sea.' His voice was trembling. 'Have I done something wrong? If so, I am sorry. I meant no harm.'

Gallagher pulled the camera out of his hand and examined it. It was a simple Brownie in a cardboard case, the kind one could buy in any department store. 'You are under arrest,' he said. 'Mr Hamilton, find a nice quiet cabin where we can lock this gentleman up.'

Hamilton nodded. 'We'll put him in Nelson,' he said.

CABIN B111, called Nelson by the crew because it had 'one of everything', was an inside cabin on the promenade deck, well away from the other passengers. Located next to the engine hatch and not far from the water closets and drying room, it was regarded as the least salubrious cabin on that deck and was rarely used unless the ship was completely full. Inside the cabin, Hamilton locked the door behind them. 'Sit down,' Gallagher said.

The man sat on the edge of the bed, hands clasped in his lap. He was young, Gallagher saw, probably only in his mid-twenties. His knuckles were white with strain. 'What is your name?' Gallagher asked.

'John Crossland.' The voice was low and quiet. 'I'm from Pittsburgh, Pennsylvania.'

Gallagher nodded. 'Listen carefully,' he said. 'We are on the high seas, in a time of war. The usual legal customs do not apply here. The captain's word is law. If I report that you are a German spy, he will have you shot immediately and your body thrown overboard. No one will ever know what happened to you.'

The young man said nothing. His hands were whiter than ever and his eyes were sick with fear. 'Tell me the truth,' Gallagher said. 'If you do not, in five minutes' time you will be dead. Understood?'

The young man nodded.

'Now, let's try this again. What is your name?'

'Leutnant Georg Kreutzer,' the young man said finally.

'I assume you are in naval intelligence. Do you work for Captain von Rintelen?'

'Yes.'

'What were you looking for? What were you photographing?'

Silence. Gallagher looked at Hamilton. 'All right. Send word to the captain, and ask him to assemble a firing party.'

The blood drained from Kreutzer's face. 'I was looking for the guns,' he said.

Gallagher stared at him. 'Guns? What are you talking about?'

Kreutzer looked blankly back at him. 'Surely you already know. You must know.'

'Let's pretend I don't.'

'We have information that the Royal Navy intends to convert this ship into an armed merchant cruiser. She is to be fitted with a battery of quick-firing guns. I was looking for evidence to confirm this.'

'And what did you find?'

'I did not find the guns. But I discovered the mounts for them on the forward deck, concealed beneath coils of rope.'

Gallagher looked at Hamilton. The purser closed his eyes and opened them again, confirming what had been said. 'And if you found evidence, what were your orders?' Gallagher asked.

'I was to send a telegram to an address in New York, in code. The information would be passed to Captain von Rintelen.'

'Then what?'

'I don't know. That was not in my orders.'

Gallagher studied him. Something was wrong here, that was certain, but Kreutzer's fear was very real. 'So,' he said. 'You have confessed to being a German spy. You know what happens next.'

'No,' Kreutzer said quickly. Gallagher watched his face, and saw the moment when he made up his mind. The words came tumbling out in a rush. 'No, don't kill me. I can give you information. Please, you must listen to me.'

Gallagher let a few moments pass. 'Information about what?'

'There is a traitor among your people. Someone on the consul's staff in New York. He is working with us.'

Gallagher nodded, pursing his lips. 'What is this man's name?'

Kreutzer stared at him. 'Who do you work for? The secret police?'

Gallagher said nothing.

'I want a guarantee,' Kreutzer said. 'A formal promise, in writing, that my life will be spared. Give me that, and I will tell you his name and everything else I know.'

'Your life is important to you,' Gallagher said. 'More important than duty to your country?'

'My life is the only thing of value that I have left,' Kreutzer said quietly.

The deck beneath their feet rose and fell slowly. Kreutzer was afraid, but he was also smart enough to know that he held a bargaining chip. Chalfont had never denied knowing Rintelen, only that he was a traitor. If Kreutzer could give evidence to show, one way or the other, whether Chalfont had been working with Rintelen, then he was an asset worth preserving. Of course, Gallagher thought, he might be a plant; Rintelen might have put him here deliberately, hoping he would be caught and spin a false story.

On the heels of the thought, Kreutzer spoke. 'May I ask a question? Who betrayed me?'

Gallagher looked surprised. 'No one betrayed you. One of the passengers saw you, and thought you were acting suspiciously. He reported it to us.'

Kreutzer said nothing, but he did not look convinced. 'Very well,' Gallagher said after a moment. 'I shall tell my superiors that you are offering a deal. The final decision rests with them. You will remain locked in this cabin. Stewards will bring your meals here, and a chamber pot. Do not be so foolish as to attempt to escape.'

Kreutzer spread his hands. 'We are in the middle of the Atlantic,' he said. 'Where would I run to?'

IN THE PRIVACY of the purser's office, Gallagher looked at Hamilton. 'What's this about guns?'

The purser looked glum. 'He's telling the truth, or most of it. The Admiralty issued orders to arm the ship at the start of the war and the mountings were installed, but then they changed their mind.'

'If this ship is armed, then technically it is a warship. And the Germans are perfectly within their rights to sink her without warning.'

'The guns aren't on board,' Hamilton said. 'I told you, they just put in the mountings, that's all. The question is, how did the Germans find out about it?'

'No idea,' said Gallagher.

'You could have battered him. Made him tell what he knows.'

'I could. But in my experience, that is usually the least reliable way to get information out of someone.'

'Is that so? Easy to tell you didn't grow up in the Gorbals.'

Gallagher smiled. 'I have other ways of getting what I want. Take good care of him, Hammy. Treat him with respect, feed him well, give him everything he asks for, within reason.'

The purser looked at him suspiciously. 'What are you up to now?'

'Something sneaky and underhand,' Gallagher said. 'It might even work, too.'

'What are you talking about?'

'Kreutzer gave in rather quickly, don't you think? And I reckon I know why. He is afraid, yes, but he is also angry. He thinks someone may have betrayed him deliberately, and he may have been right. Is Schurz still here?'

'I saw him lurking in the foyer when we came in. Doubtless he's waiting to hear what happened.'

'May I borrow your office for a moment? I want to speak to him. And pass the word to Captain Turner. I'll need to report to him as well.'

Schurz was shown in a few minutes later. 'Thank you for reporting what you saw,' Gallagher said, gesturing towards a chair. 'Please, have a seat.'

Slowly, Schurz sat down. 'Who you are, Mr Gallagher? Are you with the police?'

Gallagher shook his head. 'I'm a civil servant,' he said. 'The captain and his officers have other things on their plate, as you can imagine. I know Captain Turner well, and he asked me to handle this matter.'

'Did you arrest the man I saw?'

'Yes, we have him in custody. He will be handed over to the police when we reach Liverpool.' Gallagher paused for a moment, thinking about how to play this. Schurz was suspicious, and he needed to play down those suspicions. 'Can you tell me again when you saw this man and what he was doing?'

Schurz repeated his story and Gallagher wrote it down carefully on a sheet of paper. 'Out of curiosity, what were you doing out on deck? Exploring the ship?'

'No, I have sailed on *Lusitania* before. I was simply getting some fresh air. I hate being cooped up inside for too long.'

'I quite agree. Mr Schurz, do you mind if I ask a few more questions? The police are bound to want to know certain things, and if I ask you now, perhaps we can prevent them from bothering you later.'

'Of course,' Schurz said stiffly. 'I am prepared to help in any way I can.'

'That is very generous of you. Now, you said you were a consulting engineer. What exactly does that mean?'

'I am an efficiency expert. I help companies to implement the principles of scientific management in order to improve productivity. I am considered one of the pre-eminent men in the field.'

Gallagher raised his eyebrows. Schurz stiffened again, as if his veracity had been questioned. 'My engineers have worked with more than a hundred companies across America, with very positive results. Many of my clients have sent letters of testimonial.'

'Very impressive. And you are travelling to Britain to advise British companies on how to do the same?'

'It is more than that.' Schurz seemed to visibly swell with self-importance. 'Your government is establishing a new department, the Ministry of Munitions, to improve the supply of artillery shells to your army in France. I have been asked to advise the minister, Mr David Lloyd George.'

Gallagher looked perplexed. 'I don't quite understand. Why do they need you?'

'Because your army is in desperate straits. Back in March you nearly ran out of shells at the Battle of Neuve-Chapelle, and if the shortage continues, you may well lose the war.'

'And you are the man who can solve the problem?'

'I am a specialist in the armaments industry, especially shell production. I was one of the lead engineers on the project to introduce scientific management at Watertown Arsenal, and I have worked with most of the other American munitions factories since, Dupont, Union Metallic Cartridge Company, Remington, Austin Powder Company, Nobel. I am probably the world's leading authority in this industry.'

Gallagher smiled. 'Then we are very lucky to have you. Will you please tell me your nationality, Mr Schurz?'

'I am American,' Schurz said. He sounded like he was used to answering this question. 'I was born in Cincinnati, Ohio. Yes, my surname is German, my family on both sides are German immigrants, but they moved to America more than sixty years ago, before the Civil War. My grandfather served as an officer in the Union Army during the war.'

'Would you describe yourself as a patriot?'

'No.' Schurz spoke with surprising force. 'Patriotism is emotional nonsense, Mr Gallagher, and I have no time for it. I am an engineer, a positivist and a scientist, and I deal only in matters of proven fact, rational calculations backed up by weight of evidence. Patriotism is nothing more than vapid superstition.'

Schurz paused, considering his own words. 'Your pardon if I have offended you, Mr Gallagher. You are, after all, a servant of your country.'

'Service and patriotism are not necessarily the same thing,'

Gallagher said. 'On the whole, Mr Schurz, I am inclined to agree with you. Thank you for your time and patience. May I ask one more favour?'

'Yes, of course.'

'Please keep this business to yourself. As you can imagine, many of the passengers are feeling rather nervous. I would not wish to add to their fears.'

'THE MAN WE arrested has admitted to being a German spy, sir,' Gallagher said a few minutes later. 'His name is Kreutzer, and he is an agent of German naval intelligence.'

They were in the captain's day cabin. Light glinted off the four gold stripes on the sleeve of Turner's dress uniform; he was about to conduct the Sunday service. 'Where is he now?' the captain asked.

'We've locked him up in Nelson.'

'Good. Tell the master-at-arms to put a guard on the door.'

'With respect, sir, I would rather not. A guard will be noticed by the other passengers and will get them talking. I'd rather this was kept as quiet as possible. And I don't think Kreutzer will attempt to escape.'

'Mmm. Very well.' The captain thought for a moment. 'And he was looking for the gun mounts, you say.'

'Those were his orders, sir. But I'm convinced it was a set-up. Kreutzer was a pawn to be sacrificed.'

'Do you know why?'

'Not yet, sir. I'd like to interrogate him more fully, but I will need to contact London and ask for instructions first.'

'Your service will handle this business as it thinks best, I am sure. But if you discover anything that presents a threat to this ship, I want to know about it *immediately*. Understood?'

'Of course, sir,' said Gallagher.

6

SUNDAY WORSHIP FOR first-class passengers was held in the saloon. According to tradition at sea, divine service was led by the ship's captain and so Captain Turner, reluctant servant of the Lord, stood beside the piano and rattled through the service in his gruff voice, bowler hat clenched in his hands in front of him. He escaped the moment the service was ended.

Chalfont had not been in attendance. Gallagher knocked twice at his cabin door but received no answer. He stopped a passing steward. 'Have you seen Mr Chalfont this morning?'

'He hasn't left his cabin, sir.'

Judging by yesterday, it seemed likely that Chalfont had drunk himself into a stupor and had not yet regained consciousness. Best to catch him later, Gallagher thought, when he was hungover and vulnerable. As he had told himself before, there was plenty of time.

He found Hamilton in the purser's bureau. 'Any luck with those keys, Hammy?'

Hamilton nodded towards his office. 'You'd better come in.'

They walked into the office and the purser closed the door behind them. 'What is it?' Gallagher asked.

'None of the keys to Dowrich's cabin are missing,' Hamilton said.

Gallagher stared at him. 'Are you certain?'

'Dead positive, son. We keep two copies of every key. One is issued to the passengers when they arrive. The other is kept here at the bureau in case they get careless and lose the original. Dowrich's spare key is here, hanging on its hook under the counter. The other key was on the sideboard of his cabin, locked in with him.'

'The pass keys?'

'All accounted for.'

Gallagher was silent for a moment. 'Someone killed Dowrich and then escaped from a locked cabin without a key. Or, the door was unlocked and they walked out, but somehow they locked the door behind them. Again, without a key.'

'Both of those things are impossible,' Hamilton said.

'Schurz heard something shortly before ten P.M., probably the shots that killed Dowrich. Did the stewards see anyone around that time?'

Hamilton shook his head. 'I spoke again to the steward in the portside pantry, the same one who found the body. He saw two passengers come through at about nine thirty, but they went straight to their cabins. Later, when he was doing his rounds, Mrs Markland came up and asked for a carafe of water to be delivered to her cabin. Everyone else seems to have been upstairs, either in the smoking room or listening to Señor López.' Hamilton scratched his chin. 'There's another possibility. I don't like it, but . . . it's possible that one of the stewards or stewardesses could have done it.'

'Why?'

'They were trying to rob the cabin and got caught, perhaps? It's never been known on my ship, but I've heard of it happening on others.'

Gallagher shook his head. 'Dowrich knew the person who killed him. He was preparing to pour them a drink; remember the glasses and the open decanter? Also, nothing had been touched in the cabin. There are some fairly expensive cufflinks in the wardrobe, and there's about five thousand dollars stuffed under the mattress.'

Hamilton's eyes opened wide. 'Bloody hell, Pat, when were you going to tell me about that?'

'Can you put the money in the safe, Hammy? There's a gun there, too, you can take that as well.' Briefly, he told Hamilton the contents of the telegram from London. 'Dowrich was rotten through and through, and I think that's why he was killed.'

'Somebody had it in for him.'

'Yes. He told me had information about some of the passengers, something he was keen to pass on to me.'

'Any idea which ones?'

'There are several possibilities . . . Can you do me a favour? A couple of people caught my eye last night. A big fellow with a sand-blasted face who looks a bit like a gunslinger, and a Latin type with a moustache who seemed to be watching the Lópezes. Can you find out who they are?'

'Of course. I reckon you could be on to something about the Latin type. Old López was around the office this morning, asking if he could see the passenger register. I told him no, of course.'

Gallagher frowned. 'Did he say why he wanted to see it?'

'No. Just held up his hand and apologized, all very courtly, and asked me to forgive him for taking up my time. I'm not sure about him, though.'

'What do you mean?'

'Well, it's just an impression, but . . . under those impeccable Spanish manners of his, I'd say he was frightened of something.'

*

IN THE CORRIDOR outside the purser's bureau, a white-jacketed medical orderly saluted Gallagher. 'Dr Whiting's compliments, sir, and would you call on him as soon as is convenient?'

Whiting sat hunched over the desk in his office. A single sheet of paper lay before him, along with two small dark objects. 'I have the post-mortem report,' he said. 'I'll give you the high-lights. Shot twice in the chest at very close range; judging by the amount of powder residue, the gun must have been no more than an inch or two from his waistcoat. One bullet pierced the renal artery, meaning he would have bled to death in a few min-utes. He had no other injuries, and to all outward appearances was entirely healthy.'

He gestured towards the two objects. 'These are the bullets.'

Gallagher picked them up. Both were black with dried blood, but it was possible to see the rifling marks on the sides. 'I measured them for you,' Whiting said. 'They're .41 calibre, weight about a hundred and thirty grains.'

'Probably from something like a pocket pistol,' Gallagher said. '.41 Short is a popular calibre for derringers. I imagine there will be dozens of them on the ship, brought along by damned fools who think they can defend themselves against a U-boat.'

Whiting nodded. 'I heard there was a problem with another passenger this morning.'

Gallagher rolled his eyes. 'Someone messing about. He went up onto the bow to take photographs of the sea and nearly got washed overboard. Hamilton and I escorted him to safety.'

'Some of these people don't understand they're not still in Hyde Park,' Whiting said. He handed over the report. 'Let me know if you need anything else.'

SUNDAY, 2 MAY 1915
12.32 P.M.

ALREADY THE PASSENGERS were getting into their routines.
There were the men who strode purposefully around the boat
deck every morning, determined to get their daily exercise
regardless of the weather. There were the women who sat in the
saloon and embroidered garments of indeterminate nature with
fine silk stitches, or the elderly lady dressed all in black who
sat by the windowsill and painted blown eggshells in brilliant
intricate patterns like Fabergé eggs. There were the gentlemen
who sat and talked in droning monotones, not really listening to
each other, or the ones like Ripley who drank and played endless games of cards, all of them thinking in some small part of
their minds about what would happen on Friday morning when
the ship reached the war zone.

Their lives were confined to these small spaces; library and
smoking room, saloon and dining room, the outside deck if
the weather ever cleared, their own cabins. In this atmosphere
of elegant claustrophobia one could smell both ennui and fear
in equal measure. 'I have never known a voyage like this,' said
Maurice the maître d'. 'Another three or four days and they will
be climbing the walls.'

'Or chewing each other's legs off,' Hamilton said.

'Or both,' said Gallagher. 'Hammy, I've sent another telegram, this one to London. If a reply comes in from either
London or New York, have a messenger bring it to me at once.'
He needed to know more about Dowrich's time in America, and
he needed instructions about how to handle Kreutzer, before he
could move.

Lunch was as lavish as ever; potted shrimps, foie gras and

sardines followed by a choice of four different kinds of soup, omelettes, curried pheasant, a further choice of lamb chops, rump steak, leg of mutton or a selection of cold dishes including roast grouse, lobster mayonnaise, pressed beef and boar's head, followed by a range of desserts. Chalfont did not come to the table, nor did Franklin; scanning the dining room, Gallagher could see no sign of the young woman, Billie Dolan, either. The most likely explanation for her absence, he thought, was probably the obvious one.

The Lópezes were absent too. 'I saw Señor López this morning,' Mrs Markland reported. 'His wife is unwell. She has both asthma and a weak heart, poor thing.'

The results of the sweepstake on the distance travelled were announced, to cheers at another table. Gallagher carefully tore his ticket into small pieces and laid them on the tablecloth. Maurice caught his eye and grinned at him.

'This whole sweepstake thing is a sham,' Ripley grumbled. There was a smear of mayonnaise on his goatee beard. 'I'll bet the stewards pocket all the money and share it out between them.'

'They don't,' Dolly Markland said. 'The money goes to the seamen's mission in Liverpool. If you don't approve, Mr Ripley, don't buy a ticket.'

Ripley sniffed but, somewhat to Gallagher's surprise, he resumed eating in silence. At the end of the meal he belched loudly, said he had to see a man about a dog and departed. Schurz followed him soon after. Mrs Markland visibly relaxed.

'If you find him objectionable, I am sure you could move to another table,' Gallagher said.

'I must confess that was my first instinct,' said Mrs Markland. 'But I am sure I can bear it for a few days. If Ripley is prepared to let bygones be bygones, so am I.'

He wondered what lay between her and Ripley, but he changed the subject. 'Will you cross to France to join your husband, or will you stay in London?'

'That depends on Arthur. He has promised to take some leave when I arrive, and we will meet in London and make plans, or try to. God knows how long this accursed war will last.'

'Not long,' Gallagher said, smiling. 'Mr Franklin will soon sort things out.'

Her smile matched his. 'Of course. How could I forget?' Her smile faded. 'I wish I could believe him. I want this to end, Mr Gallagher. I want my life back the way it was. If you only knew how hard . . .'

She stopped, biting her lip. Gallagher watched her, seeing the struggle going on inside her. Franklin had talked about the soldiers dying at the front, López had recounted the horrors he and his wife had seen; Dolly Markland saw the war mostly in terms of how it affected herself . . . No, he thought suddenly, that is too facile. I see pain and hurt here, and also fear. Is she afraid for her husband, perhaps? That might explain why she had snapped at Dowrich.

'Are you married, Mr Gallagher?' she asked.

He shook his head.

'I thought not,' she said. 'You don't look like the marrying kind . . . I'm sorry, that was very rude of me.'

'You are right, as it happens. To be fair, *not* marrying wasn't a deliberate choice. It just seems to have happened.'

'Where are you from? If you don't mind my asking.'

'I'm not really from anywhere. My mother and stepfather live in Hampshire, but I have spent very little time there. As a boy, I ran away from school to join the marines, and spent ten years in the service. After that I was with Cunard for several years before I joined the civil service. There you have it, the story of my life.'

It was a heavily edited account, and she knew it. She regarded him sceptically. 'Are you not tempted to join up? No, don't worry, I'm not going to show you a white feather.'

'I've been told I'm not allowed to join up. It seems I'm in some sort of critical occupation.'

'The Paymaster General's Office does vital war work?'

'Apparently. I'll tell you more about it, just as soon as I find out what it is.'

'What you are telling me is that I should stop prying. Very well, I shall mind my own business. Thank you, Mr Gallagher. I have enjoyed talking with you.'

They rose and Mrs Markland departed. A steward arrived, bearing a telegram on a silver salver. 'This has just come in, sir.'

The message was from the service in London. His instructions regarding Kreutzer were brief and blunt. He was free to offer the spy a deal, on whatever terms were required; the important thing was to get him to talk about Chalfont. What London wanted was quite clear: proof of Chalfont's involvement with German intelligence, one way or the other, and the whole case wrapped in a nice neat package and tied up with a ribbon and bow by the time *Lusitania* reached Liverpool.

That was expected, and he turned to the rest of the telegram. As a precaution, he had asked if the service had a file on Charles Schurz. It did, and the summary of contents made interesting reading. Schurz was a prominent member of the Deutscher Bund and several other German social and cultural organizations in New York, Pittsburgh, Cincinnati and Milwaukee, all cities with large German populations. He was also friendly with many prominent German-American industrialists and scholars. The service had strongly objected to his appointment to the proposed Ministry of Munitions in Britain on the grounds that his associations made him a security risk, but had been over-ridden by officials from the office of the Minister, Mr Lloyd George; according to them, Schurz was the best engineer in the business, and that was all that mattered. The final line of the telegram noted that many of the companies where Schurz had served as consultant had also experienced problems with labour unrest.

He climbed the ornate stair to the promenade deck, hearing the whine of the electric motor as the lift rose beside him. Hamilton was behind the desk in the purser's bureau. 'I saw the message from London,' he said. 'Is that about our friend from this morning?'

'Yes. I need to see him again, Hammy. I might need to look into Dowrich's cabin again, too.'

'I'll give you a pass key. That way you can come and go as you like.' Hamilton handed over the key. 'Don't lose it,' he said straight-faced.

'I'll do my best.'

KREUTZER WAS LYING on the bed when Gallagher entered the cabin, hands clasped behind his head and staring up at the ceiling. He sat up quickly when he saw who his visitor was. 'May I come in?' Gallagher asked.

The German forced a smile. 'You may do as you wish. Have you come to interrogate me?'

'I would like to talk to you, yes.'

Lusitania rolled through another heavy swell, and Gallagher braced himself a little as he sat down in the chair opposite the bed. Kreutzer saw the movement. 'You have been at sea before, I think,' he said.

'Ten years in the Royal Marines,' Gallagher said. 'I also worked for Cunard for a time. And you?'

'I joined the Kaiserliche Marine four years ago. I was a junior officer on the *Scharnhorst* until the war broke out. Then I was detached for . . . special duties.'

'You're a lucky man,' Gallagher observed. Five months earlier, the armoured cruiser *Scharnhorst* had been sunk at the Battle of the Falklands. None of the 800 men aboard her had survived.

'Somehow I do not feel lucky,' Kreutzer said.

Silence fell. In the distance, the ship's fans hummed gently. 'Your offer has been accepted,' Gallagher said. 'Your life in exchange for what you know about Harry Chalfont.' He paused. 'That is the man we are discussing, is it not?'

'I want something in writing,' Kreutzer said.

Gallagher rose and went to the writing desk. Picking up a fountain pen, he wrote a short note certifying that Georg Kreutzer was under the protection of the Secret Service Bureau and was henceforth to be treated as a prisoner of war. Signing the letter, he handed it to the German. 'Satisfied?'

'What is to prevent your masters from tearing up this letter once we reach England?'

'Nothing,' said Gallagher.

Kreutzer searched his face for a long time, looking for reassurance and finding none. Finally he nodded. 'Very well. In for a penny, in for a pound, as the English say. Where do you want me to begin?'

'Let's start with you,' Gallagher said. 'Where are you from?'

'Thüringen, in central Germany. I later attended the University of Heidelberg, where I studied liberal arts and foreign languages.'

'Is that where you learned English?'

Kreutzer nodded. 'I had thought of becoming a diplomat, as I wanted to travel. Instead, my friends persuaded me to join the navy. We joined together, five of us on the same day. By chance, we were all assigned to the same ship.'

'The *Scharnhorst*,' Gallagher said quietly.

'Yes.' Kreutzer looked down at his hands.

So far, so good, Gallagher thought. He had answered clearly and, so far as could be told, honestly. 'This detached service you spoke of. Were you sent immediately to New York?'

'Yes. I was seconded to the service of Captain von Rintelen of the Nachrichten-Abteilung. As you know, he is the senior German intelligence officer in America. As well as intelligence-gathering, he was also ordered to disrupt the flow of artillery shells from America to the Allies, by whatever means.'

'What was your role?'

'I posed as an arms dealer, a buyer of munitions.'

'What name did you use?'

'I called myself Anders Kohlbach.'

Gallagher nodded; he had seen the name in the file on Rintelen. 'What did you do?'

'On the captain's orders, I bought large quantities of artillery shells, which might otherwise have been sold to the British or the French. We were trying to deny the enemy access to munitions. We then disposed of the shells by dumping them secretly in the sea.'

'You didn't send them to Germany?'

'Your blockade of German ports and harbours is quite thorough. Nothing would have got through. It was judged best to destroy the shells to keep them out of your hands.'

'What was Chalfont's involvement?'

'Harry Chalfont approached me at the Deutscher Bund

about three months ago. How he discovered who I was, I do not know. But he offered to help the operation.'

'How did he gain admittance to the Deutscher Bund?'

'He speaks German fluently, and professes to be a great admirer of German culture. He has read all the classics, Goethe, Schiller, Herder.'

'Sturm und Drang,' Gallagher said. 'What did Chalfont do?'

'He arranged deals with armaments manufacturers. He knew many of the directors of these companies personally, and could find out who their clients were and who was placing orders. He helped us to identify which companies were selling to Britain, but the best service he performed was to discover that one manufacturer was also selling shells to the Mexican rebels, especially to Pancho Villa and his Northern Division. This was later confirmed by our agent in Mexico City.'

'What is the name of this agent?'

'Colonel Maximilian Kloss,' Kreutzer said without hesitation.

'Which manufacturer was supplying Villa?'

'The Union Metallic Cartridge Company in Bridgeport, Connecticut. They had received an order for several thousand eighteen-pounder artillery shells.'

Gallagher thought about the business cards that he had taken from Dowrich's cabin, and the cryptic note on the back. *Ask him about White Star.* 'What did you do with the information Chalfont gave you?'

'I don't know all of the details, as I was not directly involved in that operation. Chalfont handled most of it himself. But somehow, the consignment that was meant for General Villa was diverted instead to the Mexican government. General Villa received instead a consignment of duds, shells that would not explode. When Villa attacked the government forces at the Battle of Celaya, his guns were useless. He lost most of his army.'

'What happened then?'

'The American authorities learned about the switched consignments; again, I do not know how, but the Bureau of Investigation began taking an interest in us. Chalfont was aware that the British and American authorities both suspected him. He advised us to shut the operation down.'

'Did you know he is on board this ship?'

'Yes. That is why I travelled third-class, to keep clear of him.' Kreutzer met his eye. 'Is Chalfont the man who spotted me? Did he betray me?'

'No. What makes you think you were deliberately betrayed?'

'Because I know how Captain von Rintelen's mind works,' Kreutzer said.

And that, my boy, is going to be very useful, Gallagher thought, once we get you back to England and start extracting information from you. 'Just a few more questions,' he said aloud. 'At the Deutscher Bund, did you ever encounter a man called James Dowrich?'

Kreutzer thought. 'I'm sorry. The name means nothing to me.'

He appeared to be telling the truth. 'What about an engineer named Charles Schurz? Did you meet him?'

The young man nodded immediately. 'Yes, several times. He was a consultant to some of the armaments makers we dealt with, including Union Metallic. We learned a great deal from him.'

Gallagher's eyebrows rose. 'Did he know who you were?'

'No. I was very careful to keep my identity a secret. Schurz thought I was another businessman in the arms trade. He was quite happy to talk. He liked to show off how clever he was. But he had no idea we were German agents.'

'One last thing. Does the name White Star mean anything to you?'

'Do you mean the British shipping line?'

'Possibly. Or it might mean something else.'

'I cannot think what it might be. If it is a code name, I do not know what it signifies.'

Gallagher rose to his feet and stood for a moment, balancing against the roll of the ship. 'You have given us all this information very freely,' he said. 'But you are an officer in the German navy, sworn to protect the Fatherland. I asked you this once before, but I must ask again. Does your duty to your country mean so little to you?'

'My duty to my country,' Kreutzer repeated slowly. 'My country, that sent my friends to die on the *Scharnhorst*. A cruiser with no more than a few inches of armour, against the twelve-inch guns of British battleships. They were lambs to the slaughter. No, Mr Gallagher, I am no longer interested in my country, only in my own little village in Thüringen, and a girl called Jeni who once gave me a paper heart.'

'Jeni. A nice name,' Gallagher said quietly. 'Is she your sweetheart?'

'She was once. I hope she will be again.'

Gallagher nodded. 'The war won't last for ever,' he said. 'When the end comes, hopefully sooner rather than later, you will be reunited. Are the stewards treating you well? Is there anything you need?'

'No, thank you.' Kreutzer looked surprised. 'But it is kind of you to ask.'

'War doesn't have to mean the end of civilized behaviour,' Gallagher said. 'We may be on opposite sides today, but we have both been to sea. I served with German sailors and marines in China during the Boxer Rebellion.' He touched the scar on his temple. 'I fought alongside them the day I got this. They were good comrades.'

'Yes. As you say, the war will not last for ever. Perhaps we will be comrades too, one day.'

'I hope so,' Gallagher said. He pointed to the service bell. 'Make yourself comfortable, and ring if you need anything. No, please, don't get up. I'll see myself out.'

7

DOLLY MARKLAND DONNED her cloak and went out onto the starboard promenade. The weather was still vile; the covered promenade kept out the rain, but even sixty feet above the sea she could taste the salt spray on her lips. At times the waves seemed like mountains, rearing up and flinging themselves at the ship, but *Lusitania* simply battered through them, steel hull quivering with the power of her mighty turbines. High over-head the wind in the Marconi aerials hummed a dark threnody.

She wondered where Arthur was now. Arthur Markland was a quietly kind man whom she had married a few months after she fled New York. People described it as a whirlwind romance, but there was nothing tempestuous about it, just a meeting of minds between a man who wanted a settled life and the comforts of home and a woman seeking to forget the past and find peace.

Arthur did not know her history, of course; none of them did, the smart Toronto set with whom they dined and played cards in their fashionable houses in Rosedale. He was an actuary by profession, who had become president of an insurance company and was accounted wealthy by modern standards; he had given her a fine house and a life of luxury, but most all he had given her things she had never experienced before, things like stability and certainty. Others might have described her life as monotonous and routine. She had clung to that routine like a drowning woman to a life raft, because to her it represented a fresh chance, a clean break with the past.

Then the war came. Once a month for all the time she had known him, Arthur had turned out for drill as an officer in a militia regiment, the Queen's Own Rifles of Canada. No one had been more surprised than himself when he was selected for the first contingent of the Canadian Expeditionary Force to France. Not for the first time, she wondered how someone as gentle and unimaginative as Arthur could ever have been appointed as a senior staff officer. She knew the answer, of course; General Currie, his commander, was also an insurance man.

His letters, since he had sailed, had been few and guarded. She had known he was in France, but for reasons of military secrecy he could not tell her where. Now, everyone knew the Canadians were in the thick of the action at Ypres; newspaper reports spoke of gallant deeds, bayonet charges and trenches held against overwhelming odds, but there was also talk of heavy casualties and, of course, the terrible new weapon, poison gas. She imagined Arthur in a muddy trench, holding a handkerchief soaked in his own urine against his face and trying to breathe through clouds of chlorine, but she shook the image off. As a staff officer he would be far behind the front lines, and safe. Wouldn't he?

The ship rolled and she clutched at the salt-damp railing, her knuckles white. She did not love Arthur Markland and had never pretended that she did, but she needed him, needed the comfort and security he provided like a drunk needs a lamp post to cling to for support; or, if she was honest with herself, sometimes to piss against. She treated Arthur abominably, but he always responded with a kind of stoic patience. She hoped, desperately, that he really was safe, because she was not sure what she would do without him.

She stood on the deck for perhaps an hour while her cloak grew sodden with spray, gazing out over the foaming peaks and wide ragged valleys of the sea, forcing herself to be calm. *Arthur will be safe. Arthur will be safe . . .*

'He will be safe,' she said aloud. 'And I will do whatever is necessary to keep him safe.'

The cold was beginning to bite. She went inside and into her cabin, shivering as she hung up the sodden cloak. I mustn't catch a chill, she told herself. I shall have a hot bath. She undressed and pulled on a dressing gown, and was just tying the belt when someone knocked hard at the door.

She frowned. 'Who is it?'

'It's Ripley. Open the door.'

Just for a moment Dolly Markland froze. She had hoped Ripley would spend the voyage playing cards and would pay her no further attention. She should have known better.

'Go away,' she said sharply. 'I'm not decent.'

'You never were. Open the god-damned door,' Ripley hissed, 'or I'm gonna break it down.'

Suddenly angry, she pulled the door open. 'What do you want?'

Ripley pushed past her and into the cabin, slamming the door behind him. He paused for a moment, looking at her. 'What's wrong with you? Seasick?'

'I was about to have a bath. Not that it's any of your business. What do you want?' she repeated.

'I want money,' he said. 'Fifteen thousand bucks, to be precise.'

She stared at him. '*What?*'

'Fifteen thousand,' Ripley repeated. 'And you, Dolly-doll, are gonna get it for me.'

'Ripley, what in God's name are you talking about?'

'For Christ's sake, how many times have I got to say it? I need money. I'm in big trouble, Dolly, and you're gonna help me.' He pointed a finger at her. 'Cuz if you don't, and I go down, I'm taking you with me.'

'Are you trying to blackmail me, Ripley? Because if you are, you can go to hell.'

Grabbing her arm, Ripley pulled her close and yanked her dressing gown over one shoulder, then hauled her camisole down and lifted one breast in his hand. There, just above her nipple, dark against the blue-veined cream of her skin, was a small tattooed rose.

'Ripley's Roses,' he said, and he smiled like a shark. 'My brand. My property.'

She pulled away, dragging her dressing gown closed once more. 'You stinking son of a bitch. You don't own me.'

'Don't I, though? What does your husband think of that tattoo?'

'He has never seen it.'

'Gordon Bennett.' Ripley stared at her. 'You been married to him for five years, and he's never seen your tits?'

'Get out!' she said violently. 'Or I shall ring for the stewards and have you thrown out.'

Ripley shook his head. 'No. You're gonna listen, and then you're gonna help me.'

'Or what? You'll expose me? Tell everyone I used to be a chorus girl? Well, go on then, do it! I don't give a damn. My husband will forgive me, and I don't care about the rest.'

A slow smile of malevolence spread across Ripley's face. He reached into his pocket and pulled out a black cigar, struck a match and lit it. 'A chorus girl,' he said. 'Sister, that is just the beginning. Oh yes, you were a damned good chorus girl. You could sing, you could dance, you could act, and my God, what you could do in bed defied the imagination. But you were more than just one of my Roses. I think people are going to be really interested in what you did after you stopped dancing, and became my partner.'

'You scum,' she snapped. 'You fucking piece of shit.'

Ripley blew out smoke. 'Yeah,' he said. 'Beneath the airs and graces, you're still the same old Dolly. Mouth like a sewer, you had. Well, whatever I am, you're the same, sister. There's nothing to choose between us. Especially not when it comes to Billie Dolan.'

She stood absolutely still. 'Billie Dolan,' Ripley repeated. 'The one you gave it all up for. I never understood that, you know. I mean, she was good; of course she was good, you trained her. But what was so special about her?'

'You wouldn't understand.'

'Maybe I wouldn't. Maybe I don't really care, if I'm honest. Anyway, here's my point. Billie is here, did you know that? Here on the *Lusitania*.'

'How do you know?'

'Cuz I seen with my own eyes, that's how. And you know why she's here?' Ripley puffed on his cigar again. 'This is the very special bit I saved up just for you. She's here cuz she's the mistress of Mr Edwin Peabody Franklin.'

'God damn Franklin.' Her voice seemed calm. 'He should never have brought her with him. He has no right to risk her life.'

Ripley looked disappointed. 'You already knew?'

'Of course I knew, you fool. But why did the stupid bastard decide to drag an innocent young woman into a war zone?'

'Don't ask me. Now look, here's the thing. I reckon I can get her away from him,' Ripley went on. 'When we reach England, he's gonna be so busy hobnobbing with kings and kaisers, if Billie does a flit, he ain't even gonna notice. Besides, he'll probably have a couple more bits of skirt stashed away somewhere, waiting their turn. Men like him always do. And you two lovebirds can enjoy your reunion.'

'What do you want, Ripley?'

He took a step towards her. 'I told you what I want. I want fifteen thousand bucks, and I want them now. That's my price for getting Billie back for you.'

'Oh, fuck you! Where am I going to get fifteen thousand dollars?'

'Come on. Your husband owns an insurance company. And if you can't figure out a way to extract money from his bank account, you ain't the girl you used to be. I need a wire transferring the money to my account. I'll write down the details for you.'

'Why do you need that much money?'

'I'll level with you,' Ripley said. 'Thing is, my last show was a bit expensive to put on. And now, my backers are wanting their money.'

'You lying prick. You said *Hop-Scotch* was a hit.'

'Oh, it was. In my view, it absolutely was. Trouble is, the critics and the audiences didn't agree with me. We had to pull the show after two weeks. On top of which, me and the critics and audiences hadn't seen eye to eye about a couple of other recent shows too, and I was finding it hard to get money from the banks.'

'What's the problem? Have your Roses begun to wilt?'

'Yeah, some of them have got a bit long in the tooth. Twenty years old in a chorus line is practically a grandmother, as you know, and since you left I haven't been able to recruit as much fresh talent. To cut a long story short, I borrowed the money from a . . . from a consortium of private investors. When I couldn't pay it back, I thought I'd go to Europe and wait till things cooled down. Unfortunately, the consortium decided to sell their debt to a gentleman named Paul Kelly. That's *the* Paul Kelly, the boss of the Five Points Gang. These days, they're just about the biggest gang in New York.'

'And Kelly sent someone after you. So what? I think I'll just do nothing, and let them kill you. I'll enjoy dancing at your funeral.'

Ripley seized her wrist again and held it hard, resisting her efforts to pull away. 'Don't fool yourself,' he said. 'Like I said, if I go down, I take you with me.'

'Fuck you,' she said again.

'Oh, I love a girl with spirit, but it ain't gonna do this time, you hear me? I'll leave a nice exposé for the papers, and I'll make sure Billie Dolan is front and centre of the story. Do you suppose Mr High-and-Mighty Franklin will keep her, once he finds out about her past? Not a chance. He'll beat the hell out of her, and then he'll throw her out in the street and let her starve. Think about that, Dolly-doll, and then after you've finished thinking, go and find that god-damned money. You understand me?'

'Yes,' she said. 'Now get out.'

Ripley bowed sarcastically. 'Good seeing you again, Dolly. Just like old times.'

SUNDAY, 2 MAY 1915

3.02 P.M.

THE PURSER HAILED Gallagher as he walked past the bureau. 'That other telegram you were expecting, Pat. It's just arrived.'

Gallagher followed him into the office and Hamilton handed over the buff paper form.

'Have you figured out how they did it yet?' the purser asked.

'How who did what?'

'Killed Dowrich and got out of a locked room without a key. I'm racking my brains and I can't figure it out.'

The telegram was from Captain Peters of the New York Police Department. Arriving in America, James Dowrich had begun to mix in political circles – how did he manage that? Gallagher wondered – and developed connections with Tammany Hall, the powerful political society that dominated New York and ensured the Democratic Party's iron grip on power. Dowrich had clearly done well for himself in the intervening years; he was said to be close to Charles Murphy, the unofficial leader of the society, who relied on him as an advisor. He was, in short, a highly respected citizen, and Gallagher could almost hear the irony dripping from Steve Peters' voice as he read the words.

The second half of the telegram concerned Jonathan Buckland. He had been managing director of the Union Metallic Cartridge Company for twelve years. Married with three children, he lived a blameless life, if one discounted the fact that he was an arms merchant. The company was thriving under his leadership, and had recently won several large contracts for export. Buckland was a strong supporter of the Democrats and had donated to party coffers for many years, including helping to fund William Randolph Hearst's campaign for the presidency in 1904.

'Anything useful?' Hamilton asked.

'Yes,' Gallagher said slowly. 'Yes, I think so.'

Dowrich had wanted to talk to him about the other passengers. The clues had suggested he was referring to either Chalfont or Schurz and very possibly both. But as a high-ranking member of Tammany Hall, he would have had access to many secrets. Might there be more to it than this? And where – if anywhere – did Kreutzer fit into the picture?

Time to find out, Gallagher thought, and he went looking for Harry Chalfont.

HE TRIED THE smoking room first, but there was still no sign of Chalfont; the barman said he had not been in all day. Going back downstairs, Gallagher knocked on the ex-vice consul's cabin door.

'Come in,' said a husky voice. 'And if you have any whisky, bring it with you.'

Gallagher stepped inside the cabin, closing the door behind him. The decanters on the sideboard were empty. 'I reckon you've probably had enough whisky.'

Chalfont stared at him, red-eyed, his lined face blotchy. 'For your information,' he said, 'there is no such thing as *enough whisky*. Ring for the bloody steward and have him fetch a bottle. Either that, or get out.'

Gallagher clicked his tongue. 'You promised you would give me no further trouble. Your word as a gentleman, you said.'

Chalfont's shoulders slumped, and he sighed. 'So I did. Your pardon, dear boy. It's just that this blasted deck keeps moving and heaving, and whisky is about the only thing that makes it bearable. Never mind. What can I do for you?'

'I wondered if we might have a little talk.'

'A little talk. What about, I wonder? Ah, let me guess. The high crimes and treasons of Mr Harry Chalfont, late of His Majesty's diplomatic corps. I thought your orders were to escort me to Liverpool, not to interrogate me.'

'My orders allow me a great deal of latitude,' Gallagher said, truthfully.

'Very well. Ask away and I will attempt to answer, insofar as my dilapidated mind will allow.'

Like Kreutzer, Chalfont was being unexpectedly coopera-tive. Or, Gallagher wondered, is it really unexpected? Both men must know that their only chance of staying alive is to tell the truth; either that, or a lie so convincing the authorities will swallow it whole. Kreutzer had given one version of the story. Time to see what Chalfont could come up with.

'Tell me about yourself,' he said.

Chalfont looked surprised. 'You've read my file. What else do you want to know?'

'You had a long history in the diplomatic service without ever quite making it to the top. Chargé d'affaires in Istanbul, second secretary in Berlin, consul in Trieste, then in Florence. Vice-consul in New York must have felt like a demotion. What went wrong?'

'Wrong? Nothing went wrong.' Chalfont reached into his pocket and pulled out his cigarette case and offered it to Gal-lagher, who shook his head. Removing a cigarette, Chalfont lit it and puffed out smoke.

'Nothing went wrong,' he repeated. 'I simply didn't care. Diplomatic service was never a career for me. It was more of a . . . pastime. It allowed me to indulge myself in the things I did care about.'

'Such as?'

'The usual. Horses, women, whisky, fast cars, women, rou-lette, women . . . And then, finally, when I had begun to think it was too late, along came *the* woman, the one I had spent most of my life dreaming of. Her name was Nancy and believe it or not, it was love at first sight. We were engaged inside a week, married in a month, and spent eight blissful years together until she died.'

'Yes. Cancer, I understand. That must have been a terrible time for you.'

Chalfont gazed at the smoke curling from his cigarette. 'I won't elaborate on my feelings, if it is all the same to you. If you have ever lost someone, you will understand. If you haven't . . .'

'I understand,' Gallagher said.

Chalfont looked at him, bloodshot eyes suddenly shrewd. 'Do you? Then I assume you will also understand why I went to New York. I took the first post, any post, that would get me as far away as possible from the places where we had been happy together. I didn't give a damn about rank or pay or promotion. I just wanted out.'

'According to reports from your superiors, you began drinking heavily.'

'True. Although given how dim most of my superiors were, I'm surprised they noticed.'

'When and where did you meet Franz von Rintelen?'

'At the Deutscher Bund, about four months ago.' The answer came smoothly and easily, almost as if Chalfont had not noticed the change in line of questioning. 'He was calling himself Hansen, just as you said.'

'Tell me how it happened,' said Gallagher.

'I knew the situation, of course,' Chalfont said. 'Our arms factories, like our army, were desperately unprepared for war. The shortage of artillery shells was already starting to bite last December, and by March this year we were facing a full-blown crisis. To survive, we had to import shells and explosives quickly, and that meant America. It was obvious that the Germans would work this out and send a team to America to interrupt the supply line. So, I tried to get a line on who they were.'

'Did you inform your superiors? Sir Courtenay Bennett, or the Foreign Office?'

Chalfont shook his head. 'That was my first mistake, you might say. But I knew I would be fishing in some fairly murky waters, and I needed the Germans to trust me. I didn't know who might be watching me or reading my letters. So, I told no one. I went underground.'

'What did you do?'

'My first port of call was the Deutscher Bund. The vast majority of Germans living in America are loyal citizens, but there are a few, a smattering, who support the Kaiser and the Fatherland, and I reckoned some of them could be German agents. So I hung around the bar, buying drinks and reminiscing about life in Berlin, waiting for a fish to bite. Finally, one did.'

'Who was he?'

'He called himself Kohlbach and he professed to be a dealer in arms and explosives, but it was pretty obvious he was an agent. A brand new one, too, still wet behind the ears. He stuck out a mile. I approached him, and a few days later he introduced me to his chief, Captain von Rintelen.'

Silence fell. Chalfont lit another cigarette. 'Kohlbach's real name is Kreutzer,' Gallagher said. 'He is a lieutenant in the German navy. We have him in custody.'

Chalfont gazed at him for a moment. 'Do you? I wondered what card you had up your sleeve. If so, then you presumably know what happened next.'

'According to Kreutzer, you helped him and Rintelen purchase consignments of artillery shells that might have been sent to the Allies in France, and destroy them. Did you?'

'Yes,' Chalfont said.

The silence lasted for quite a long time. 'It wasn't just filled shells,' Chalfont said finally. 'We bought shell casings, powder, explosives, fuzes, the lot. Then we loaded them onto barges in New Jersey, towed them out into the bay and threw them overboard.'

'All of which could be classed as aiding and abetting the enemy in a time of war.'

Chalfont made an impatient gesture. 'Like I said, I had to win their trust. Every time we destroyed another consignment, they trusted me a little more. What Rintelen and Kohlbach didn't know, because I ran bloody rings around them, was that for every consignment we destroyed, many others slipped away under their noses, destined for British ports. Through an intermediary, I bribed American customs officers to approve false manifests for neutral ships, and we smuggled the munitions aboard them. Very often those ships carried contraband explosives and shells into British ports without their owners or captains ever knowing about it. It wasn't enough, of course, it was never going to be enough to avert the shell crisis. But at least I did my bit, and hopefully some of our troops in France are still alive today thanks to my efforts.'

'Can you prove any of this?' Gallagher asked.

Chalfont shook his head. 'No. I was careful not to leave a trail. If Rintelen had known what I was up to, I would have been at the bottom of the Hudson River in fairly short order, with a concrete block tied around my neck to keep me there. As you pointed out yesterday, none of the people who worked with me is willing to testify in my defence. They all have too much to lose. Their lives, for a start.'

'Was Union Metallic Cartridge Company one of the firms you worked with?'

'Yes. Rintelen had some sort of inside line there. I was never able to discover what it was.'

'Were you involved with the Mexican shipments? What happened there?'

Chalfont grimaced. 'That really *was* a mistake. Rintelen discovered there was a chance to intercept one of the shipments of munitions the Americans were sending to Pancho Villa's army. Unfortunately, it all went wrong and Villa complained to the Americans, who started tracing the movements of the munitions. The Bureau of Investigation put the finger on me and informed Sir Courtenay Bennett, who in turn informed London. And now here I am, quite literally hoisted by my own petard.'

Gallagher studied him for a moment. 'It's a good story.'

'I do hope so, dear boy. Because it is the only one I have.'

'Our table companion, Mr Schurz. Did you ever meet him at the Deutscher Bund?'

Chalfont sucked in smoke and blew it out in a long cloud. 'We never met, no. At least, I don't remember seeing him, and he seems to have no recollection of me. But I heard others mention his name. Kohlbach, or Kreutzer, or whatever his name is, spoke of him several times. He was an excellent source, or so they said.'

'Was Schurz working with the Germans?'

'That is the question I am pondering myself. I don't recall hearing either Kreutzer or Rintelen saying as much. To them, he was just a puffed-up engineer who didn't really understand the meaning of the word *discretion*. He talked about his new job with the Ministry of Munitions, absolutely boasted about it all over town. I can't imagine that will make your chaps very happy. Or the US government, which is trying to be neutral.'

Gallagher nodded. 'James Dowrich met someone at the Deutscher Bund on the afternoon of the tenth of February. Was it you?'

Chalfont chuckled. Stubbing out his cigarette in the glass ashtray, he reached for another and lit it. 'How did you find out?'

Gallagher ignored the question. 'At dinner last night, you gave no sign of recognizing him.'

'Nor he me. If he wants to keep quiet about knowing me, that's up to him. But he certainly didn't conceal the fact that he knew Ripley. I wonder why?'

'Don't change the subject. How well did you know Dowrich?'

'I had met him a few times before, at social events. If you have done your background checks, you will know he's a Tammany Hall man, a fixer for Boss Murphy and Big Tim Sullivan. Anything they want doing, he does it. Vote rigging and ballot fraud are his specialties; if you want to win an election in New York, Dowrich is the man for the job. Or was.'

'What do you mean?'

Bloodshot eyes fixed on Gallagher's face. 'You spoke of him just now in the past tense. Was that a slip on your part, or deliberate? Either way, I'm guessing he's dead. Am I right?'

'Yes,' Gallagher said quietly. 'But keep it to yourself.'

'My dear fellow, keeping secrets is one of the things I'm good at. May I ask what happened?'

'He was shot.'

'Ah! Interesting. Am I by any chance on the list of suspects?'

'Do you know how to get out of a locked cabin without a key?'

'Do I look like bloody Houdini? Let me put your mind at rest. I didn't know Dowrich well enough to want to kill him. We met at the Deutscher Bund that afternoon because I needed his help. I told you I used an intermediary to bribe customs officers. Dowrich was that intermediary. He used his Tammany Hall connections, and I paid him a handsome commission for doing so.'

'Did he know what cargos you were shipping to Europe? Did you tell him about the munitions?'

'I didn't tell him, but of course that doesn't mean he didn't know. He would have had his own source of information.'

'What do you know about White Star?'

Just for a moment the cigarette in the other man's hand was unsteady. 'Why do you want to know?'

Gallagher said nothing.

'White Star is the very latest in industrial savagery,' Chalfont said. 'It is a type of gas shell, developed by our people but manufactured under licence elsewhere. It contains a mixture of two kinds of gas, chlorine and phosgene. Chlorine isn't as deadly as phosgene, but when you inhale the mixture the chlorine makes you cough, sucking in more air. That carries the phosgene into your lungs, and kills you.'

'Does Union Metallic manufacture these shells?'

'They do. So do other companies, of course. What has this to do with Dowrich?'

'The man has been murdered,' Gallagher said. 'Everything has to do with him.'

'Don't try to be glib, dear boy, it doesn't suit you. So what is your priority now? Extracting a confession from me, or finding out who killed Dowrich?'

'Nothing says I can't do both. Why do you think Dowrich was on this ship?'

'I don't know for certain, but one thought occurs to me. Dowrich did more than just rig elections. He cleaned up messes, for Tammany Hall and for other people too. Has it occurred to you that he might have taken passage on *Lusitania* in order to kill me?'

'If he did, you're safe now.' Gallagher rose to his feet, hand resting on the cabin door. 'Just one more thing. You said last night that Dowrich disliked me. Why, do you think?'

Chalfont's eyes twinkled for a moment. 'Did I say that?

I can't imagine why. Of course, it is possible that I was not entirely sober.'

Gallagher nodded. 'I'll send for that whisky now,' he said.

'Thank you,' Chalfont said. The twinkle faded and he sounded suddenly tired. 'That would be most kind.'

8

'GUTEN TAG, HERR Schurz. Unterbreche ich Sie?'

Schurz lowered his newspaper. 'Nein. Ich wollte gerade gehen.'

They were in the smoking room, the afternoon light dim through rain and spray.

'I must say, your German is excellent,' Gallagher said, smiling. 'Better than mine, certainly. Do your people still speak the language?'

Schurz looked puzzled by the question. 'They speak nothing else. I'm the first of my entire family to be truly fluent in English.'

'Really? I am surprised.'

The engineer shook his head. 'German immigrants tend to keep to their own communities. They are proud Americans, but they speak German, think in German, educate their children in German. Did I mention some of my family fought in the Civil War? There were entire regiments raised in Pennsylvania and Ohio where not a word of English was spoken. Even the generals had to have interpreters. We lost the battle of Chancellorsville because one of my ancestors misunderstood orders given in English and turned his brigade the wrong way.'

'And I imagine fluency in German also helps you with some of your clients. You mentioned last night that you are a member of the Deutscher Bund.'

'It's not the language, it's the cultural connection. My clients like to feel they are doing business with people like themselves, people they can trust.'

'I understand. Of course, not everyone who went to the Deutscher Bund was German. Chalfont tells me he used to go there quite often. He met Dowrich there once.'

Schurz looked blank. 'Did he? I didn't realize they were acquainted.'

'Oh, yes. Did you ever happen to see them there, Mr Schurz?'

'No. I had never laid eyes on either of them until we sat down to dinner last night.' Schurz's eyes narrowed a little. 'Why are you asking these questions? You're not really a civil servant, are you?'

Gallagher spread his hands. 'I'm sorry, I know this is intrusive. You see, I used to work for Cunard, and Captain Turner knows me. He needs to provide a full report on the man you spotted, and he has asked me to collect some information. I don't particularly want to do it, but Turner isn't the sort of man who takes no for an answer.'

That's one thing detectives and actors have in common, Roxanne had said. *We're both very good at lying.* He had been puzzled, and a little offended. *I thought acting was about finding new ways of expressing the truth*, he had said, and she had smiled and replied, *That's not what I am talking about.* He had not understood her, at least not at the time.

'Did you ever meet a man called Anders Kohlbach?' he asked.

Schurz's voice became still more guarded. 'I know him, yes.'

'Is he a friend?'

'Hardly that. I met him socially, that's all.'

Gallagher nodded. 'Did you not recognize him this morning?'

'What do you mean?'

'Kohlbach is the man you spotted on deck. The man we detained.'

Schurz stared at him, open-mouthed with astonishment. '*That* was Kohlbach?'

'The very same. You really didn't know it was him?'

Schurz recovered. 'Of course not,' he said coldly. 'He was some distance away, one deck below me and with his back to me, dressed in a rather shabby coat and hat. It never crossed my mind it could be Kohlbach.'

'And the light was poor, and there was quite a lot of spray flying around,' Gallagher mused. 'Yes, I can quite see why you missed him. And he's a fairly ordinary-looking fellow, isn't he? Nothing about him stands out.'

'I suppose so.' Schurz was still miffed. He folded his newspaper and laid it on the table. 'Have you established why he is on this ship?'

'Well, it seems fairly obvious from what you saw and from our subsequent enquiries that he is a German agent of some sort. You said you met him socially. May I ask what you talked about?'

Schurz was immediately defensive again. 'Business, mostly. Technical matters, too. I recall he was very interested in data comparing various explosives, trinitrotoluene, amatol, lyddite and so on. I told him nothing that would compromise your security, if that is what you mean.'

Gallagher wondered how he could be so sure of this. 'Did you mention your appointment to the Ministry of Munitions in Britain?'

'I may have done. There's nothing secret about it.'

'No,' Gallagher agreed. 'Of course not. Thank you, Mr Schurz, for your time. Once again, please keep this conversation under your hat.'

'If I must. There is altogether too much mystery on this

ship,' Schurz complained. 'I am a man of science. I do not like mysteries.'

'What do you mean?'

'Mrs Markland, for a start. I encountered her half an hour ago and greeted her, but she simply brushed past me. Her face looked like she had seen a ghost. Then there is that fellow Ripley. I overheard him arguing with the purser this morning, and ever since then he has been prowling around the ship staring at the other passengers. He is making some of the women feel quite uncomfortable.'

Ripley was at the bar, cigar in one hand and brandy glass in the other, talking to a group of men. All of them were laughing. Ripley made a gesture in the air, describing a shape like an hourglass, and they laughed again. 'Some of the men, on the other hand, seem to find him amusing,' Gallagher said.

'Perhaps. He is certainly not to my taste.' Schurz rose. 'Now, if you will forgive me, Mr Gallagher, I must go. I have some technical papers to read before dinner.'

After a moment Gallagher rose and walked over to the bar. Ordering coffee, he stood and listened to Ripley describe the various hit shows he had put on over the years. None were familiar to Gallagher; they had names like *Dulcibella*, *Bye-Bye Mabel*, *Enchanted April*, *The Girl Who Knew Too Much*. He wondered what Roxanne would have thought, and could almost hear the acid in her voice, commenting.

After a while the other men moved away. Gallagher smiled at Ripley. 'You've enjoyed a great deal of success in your career, haven't you? You and your Roses.'

'I sure have.' Ripley banged his brandy glass down on the bar and called for another. 'The King of the Great White Way, they call me, and they're absolutely right.'

'I'm sure. But tell me, what was Dowrich going on about

at dinner last night? Your last show, *Hop-Scotch*. He seemed to think it had been a flop.'

Ripley waved his hands. 'He was just taking a poke at me. He's one of those people who can never see someone else being successful without wanting to take them down.'

'Oh, so you know him?'

'Yeah, sure I do. He used to come to some of my shows, him and his big noise friends from Tammany Hall. It was good at first, they brought in business. It took me a while to realize what a snake in the grass Dowrich was.'

The brandy arrived. Gallagher picked up the chit and signed for it before Ripley could move. 'Did you have a falling out?' he asked.

Ripley was drunk, just drunk enough not to realize he was talking too much. 'Look . . . O.K., he was right about *Hop-Scotch*. Things have changed since the war came. People want different kinds of shows. I got it wrong, with that show and a few others. To tell the truth, the main reason I'm going to Europe is to get things back on an even keel again. If I can stage a few hits, fill some theatres, I'll recoup my losses.'

'Does Dowrich know you have debts?'

'Yeah, the slimy bastard. He helped me arrange a loan from some of his rich friends at Tammany, Big Tim Sullivan and that lot. When *Hop-Scotch* didn't work out, I asked for a bit more time to pay the loan back, but they weren't having it. When I couldn't pay up they sold the loan to Paul Kelly.'

'The Five Points boss?' Gallagher whistled quietly. 'I'd say you're in deep trouble, Mr Ripley.'

'You said it, brother. I thought I'd give them the slip by going to England, but no such luck. Yesterday afternoon Dowrich walks up to me and says Kelly has authorized him to collect the money. I've got to hand it over, or else.'

'Where are you going to get the money while we're at sea?'

Below the absurdly waxed moustache, Ripley bared his teeth like a dog. 'Don't worry. I've got a plan.'

'I think I'd be worried all the same, if I were you. What about your safety? Do you have a gun?'

'Me? No, I never carry a gun.' Ripley leaned closer, exhaling brandy fumes. 'This accident of Dowrich's. You don't suppose somebody arranged that, do you?'

'Why? Does he have enemies?'

The other man snorted. 'Brother, ain't you been listening? He's from Tammany Hall. They're not even good honest crooks up there, they're politicians, and that makes them the most devious kind of polecat that ever walked God's earth. Of course he has enemies, plenty of 'em.'

Over by the windows a group of men were gathering to play poker. Someone called to Ripley, who ordered another brandy and went off to join them. Gallagher stirred his coffee, watching him. Ripley's story, and he reckoned most of it was true, opened up another line of enquiry. Ripley clearly had motive to kill Dowrich. He claimed not to have a gun, but he could of course be lying.

There were two problems. If Ripley had killed Dowrich, he was hardly likely to incriminate himself by giving himself a motive for the murder. Also, Dowrich had been shot in his cabin between nine thirty and ten fifteen, and according to Mrs Markland, Ripley had been playing cards in the smoking room the entire time. Even if he was clever enough to find his way out of a locked room, which Gallagher doubted, had he also discovered the secret of being in two places at once?

And did it matter? Chalfont, of all people, had been right; Gallagher's duty was to his service and his country. A small-time criminal and political fixer had been found shot dead in his cabin; if no one ever knew the truth, would it really matter? Probably not, he told himself. But he knew that was not true.

SUNDAY, 2 MAY 1915

7.30 P.M.

DINNER WAS THE usual lavish array of hors d'oeuvres, consommé, potage Saint-Germain, turbot with lobster sauce, sole mornay, veal sweetbreads, lamb cutlets, ox tongue with spinach, roast chicken, haunch of mutton, sirloin of beef and a dazzling range of desserts. Gallagher looked at the menu and thought about the queues outside the butchers and the bakeries in London.

The Lópezes were once again absent, and so – surprisingly – was Mrs Markland. Schurz arrived late and said almost nothing throughout the meal, apparently brooding on some inner thoughts of his own. Chalfont sat hunched over his plate, glass of whisky in hand. Ripley seemed to have lost some of his ebullience at first, but a dozen oysters and half a bottle of champagne soon perked him up again. Franklin talked, mostly about himself.

'People often ask me, what is my philosophy of business? What is my secret? To me, the essence of business, and the reason why I have enjoyed a modicum of success, can be summed up in a single word: service. The modern businessman is not the people's master. He is their servant. I can honestly say that there has never been a single day in my business career when I have not thought about the people and their welfare, and how I may contribute to it.'

'So how come you're here playing the peacemaker, instead of back home running your business?' Ripley asked.

'Jesus,' muttered Chalfont under his breath, 'don't encourage him.'

'I am not *playing* at anything, Ripley. Service is not just a matter of commerce, it is a higher calling. Those of us who are privileged to hold power, as I am, have a duty to use that power wisely. I owe it to the people to act in their best interests in all that I do, not just in commerce, and that leads me naturally to pacifism.'

'Here we go,' murmured Chalfont.

'For centuries past, philosophers have argued that peace is the natural condition of humanity. Peace is good, Hobbes said, and therefore also the way to peace is good. To be at peace is to be in a state of virtue, whereas violence is the product of acts of sin. Look at the causes of any war, from the Trojan War to the present catastrophe, and what do we find? All the deadly sins, greed, anger, lust, pride; these are where conflict has its roots. Some, like Mr Schurz, have argued that war is a natural state of human affairs, but they are quite wrong. The weight of philosophy and the evidence of history are against them. That is why I intend to use my powers to bring this war to its end, and return us all to a state of grace.'

'Care to comment, Mr Schurz?' Chalfont asked.

'Eh?' Schurz looked up from his plate. 'I'm sorry. I'm afraid I wasn't listening.'

Franklin looked irritated but carried on. Ripley devoted himself to his food, smacking his lips from time to time. 'Dear God,' Chalfont murmured to Gallagher. 'How much longer do we have to put up with this?'

'Six more days to Liverpool.'

'I tell you what, dear boy. Suggest to your secret service chums that instead of pulling out my fingernails, they lock me in a room with this lot. I swear to God, in no time at all, I'll be singing like a canary.'

After dinner most of the passengers retired upstairs to the boat deck. As usual, many of the men disappeared into the smoking room to play cards, while the others and the women gathered in the lounge to drink coffee and listen to one of the American ladies play the piano, a beautiful arabesque unmistakeably by Amy Beach. Gallagher knew her well; Roxanne had introduced them when she was in Boston, playing Helen of Troy at the Globe, and they had remained friends ever since. Once, sitting in the audience watching Roxanne illuminate the stage, Mrs Beach had leaned over to him and whispered, 'Is she real? Or is she something from the spirit world?'

'I don't know', Gallagher had said.

Her cheeks dimpled as she smiled. 'And you don't care,' she said.

No. He had never cared what Roxanne was, or who she was. All that mattered was she had existed.

Chalfont appeared beside Gallagher, carrying two large glasses of brandy. 'One of these is for you.'

Reluctantly, Gallagher took the glass. 'To what do I owe the pleasure?'

'For treating me in a civilized manner. Far more civilized than I probably deserve.' He nodded towards the piano. 'Good. Not as good as old López, though. I was sorry not to see him and his wife at dinner.'

'They've had a rough time. Perhaps they just want a little privacy.'

'If you want privacy, an ocean liner is the last place to find it. Everyone on this tub knows everyone else's business, down to the last dotted i and crossed t. You get jolly sick of it after a while, don't you?'

A goldfish bowl, Mrs Markland had called it. 'It will be better when the weather clears and we can spend more time out on deck,' Gallagher said. 'You're not playing cards with the others?'

'I lost my taste for cards when Nancy died. Lost my taste for a lot of things, come to that. Sláinte.' He clinked his glass against Gallagher's and sank half his brandy at a gulp. 'What about you, dear boy? What arouses you? What passions lurk beneath that quiet exterior? Or is the prisoner allowed to ask such questions of his gaoler?'

'I'm not your gaoler. Only your escort.'

'Come on, dear boy, undo your top button. I know you have a romantic side, I watched your face when López was playing. Are you a musician yourself?'

Gallagher sipped his brandy. 'Can't play a note,' he said. 'I used to paint a bit, and I loved the theatre.'

'Oh? Were you fond of the classics, or were your tastes more modern? I'm betting the latter.'

Gallagher shook his head. 'It didn't matter. Shakespeare and Shaw and everything in between, I watched it all.'

'The theatre,' Chalfont said reflectively. 'A world of pretence and make-believe, special effects and illusions, smoke and mirrors. What attracted you to it, do you suppose?'

'Do you think it might have something to do with my job?'

'Touché.' Chalfont sipped his brandy. 'Well? How am I doing? Marks out of ten.'

Gallagher shook his head. 'It's not down to me. There's others you will need to impress. They're the ones who make the decisions.'

'Bravo,' Chalfont said. 'Not even a politician could have passed the buck more skilfully.' He studied Gallagher for a moment. 'How did you end up in the service? A burning desire to serve king and country?'

'I've never been much of a patriot,' Gallagher said. 'But my chief was a man I could trust. That was good enough for me.'

'That's not much of an answer. Look at your career: marines, Special Branch, secret service. I don't know what you did for Cunard, but I imagine it was something similar. Why choose that life?'

Gallagher paused. By opening up a little he might win Chalfont's trust, and persuade him to do the same. 'I never had much of a home life,' he said finally. 'When I was eleven years old, I ran away from school to go to sea. After that I wandered from one thing to another, looking for something.'

'Did you ever find it?'

'Yes, for a while. Like you, I met the woman of my dreams. And then she died.'

'Ah,' Chalfont said quietly. 'Forgive me, dear boy. My questions were rude and intrusive.'

'Not at all. I know how empty life can be after a tragedy. Like you, I also understand how quickly the sense of purpose slips from our grasp and vanishes.'

'Yes . . . I begin to think we are more alike than we first realized.'

'There is a line from Baudelaire that fits us both, I think. *Damaged goods, made in a worthless age.*'

Chalfont looked around the glittering room, lamplight reflecting off the polished wooden walls and the glass skylight. 'That probably sums up most of the rest of us, would you not say? Except for men like Franklin, and Schurz. They're not damaged, they are the producers, the makers of the machine age that stamps its imprint on people like you, and me, and the Lópezes. We can harm people so much more efficiently now, so much more swiftly and in such greater numbers. And we do it all in the name of progress.'

'You don't believe in Franklin's utopia?'

'Of course not. Neither do you. Neither does Franklin. The man is a megalomaniac, pure and simple. He believes in nothing except his own greatness.'

'Mrs Markland said something very similar. I find it hard to disagree with either of you.'

'Franklin is a product of our times,' Chalfont said. 'In no other era of human history could a tractor salesman imagine himself to be the world's saviour. No wonder the world is going to hell.'

Chalfont stopped suddenly, and shook his head. 'Listen to the voice of an old man talking. I sound ancient as a fossil.'

'Let me get you another drink.'

'Thank you, but no. I feel suddenly tired. I shall be sensible for once, and make an early night of it. Goodnight, dear fellow.'

Hamilton came up and touched him discreetly on the arm. 'There's something you need to see, Pat.'

Gallagher followed him out into the foyer. 'What is it?'

'The electrical current to the Marconi station has failed. We can't send or receive messages.'

'Have you discovered why?'

'Yes. Take a look.'

A floor-to-ceiling mahogany cabinet stood on the port side of the foyer, its inlaid decoration concealing its real function. 'The wires run up from the generator through here to the Marconi instrument, and also to the electric lights in the station,' Hamilton said. 'The telephone wire is on a separate conduit down to the exchange on the promenade deck.'

He opened the cabinet. The two of them stood close, shielding the interior from the gaze of any passers-by. Running down the wall were half a dozen wires covered in thick braided cloth insulation. In places the insulation had been scraped and scratched away, exposing bright aluminium wire, and here and there the wires had parted, leaving frayed silver strands hanging in the air.

Small black pellets lay on the floor of the cabinet, along with strands of insulating fabric. Gallagher picked one up and examined it in the palm of his hand. 'Still haven't got rid of those damned rats, I see.'

'God knows we've tried everything,' Hamilton said morosely. 'They've been a bloody plague since the beginning.'

'Could rats have chewed through the wiring?'

'Of course they could. Don't you remember?'

'I do.' A fire had broken out during *Lusitania*'s maiden voyage when rats gnawed through the electrical cabling. There had been other incidents since. 'On the other hand,' Gallagher said, 'an enterprising person could have used a file to scrape through the insulation and wiring, and put a handful of rat droppings on the floor to make it look more realistic.'

'Yes,' the purser said. 'That's exactly what I was thinking. What do you reckon, Pat? Be level with me now. I have thirteen hundred passengers and three hundred victualling crew in my care.'

'Kreutzer was a dummy,' Gallagher said. 'I'm absolutely certain of it now. We were meant to find him. That means there is another German agent on this ship.'

Hamilton gestured towards the cut wires. 'If so, they've shown their hand a bit early.'

'Yes. Although that may not have been the intention. They did try to make it look like rats.'

The purser was still staring at the wires. 'They want to stop us from sending messages.'

'Or receiving them. Or, possibly, from overhearing any chatter that might be going on around us. Do the Marconi operators scan all frequencies?'

'Yes. We listen to the German naval frequencies all the time. We got away from a German cruiser last autumn because we overheard her chatter even before she came in sight.'

'Then that's it. Someone is sending a message they don't want us to hear. How long before the Marconi station is working again?'

'I've sent for an electrical fitter. Probably only a couple of hours.'

'Good. Once it is up and running, tell the operators to keep their ears open. They might still hear something.'

9

Morning brought more wind and rain, rattling on the port-hole glass. Dolly Markland rose from her bed and looked out at the heaving waves in the dim light, slate-grey and frosted with foaming white. She thought about the abyss below the waves, the countless fathoms of darkness, and shuddered. Some of the other passengers enjoyed being at sea; Gallagher, for example, was at home here. She found the sea huge and terrifying.

She washed, dried her face and sat down at her dressing table where she used cosmetics to erase all traces of a sleepless night and restore her face to its usual emotionless mask. Putting on her cloak, she went out on deck. The hour was too early and the sea too rough for anyone else to be up yet; she found a sheltered corner on the forward part of the promenade deck and huddled there, listening to the wind scream in the Marconi aerials overhead.

Fear had kept her awake last night. Not fear of the sea, and certainly not fear of Ripley; she knew Ripley, and could handle him. Long ago when she was young and stupid she had found Ripley exciting, a rule-breaker and risk-taker who had encouraged her to do the same; not that she had needed much encouragement. Now she found him repulsive and ridiculous in equal measure. She was not frightened by his threats.

Her fear, if she forced herself to be honest – not a thing she was used to doing – was for herself. She had spent the last five years inventing a new life for herself, protecting her marriage, protecting Arthur; protecting herself. She had tried to put Billie Dolan behind her, and for the most part she had succeeded. There were occasional moments, flashbacks to the past when she felt the familiar longing gnaw at her bones, but she had learned to suppress these.

The news that Billie would also be on *Lusitania* had been a shock, but she thought that after all this time she could probably handle it. Ideally, she would get through the voyage without having to meet her face to face. It should be possible; if she dropped out of sight completely, people might begin to ask questions, but she could take some of her meals in the dining room, sitting with her back to the room, and order the rest in her cabin. Franklin's presence at the dinner table was repulsive, but she had proved on Saturday that she could live with it. She would avoid the saloon and library now, the places ladies frequented, and if the weather cleared, there were quiet places on deck where she could be alone.

To be alone, she thought. To be truly alone, dependent on no one, at no one's beck and call. I wonder what that is like?

Lusitania lurched in the trough of a larger wave, hull shuddering and vibrating while fountains of spray rose in the air. The wind shrieked. Dolly thought once more about the black empty depths beneath her, and shivered again. She turned and went inside.

MONDAY, 3 MAY 1915
8.07 A.M.

THE AIR IN the dining room smelled of bacon and hot coffee. There were more passengers than yesterday, but most of them were subdued, talking in quiet voices. The ship was four days from the war zone.

Chalfont and Dollie Markland were absent from the breakfast table but the Lópezes were there, the pianist picking at a piece of smoked fish, his wife sitting beside him. She had taken the top off a boiled egg, but she did not look like she intended to eat it. 'I hope you are feeling a little better, señora,' Gallagher said.

'I am much improved.' She did not look it; her face was pale grey, her lips bloodless. 'Perhaps what you said is true. I am getting my . . . what did you call them? My sea legs.'

'I hope so. But there was no need to come down here. You could have asked the steward to bring you breakfast in your cabin.'

'You are kind to think of this. But we thought it best to come down. We do not wish to draw attention to ourselves by remaining in our cabins.'

López looked at her sharply. 'What do you mean?' Gallagher asked.

Señora López looked confused. 'I am sorry. My English is not good, I do not always have the right words. I think I mean to say, it is very bad manners of us to sit in our cabin all day. We must be with our fellow passengers.'

'I am sure no one will think the worse of you,' Gallagher said.

'You are kind,' she repeated, and looked down at the glistening yellow eye of her egg.

After breakfast Gallagher called at the purser's office. 'Is the Marconi system working?'

Hamilton nodded. 'They had the electricity restored by midnight. And you were dead right, son. As soon as the system was up and running, the operators did a scan of all frequencies.

They picked up the tail end of a transmission on a frequency used by the German navy.'

Gallagher's scalp prickled as he picked up the telegram form. 'Have you informed the captain?'

'Yes. He ordered the intercept to be forwarded to the Admiralty, but he also said to give it to you and see what you made of it. It's in code,' Hamilton added.

'Yes, I recognize it. It's the SVB Code, an old one. German naval attachés abroad still use it. It's a simple substitution code, easy to break.'

Hamilton waited.

'... *fehlen klare Informationen über die Schiffspassage, ob die Fracht in Liverpool abgeladen wird. Am dringendsten an das Oberkommando Kiel weiterleiten*' Gallagher read. '... lack clear information about the ship's passage, or whether the cargo will be offloaded at Queenstown. Forward most urgent to the High Command in Kiel.'

'That's the telegram they didn't want us to intercept,' Hamilton said. 'Someone in New York is signalling about our movements.'

'Yes. But they're not certain. I don't understand the reference to Queenstown. We drop off the mails there, but everything else is always offloaded at Liverpool.'

'Maybe the Germans don't know that.'

'No. Perhaps not.' Gallagher looked at the purser. 'There's something else you're dying to tell me, isn't there?'

'Yes, although I'm not sure how helpful it is. You remember those two passengers you asked me to look out for? I've clocked them both. The one with the 'tache is registered on the passenger list as Juan Arango. No occupation, but his place of residence is given as El Paso, Texas.'

'El Paso,' Gallagher said. 'That's down on the Mexican border, isn't it?'

'So I understand. The other one, the big fellow, is Jan Steen, Dutch national and resident of Ijmuiden in the Netherlands. He's a business promoter, apparently.'

That would explain why he was listening to Franklin on Saturday night, Gallagher thought. When Franklin wasn't lecturing about pacifism he was usually giving monologues about his business philosophy and why he was so successful. 'Anything unusual about him?'

'Not that I've seen. He looks a bit rough around the edges, but the stewards say he's been a model passenger.'

'There's something dodgy about Arango, though. The Lópezes know it, too. She was watching him pretty closely on Saturday night.'

'Maybe there's something dodgy about the Lópezes,' Hamilton suggested, a note of humour in his voice. 'They're wanted criminals on the run, and Arango is a bounty hunter come after them.'

'Is there anything to connect either Arango or Steen to Dowrich?'

'Nothing that I can see. Like I said, I'm not sure how useful this is.'

Gallagher shook his head. 'I'm chasing my tail. Dowrich said he wanted to talk to me about some of the passengers, but which ones? He knew Chalfont and he knew Ripley, both of whom potentially have a motive for killing him.'

Hamilton looked surprised.

'According to Ripley, Dowrich was trying to shake him down,' Gallagher said. 'Which reminds me, Ripley has some scheme for getting money to pay off a debt. I suspect he's trying to run a grift on one of the other passengers. You might want to keep an eye on that.'

'Thanks for the warning. Of course, he also knew another passenger. You.'

Gallagher shook his head. 'Not well. We were shipmates for about six months, but he was navy and I was a marine. You know how it is, Hammy. Bootnecks and tars don't mix.'

He frowned. 'Yet all evening he kept insinuating that we were old mates. And at the same time, Chalfont thought he had something against me.'

'Did he know who you really are? The secret service and all that?'

'Possibly . . . What's the real story, Hammy? Why was Dowrich really on this ship?'

'Search me. What do you want to do about Arango and Steen?'

'Ask the stewards to keep an eye on them. Something may come up.'

Going forward along the promenade deck, Gallagher used the pass key to let himself into Dowrich's cabin, where he put on a pair of gloves and conducted a second, much more detailed search of the dead man's possessions. He examined the trunk carefully for concealed compartments, felt along the seams of the jackets and trousers to see if the lining had been re-stitched, bent the covers of the books backwards to see if anything fell out of the bindings. A little gingerly, thinking of White Star, he opened the bottles of toiletries and sniffed them but found nothing amiss.

The ship rolled again, and the cabin key on the sideboard clinked against the decanters. Gallagher flipped through the books page by page. Dowrich was clearly a man who liked to make notes, but was not organized enough to keep a proper diary; instead, he wrote things down on scraps of paper, like business cards or matchbooks or the margins of books. The book on shell manufacture had dozens of pencilled scribbles, numbers or sequences of letters that might have been chemical formulae, and the corners of pages relating to the filling of shell casings had been turned down to mark them. Dowrich had been a navy officer, of course, so he was familiar with shells and explosives.

The short stories and the pot-boilers had occasional notes too, mostly times and dates and initials, probably referring to people Dowrich intended to meet. In *A Connecticut Yankee in King Arthur's Court* several passages had been underlined in pencil, including a reference to the hero's home town, Hartford, his profession as a manufacturer of firearms and his eventual title in Camelot, 'the Boss'. Next to a passage where 'the Boss' humiliates Merlin the magician and destroys his reputation, Dowrich had written, *P.G. – play him.*

Dismissing more fanciful thoughts such as codes embedded in the text, Gallagher decided these were probably just expressions of amusement at coincidences in the book; the Boss probably made Dowrich think of Boss Murphy at Tammany Hall. The arms manufacturer might have reminded him of Buckland, the managing director of Union Metallic Cartridge Company, although he remembered Union Metallic was in New Haven, not Hartford.

P.G., he realized, might well mean himself. He hadn't remembered Dowrich at first, but Dowrich had clearly remembered him, and had planned a part for him in whatever scheme he was running. *Play him.* Sudden anger rose, and he thought for a moment about abandoning the case altogether. Dowrich could rot; a lonely, unexplained death was all he deserved. But he sensed this was about far more than Dowrich.

Monday, 3 May 1915
11.08 a.m.

After locking the door with the pass key, Gallagher fetched a blank telegram form from the purser's bureau and climbed up to the boat deck. The rose-carpeted reading room was quiet; two men were reading sporting magazines and a trio of women sat knitting silently in a corner, but that was all. A waiter brought him coffee and he sat for a moment, staring out over the sea and trying to compose a message in his mind. He needed the help of Captain Peters and the New York police again, and this time it was a little more complicated. The business card and matchbook had given him a hunch about Dowrich and Jonathan Buckland, the arms manufacturer, and he needed someone to test it. He also wanted to know the official American view of Charles Schurz. There was not a speck of evidence to connect Schurz with Dowrich's murder, but Gallagher still felt uneasy about the engineer.

Outside, the grey and white waves billowed to the horizon, but he thought the wind was down a little, and the clouds were higher and lighter. His mind wandered. He watched the fractal patterns of light and shade on the surface of the waves and saw how the patterns changed constantly, like particles flying apart and coming together. In his mind's eye he boxed out a particular quadrant of the sea and imagined how it would frame. To his surprise, the restless urge to paint which had once dominated most of his waking hours was starting to leak back into the fissures of his brain. He could imagine mixing colours, lead white – perhaps platinum white, which was a little less brilliant – and carbon black in careful dots to achieve those various shades of grey from slate to silver. Dots, that was it. How would a pointillist approach this subject? Signac had painted many seascapes, but they were always calm Mediterranean seas, not the wild North Atlantic. Yes, that would be a challenge.

Why am I thinking about painting again? he wondered. Perhaps it was being back at sea, for the first time in years. Earlier he had thought that the sea was no longer his home, but he wondered now if he was wrong. So much of his early life had been spent at sea that it had become part of his soul. There was no doubt that he missed it, like he had missed so many things since Roxanne . . .

He heard a sudden, soft noise behind him and turned, then rose quickly to his feet. A young woman stood before him, hands clasped in front of her, and just for a moment he was reminded of Roxanne, but this girl was taller and she had the face of a young angel. She wore a white skirt and a blouse of bronze-coloured silk, with fair hair piled up on top of her head. He realized this was the girl who had walked past the table on the first night of the voyage, the one Schurz said was Franklin's mistress.

'Mr Gallagher?' Her voice was soft as ripe fruit, with a trace of the South. 'My name is Billie Dolan. May I please have a word with you?'

'Of course. Please, do sit down. How did you know my name?'

They sat. 'The purser pointed you out to me, sir. He said you might be able to help me.'

'I see.' He felt a slight sense of resignation, but he trusted Hamilton; if the purser had sent her, then this girl must be in real trouble. Out of the corner of his eye he saw Harry Chalfont come into the library, pick up a newspaper and feel his way unsteadily into a chair. So much for the early night, Gallagher thought . . . On the heels of the thought Schurz walked into the room, glanced once at Gallagher and then sat down on the far side of the room, opposite Chalfont. Both were well out of hearing, as were the gentlemen reading magazines and the lady knitters.

'What is the trouble?' he asked quietly.

Miss Dolan had seen Schurz enter. '*He* is part of it,' she said, her voice low. 'I think he is following me. Every so often, especially when I think I am alone, I turn around and he is there. He never looks directly at me, but I know he is watching me.'

Gallagher paused. Schurz *had* followed Franklin and the girl to Franklin's cabin on Saturday night; he had admitted as much at breakfast yesterday. 'Do you know him? Have you met him before?'

'I never seen him before we got on board this ship, sir.' Her hands were like claws in her lap. 'I can't understand what he wants with me.'

If it had been anyone but Schurz, the answer to that question would have been obvious, but Schurz was an unlikely ladies' man. 'I should ignore him, if I were you,' Gallagher said gently. 'I reckon he's pretty harmless.' He met the girl's eye for a moment. 'And if not, you have Mr Franklin to protect you.'

She stared at him in alarm. 'It's all right', he said gently. 'I understand, and I promise not to tell anyone. Believe me, I know how to keep a secret.'

Whether her relationship with Franklin was indeed a secret was highly doubtful, but she relaxed a little. 'Yes, sir. But it's not just Mr Schurz. There's another man too, Mr Ripley. I . . . I used to work for him a while back.'

'As a chorus girl?' She looked alarmed again and he said,

'Miss Dolan, if I am to help you, you need to tell me what is going on.'

'Mr Ripley is trying to get me to leave Mr Franklin, and . . . oh, sir, if Mr Franklin finds out, he's going to get awful mad.' She swallowed. 'I need to get off this ship, sir. I need to get away.'

Her accent increased with her distress. Gallagher began to feel sorry for her. 'Get away from whom? Schurz, or Ripley?'

'Both of them. And from Mr Franklin, too, sir. I want to get away from him, from all of them. I just want to go somewhere, anywhere, and make a fresh start. I feel like my soul is covered in mud. I want to wash it clean, sir, and I want to make my peace with God and live my life free. But I can't do nothing, not with all of them hanging over me. I'm so desperate, sir, I don't know how to begin to tell you.'

'You don't have to,' he said gently. 'I know this is hard, Miss Dolan, but can you help me understand a few things? I can better assist you if I know what's going on.'

Mute with misery, she nodded.

'Why does Mr Ripley want you to leave Mr Franklin?' Gallagher asked.

Her hands began to twist, knuckles white with pressure. 'Mr Ripley says he needs money, sir. And he says he can only get it if I leave Mr Franklin.'

Gallagher was puzzled. 'I don't understand. Is he trying to get the money from Franklin?'

'No, sir, at least not now. He came to see Mr Franklin on Saturday afternoon, after we sailed, and he asked Mr Franklin for some money but Mr Franklin turned him down.'

Something stirred in the back of Gallagher's mind. 'Were you there when this happened?'

'I was in another room in Mr Franklin's suite.' Her distress was making her accent grow stronger. 'I was tryin' not to eavesdrop, I know it's wrong to do so, but they was shoutin' so loud I couldn't help overhearing. Mr Ripley was yellin' and sayin' this is all your fault for bringin' that lousy skunk into my theatre, and Mr Franklin was sayin' if you were damn fool enough to borrow money from Jimmy Dowrich, that's your lookout. There was a lot more like that.'

'Do you know what they were talking about?' Gallagher asked.

'Yes, sir. Mr Franklin used to come to the theatre a lot. He used to bring friends too, real high and mighty folk from Tammany Hall. That was back when he was thinking about going into politics, you see.'

'I didn't know he was.'

'Oh, yes, sir.' Now that the conversation was not about her, she was relaxing a little. 'He was planning to run for a seat in the Senate. The Tammany Hall folks were all for it, and they even put up the money for his campaign. Mr Franklin decided not to run in the end, but that didn't stop him from keeping the money.'

Gallagher was intrigued. 'He couldn't afford to finance the campaign himself?'

'Oh, he could, sir, but Mr Franklin never pays for anything if he can get someone else to do it for him. I reckon that's why he's so rich.'

Gallagher suppressed a smile. 'So what happened with Dowrich?'

'It was Mr Dowrich who introduced Mr Franklin to Mr Ripley. They were all three of them friendly for a while, but then there was a big bust-up. I don't know for sure what it was about.'

'This conversation on Saturday. Did they discuss Dowrich again?'

She looked surprised. 'Why, they were talking about him all the time, sir. Mr Franklin finally said he'd give Mr Ripley some money, but only if he'd get rid of Mr Dowrich. Mr Ripley said he wasn't getting into all that again, and they went back to shoutin' at each other.'

'Get rid of him?'

'Make him go away, I guess.'

'So Ripley didn't get his money.'

'No, sir. Mr Franklin is real careful that way, he never gives money unless he gets something in return. The only time he ever actually paid Mr Ripley money was when Mr Ripley had something he wanted real bad.'

'And what was that?'

The misery was back in her face. Her voice dropped to little more than a whisper. 'It was me, sir.'

Gallagher looked out the window at the heaving seas, thinking hard. 'We are three hundred miles south-east of New-foundland,' he said. 'The captain won't change course, not now.'

'I wouldn't expect him too, sir.'

'Today is Monday. On Friday afternoon we call at Queens-town in Ireland for a few hours before we sail on to Liverpool. When we reach Queenstown, I will help you get ashore and prevent the others from following you.'

How, he was not sure, but secret service agents were sup-posed to be resourceful; he would think of something. 'Do you have money?' he asked.

'A little.'

'I'll lend you more if you need it.' He could always claim it back from petty cash. 'I have friends in Ireland who will look after you and help you get settled. Until then, I'll ask the purser to move your accommodation. We might put you in third class, where no one will ever find you. It won't be comfortable, but can you tough it out for a few days?'

'I don't mind discomfort, sir, but it won't do. If I disappear, Mr Franklin will just demand that the captain hand me over. And the captain won't have no choice but to obey, will he?'

'While we are at sea, the captain's word is law.'

'But when we get to port, Mr Franklin will go to the authorities and make awful trouble for the captain, and you, and everyone. He's got powerful friends, sir, everywhere he goes. They can destroy you.'

No, they can't, Gallagher thought of saying; but it was quite probable that Franklin could damage Captain Turner's career, and the country needed seamen like Bowler Bill. He hesitated. 'Leave me where I am, sir,' she pleaded. 'I been survivin' for so long, I can survive a few more days. When we get to Queenstown, you can say I ran away and there was nothing you could do to stop me. Mr Franklin will still be mad, but he won't have no reason to harm you or the captain.'

Gallagher looked at her, doubtful. 'Are you sure?'

'Yes, sir, I'm real sure. I don't want you or anyone to come to harm because of me. I'm not worth it, sir.'

'All right,' he said finally. 'We'll do it your way. And will you do me a favour? If you remember anything more about Mr Ripley and Mr Franklin's conversation, especially anything they might have said about Mr Dowrich, will you tell me? It could be important.'

Lost in her own pain, she did not ask why. She nodded. 'I'll try, sir.'

After she had gone he sat for a while trying to work out the implications of what he had heard. Which was she more afraid of, he wondered, Ripley or Franklin? On balance, probably Franklin. He could understand why; Roxanne had educated him, telling him how powerful men like Franklin tended to be jealous possessors. They liked their women submissive and silent, clear reflections into which they could gaze and admire themselves. Roxanne herself had been strong enough to avoid becoming a victim, but she knew of many others who had not. *Behind the footlights lie some very dark places*, she had said, and he could still hear the quiet sorrow in her voice.

Sighing, he picked up the telegram form and began to write his message to Captain Peters. Chalfont rose and left the room. Schurz sat for a few minutes, gazing out through the salt-stained windows, and then followed him.

10

Lunch in the great domed dining room, the same pageant of white-coated waiters bearing silver trays balancing on the rolling deck as they moved to and fro, was not a convivial meal. Ripley gobbled his roast quails, muttering under his breath and glancing every so often at Dolly Markland, who picked at a plate of chicken mayonnaise and sipped a glass of water. Even Franklin was quiet, and in the silence Gallagher fancied he could hear the wheels of the great man's mind, clicking as they turned.

They rose at the end of the meal and Franklin turned. 'Mr Gallagher, can you spare me a moment of your time? There is something I wish to discuss with you.'

Gallagher was briefly surprised. So far as he knew, Franklin had never invited any of the others for a tête-à-tête; the shouting match with Ripley presumably did not fall under that heading. 'I am at your service, Mr Franklin,' he said.

They took the lift up to the boat deck and walked along to the smoking room, where Franklin ordered a malt whisky on the rocks and a cigar. He shook his head when Gallagher refused both and asked for coffee. 'You're an abstemious man, Gallagher.'

'I tried smoking a pipe when I was in the marines. Someone

told me it was the manly thing to do. I gave it up after about a week.'

'Are there no other pleasures in your life? What about women?'

'There was a woman once,' Gallagher said.

Franklin did not ask what had happened to her; it was clear that he did not really care. He puffed on the cigar and took a sip of whisky, ice cubes clinking in the crystal glass. 'What do you make of our friend Schurz?' he asked.

Gallagher wondered where this was going. 'I know little about him. He is a very successful engineer, it would seem.'

'Successful? Yes, you could say so. Successful at making weapons and shells that will kill and maim thousands of people, and earn a fat profit for the armaments makers.'

'You earn profits yourself,' Gallagher pointed out.

'I do, by making tractors and harvesters that allow people to put food on the table. As you know, I believe in industry as a powerful force for good in the world. But men like Schurz are threatening to undo all the good that men like myself have accomplished.'

'By helping arms makers?'

'It's not just that, it's his methods. He claims his work is grounded in rational science and is rigorously tested, but that is rubbish. He is little better than a snake-oil salesman. By dehumanizing work, he actually makes the workers less productive than they were before, but somehow he manages to persuade his clients otherwise.'

'Schurz would disagree. He also argues that his methods improve the lot of the workers, so they are less fatigued and better paid.'

Franklin snorted. 'Really? Then why is it, Mr Gallagher, that everywhere Schurz goes he creates unrest? Every single factory where Schurz worked has had labour trouble, every one. Strikes, walkouts, protests, the lot. When he introduced his methods at the Union Metallic Cartridge Company the workers attacked his time-and-motion men, beat them up, stole their stopwatches and threw them out of the factory. The governor had to send in the National Guard to restore order. If Schurz's work is benefitting the workers, the workers sure as hell don't know it.'

Franklin took another ship of whisky. Thin skeins of cigar smoke rose towards the ceiling fans. 'The problem has been particularly bad in the armaments industry. I understand Schurz is going to Britain to help your factories produce more shells. Mark my words, by the time he's done, there will be so much ferment on the production lines that you'll have fewer shells than before. That should make the Germans happy, at least.'

Gallagher watched him. 'Are you suggesting Schurz does this deliberately? Introduces working practices he knows will be unpopular, so as to cause unrest and slow production in the shell factories?'

'I don't know if he does or not. But if he does, he's doing a damned good job of it.'

'Clearly you care a great deal about your workers, and all of the working classes. Why not serve them more directly? You could enter politics, for example. A man of your abilities would find it easy to find a seat in the House of Representatives, even the Senate.'

Franklin tapped the ash of his cigar into an ashtray. 'As it happens, I once considered doing so. But I decided politics was not for me.'

'Why not?'

Franklin appeared not to have noticed the change of

direction; he was talking about himself now, the only subject that mattered. 'For one thing, I realized I have more power where I am. As an industrialist, I am not chained to any party or any ideology. I can go where I wish and I can speak my mind freely. People will respect me for who I am, not what I represent. Hence, my present mission to bring about peace.'

Gallagher nodded. 'But also, as I discovered, politics is a bottomless pit of corruption,' Franklin continued. 'Political machines like Tammany Hall and their partners in the criminal gangs control access to power. These are not people I would care to be associated with. I have high standards, Gallagher.'

Not so high as to prevent you buying a young woman like a slab of meat in the marketplace. Gallagher looked thoughtful. 'I understand what you mean about Tammany Hall. Our absent dinner companion, Mr Dowrich, is part of that set-up. Between you and me, Mr Franklin, I don't care for him much.'

'You would do well to stay away from him. As it happens, I am acquainted with Dowrich. I pretended not to recognize him, of course, I wasn't going to give a man like him the satisfaction of claiming to know *me*, but I can't imagine why I have to sit at the same table as him. If there was a proper captain's table on this ship, that would never have happened.'

Gallagher raised his eyebrows. 'You really don't like him.'

Franklin looked irritated. 'I dislike him in the same way one dislikes certain pernicious insects, like ants and wasps. And when men like Dowrich get in my way, I treat them exactly like insects. I squash them.'

The industrialist drank some more of his whisky. 'However, I digress,' he said. 'Dowrich is no longer in any position to bother me. My concern now is with Schurz.'

Gallagher waited. Franklin leaned forward a little. 'You may recall me mentioning that Mrs Franklin has chosen to stay at home while I travel to Europe,' he said.

'I do, yes.'

'However, I am not unaccompanied. Perhaps you are already aware of this.'

'I am. You are a fortunate man. She is a remarkably beautiful young woman.'

'You know who she is, then.'

'To be honest, Mr Franklin, I think it is a bit of an open secret.'

Franklin considered this for a moment, reflecting perhaps on whether this was to his advantage. 'Yes. It's hard to keep a girl like Billie Dolan under wraps. Are you sure you won't have a drink?'

Gallagher shook his head. Franklin caught the waiter's eye and signalled for another whisky. 'Schurz has some grudge against me,' he continued. 'No idea what it is. Jealousy, perhaps, because I am the more successful man, or because I called him out that first night at dinner and he failed to defeat me in reasoned argument. Or perhaps he is loyal to his war-mongering friends and rejects me for my pacifism. Whatever the reason, he has decided to attempt some form of retaliation. Rather pathetically, he is now making a nuisance of himself to Miss Dolan. He has started following her around the ship.'

'I see,' said Gallagher. 'Why are you telling me this?'

'I want you to talk to Schurz. Be diplomatic, but make it clear to him that he is to leave Billie alone.'

'Again, why me?'

'Oh, come, Gallagher, surely it is obvious. You're about the only competent person I've met on this ship. Chalfont is a drunk, Ripley is a clown pretending to be a ringmaster, and the old Spanish couple don't have much about them; he can play the piano a bit, but that's about all. I don't what the Markland dame's problem is; if I didn't know she was married, I'd say she was someone's spinster aunt. The rest of the passengers are sycophants and bottom-feeders. But you I can talk to.'

Talk to as an equal? Gallagher wondered. No, that would surely be asking too much. 'Men sometimes become obsessed with women. I can try to warn Schurz off, but there is no guarantee that he will listen.'

'Then explain to him what will happen if he does not,' Franklin said. 'Billie belongs to me. She is my possession. And I will defend what is mine, with whatever force is necessary. You may tell Schurz as much.'

Gallagher stared at him. 'You talked earlier about squashing Dowrich, and now using force against Schurz. What happened to your fine words from last night? Peace is the natural order of affairs, violence is the product of sin? Did you actually mean any of that?'

'Of course I did,' Franklin said calmly. 'I meant every word. Society has a natural order and is governed by its rules.'

'And yet you are willing to threaten Dowrich and Schurz.'

'Oh, come, Mr Gallagher, surely it is obvious. These rules, these arbitrary moral codes, are meant to apply to the common mass of people, not to men like me. I am above all that. I make my own rules.' He raised one finger. 'When I speak, Mr Gallagher, my word is law. Remember that.'

Gallagher paused. Megalomaniac, Chalfont had said, and he had not exaggerated. His first instinct was to tell Franklin to go to hell. But however deeply one despised the man, he did have influence and power. And, of course, there was the girl herself, who seemed to need protecting from the entire world.

'I'll see what I can do,' he said.

*

133

IT DID NOT take him long to find Schurz. The latter was in the reading room, sitting upright in an armchair reading a magazine; *The Engineer*, Gallagher saw. Chalfont was in a window seat, ostensibly asleep with an illustrated newspaper over his face, oblivious to the heave and roll of the ship. Billie Dolan sat in a corner of the big room, gazing out over the wild seas; she did not notice Gallagher enter.

'Good afternoon,' the engineer said, without enthusiasm. 'What can I do for you?'

'I've just had a word with Franklin,' Gallagher said, sitting down opposite him. 'He seems to be under the impression that you are following Miss Dolan.'

Schurz looked at him as if he had lost his mind. 'What? *Her?*'

'Her. The woman you correctly identified as his mistress.'

'Why on earth would I want to follow her?'

Gallagher glanced at Billie Dolan. 'Because she's the sort of woman that men follow. The face that launched a thousand ships, and burned the topless towers of Ilium.'

'What utter nonsense,' Schurz exclaimed. 'I'm not following her. For God's sake, I've a wife and three children back in Connecticut. I'm not interested in other women. And tell Franklin if he wants to make a complaint, come and do it to my face, rather than employing other people to do his dirty work.'

'On the whole, I think you'll find it rather more pleasant facing me than Franklin,' Gallagher said. 'You are quite certain you are not following Miss Dolan?'

'For God's sake, Gallagher. No, I am not following her. If you want to know the truth,' he said, nodding towards Chalfont, 'I am following *him.*'

Gallagher looked puzzled. 'Chalfont? What on earth for?'

'Because there is something fishy about him. You've spent

time talking with him, haven't you noticed? When he isn't asleep or dead drunk, he wanders around the ship like a lost soul. I found him yesterday afternoon on the promenade deck back near the barbershop, knocking on cabin doors. Most of those cabins are empty, aren't they? So what was he doing there?'

Gallagher came alert. Kreutzer was in one of those cabins; they had put him there to keep him away from the other passengers. 'Haven't a clue,' he said. 'Forgive me for asking, Mr Schurz, but why does it matter?'

'I told you, I don't like mysteries. There's something wrong on this ship. That fellow you arrested, that old Spanish couple always looking over their shoulders like someone is following them, that Mexican who keeps wandering about staring at people, and now Chalfont. It's getting on my nerves.'

Gallagher took his time before answering. 'Which Mexican?'

'I don't know his name. I saw him talking to Ripley yesterday afternoon. He's another thug, in my opinion.'

Gallagher nodded. 'You may be right,' he said. 'But here is a piece of friendly advice. Stay away from Chalfont.'

'Why?'

'Because he is under British government protection.' He saw Schurz open his mouth, and forestalled him. 'Sir, I strongly advise you not to ask further questions. Not unless you want to jeopardize your own contract with the British government.'

Slowly, Schurz closed his mouth. 'I understand,' he said in his usual stiff manner. 'You may rely on me.'

'Good. Concentrate on your work, Mr Schurz. I'll deal with Chalfont.'

Billie Dolan rose and walked out of the reading room, stumbling once as the ship rolled. Gallagher rose too and crossed to where Chalfont lay sleeping in his chair, lifting the newspaper from his face. 'Hullo, Harry.'

Bloodshot eyes opened, dark irises swimming in seas of crimson. 'Dear boy. Are we on first-name terms now?'

'Why were you wandering around knocking on cabin doors yesterday afternoon?'

'Yesterday aft— Hmm. Yesterday afternoon. To be honest, the period between lunch and dinner is a bit of a blur to me. Not sure I can tell you with any great certainty.'

'Try.'

'Don't be so peremptory, dear boy. Give me a chance to think. Now, let me see . . . I went up to the smoking room after lunch and had a couple of noggins, and it was then that things started to get a bit hazy. I couldn't remember which was my cabin, so I wandered along and tried my key in the lock of each one I came to, but none of them would open. In the end I resorted to knocking on doors, hoping to scare up somebody who could tell me where I belonged.'

'Did you?'

'No. Not one of the blighters answered, which is jolly rude when you stop and think about it. Never did find my cabin. Came back up here and passed out in a chair.'

That was probably true; the stewards could confirm it. The rest of the story seemed plausible, but the last thing he wanted at this delicate stage was Chalfont learning that Kreutzer was on the ship. He had been reluctant to put a guard on Kreutzer's door because he didn't want to draw attention to what or who might be in the cabin, but he might have to rethink that.

'Are you making a nuisance of yourself with Miss Dolan?' he asked.

Chalfont grinned at him. 'A nuisance? Dear boy, of course not. I am behaving like a perfect gentleman.'

'You're following her around the ship, aren't you?'

'When I am sober enough to recognize her, yes. Why not? I know I don't stand a chance, but I can still dream about what I would do if I were thirty years younger. Or even twenty, or ten. A girl like her wants someone better than that horse-face Franklin.'

'Or an old drunk.'

'A little less of the *old*, dear boy. Age is relative, you know. Do you happen to know the ship's present position?'

The question surprised Gallagher. 'We're about nine hundred miles from New York.'

'And how far to the edge of the war zone? Eleven hundred miles, or twelve hundred? Do you find yourself wondering what will happen when we get there?'

'No,' Gallagher said. 'I find myself wondering why I don't lock you in your cabin on a diet of bread and water. Stay out of trouble, Harry. Or I might change my mind.'

FRANKLIN WAS STILL in the smoking room. 'I have delivered your message,' Gallagher said. 'There has been a misunderstanding, but it has now been cleared up. You should have no further trouble.'

'I am glad to hear it,' Franklin said calmly. 'I expected you would find a way.' He blew out smoke. 'You are a resourceful man. I could use someone like you in my business.'

'To do what?' Gallagher asked. 'Fetch and carry? Run errands for you? Or as a bully boy, to keep people away from your mistresses?'

'I would pay you very well,' Franklin said, his voice still calm. 'Far more than you earn now. You can name your own salary.'

'You can't buy people, Franklin.'

'Of course you can. Everyone has their price, Gallagher. Name yours, and I will pay it.'

Gallagher stood up. 'I spoke to Schurz because I was concerned about Miss Dolan,' he said. 'I have no further interest in your affairs, Franklin, and no power on earth could persuade me to work for you. Good afternoon.' He turned on his heel and walked out of the room.

11

'I SPOKE TO the girl,' Gallagher said to Hamilton a little later, when they met up in the latter's office. 'I told her we would get her off the ship at Queenstown. I'll make sure she's looked after once she is ashore, but we need to make sure no one knows she has gone until after we sail for Liverpool.'

'If she doesn't mind a wee bit of discomfort, we can send her out in a mailbag,' Hamilton said. 'We've done it before.'

'Have we?'

'After your time. A runaway bride discovered her fiancé's family had sent detectives on board to bring her back. The master-at-arms and I put her down the mail chute, and the postmaster in Queenstown helped her out and gave her money to get away.'

'Hammy, you old romantic.'

'I had to do something. Same as this lass. She was pretty desperate when she came to see me, that's why I suggested she talk to you. I was worried she might be a jumper.'

It happened sometimes that passengers slipped over the rail at night or during bad weather, taking what they imagined was the easy way out of their troubles. Gallagher remembered one horrific case in particular. For some people, being at sea meant freedom from their everyday cares; for others, life on board ship felt like living in the jaws of a trap. And on this voyage, of course, the strains were greater than ever.

'Can you square this with the captain, Hammy? God knows I have enough else on my plate.'

Hamilton nodded, picking up a telegram form. 'This came in from your pal in New York. The barman said you were in confab with Franklin, so I held on to it until you were free. Was it an interesting conversation?'

Gallagher shook his head in distaste. 'Even if I wasn't already inclined to help Billie Dolan, half an hour in Franklin's company would have changed my mind.'

The telegram began with a complaint from Captain Peters to the effect that the New York Police Department's resources were limited and if Mr Gallagher wanted any further sleuthing done, would he kindly return to the city and do it himself. Gallagher smiled a little; caustic and sarcastic, Steve Peters was also the kind who would never let a friend down. He would pay the favour back one day.

His hunch about Buckland and Dowrich, based on the business card and the matchbook, had been correct. The managing director of Union Metallic Cartridge Company often came to New York on business, and Shanley's Oyster House was one of his favourite watering holes. Staff recalled him meeting James Dowrich – himself a very recognizable figure in Manhattan – late in January. The two men had lunch together; no one knew what they had talked about, but they had parted on amicable terms. One of the waiters thought he had seen them together before.

Gallagher paused. That last point was entirely likely; Buckland had connections with the Democratic Party, and he was bound to have run across Dowrich at some point. Those connections were probably good for business too. Dowrich had gone on to meet Chalfont a few weeks later; of course Chalfont already knew Dowrich too, but it was hard to avoid the feeling that all these meetings were connected.

He read the rest of the telegram. Charles Schurz was listed as the general manager of Charles Schurz Engineering Ltd, a consultancy based in Hartford, Connecticut, where Schurz also lived. *The Connecticut Yankee*, Gallagher thought. He also had offices in New York, Chicago and Cincinnati and employed about forty engineers, making his business one of the largest consulting engineering practices in the United States, rivalled only by Emerson and the Gilbreths. The Hartford office was the largest and dealt mostly with arms manufacturers. That made sense; this was the centre of the American armaments industry. Union Metallic was only a few miles away in Bridgeport, the famous Winchester company was located in nearby New Haven, and the big government armoury at Springfield was just over the border in Massachusetts to the north.

The final note gave Gallagher further cause for thought. Schurz too was a highly respectable citizen, but that was not always true of his contacts. One man in particular, a professor named Hugo Münsterberg, was a person of interest to the American authorities thanks to his pro-German views. He and Schurz had met several times, most recently in February of this year.

'Anything useful?' Hamilton asked.

Gallagher folded the telegram and put it in his pocket. 'Damn it, Hammy, I don't know. Dowrich seems to have known everyone in New York, and to have fallen out with most of them.'

'If he was a bagman for Tammany Hall, I'd say that was hardly surprising.'

'It now turns out he had history with both Franklin and Ripley, and was on bad terms with both.'

'Bad enough for either to have killed him?'

'Ripley certainly had motive for murder, but he was playing poker in the smoking room when Dowrich was shot.' At least, that was what Mrs Markland had said. 'And Franklin said something damned odd. *Dowrich is no longer in any position to bother me*, he said. What did that mean? Does he know what happened to Dowrich?'

'Or did he do it?' Hamilton asked.

'Not unless he shot Dowrich, swallowed the gun and crawled out through the keyhole. Next thing we know, it will turn out Dowrich has some past connection with Mrs Markland, or the Lópezes.'

'Maybe he's the bounty hunter sent to find the Lópezes,' Hamilton suggested.

'That isn't funny.' But a hare had started running in his mind.

MONDAY, 3 MAY 1915
3.16 P.M.

BILLIE DOLAN HAD gone to the reading room hoping some light and air would lift her spirits, but if anything the open spaces had made it worse. As soon as she left the reading room she fled down the ornate stair to the promenade deck, where she locked herself in her cabin, threw herself down on the bed and began to weep.

Four days until they reached Queenstown. In a moment of desperation she had poured her heart out to Gallagher, a complete stranger, and almost at once she had regretted it. The problem was not Gallagher; he struck her as a man who kept his word, and she had no doubt that he would try to help her escape. For a few brief moments this morning she had believed him, believed that freedom awaited her in Ireland, but over the years Billie Dolan had come to realize that hope is a brutal illusion. She would not escape; despite Gallagher's efforts, Franklin would prevent her from doing so. Nothing would change. The endless days of humiliation and fear would go on.

Someone knocked at the door. She sat up quickly, heart pounding, but realized it was not Franklin's knock. 'Who is it?' she called.

'It's Ripley. Open the door.'

Why had God turned his back on her? Why had He put her on this ship with the people she hated most in the world? 'Stay away from me!'

The doorknob rattled. 'Come on, I need to talk to you,' his voice hissed. 'Just for a minute, that's all. Hurry up, for Christ's sake! If Franklin finds me, you know what he'll do to both of us.'

Scrambling to her feet, she unlocked the door and pulled it open. Ripley hurried inside, pushing the door shut behind him. The ship rolled and he put a hand on the wall to steady himself. He smelled of stale smoke and brandy, as he always had.

Ripley stared at her. 'What's wrong with you?'

'Nothing.' Billie wiped her face with the back of her hand. 'Say what you want to say, Mr Ripley, and then go away. Like you said, Mr Franklin mustn't find you here.'

'I need you to do something for me.'

She looked at him, dully. 'What is it?'

'Did you know Dolly is on this ship? Dolly Markland, she calls herself now.'

'No,' Billie said after a long time. 'I didn't. I haven't seen her.'

'That's because she's being discreet. Keeping out of your way,

I expect, and trying to keep out of mine, too. I need you to go see her.'

'Why?'

'Really, kid? I know it was five years ago, but ain't you got nothing left inside you?'

'No,' she said in a voice of icy misery. 'I've got nothing left, Mr Ripley. You beat it out of me, remember? Why would I want anything to do with Dolly now?'

'Because you two lovebirds are going to run away together,' he said. 'Just like you were going to do back in the day. Well? Isn't this what you wanted?'

She stared at him. 'No. Anything you want me to do has got to be poison.'

Ripley growled in his throat. He took a step closer to the girl, who flinched and moved back, her hands pressed against the wall behind her. 'Don't cross me,' he said. 'Do as I say, and everything will be O.K. Refuse, and I'll make you wish you'd never been born.'

'You can't touch me. I belong to Mr Franklin now.'

'I won't lay a hand on you, kid. I don't need to. But if you don't agree to go with Dolly, I'll go straight to Franklin. See what I'm saying? You agree to go with Dolly, I'll keep your secret until you're away and safe. You don't agree, I'll tell Franklin you're planning to leave him. And he's not gonna like that.'

'You bastard,' she whispered.

'Dolly is up in that café on the boat deck. Pull yourself together, make your face pretty and go see her. Tell her I'll make all the arrangements to get you and her off the ship. In return, all she has to do is give me fifteen thousand bucks.'

He pulled out his watch and looked at the dial. 'Tell her she has an hour,' he said.

*

MOST OF THE passengers were gathering on the promenade deck below, drinking tea from cups that rattled in their saucers and eating sandwiches and petit fours with unsteady fingers. Up on the boat deck, the verandah café was empty apart from a single woman sitting and staring at the rain-streaked glass. A book lay on the table at her elbow, unopened.

Billie Dolan stopped a dozen feet away. 'Dolly,' she said, low-voiced.

The other woman's back stiffened, but she did not move. 'Dolly,' the girl said again. 'It's me. It's Billie.'

'I know who it is. What do you want?'

'Mr Ripley sent me,' Billie said.

'He what?' Dolly rose sharply, turning to look at her, and Billie saw her face for the first time. She was older, and thinner; her cheekbones looked like they were trying to cut through the skin of her face. Her lips were set in a thin, bitter line.

'Tell Ripley to stay away from me,' Dolly said. 'If he doesn't, he'll get hurt. So will you.'

Gallagher had offered to hide her on the ship. But there was nowhere to hide, not from people like Ripley and Dolly. 'You're right,' Billie said. 'I will get hurt. Ripley will see to it, he said so. Just like last time.'

She saw Dolly's fists clench. 'What do you mean, last time?'

'We were going to run away together, remember? You planned it all. We'd leave the theatre separately to avoid suspicion, and meet at Grand Central Station. You'd booked tickets on a train for Canada. We'd be free there, you said, free to be together.'

'I remember very well,' Dolly said, and there was a fine edge of anger in her voice. 'I waited for over an hour, until the train was ready to depart, but you never came. You didn't even send a message to tell me why you were staying behind. Why, Billie? What did they offer you to change your mind?'

'I never changed my mind,' Billie said quietly. 'I tried to go to the station, Dolly. But Mr Ripley saw me go, and he sent men after me and they dragged me back. And then they held me down, and he beat me with a cane until I bled. By the time I was well enough to walk again you were gone, long gone, and I had no idea where in Canada, and even if I had wanted to come after you, Mr Ripley wouldn't let me leave.'

'I wrote to you. I must have sent a dozen letters, asking if you were well, telling you where you could reach me. Why didn't you reply?'

'The letters never reached me. Mr Ripley must have destroyed them. Honest, Dolly, once you left, I never heard from you again. I never knew what happened to you. I just assumed you had forgotten all about me.'

'I never forgot you,' Dolly Markland said. The anger was still plain, but there was something else in her voice too, echoes of a long-suppressed pain. They stood in silence for a long time, staring at each other.

'What happened?' Dolly asked finally. 'Did you go back on stage?'

'For a little while. But I wasn't Mr Ripley's favourite no more. I was trouble, he said, and he wanted rid of me. After a while he sold me to Mr Franklin.' She swallowed the sour taste in her throat. 'I think that was part of my punishment.'

Dolly stared at her. 'He *sold* you?'

'Mr Ripley had some debts, like he always does. Mr Franklin cleared them, on the condition that I went with him.'

'Jesus Christ,' Dolly said. The anger was gone now, melted away. She looked down at the deck for a moment. 'What is Ripley offering now?'

'He said we can go together. He'll help us get off the ship, get me away from Mr Franklin. But before he does that, you have to give him the money.'

'He sold you to Franklin, and now he wants to sell you to me.'

'I guess so,' Billie said.

Slowly, as if she was very weary, Dolly sat down again. 'We can't trust Ripley. He'll take my money and double-cross us.'

'That's what I was thinking, too,' Billie said. 'But he says if you don't give him the money, he's going to tell Mr Franklin that I want to leave him.'

Dolly tapped her fingers on the table for a moment. When she looked up, her face had gone hard again. 'Leave Ripley to me,' she said. 'I'll deal with him. First of all, we need to get you away from Franklin.'

'Dolly—'

'You must move out of your cabin at once. I'll speak to the purser and find another cabin for you. Don't worry, I'll pay for everything. From now on, I am your protector.'

'And what does that mean?' Billie asked. 'Are you replacing Mr Franklin?'

They stared at each other. Billie Dolan looked into the other woman's face and saw the old hunger in her eyes. 'Do you want us to go back to the way things were?' she asked. 'Are you proud of what you did, Dolly?'

'I am not proud.' Dolly Markland's voice scraped across her throat. 'I have had five years to remember and reflect, and regret. I wish I could do things differently, and given another chance, I would. I still care about you,' she added quietly.

'You care about me? Back in the day you told me you loved me. Was that true?'

The ship rolled in the grey seas and the wind moaned in the Marconi aerials. 'Yes,' Dolly said. 'Yes, Billie, I loved you.'

'Then why didn't you come back? Why didn't you come to help me get away, or even just share my pain? No, you high-tailed it off to Canada and safety. Is that what you call love, Dolly?'

The other woman said nothing. 'I clung to you because you were my hope of safety, and you failed me,' Billie said. 'I came to see you today because I hoped against hope that you might be able to help me. But all you want to do is own me, just like the others. Well, you can leave me alone. I'll look after myself, like I always have done.'

'What will Franklin do if he finds out?'

'Same things as he always does.' Billie Dolan turned and walked out of the café, leaving Dolly Markland behind her, motionless, staring blindly out over the sea.

Ripley found her there half an hour later, still sitting and watching the rain beat the rolling seas to froth. 'Well?' he demanded. 'You got the money?'

'I'm still waiting to hear from Toronto.'

Ripley stared at her. 'Are you really? You're not trying to cross me now, are you?'

'Of course not,' she snapped. 'You gave me no choice, remember?'

'I need that money, Dolly-doll.'

'I am not responsible for delays to the Marconi service, Ripley. Perhaps the weather is affecting messages.'

'I don't give a god damn about the weather. I need the money,' Ripley repeated.

She turned her head and looked at him for the first time. 'Why is this so urgent? We're in the middle of the Atlantic, after all. Are they leaning on you?'

'They told me if I don't cough up the money by the time we land at Liverpool, I won't be getting off the ship. Trust me, sister, if anything happens to me, Franklin is gonna hear everything about you and Billie. I've already arranged that.'

'Who told you this? I don't see many Five Point gangsters on this ship.'

'And you'd recognize one, would you? Yeah, you probably would . . . It was that bastard Dowrich. He's the one who's threatening me.'

Dolly Markland laughed with a sound like breaking glass. 'Dowrich? He's no danger to you, or anyone else. Forget him.'

Ripley's eyes narrowed. 'What do you mean?'

'I mean, Dowrich is in hospital with a broken head, remember? He can't hurt you.'

'Dowrich ain't the only one,' Ripley persisted. 'There's others. They'll keep coming after me.'

'I don't believe you, and even if I did, I wouldn't care. Admit it, Ripley, this is a shake-down. Right?'

Ripley said nothing. 'Fine,' Dolly said. 'We know where we stand. You'll get your money when it's ready. Now, fuck off and leave me alone.'

Ripley walked away. Dolly Markland waited until he was gone, then took from her pocket the telegram she had written but not yet sent. Rising, she opened the glass door onto the open deck and stood for a moment with the wind whipping around her. Holding up the telegram, she started to tear it in half. But her trembling hands would not obey her.

After a long moment she folded the telegram and put it back into her reticule, and stood with her hands clenched at her side. Memories washed over her, memories full of shame and horror, but there was also the reawakening of desire, a hunger that gnawed at her nerves and stretched the hair of her scalp tight across her head. She swallowed, tasting bile in her throat, wanting to be sick, hating herself and longing for Billie at the same time.

I can't do this anymore, Arthur. God help me, I've tried for five years, but I can't do this. Not anymore.

12

The weather changed during the night, and a pastel-coloured dawn found *Lusitania* ploughing through calm seas, white water foaming around her black hull as she raced eastward. Having slept badly, Gallagher rose early and went out on deck. The sun was a dull light gleaming through banks of haze, tinting the oncoming waves with splashes of silver and lighting the effervescent foam at their crests.

For a moment again he imagined himself as a painter, trying to capture that emanant light, the softness of the mist above the harder contours of the sea. This time the thought disturbed him, and he stopped.

The sea is your mirror, Baudelaire had written. *You contemplate your soul in the infinite unrolling of its waves.*

Water rushed and hissed past the hull. The sun was shining brighter now, breaking free of the haze. The day might turn out fine, Gallagher thought. Back home it would be spring, with flowers in the meadows and hedgerows and birdsong filling the air, with everyone trying to pretend that life was normal and forget the bitter horrors being enacted in France.

He sighed. He had slept badly because he could not stop thinking about Billie Dolan. She reminded him of Roxanne. Not physically; apart from the fair hair, there was little resemblance. Billie Dolan was tall and full-figured, whereas Roxanne was so slight that he sometimes worried that a puff of wind would carry her away. But there was something familiar about the loneliness and fear and desperation. Roxanne had told him something of her own dreams and nightmares, when she had given him the copy of *Les Fleurs du Mal*.

The sweetest flowers bloom in solitude, beheld by no one. Roxanne had been like that. He wondered if Billie Dolan was too.

A movement caught his eye. He turned his head to see Mrs Markland coming out on deck, wrapped in a black cloak. She appeared not to notice him at first, but finally she looked at him and smiled. 'Good morning, Mr Gallagher.'

Despite the smile, her face looked hard and strained. 'Good morning, ma'am,' he said. 'How pleasant it is to see the sun.'

'I was thinking the same. It is so nice to get outside and breathe some fresh air. I find the atmosphere inside the ship more oppressive with every hour that passes.'

He smiled in turn, gesturing towards the sea. 'Enjoy the tranquillity while you can.'

'Yes. Three more days to the war zone. Half our fellow passengers are pretending to ignore the fact, the other half are jumpy as cats. I can't tell which I find more irritating.'

'Is that why you spend so much time on your own?' She looked at him, and he bowed his head. 'Forgive me. I used to enjoy having time alone when I was at sea.'

'What did you do in your solitude? Gaze at the waves and think profound thoughts?'

'No. I painted, or at least I attempted to.'

She blinked. 'Mr Gallagher, you never cease to surprise me . . . Were you any good?'

'No. I enjoyed it, though. It brought me peace.'

'Peace,' she said reflectively. 'You were lucky. I barely recall what peace is.'

'None of us do. Everywhere we turn, the world around is burning. Peace will soon be nothing more than a folk memory, a tale old people tell their grandchildren.'

'Some of us live their hells in public,' she said quietly, 'and some of us endure a more private form of perdition.'

He considered this for a moment. She wanted to talk, he sensed, but something was holding her back. 'Which do you do?' he asked.

'A bit of both, I suppose. I am worried for my husband, of course. Not a day goes by when I don't imagine him dead in a trench somewhere.'

'That is understandable.' He watched her for a moment. 'There's something else, isn't there?' he asked. 'You are afraid of something in your past.'

'Everyone is afraid of something in their past. Aren't you?'

'Of course. In my case it was someone I had sworn to protect, but who died on my watch. It happened here, on the Lusitania.'

Her eyes searched his face, wanting to know if she could trust him. 'I have spent five years trying to cut myself off from my past,' she said. 'But as soon as I returned to New York, even before I boarded the ship, it began to catch up with me. And I no longer know if I am strong enough to resist it.'

'Does your past concern Ripley? Pardon me if I am intruding.'

'No. I don't mind talking, not to you. You see, I used to work for Ripley.'

'You were a dancer?'

'At first, and then after I got too old I became his assistant.

I helped recruit and train new dancers. I enjoyed it, at least at first. I was young and impressionable, and I thought the life was glamorous and exciting. I suppose it was, in some ways.'

'Why did you leave?'

'I opened my eyes,' she said. 'I discovered that the glamour and sparkle and bright lights were built on rotten foundations. You don't know what it's really like in the theatre; you only find out when you see it from the inside.'

He wondered why her years of working for Ripley had left such deep scars on her soul. 'I know.'

'Do you? Yes, I think you do. You have more capacity for empathy than most men.'

'And you realized that if you stayed in that world, in time it would corrupt you.'

'No. I was already corrupted. That was the revelation I finally came to, and in that moment I knew I had to get out.'

I feel like my soul is covered in mud, Billie Dolan had said. He wondered if Mrs Markland felt the same. 'You must have been horrified when you realized you were sitting at the same table as both Ripley and his old pal Dowrich. You knew Dowrich too, I assume.'

Her face had gone still. 'Yes, I knew him . . . Has he regained consciousness?'

It was a curious question, Gallagher thought. 'No. There is a chance he might never do so.'

'Then the world will truly be a better place.' More people were coming out on deck, the morning exercise brigade striding out briskly, walking sticks tapping on the mahogany planks. At the sight of them, Dolly Markland seemed to recoil physically. 'I will bid you good morning, Mr Gallagher,' she said abruptly. 'It has been nice talking with you.'

TUESDAY, 4 MAY 1915
8.02 A.M.

SHE DID NOT join the others for breakfast. The Lópezes did, sitting silently while Franklin lectured them all on pacifism. Neither Schurz nor Chalfont challenged him this time; presumably they had realized by now that nothing they said to Franklin would have any impact, or make even the slightest mark on the impenetrable wall of his ego. Gallagher glanced at the Lópezes and saw they were watching someone on the far side of the dining room. Following their gaze, he saw the dark-eyed man with the moustache, the one Hamilton had identified as Juan Arango, cattle dealer from El Paso, Texas. He was sitting sideways on, apparently absorbed in the conversation at his table and paying no attention to the Lópezes or anyone else in the room.

Señora López's face reminded Gallagher of a rabbit hypnotized by a snake. Schurz had been right about the Lópezes, he thought suddenly; they seemed afraid, all the time. It had nothing to do with him, of course; despite Hamilton's joke, there was absolutely nothing to connect López and Dowrich. But all the same, his antennae were twitching, telling him something was going on.

Restless, Gallagher took the lift up to the promenade deck and walked aft through the ship, down the long passageways past the cabin doors with their numbers picked out in brass letters. He came to the cabin where Kreutzer was incarcerated and checked the door; all was secure. He walked on aft, past the drying room where the stewards aired and ironed laundry, and came to the barbershop. If Chalfont had been snooping around Kreutzer's cabin, the barber might have seen him.

The barbershop was small but comfortable, smelling of leather and soap and eau-de-cologne. Another man was already in one of the high chairs, reading a newspaper while the barber stood behind him wielding scissors and razor. The barber, a grave-featured black man who remembered Gallagher from previous voyages, nodded pleasantly. 'Sit yourself down, Mr Gallagher. I'll attend to you after I finish with this gentleman.'

'No rush, Joe,' said Gallagher, settling himself in the other chair. He glanced at the other man, and realized that it was the Dutchman, Jan Steen. Seen close up, his red face looked rather weather-beaten and there was an old white scar, partially obscured by sunburn, on the back of one hand. He was reading the *New York Times*; the article, Gallagher saw from the headline, was about the fighting around Ypres.

He cleared his throat. 'Bad business, that,' he said.

'Ghastly,' said Steen. His Dutch accent was a soft slur, barely noticeable. 'The Germans broke through at Gravenstafel Ridge, and high command sent two Canadian battalions to counterattack at Kitchener's Wood. Cowboys from Alberta and backwoodsmen from British Columbia, going up against machine guns and barbed wire and poison gas. I spent some time in western Canada, years ago. I probably know some of those fellows.'

'It really brings it home, when friends start to die,' Gallagher said quietly.

'It's the waste that appals me. The people in charge are clearly incompetent. No brains, no planning, no thought, just throw men into the mill. I've seen it before.'

Behind him the barber worked patiently, snipping hair. 'You're a military man, sir? My name's Gallagher, by the way.'

'Steen,' said the Dutchman. 'Yes, I saw service in South

Africa.' He smiled a little. 'I'm afraid I was on the other side. No hard feelings, I hope.'

'None whatever.'

'After that I knocked around a few places, Kenya, the East Indies and so on. I managed somehow to get involved in the Chinese Revolution too. That didn't go well.'

Gallagher nodded. 'I was out in China earlier, during the Boxer affair.'

'The Boxers? Was that the shambles they say it was?'

'Worse.' They talked for a few minutes about China, and Gallagher said, 'Are you on your way home?'

'Back to the Netherlands to settle down. I made a fortune in rubber out in the Indies. Now I'm going home to make another one in steel.'

'I didn't know the Netherlands had a steel industry.'

'It doesn't. I'm going to start one.' Steen smiled. 'So long as the war lasts, there's plenty of money in steel. Ships, guns, shells, you name it.'

'The Netherlands is a neutral country,' Gallagher said.

'So is America,' said Steen, and he smiled again. 'Where there's a war, there's a profit.'

The barber stirred up lather and began carefully applying it to Steen's chin and jaw. 'Are you enjoying the voyage?' Gallagher asked.

'It's comfortable enough. Food's good, and there's plenty of it.'

Gallagher looked dubious. 'I'm not sure about some of the passengers, though,' he said. 'There's some damned odd people on board this ship.'

'Tell me about it.' The Dutchman spoke carefully, lips barely moving as the razor glided along his neck. 'There's two of them at your table.'

The antennae twitched again. 'Oh? Who do you mean?'

'Isn't it obvious? Franklin, and that engineer fellow, Schurz.'

'Franklin is an egoist,' Gallagher said. 'Boring but harmless, I would say.'

'Is he? A man who thinks he can single-handedly bring about peace between Germany and Britain is mad enough to attempt anything. And I don't think Schurz is all he seems to be.'

'Oh?'

'I tried to engage him to work for me. I knew his reputation from management circles. He's a good efficiency expert, if a trifle heavy-handed with the men. I offered him a handsome fee, passage paid to the Netherlands, everything he could want. He turned me down flat.'

'He has a contract with the British government,' Gallagher said.

'I know all about that. They will pay him half what I offered. I've never yet met a consulting engineer who didn't follow the money.'

'Perhaps my government has offered him something more important than money.'

The barber wiped the last soap from Steen's chin and held up a mirror. 'Like what?' Steen asked. 'A knighthood? A peerage? A place in paradise? I would imagine all of these are in the gift of the British government.'

Gallagher smiled. 'Only the first two, I'm afraid. Schurz is annoying, but you should not be concerned by him.'

In other words, mind your own business. Steen smiled too, rising to his feet. 'I guess you're right,' he said, handing the barber a generous tip. 'Well, nice meeting you, Mr Gallagher. As they say in America, I'll see you around.'

There was a moment of silence after Steen had gone. Gallagher turned to the barber. 'It's a strange thing, isn't it, Joe?

Men who might otherwise be the soul of discretion will say absolutely anything in front of their barber, like he isn't even there.'

'I reckon they think we're all deaf,' said the barber. 'You wantin' a haircut, Pat, or somethin' else?'

'Something else. Have you seen anyone snooping around the cabins down this part of the deck?'

'Yeah, that old drunk fella, Chalfont, he was down here day before yesterday. Came in here sayin' he couldn't remember where his cabin was. I told him where to find it and gave him a steer. Never did find out if he got there.' Joe paused. 'Is he trouble?'

'If he is, he's my trouble,' Gallagher said. He nodded towards the door. 'What did you make of that fellow?'

'Tips real nice. But if he's a steel baron, then it's me that's the Dutchman. That boy's a fightin' man. I could smell it a mile off.'

Gallagher clapped him on the shoulder. 'Joe, you're in the wrong trade. When the war is over, sell up, go to Vienna and become a psychoanalyst.'

Joe sniffed. 'Reckon I'm better off as a barber on Big Lucy,' he said. 'Anyway, I don't see them two jobs bein' much different, do you?'

QUESTIONS, QUESTIONS, GALLAGHER thought as he let himself into Kreutzer's cabin. But never enough answers.

Kreutzer was seated at the writing desk, writing something on the ship's headed stationery with a fountain pen. Gallagher raised his eyebrows. 'Writing your memoirs?'

'My last will and testament,' said Kreutzer. 'Not that I have much to leave behind, but there are few things I would like people to remember me by.'

'You're not going to die,' Gallagher said. 'We promised you your life, remember?'

'I believe you.' Kreutzer wafted the paper in the air to dry the ink and then folded it and handed it to Gallagher. 'All the same, this is wartime and things happen. Keep this safe for me, will you, please? There is an address in Weimar where you can send it, if something happens.'

'I'll do my best,' Gallagher said.

'Thank you. To what do I owe the honour of this latest visit?'

'I have a couple of names for you. Have you ever heard of Jan Steen? A Dutchman who claims to be in the steel industry?'

Kreutzer shook his head. 'I am sorry.'

'The second is an American, or more likely a Mexican. His name is Juan Arango.'

Kreutzer sat up straight. 'Ah. Now you have my attention.'

'You know him?'

'I have never met him, but I know who he is. He is a staff officer with the Northern Division, an aide-de-camp to General Pancho Villa. He also played an important role in securing American arms shipments to Villa's army.'

'Would he know who you are?'

'I don't think so. As I said, we never met, and I had no direct involvement with Mexico.' Kreutzer paused for a moment, thinking. 'He might know Chalfont. I don't know for certain, but I have an impression that Chalfont was involved in the operation to send shells destined for Villa's army to the Mexican government instead.'

Chalfont had said as much himself. 'There's one more thing while I'm here. Charles Schurz. You said he was a useful source of information. Is there any chance he knew you were really a German agent?'

Kreutzer considered this for a long moment. 'I do not think so, no. He approached me several times, looking for contracts; he seemed very eager for work. He was only ever interested in business. He did not care who he dealt with.'

'You say he was looking for work?'

'Very much so. He is quite ambitious. I would say he wants to make a name for himself.'

And yet he had turned down a lucrative offer from Steen. Assuming Steen was telling the truth. *Jesus Christ, more questions.*

CHALFONT WAS IN the smoking room leaning against the bar, a glass of whisky before him. Sunlight poured in through the tall windows, shining blue through the fog of smoke from pipes and cigars. Gallagher looked at the glass. 'Hair of the dog?'

'Dog. Bloody great wolf, more like. I suppose it's no use asking you to join me.'

'No, thanks.'

'You might as well, you know. It's all free. Shall I tell you a secret, dear boy?' Chalfont leaned closer. 'I left all my money in New York. I have exactly six shillings to my name. When we reach Liverpool, His Majesty's government will have to pay my bar bill.'

'I see. You're trying to bankrupt the country, so we are forced to stop the war and sue for peace with Germany.'

'Exactly. I'm secretly in collusion with Franklin. We're all pacifists together.'

Gallagher smiled briefly. 'You said the other day you thought Dowrich might have been on board *Lusitania* to kill you. Why? Who would want you dead?'

'How long do you have?'

'Let's eliminate the obvious. The German spymaster, Rintelen, might have discovered you betrayed him – if you did betray him – but he wouldn't have let you live long enough to board this ship. I know Rintelen's methods, and they tend to be swift and direct.'

Chalfont watched him, eyes half closed. 'Who else do you have in mind?'

'You said Dowrich cleaned up messes for Tammany Hall. Did you do anything to annoy Boss Murphy, or any of his associates?'

'Not that I am aware of.'

'What about their friends in the gangs? Murphy and Sullivan are close to Paul Kelly of the Five Points Gang. Do you know him?'

Chalfont paused, calculating, wondering how much Gallagher already knew. 'My job required me to gather information from many different sources, high and low,' he said finally. 'Kelly is deeply involved in both the criminal underworld and New York City politics. At times, indeed, it is difficult to tell them apart. To give you a direct answer, yes, I have met Kelly. And no, I have given him no reason to kill me.'

There was something here, Gallagher thought, but he could sense Chalfont was digging in his heels. 'Have you ever heard of a man named Jan Steen?'

'Yes, I met him the other day. Good solid piece of Dutch beef. Looks like he might have been a prizefighter, don't you think?'

'What about Juan Arango.'

There was another pause. For a moment Chalfont seemed almost sober. He looked around, but the barman was busy at the other end of the bar. 'Why would you want to ask about Juan Arango?' he asked quietly.

'To find out what you know about him.'

'Don't be glib, dear boy. It doesn't suit you. Major Juan

Arango, as you most certainly know already, is a member of Pancho Villa's staff. He handled the transport of munitions from the American suppliers to Villa's army on the front lines.'

'Where did the munitions cross the border? El Paso?'

'You see? You do know already. What else can I tell you?'

'Did you ever meet Arango? Do you know what he looks like?'

'I had no direct dealings with him. Rintelen discovered his role in the munitions shipments, I don't know how. After that we tried to keep a low profile.'

'Nevertheless, Arango must know about the munitions swap. Is it possible that he has connected you with it? If the Americans suspect you, then Villa and his officers may suspect you as well.'

Chalfont considered this for a moment. 'What are you not telling me, dear boy?'

'Arango is on this ship, Harry. He could be looking for you.'

He waited for a reaction. The ship rolled a little and Chalfont gripped the bar, steadying himself. 'Really?' he said. 'Well, well. How fascinating.' He raised his glass. 'It's a good thing I have you to keep me safe.'

GETTING CHALFONT TO take anything seriously was like banging one's head against a brick wall. Irritated and frustrated, Gallagher went back upstairs and walked aft to the verandah café, where he sat down and ordered coffee.

The sun was warm on his face; it really was starting to feel like spring. Some of the frustration began to seep away. He studied the sea and sky, intrigued as he so often was by the purity of colour in nature that was so hard to create in painting. But of course, painting was another illusion, just like theatre, unless you could find that elusive truth that lay hidden beneath. It was easy to match the pigments; ordinarily it would be Prussian blue for the sea, but that was a bit unpatriotic these days, so perhaps ultramarine instead. The sky was cobalt overhead, lightening to cerulean on the long circular sweep of the horizon. Yes, the colours were easy. But how did you make them live? That was the secret that had always eluded him.

I'm a good painter, he had said to Roxanne. *But I will never be a great one, until I understand that.* And she had said, very seriously, *Don't think so much. Listen to the subject of the painting, let it tell you want it wants.*

Don't think so much . . . He had smiled at the time. It was an occupational hazard in his line of work. Pondering now, he wondered what to do with his suspicions. He knew his options were limited. It was easy to interrogate Chalfont and Kreutzer; one was a British citizen and a suspect, the other was an enemy officer and prisoner. But Steen and Arango were neutrals. He had no official reason to question them; if he tried to do so, he could find himself in the middle of a diplomatic incident.

And then there was Schurz. Chalfont thought he was suspicious, but then Chalfont might be saying that to cover his own tracks. Kreutzer thought he was an innocent dupe; but then again, Kreutzer could be lying. Something about Schurz annoyed Gallagher, and it was not just his smugness or his prudish way of reminding everyone of his neutrality. For someone who was about to go to work for the British government, 'neutrality' rang rather hollow. And yet, there was no reason to believe he was not absolutely genuine.

He sat for an hour, fidgeting, his thoughts broken and restless and tinged with premonitions of disaster.

The telephone behind the bar rang. The barman picked up the receiver, listened for a moment and then turned. 'Mr Gallagher? Mr Hamilton asks if you would be so good as to join him in his office, as soon as is convenient.'

Which meant, right away. The premonitions increased.

Hamilton was waiting outside his office, looking even more dour than usual. 'What is it?' Gallagher asked.

'I have Señor and Señora López in the office. They're both scared out of their wits.'

'What happened?'

The purser nodded. 'Come and hear for yourself. I told them you are a civil servant, by the way, but you used to be a policeman and you're an old friend of the captain. I think they bought it.'

The Lópezes were seated in the office, Señora López holding her husband's hand tightly. 'Please,' Gallagher said as they started to rise, 'don't get up. Now, tell me what happened.'

'Señora López and I went on deck,' López said, 'to walk a little and get some fresh air. When we returned to our cabin we found it had been ransacked. Our belongings had been pulled out of the wardrobe and hurled onto the floor. Señor Gallagher, we fear that our lives may be in danger.'

13

Gallagher sat down. 'Why would anyone want to harm you?' he asked.

The couple glanced at each other. Their fear was obvious; Señora López held their cabin key in her hands and she kept tugging at it with shaking fingers, pulling the snap ring open and shut with soft metallic clicks. Yet somehow, Gallagher was certain that they had rehearsed their story before coming to see Hamilton.

Hamilton remained standing by the door. 'Because of our politics,' López said. He hesitated. 'I do not know your own political views, señor.'

Gallagher smiled a little. 'I try not to have any. But I have nothing against those who do.'

'My wife and I are both committed communists, and have been for many years.' He looked at Gallagher a little timidly, almost as if seeking approval. 'My father was a labourer, and Corazón's father worked for the railways. They toiled for six days a week, often for ten and twelve hours a day, and yet they spent their lives in hardship and poverty. All we seek is a world that is fair and just, where labour receives its proper reward.'

'I am not unsympathetic,' Gallagher said. 'You have been active in the labour movement?'

López nodded. 'For many years,' he said. 'You might say we

inherited the profession from Corazón's father, who organized the first railway union in Spain. We helped to organize a syndicalist federation, Solidaridad Obrera, the Workers' Solidarity. Six years ago there was a general strike in Barcelona. The government sent soldiers, and when our people resisted the troops opened fire. Many of our friends were killed. We still refer to that time as the Tragic Week.'

'Was that when you went to Mexico?'

'We went into exile, yes. At first we resolved to stay out of politics. But as the situation in Mexico began to grow worse, we saw that the workers needed to organize in their own defence. We raised money from friends in Mexico and America, and we founded the Casa del Obrero Mundial, the House of Workers of the World. We helped many of the workers organize in the mines and on the railways.'

'Did you support the revolution?'

'What happened in Mexico was not a revolution, señor,' said Corazón López. 'It was an attempted coup d'état. When General Villa's troops occupied Mexico City, they committed terrible crimes. We escaped with our lives. Many others were not so fortunate.'

She tugged at the snap ring again, and this time the key slid off the ring and fell to the floor. Hamilton picked up the key and helped her reattach it to the silver tag. Hastily, she put it into her reticule. Gallagher watched her, a thought forming in his mind.

'The government promised greater rights for workers, so we supported them,' López said. 'We raised troops, the Red Battalions, and sent them to join the government army. I am proud to say they played a leading part in the Battle of Celaya, where Villa's troops were defeated. But after Celaya, the general blamed the Red Battalions for his defeat and put a price on our heads. A bounty of ten thousand pesos to whoever kills us.'

There was no easy way of confirming this; the British embassy in Mexico had closed at the outbreak of the revolution. 'Is this why you decided to return to Spain?'

'Yes. We have received assurances that we will not be prosecuted for the events of the Tragic Week. We hoped that by travelling to New York and taking ship there, we would escape the attentions of General Villa's bounty hunters. Alas, we fear we have not.' López looked timidly at Gallagher again. 'Señor Hamilton says you can speak to the captain and ask him to help us. Is this so?'

'Of course. Have you any idea who might be following you?'

'There is a man aboard this ship who is known to us,' said Corazón López. 'His name is Major Arango, and he is one of General Villa's officers. We think it may have been him who searched our room.'

Gallagher nodded. 'What do you think he was looking for?'

The couple looked at each other. 'We do not know,' said López.

Why I am so certain he is lying? Gallagher wondered. 'I will speak to the captain,' he said. 'I do not think this Major Arango will bother you again.'

After the couple had gone, Hamilton looked at Gallagher. 'What did I tell you? They're on the run, and Arango is the bounty hunter.'

'I'll never doubt you again, Hammy. Since you're so perceptive, I have another question for you. What weren't Señor and Señora López telling us?'

Hamilton rubbed his chin. 'You're right. They're holding something back, aren't they?'

'Everyone is holding something back,' complained Gallagher. 'Why do people have to have so damned many secrets?'

Hamilton grinned. 'Aye. There's the pot calling the kettle black. Are you going to speak to the captain?'

'There's no need to bother Turner with this. I shall have a little word with Major Arango myself. While I'm out, Hammy, can you do me a favour? Find out if any of the passengers have asked for their spare key.'

'What? All of them?'

'Just first class, for the moment. It will be worth it, I promise you. I think I've figured out the secret of our locked room.'

JUAN ARANGO LEANED on the rail on the promenade deck, sipping coffee from a china cup and watching the sea. The sunlight reflecting off the long low swells was so bright it made his eyes ache, and the deep blue waves were shot with silver diamonds. In the distance, low black shapes broached the surface of the water, shooting thin white spouts of spray into the air. Other passengers had stopped to watch them too.

Arango pointed as Gallagher came up beside him. 'There is a curious sight. What do you suppose it can be?'

'It's a pod of whales,' said Gallagher. 'Pilot whales, I believe. They're sometimes called blackfish.'

'Whales!' Arango stared for a moment, marvelling at them. 'This is amazing,' he said finally. 'I have never seen them before. My home is far from the sea, and all of this is very new to me.'

He looked at Gallagher. 'How do you know about whales, señor?'

'I've seen them a few times,' Gallagher said. 'I have spent much of my life at sea, one way or another.'

'I think you are a fortunate man. I find the sea fascinating, even in storms. Endlessly variable, endlessly changing, unlike the deserts and mountains of my home, which never change.'

Arango paused, still watching the whales. Two of them broached, leaping half out of the water before plunging back in fountains of spray. Some of the passengers applauded. 'Ah, beautiful,' Arango breathed. 'Magnificent . . . How strange to look at them, playing in the sun. They do not know there is a war on, and even if they could know, they probably would not care.'

Gallagher smiled a little. 'Which war, señor?'

'To the whales, what difference does it make?'

'Fair point.' He was a curious sort of assassin, Gallagher thought; courteous, friendly, interested in whales, intrigued by the romance of the sea. 'My name is Gallagher, by the way.'

'Major Arango.' The other man bowed a little, clicking his heels. Seen close up, he was younger than Gallagher had realized, not much more than twenty. Young to be a major, Gallagher thought.

'You mentioned your home. May I ask where you are from?'

'Mexico. Originally I am from Chihuahua, in the north of the country.'

'Ah, yes,' Gallagher said. 'And I think you also have a house across the river in El Paso, Texas. At least, that is what it says on the passenger list.'

Arango lowered his coffee cup and turned to look at him. 'How do you know this?'

'It is my job to know,' Gallagher said.

'Who are you? Police?'

'No. Just a civil servant.'

'I am a cattle dealer,' Arango said. 'I do much business with the Americans, and I have a house in El Paso where I stay when I go across the border. I use that address when travelling in America. It makes things easier with the authorities.'

'I'm sure it does. May I offer you a piece of advice, señor?'

'I am listening.'

'You know the elderly Spanish couple, Señor and Señora López? Someone searched their cabin this morning, and made no attempt to conceal it. They believe someone is pursuing them because of their political connections in Mexico.'

'I see.' Arango handed his cup and saucer to a passing waiter. 'Myself, I try to stay out of politics. As I said, I am only a humble cattle dealer. Affairs of state do not concern me.'

'I am glad to hear it, señor. Fortunately, I know who is responsible for the ransacking of their cabin. If anything happens to either of them, if a hair on either of their heads is harmed, I will have no hesitation in locking this man up and handing him over to the authorities when we land.'

Arango looked at him. 'Have you the power to do this? I thought you were a civil servant.'

He really is young, Gallagher thought, and naive to boot. 'This is a British ship, at sea in a time of war. The captain's word is law. And on this matter, the captain speaks through me. Am I understood, señor?'

Major Arango nodded slowly. 'You are understood,' he said.

Arango waited for a while after Gallagher had gone, thinking hard. Then he went inside and walked along the passageway to cabin B6, where he knocked twice at the door, waited a moment and knocked twice again.

The door opened at once. 'What are you doing here?' the man inside demanded. 'We're not supposed to be seen together.'

'We have a problem,' Arango said, entering the cabin and closing the door behind him. 'There is a man on this ship called Gallagher. Do you know him?'

'I know who you mean, yes.'

'Do you know who he is?'

'I have a fair idea. I've done my share of intelligence work, and I know the type. What is the problem?'

'He knows who *I* am,' said Arango, 'and he knows why we are here. He warned me off just now.' He smacked his fist into his palm. 'How in hell did he find out?'

'Any of a dozen ways. You've hardly been subtle, Juan. You didn't even bother to change your identity.'

'I did not think anyone would know me here,' the young man said sullenly.

'Well, no point in worrying about it now. The damage is done. Did you get into their cabin?'

'It was not easy. I am a caballero, not a burglar. I was in the midst of my search when one of the stewards came to the door. I had to hide in the wardrobe, and then escape quickly before the old couple returned. They know for certain the cabin was searched.'

'So you really have blown your cover,' the other man said. 'Did you find anything useful?'

'No,' Arango said curtly. 'But that does not mean there is nothing to find. The general was quite sure it is them.'

'The general was certain we would be victorious at Celaya too, and look how that turned out. Gallagher will be watching you, Juan. That means you stay away from the old couple, and you stay away from me. So long as my cover is intact, we still have a chance of finding out what really happened.'

'What are you going to do?'

'Wait until the dust settles. Let a little time pass before we make our next move. Keep your head down, Juan, and stay out of trouble.'

Tuesday, 4 May 1915
11.56 a.m.

Letting himself into Dowrich's cabin with his pass key, Gallagher looked around for a moment. Nothing had been disturbed; the key still lay on the sideboard next to the decanters. The number on the silver tag read *RMS Lusitania B16*, the number of this cabin. He picked up the key and attempted to insert it into the keyhole.

It did not fit.

'God damn it,' he said in soft anger. 'Someone has swapped the keys.'

He returned to the purser's bureau. 'Were you able to check on those spare keys, Hammy?'

The purser nodded. 'Four first-class passengers have requested replacement keys, but three later found the originals and returned the spares. The only one still missing belongs to your impresario friend, Ripley.'

'When did these people lose their keys?'

Hamilton shook his head. 'We don't keep records of that, Pat, and my assistants can't be expected to remember. They have hundreds of keys to look after, and a thousand other things to do as well.'

Gallagher sighed with exasperation. 'All right. Can you call up to the smoking room and see if Ripley is there?'

Hamilton picked up the telephone and spoke to the switchboard, then to the bartender in the smoking room. He nodded, looking at Gallagher. 'He's there, playing cards as usual. What are you doing, Pat?'

'I'll explain later. Which cabin is Ripley's?'

The purser checked his list. 'B14.'

B14 was an inside cabin on the promenade deck, across the portside passageway from Dowrich's cabin and only two doors along from Schurz. We're all in here cheek by jowl, Gallagher thought. For such a big ship, there were times when *Lusitania* could feel very small. Drawing breath, he took the key he had removed from Dowrich's cabin and fitted it to the keyhole.

The lock turned without resistance and the door swung open.

Around him all was silent save for the hum of ventilation fans. Closing the door, Gallagher began to search the cabin. He began with the washstand and writing desk, emptying each drawer but finding nothing of interest. The wardrobe was full of clothing, all in Ripley's usual colourful style; one drawer contained more than thirty sets of cufflinks, which seemed excessive. A shoe rack held a dozen pairs of shoes and boots from an expensive New York bootmaker. Beneath the shoe rack was a cast-iron strongbox with a Yale lock.

Picking the lock with an ease acquired through years of training and practice, Gallagher opened the box and began removing the contents. There was an account book, with personal expenses minutely noted, and a sheaf of carbon copies of typewritten letters, mostly to theatrical agents and fellow impresarios; he recognized some of the names. Other letters were to potential investors in Britain, people whom Ripley intended to persuade to finance his shows. There were some theatrical bills, usually showing pretty young women in glamorous costumes with exotic backdrops, along with lists of star names appearing in the shows.

At the bottom of the box he found the gun. It was a type he had seen many times before, a Remington Model 95 over-and-under derringer. This one had seen hard wear; the wooden grips were chipped and the bluing on the steel barrels was scratched and worn. Breaking it open, he saw two empty chambers, and when he raised the gun to the light he could see powder residue in both barrels. The gun had been fired, and not cleaned since.

Beside the gun was a plain waxed paper box. Opening it, he found rows of gleaming brass .41 Short rimfire cartridges, each with a letter U stamped on its base. Each was also loaded with a snub-nosed bullet identical to the two that had killed James Dowrich. The U, he knew, stood for the Union Metallic Cartridge Company.

Wrapping the revolver in his handkerchief, he put it in his pocket. He replaced the contents of the strongbox and searched the rest of the cabin. He found nothing else of interest.

Back in the purser's office he handed over the gun to Hamilton. 'Put it in the safe with the other one, if you would.'

Hamilton nodded. 'Is this the gun that killed him?'

'It might be. We'll know for certain when we reach Liverpool and can run some tests.' Gallagher dropped the key on the purser's desk. 'Better keep this safe too, it's evidence.'

'Are you going to tell me how they did it?'

'I think Dowrich let the killer into his cabin, meaning it most likely was someone he already knew. The killer shot him, then swapped the tag from Dowrich's key to Ripley's and vice versa. They left the dummy key for us to find, and used Dowrich's real key to lock the cabin door behind them.'

'Very neat,' Hamilton said. 'Where do you reckon the real key is?'

'At the bottom of the Atlantic, probably.'

'So, it's Ripley.'

Gallagher shook his head. 'According to Mrs Markland, Ripley was in the smoking room during the period when Dowrich was killed. The other alternative is that someone else took the spare key to Ripley's cabin. I know it's a stretch, Hammy, but can you try to find out when that key was taken, and who asked for it? Whether it was Ripley or someone else?'

'I can try,' Hamilton said dubiously. 'But I can't make any promises.'

'I know.' Gallagher thought for a moment. 'Either Ripley did kill him, or someone else did it and used Ripley's key in an attempt to frame him. In which case we might not have the right gun after all. But Ripley lied to me about one thing.'

'What's that?'

'He told me he never carries a gun. Maybe he didn't have it on his person when he met Dowrich, but he sure as hell owns one.'

Hamilton studied the derringer again. 'If Ripley didn't do it himself, that begs a question. Who hates Ripley enough to set him up for murder?'

'I can think of one person who might,' Gallagher said. 'Billie Dolan.'

Tuesday, 4 May 1915

3.32 p.m.

She knew it was the worst idea in the world, but she could not help herself. All her resolutions, all her defences were gone. Trembling like a woman in a fever, Dolly Markland knocked at the cabin door.

A moment passed before the door opened and Billie stood in the doorway, her eyes wide with surprise. 'I must speak with you,' Dolly said.

'No,' Billie whispered. 'It isn't safe. Please go.'

'I must speak with you,' Dolly repeated. Her voice was

breathless with tension. 'Please let me in. I promise . . . I promise I won't be long.'

After a moment, Billie stepped back and let her into the cabin. 'What is it?' she asked, closing the door.

'I'm leaving my husband,' Dolly said. 'I want you to give me a second chance.'

'Whatever are you talking about?'

Before the other woman could move Dolly seized her hand and held it in a tight, crushing grip. 'You were right,' she said, the words tumbling over each other like water. 'I shouldn't have left you. I should have come back for you. I did love you, Billie, and I still do. Please, please forgive me and take me back. That's all I ask.'

'I can't.'

'Billie, Billie, please!' There were tears in Dolly's eyes now. 'I know how to get money, we'll have everything we need. We can go anywhere in the world, Billie, anywhere at all, and we can be safe from all of them, Franklin, Ripley, everyone. We can be together for the rest of our lives, just you and me, no one else! No one will come between us, ever again!'

'They can,' Billie said. 'And Dolly, they will.'

'What do you mean?'

'If we go together and you don't give Mr Ripley the money, he'll tell Mr Franklin, and he'll come after us. Maybe they both will. It's no good, Dolly, it won't do!'

'But I'll protect you! I know I failed you before, but never again, never. When we reach England I'll do whatever it takes, but I will get you away from Franklin. Run with me, Billie!'

'I'm telling you, I can't! If I leave him, he'll hunt me down like a dog. He said so once, when he was real mad at me. There ain't no place we can hide, Dolly! You have to stay away from me, otherwise you could get hurt, real bad. And despite every-thing, I don't want that.'

Tears were streaming down Dolly's face. 'But I love you,' she said desperately. 'Now that I have seen you again, I can't live without you. I'll give up everything for you, everything—'

She stopped. The colour surged in Billie Dolan's cheeks and she took a step towards the older woman. 'Never say that!' she snapped. 'Never, ever say that to me again!'

'But darling—'

'Don't you *darling* me! Do you even know what love is, Dolly? I don't think you do, and I sure as hell don't. I've never had love from anyone, not even you. Just . . . the other.'

Dolly drew a deep breath. 'Five years ago you wanted to come with me.'

'Only cuz you were a way out of a trap I had fallen into. That's all there was. Nothing else.'

'But I can't leave you with Franklin! The thought of you with him makes me want to vomit. I swear to God, if you won't leave him, I'll kill him myself.'

Billie looked at her with contempt. 'You ain't capable of killin' anyone.'

'Don't be too sure of that.' Suddenly, Dolly Markland was growing calmer. She took a handkerchief from her reticule and wiped her face. 'I mean it, Billie. I hate that piece of shit Franklin with every fibre of my being. I will not allow him to keep you.'

'He won't keep me.' Billie stopped, biting back what she had been about to say.

Dolly's eyes narrowed. 'You're going to run from him anyway. Aren't you? I thought you said he'd hunt you down like a dog.'

'I can look after myself,' Billie said, unconvincingly.

'So you said that just to get rid of me.'

'That's right. I did.'

A little silence fell. 'So,' Dolly said finally. 'Are you telling me there is nothing between us? Nothing at all?'

'I never loved you, Dolly. You gave me hope, for a while, just like Mr Franklin did. For a while. But in the end the hope failed, like it always does. I didn't love you, Dolly, and I sure as hell don't love you now.'

'I would have died for you,' Dolly Markland said quietly.

'Well I don't want you to die, not for me, not for anyone else! Now damn you to hell, Dolly, get out of my cabin! And stay away from me!'

Grabbing Dolly's arm, she wrenched open the cabin door and propelled the other woman out into the passageway. The door slammed. Drawing another long, ragged breath, Dolly turned and walked away. This is how addicts must feel, she thought, hating themselves, hating their obsession, unable to let go. After five years, I never thought I could want her so much. Now, I don't want anything else.

14

'Tell me,' said Chalfont. 'Why do you think that fellow Schurz is following me?'

Dinner had been another lavishly gloomy affair, the dining room half full of people counting down the hours until *Lusitania* reached the war zone. Mrs Markland did not appear for dinner; the Lópezes picked at their food and left halfway through, muttering apologies. Franklin sat in silence, contemplating the world and his own preponderance in it, and Chalfont's attempts to bait him were met with a stolid wall of indifference. Ripley slurped his way through a dozen oysters and then began telling long anecdotes about the theatre, to which no one listened. It had been a relief to escape to the smoking room.

'What makes you think he is?' Gallagher asked.

'Because every time I turn around he's there, sitting and pretending to read one of his infernal technical magazines. Look, there he is now.'

Schurz was seated by the window, engrossed in another copy of *Engineering Magazine*. The Dutchman, Steen, was not far away, hunched over a table and absorbed in a game of backgammon. 'Perhaps he finds you fascinating,' Gallagher said. 'Or perhaps he thinks you are a German spy.'

Chalfont snorted. 'If anyone is a German spy, it's him. He may claim he is neutral, but back in New York he kept some damned strange company. Do you know of a fellow called Professor Münsterberg?'

Peters had mentioned Münsterberg in his last telegram. 'Enlighten me.'

'Apparently they have something called industrial psychology nowadays. It's the latest fad. Münsterberg is an industrial psychologist, teaches at Harvard. Fellows like Schurz regard him as some sort of grand panjandrum, and flock to him for advice on how to manipulate people and turn them into machines.'

Gallagher sipped his coffee. 'You sound like Franklin.'

'Very occasionally, Franklin makes sense. Although only when he is not talking about himself. To get back to the point in hand, Münsterberg is an ardent supporter of the Kaiser, one of those few members of the Deutscher Bund who is. And the last time I saw him in New York, Schurz was all over him.'

Chalfont drained his whisky glass and signalled for another. 'You said you've arrested Kreutzer. You should ask him about Schurz.'

'I have.'

'Did you? And what did he say?'

Gallagher ignored him. 'Are you sure you should have another? You've been drinking steadily since before dinner.'

'Dear boy, you are not my nursemaid. I am not accountable for my actions to you or to anyone else. My sole responsibility is to myself. John Stuart Mill said that, I think.'

'He did. He also said that this is only true so long as your actions do no harm to others. If your drinking harms only yourself, you are at liberty to drink as much as you want. But if when drunk you become violent and harm other people, then you are also responsible to society. It is then fair to restrain you from drinking.'

Chalfont looked at him. 'Do the Royal Marines teach Mill now?'

'No, I read him in the library of the seamen's mission in Shanghai, while my shipmates were getting drunk in the French Concession. That's how I gave myself an education.'

'An autodidact. How praiseworthy. Perhaps I should have gone to sea. It might have made a better man of me.'

Gallagher smiled a little. 'Not necessarily.' In the back of his mind he turned over the information about Schurz, wondering as ever why Chalfont was telling him this, and why now.

The barman had moved down to the far end of the bar, and there was no one within earshot. 'Let's change the subject,' Gallagher said. 'Tell me again about your meeting with Dowrich at the Deutscher Bund.'

'There's not much to tell, dear boy. I asked for his help in bribing some customs agents and he agreed, for a consideration. I arranged for this to be paid, and he did the rest.'

'What did you make of him, as a man?'

'Expensive suit on the outside, small-time thug on the inside. He aspired to great things, and I reckon he hoped to take over from Boss Murphy one day. But that was never on the cards. Murphy's a subtle man, very subtle. Like I said, he uses people like Dowrich to do his work in the shadows, but he never lets them get a sniff of real power.'

'The Democratic Party wants to keep America out of the war. Does Murphy agree with them?'

'I don't know.' Chalfont regarded him with bloodshot interest. 'I never asked him.'

'I'll put it more plainly. Could Dowrich have been killed for taking an interest in the arms shipments?'

'Ah.' Chalfont sipped his whisky, thoughtfully. 'I tell you what, dear boy. Let's change places for a while. I'll be the sleuth hound and tell you what I think, and you can be the interested bystander. What do you say?'

'Go on.'

'Three possibilities exist. First, Dowrich had secretly sold out to the Germans and was working with Rintelen. The Germans know I will be unable to resist the thumbscrew and the rack and will tell your chums in the service everything I know about Rintelen's operation. Dowrich was sent to keep me from talking, permanently. With me so far?'

'Yes.'

'Second, Dowrich might have been collecting information on arms shipments to the Allies with a view to exposing them publicly and forcing the government to crack down on companies like Union Metallic, who are shipping armaments to everyone willy-nilly. Or third, Dowrich could have been interested in the arms shipments for his own reasons, and was perhaps trying to steal some of them and sell them to a third party. He has connections with gangsters like Paul Kelly; perhaps the Five Pointers are moving into the arms trade.'

Chalfont paused. 'Admit it,' he said. 'For a man with most of a bottle of whisky inside him, I make quite a lot of sense.'

'Is there enough money in selling artillery shells to attract the gangs?'

'Ordinary high explosive, probably not. H.E. shells are expensive, but you still need to deal in large quantities to make real money. But if it was White Star, now, that's a different proposition. Every army is hungry for gas shells, including our own. We don't want the Germans to be the only ones killing people in inhumanely cruel ways. We want in on the act too.'

'The shipments you dealt with, the ones you say you sent to Britain and the ones you destroyed. Did any of them ever contain White Star shells?'

'No,' Chalfont said quietly, and for a moment he seemed almost sober. 'But I know Rintelen was desperate to get his hands on some. And I don't think he intended to destroy them, either.'

He sipped his whisky again. 'It all depends on whose team Dowrich was on, doesn't it? Was he playing for Germany, for Tammany Hall, or for himself? If I were you, I'd get your secret service chums to do so some digging on him.'

'I already have,' Gallagher said. 'I met Dowrich on Saturday morning shortly after we sailed. He said he had information about some of the passengers that he wanted to share with me. I assume he intended to ask for money. What do you think he was talking about?'

The red-veined eyes regarded him again. 'You can speak plainly, dear boy. We're all friends here.'

'What if he knew the truth about you? What if he was planning to give me evidence that would prove your complicity in treason?'

There was a long silence. Chalfont tilted his head back and drained his glass. 'I used to own a pair of twelve-bores,' he said, putting the glass back on the counter. 'Lovely things they were, too, made by Cogswell & Harrison. Not so fashionable as Purdey, perhaps, but I reckon I've never seen a finer pair. I shot partridge with them for many years. Then I got too old and my hands got too shaky, and I sold them. I haven't owned a gun since.'

'I know. We searched your apartment, and your luggage before it came on board. There are other ways of acquiring guns.'

'I'm sure there are, dear boy. But as I said before, I am not Houdini. I could no more kill a man and escape from a locked cabin than I could fly.'

'Why were you fumbling around trying to fit your key into different cabin locks?'

'Because I was drunk as a lord, and had no idea where I was.

Clearly, it is possible that Dowrich had discovered something incriminating about me, or thought he had. Perhaps Rintelen fed him a false account of my activities. But I did not kill him.'

Chalfont paused. 'I could give you my word of honour as a gentleman,' he said. 'But I think we're past that, don't you?'

'A little,' said Gallagher. 'However, on this occasion, I am prepared to take your word for it.'

'Are you, dear boy? Why, I wonder? Absolutely nothing about me inspires confidence. Even I have doubts about me.' He held up his whisky glass to the light, confirming it was empty, and set it down again. 'And now, it is time for me to make a graceful exit. Goodnight, dear boy. Pleasant dreams.'

TUESDAY, 4 MAY 1915
11.44 P.M.

STARLIGHT GLIMMERED OFF the long slow slide of the sea. Overhead the constellations turned in their wheels. On the boat deck, the lifeboats creaked in their davits. Billie Dolan, wrapped in a dark cloak, stared out over the water. Her heart beat hard and painfully in her chest.

Someone else came out on deck behind her. She smelled the cigar smoke and knew at once who it was. 'Go away,' she said, and her soft voice was full of hate.

'What did you say to Dolly when you talked to her? Did you agree to go with her?'

'What we talked about was none of your business.'

'Oh, yes, it is. I want my money, Billie. Fifteen thousand bucks, waiting for me when we reach Liverpool.'

Contempt mingled with anger in her voice. 'You're pathetic, Mr Ripley. Did you ever seriously dream Dolly would give you that money? If you did, you're an even bigger fool than you look.'

'I meant what I said.' Ripley's voice was sharp. 'I'll tell Franklin she's trying to steal you away.'

'Tell him whatever you like. I'm through with you, Mr Ripley. You've got no hold over me no more. You'll never get your money, cuz you're finished. Do you hear me? Finished!'

'You crazy little bitch. Look, Billie, you've got to do this. Go back to her! Throw yourself at her feet, beg forgiveness, do whatever it takes, but get me that money. Understand? Otherwise, you're for it. So help me God, I'll see to that myself.'

She shook her head violently. 'No, Mr Ripley. I ain't doing *anything* for you! You sold me like a bag of suet, you son of a bitch, and I hate you!'

She tried to push past him, and he seized her arm. She froze for a moment, staring at him. 'Take your hand off me,' she hissed. 'If you ever touch me again, I'll kill you, I swear to God.'

Ripley released her and she hurried inside; the sound of her feet could be heard running downstairs. Ripley stood for a moment, his plans collapsing in ruins around him. Quite how or why he did not know, but fifteen thousand dollars had just slipped through his fingers. He swore under his breath and went inside.

A few yards away, another shadow detached itself from the greater blackness. Jan Steen puffed on the last of his cigar and flicked the butt away, sending it spinning over the rail towards the sea far below. Then he too went inside, turning away towards the saloon where lights still twinkled and a piano played softly, a Stephen Foster song. A woman's voice was singing.

The leaves of the forest will fade,
The roses will wither and die,

But spring to our home in the glade
On fairy-like pinions will fly.
And still I will hopefully wait
The day when these battles are o'er,
And pine like a bird for its mate,
Till Willie comes home from the war . . .

The piano trailed off. In the silence that followed, a man's voice said, plaintively, 'Can anyone else smell smoke?'

Wednesday, 5 May 1915
12.16 a.m.

By the time Gallagher reached the drying room, the fire was out. Hamilton was already there along with several stewards, inspecting the charred, soaking remains of the laundry that had been airing in the room. 'What happened?' Gallagher asked.

Hamilton indicated the stewards. 'They smelled the smoke and fetched fire buckets and an extinguisher. It could have been worse. The question is, how did it start in the first place?'

'Somebody left a hot iron lying around,' said a steward, rubbing a burn on the back of his hand. 'That's usually how it happens.'

But the steam irons were cold in their racks. Gallagher lifted a bundle of wet sheets from the floor and picked up a charred metal rod, half burned away and still warm to the touch. Swiftly, he tucked it into his pocket. 'You did well,' he told the stewards. 'Mr Hamilton and I will see that the captain is informed of your good service.'

Hamilton nodded. 'Go fetch some mops and clean up in here, and then get to bed.'

The stewards departed. 'What did you find?' Hamilton asked quietly.

Gallagher produced the charred rod. 'Thermite,' he said. 'It's used in welding, so it's easily available. I've seen it used before to start fires. They probably used a strip of magnesium as a fuse, to set the thermite burning.'

'Why the drying room?' Hamilton snapped his fingers. 'Of course. Nelson is next door.'

'Yes,' said Gallagher. 'I'm going to check on our prisoner to make sure he is safe. Can you tell the captain I need to see him?'

Kreutzer was awake and on his feet when Gallagher entered the cabin. 'Was there a fire?'

'A small one, and it is has been extinguished,' Gallagher said. 'You are safe.'

Kreutzer looked him in the eyes. 'Was this aimed at me?'

No, Gallagher thought, *but I don't mind if you think so.* Aloud, he said, 'I think it very likely. You have some charming associates, Herr Leutnant. First they deliberately betray you to the enemy, then they try to burn you alive.'

Kreutzer sat down heavily on the bed. 'I am trapped in here. If they come for me, there is no escape.'

'They won't come for you,' Gallagher said. 'I didn't put a guard on the door because I was hoping to keep your presence a secret, but I will now. Don't worry. We'll get you safely to England, never fear.'

'I wish I could believe you.'

'You can,' Gallagher said simply. 'This may sound like a strange thing to say, but we are your friends. When we caught you, you were doing your duty. I have absolutely no wish to see you come to harm. But it looks like your German colleagues don't agree.'

He paused to let this sink in. 'When we last spoke, you said that after the war we might be comrades. There is no reason why we have to wait that long.'

Kreutzer looked up sharply. 'What do you mean?'

'I think you already know,' Gallagher said. 'Goodnight, Herr Leutnant. Sleep well. We will keep you safe.'

Turner was in his cabin, in pyjamas and dressing gown. Gallagher thought he looked faintly absurd without his bowler hat.

'Someone lit a thermite incendiary in the drying room on the promenade deck, sir. Thanks to the stewards, it was quickly extinguished and little damage was done. Hamilton is putting the story around that the fire was caused by an iron. Hopefully people will believe it.'

'First the wiring, now this,' Turner said. 'We have a saboteur on board.'

'We could post guards around the ship, sir,' Gallagher suggested.

Turner shook his head. 'We haven't enough men, or weapons. We're short of seamen already, and we gave up most of our small arms last voyage to equip the infantry on the Western Front. The master-at-arms has only a handful of men at his disposal.'

He looked keenly at Gallagher. 'So far, these incidents have been minor. No one has been hurt. What is the saboteur trying to do?'

'The fire was started next to the cabin where we are keeping the prisoner,' Gallagher said. 'I have let Kreutzer think it was an attempt to kill him.'

'Oh? Why?'

'Because I hope to persuade him to defect to us. I think I have a reasonable chance. However, while I suspect the saboteur wanted us to believe they were going after Kreutzer, I don't think that was the real intention.'

'Don't speak in riddles, Gallagher. Especially not after midnight.'

'Sorry, sir. The first attack was intended to silence the Marconi system, that seems plain enough. But if they really wanted to kill Kreutzer, they would have done so. I believe this latest incident is a red herring, a distraction designed to draw our attention away from their real aim. Whatever that may be.'

'You don't know?'

'No, sir.'

'It is Wednesday now, Gallagher. By tomorrow evening, Thursday, we will be approaching the war zone. Find out.'

'Yes, sir.'

'Anything more on who killed Dowrich?'

'I know how he was murdered, sir, and I am pretty certain I know why. All that remains is to find out who killed him.'

15

WEDNESDAY DAWNED BRIGHT, fresh and calm, the wind no more than a whisper, the sea placid and still. *Lusitania*'s wake was a white scar, broadening and stretching to the horizon. The air was full of the soft noises of a ship at sea, the hum of fans and the beat of turbines, the endless bubble and rush of water past the black hull and the whimper of gulls circling in the wind. *Lusitania* was forty-eight hours from the war zone.

The passengers were quiet this morning, the atmosphere tense. With the weather remaining fine, many of them left the confined inner spaces of the ship and spread out on deck. Some read, or pretended to read, staring at the magazines in their hands with unfocused eyes. Others gazed out over the vivid blue sea, or talked in low voices. Only the woman who painted the eggshells seemed unperturbed, her fine-haired brushes steady in her hand. A gaggle of children watched her in silence.

Walking out onto the promenade deck, Juan Arango spotted the old couple almost at once. They were sitting in deck chairs with their backs to him, but he recognized the black mantilla Señora López often wore, its fringed ends hanging over the back of the chair. A waiter approached, bowing, pouring coffee from a silver service, and Arango knew a moment of righteous anger. They claim to be communists, he thought. Why are they up here, enjoying the luxury of first class? They should be down in third class with the rest of the proletarians, showing solidarity with their cause.

Another thought came to mind. The colonel had said they must have evidence; the general had been known to make mistakes. The colonel had also told him to stay away from the old couple; very well, but the colonel too had been known to make mistakes. He would not risk burgling the cabin again, but there was nothing to stop him from simply confronting the old couple and demanding the truth. Surely not even the English would have a law against this.

He waited for the right moment, staring out across the sea, wondering hopefully if there might be more whales. If there were, they did not put in an appearance.

Eventually the Lópezes rose to their feet. Arango waited while Señor López carefully wrapped the mantilla around his wife's shoulders and gave her his arm. Turning his head a little, Arango watched them go inside and walk down the passageway towards their cabin. He gave them five minutes, then knocked at the cabin door. After a moment he heard López's voice. 'Who is it?'

'Room service, sir,' Arango said, reaching inside his coat and placing his hand on the butt of the revolver he kept in an inside pocket. 'I have a bouquet of flowers.'

'Flowers? From whom?'

'The card does not say, sir. It is signed only, *a lover of music.*'

The door opened. Arango drew his revolver and placed the barrel between López's eyes. 'Not a word, señor. Move away from the door.'

López backed away. Arango entered the room, kicking the door shut with his heel. Corazón López sat in a chair, her eyes wide and her skin grey with exhaustion. 'What do you want?' López asked.

'Permit me to introduce myself. I am Major Juan Arango, on the staff of General Villa of the Northern Division.'

'We know who you are,' Corazón said quietly. 'I recognized you on the first evening.'

'You recognized me? How?'

'I saw you riding in the Gardens of Chapultepec with General Villa, the night your men came to arrest us. I did not know your name, but I knew you were the same man.'

'Put your gun away, señor,' López said. 'We are no threat to you.'

After a moment's hesitation, Arango put his revolver back in his pocket. 'I have some questions for you,' he said. 'Answer honestly, and you have nothing to fear.'

López bowed his head. 'We shall do our best.'

'Earlier this year, General Villa placed an order for a large quantity of artillery shells with an American maker of munitions. When the shells arrived, we faced the government army at Celaya. But the shells were useless. They did not explode.'

The Lópezes said nothing. 'Our cavalry attacks went in without covering fire,' Arango said. 'They were slaughtered.' Suddenly angry, he slammed his hand down on the table. 'We lost eleven thousand men at Celaya. Eleven *thousand*! All this happened because we were betrayed.'

'And you think it was us who betrayed you,' said López. 'But how could we have done this? We know nothing about artillery shells. We would not know where to begin.'

'But you organized the union, Casa del Obrero Mundial,' said Arango. 'You had informers all over Mexico. One thing I do not understand. Why would communists support the government?'

'Because they promised to work with the unions and improve

the rights of workers,' López said. 'They promised peace. All General Villa brought was violence and chaos.'

Arango made an angry gesture. 'Your informers provided you with intelligence about our forces, and you passed it to the government.'

'That is true,' López acknowledged. 'Is that why you tried to arrest us in Mexico City?'

'We knew you were organizing the Red Battalions against us.' Arango paused. 'How did you escape? We surrounded your house, and searched it thoroughly.'

'We had been forewarned of your coming,' Corazón López said. 'Friends smuggled us out of the city to safety. We admit to raising the Red Battalions, of course, but we did not sabotage your shells. Our friends are workers on the railways and the haciendas, or in the mines. They have no knowledge of artillery shells.'

'Then who did this thing?' demanded Arango. 'Very well, you say it was not you. But you know who was responsible.'

'Why are you so certain?' asked Corazón.

'We have spies of our own. Colonel Kloss, the German agent in Mexico, is in contact with other German agents in America. I say it again. If you did not order the shells to be sabotaged, you know who did.'

'May I ask a question?' said López. 'What are your orders from General Villa?'

'To find out who was responsible for our defeat at Celaya,' Arango said, and he touched the butt of his revolver. 'And to execute justice upon them.'

The couple looked at each other. 'You are right in one respect,' López said. 'We knew the munitions were coming. Some of our comrades worked at your arsenal in San Luis

Potosí and passed the word. We informed the government and also Colonel Kloss, just as you said.'

'What happened then?'

'We do not know. We heard what happened only afterwards, from Colonel Kloss.' López paused. 'He was very pleased. He knew the failed shells had contributed to your defeat at Celaya.'

Arango could feel his anger boiling up again. 'You must have been pleased also.'

López paused. 'I should have been,' he said slowly. 'After all, we had helped raise troops to fight against you. Your soldiers raped and robbed the people in Mexico City. But perhaps I am getting old. When I heard the news, all I could think of was the deaths of so many young men. It made me unbearably sad.'

There was a long silence. Arango's grip on the revolver relaxed a little. 'How were the Germans able to sabotage the fuzes? As you say, this requires specialist knowledge.'

López nodded. 'According to Colonel Kloss, the fuzes were tampered with by an American engineer who also worked for the company that made the shells.'

'On whose instructions? The Germans'?'

'No. Colonel Kloss thought it was probably the American government.'

Arango was astonished. 'The Americans? They support General Villa! Why would they sabotage our shells?'

'They didn't,' López said patiently. 'They sabotaged a consignment of shells meant for the Mexican government. Somehow those shells ended up with you instead.'

'This American engineer. Who is he?'

'If you wish to find him, señor,' Lopez said, 'it will be an easy matter for you.'

'Why?'

'Because he is on this ship. I sit opposite him every night at dinner. His name is Charles Schurz.'

Arango looked from one to the other. 'How do I know you are telling the truth?'

López spread his hands. 'What have we to gain by lying? For us, the war is over. We are two old people, spent and nearly done. All we ask now is to return to our homeland and be buried in its soil. Whatever you may think, señor, we are no longer your enemies.'

WEDNESDAY, 5 MAY 1915
10.26 A.M.

JAN STEEN TAPPED the ash from his cigar and nodded towards the window. 'That young woman is the very picture of melancholy. Would you not say?'

Gallagher glanced up from the telegram he had been reading. Billie Dolan stood on the boat deck, her shoulders slumped, her hands resting on the rail. Alarm shot through his mind; Hamilton had wondered if she might try to take her own life and it occurred to him that she might be getting ready to jump. But after a moment she raised her head a little and stepped back from the rail, and he breathed more easily.

'Do you know who she is?' Steen asked.

'Franklin's mistress.'

'Yes, I know that. Who is she apart from that?'

'She used to be a showgirl in Ripley's troupe.'

'Ah, one of Ripley's Roses. I have heard all about them from Ripley himself. She and Ripley are not on good terms now, though. Far from it.'

Something about his tone of voice made Gallagher look at him. 'What do you mean?'

Steen grimaced a little. 'The world hates a gossip,' he said. 'But I overheard them quarrelling last night, out on deck. They were threatening each other, quite clearly.'

'What was the argument about?'

'Ripley is trying to screw money out of someone, and demanded she help him. She refused, and I distinctly heard her threaten to kill him.'

Who hates Ripley enough to want to set him up for murder? Hamilton had asked. 'I expect she was speaking metaphorically,' Gallagher said.

'I hope so.' Steen puffed on his cigar.

Gallagher folded the telegram and put it in his pocket. 'Did either of them mention who Ripley is trying to con?'

'Someone called Dolly. I wondered if it might be Mrs Markland?'

Gallagher smiled. 'Now we really are gossiping,' he said.

GALLAGHER DEPARTED, WALKING aft towards the verandah café. The man who called himself Jan Steen waited for a while, finishing his cigar, and then rose and walked forward along the boat deck, frowning a little.

Juan Arango stood waiting in the shadow of Lifeboat Number 2, right at the forward end of the deck. 'I know who betrayed us,' Arango said. 'He is an engineer, by the name of · Schurz.'

'How do you know this?' demanded Steen.

'I spoke to the old couple. They explained everything that happened.'

Steen was speechless for a moment. 'I told you to stay away from them, not have a chat with them!'

'In the name of God, I had to do something. The voyage will be over in a few days. Once they reach England, they could disappear for ever. I know I took a chance, but I had to talk to them. I did not harm them, I promise.'

'What did they tell you?'

Arango repeated what López and his wife had said. 'Do not worry, I did not just accept what they said. I have talked to some of the other passengers too, including the old drunk, Chalfont.'

Something rattled on deck. Arango looked around and saw nothing, but he lowered his voice all the same. 'Chalfont told me a great deal about Schurz. It all fits together, compañero. It must be him.'

Steen shook his head. 'If Schurz is an American agent, we cannot touch him. General Villa needs American support.'

'I do not care,' Arango said in a fierce whisper. If Schurz is responsible the deaths of our compañeros, not even God can save him.'

'You have absolutely no proof about Schurz. And the old couple would say anything to save their skins.'

'Then what about this? Chalfont says that Schurz has been going down to the main deck. He spent nearly two hours there yesterday, checking the doors and bulkheads. He is looking for something, but Chalfont does not know what.'

'I wouldn't say Chalfont was particularly reliable. But even if he is right, how does that tie Schurz to our defective shells?'

'I do not know. But there is something suspicious about this man, compañero. I am determined to find out what it is.'

Lusitania's bow dipped into a heavier sea. Spray shot into the air, glistening in the starlight. 'Be careful,' Steen said. 'If what you say is true, he could be dangerous.'

Arango grinned at him, full of the confidence of youth. 'So am I, compañero,' he said.

WEDNESDAY, 5 MAY 1915
11.14 A.M.

THE GLASS DOORS of the verandah café had been opened and people spilled out onto the deck, drinking coffee and eating ice cream and pretending this was just like any other Atlantic crossing. Dolly Markland had found a table on her own near the rail, looking out over the eye-aching blue of the sea. 'May I join you?' Gallagher asked.

Dolly nodded. A waiter brought a cup and poured coffee. She looked like she had aged in the past few days, Gallagher thought; her skin was pale and grainy and her hands were so stiff he wondered if she was suffering from arthritis.

'I have a question for you,' she said. 'Why is there no smoke coming from the fourth funnel? Is something wrong with the engines?'

'No, the fourth funnel is a dummy. For some reason passengers believe ships with four funnels are safer than vessels with only three. So, today every liner has four funnels.'

'People are peculiar,' she said after a while.

'They are,' Gallagher agreed. 'Mrs Markland, I am sorry for the imposition, but I need to ask you some questions.'

The ghost of a smile passed across her face. 'Are you still maintaining the fiction that you are a civil servant?'

'Believe it or not, I truly am. You told me yesterday that you used to work for Ripley. Does your husband know this?'

'No,' she said after a moment. 'He does not.'

'Pardon me for asking, but why have you not told him?'

'Because he lives in a different world,' she said. 'They all do, him and his friends. When I married him, I joined that world too and cut myself off from the past. I trained myself to be

Dolly Markland, wife of the president of an insurance company, and I do the things the wife of the president of an insurance company is expected to do. I play bridge, I go riding, I attend the theatre, I sit on charity boards and approve grants to the sick and needy. That is who I am now.'

Roxanne had tried to live in two different worlds, and had failed. Mrs Markland was failing too; he could sense the turmoil beneath her calm front, and felt sympathy for her. 'Isn't that risky?' he asked. 'Someone from your past might appear and tell your husband about your previous life.'

Her voice was firm. 'If anyone attempted to do so, I would deal with them.'

Gallagher reached into his pocket and handed her a telegram. It was an outgoing message, written in a neat hand and instructing a firm of Ontario solicitors to transfer the equivalent of fifteen thousand American dollars from the account of Mr Arthur Markland to another account in his wife's name at the Brooklyn Trust Company in New York.

'Is someone blackmailing you, Mrs Markland?' he asked.

This was normally the moment when you saw fear in their eyes. Gallagher looked into Dolly Markland's face and saw nothing more than a flash of irritation. 'Why have you decided to pry into my private life, Mr Gallagher?' she asked. 'Do you read all the passengers' telegrams?'

'At the moment, yes. Not only are we sailing into the war zone, but I also need to find out what happened to James Dowrich.'

She raised her eyebrows. 'From your tone of voice, I take it Mr Dowrich's blow on the head has proved fatal.'

'He didn't suffer a blow on the head. Someone shot him twice in the chest at close range.'

One manicured finger tapped on the table top. 'What has that to do with me?'

Gallagher picked up the telegram. 'Dowrich intimated that he had information about a fellow passenger. I wondered if that was you. Did he ask you for money?'

'Jimmy Dowrich was always after money,' she said finally. 'It was the only thing that interested him. Getting money, making money, spending money, that was his whole life. He worked for Tammany Hall, of course, but his only ideology was greed.' She paused. 'Something was missing from that man's soul,' she said.

Gallagher thought about the five thousand dollars Dowrich had stuffed under his mattress. 'How well did you know him?'

'Not especially well. When I worked as Ripley's assistant I often saw him in the theatre. He usually came in with others, Tammany Hall bigwigs or his gang friends. Often it was diffi-cult to draw a line between them, of course.'

'Did you see him with Edwin Franklin?'

She shook her head. 'Franklin's dalliance with the theatre was after my time. I had never met Franklin until dinner on Saturday.'

'Did you know Dowrich had fallen out with Ripley?'

'I heard something about that, yes.'

Gallagher considered this. 'How?' he asked. 'You said you had cut yourself off from the past, but interestingly, you con-tinued to maintain a bank account in New York. I think you were still in contact with some of your old associates. Either Dowrich or Ripley, perhaps both. And one of them was black-mailing you.'

A gull wheeled against the sun, its long-winged shadow pass-ing over the table, quickly gone. 'To be perfectly correct, no one was blackmailing me,' Dolly said. 'Both of them tried to extort money from me, separately, but I refused.'

'Tell me what happened with Dowrich.'

'He found my address in Toronto,' she said. 'I don't know how, but he wrote to me several times. He made vague threats, telling me he could expose me if he wished, but not asking for anything specific. I arrived in New York several days before *Lusitania* sailed, and took a hotel room.'

Gallagher remembered the business cards in Dowrich's suit pockets. In his mind, another piece clicked into place. 'The Knickerbocker Hotel,' he said.

She looked surprised. 'Yes. Dowrich found me – presumably his friends in the gangs have lookouts in the hotels – and came to see me. This time he demanded money. If I didn't pay, he would inform my husband about my past. I told him to go to hell.'

'And Ripley?'

'Much the same, although he only made his move on Sunday, a day after we sailed. I gave him the same response.'

She is an unusual woman, he thought. Very few would have the strength to defy both Dowrich and Ripley, given their connections. 'That is risky, don't you think? Dowrich could have told your husband. Ripley still might.'

'I'm not afraid of Ripley. He has problems of his own to deal with.'

Gallagher tapped the telegram with his finger. 'And yet, Mrs Markland, you still transferred the money.'

'Yes,' she said levelly. 'Not to give to either of them, but to keep for myself. I have decided to leave my husband.'

'Does he know?' Gallagher asked after a moment.

'He will when I tell him.'

'And you are taking his money? If you are doing so without his consent, that amounts to theft. Do the lawyers who helped arrange this transfer know your plans?'

'My business affairs, and those of my husband, are private. I will thank you to keep out of them.'

'The Canadian police might not agree with you. I wonder how you persuaded the lawyers to help you? I wonder, too, how much this has to do with Billie Dolan.'

That shot hit home, he thought. She froze for a moment, and it was only with difficulty that she forced herself to relax. 'You told me you helped to train new dancers,' Gallagher said. 'Was Billie one of them?'

'Yes.'

Gallagher watched her in silence for a long time, studying her face. 'What else was she?' he said quietly.

'She was my lover,' Dolly said. 'There you have it. My dirty secret.'

Again, for a moment, he felt nothing but sympathy for her. It was as she had said; a different world. 'This is why Dowrich and Ripley were trying to blackmail you. Not about your professional past; the revelation that you had been a chorus girl might have been awkward, but I reckon you could have ridden that out. But this would have caused a scandal, wouldn't it?'

'I can see you don't know me very well, Mr Gallagher,' she said. 'Yes, there would have been a scandal, but I would have fronted it out. I am a lot tougher and more resourceful than people believe. But, I am tired of living a lie. I want to go somewhere fresh and new where no one knows me, somewhere I can be myself and live my own life. I am tired of it all, Mr Gallagher. I am tired of bridge and the theatre and the charity galas. I need to be alone for a while. Arthur will never miss fifteen thousand dollars, and after a few months I doubt if he'll miss me, either.'

'And the trenches, the gas? The thought that he might be killed? It no longer perturbs you?'

'No,' she said, rising to her feet. 'I freely admit that it should, but it no longer does.'

'What has changed?'

'Even if I told you, Mr Gallagher, I doubt if you would understand.'

'One more question,' Gallagher said. 'You knew that Ripley and Dowrich had fallen out. Did Dowrich tell you this?'

'Yes, when he came to see me in New York.' She looked down at the table for a moment. 'There's one other thing,' she said. 'He told me Ripley had threatened to kill him. I asked if he was afraid, and he said no, he could look after himself. He had a gun, he said, and he reckoned if Ripley came after him, he could defend himself.'

Dolly Markland looked up again. 'Sounds like he was wrong,' she said.

It was an interesting story, Gallagher thought when she had gone. Large parts of it were probably true, but one element in particular rang false. Just a few days ago she had been full of concern for her husband fighting in France. Now she was leaving him; not only deserting him but professing herself unconcerned by his fate and callously helping herself to his money. He also didn't believe her when she said she could brazen out any scandal concerning herself and Billie Dolan. In Paris or Vienna, yes; in Presbyterian provincial Canada, absolutely not.

He felt a sense of foreboding. He had seen people break under pressure, and recognized some of the signs. She had not been honest with him; largely, he suspected, because she was not being honest with herself.

And then there was Ripley. He had left the showman off his list of suspects because he had an alibi, but that alibi had been provided by Mrs Markland herself and she now had to be considered an unreliable witness. Gallagher rose and walked through the café past the bar and into the smoking room, looking around.

There were two exits from the smoking room. One led through the saloon to the main staircase and lifts; Ripley could easily have taken this down to the promenade deck and gone to Dowrich's cabin, returning the same way once his victim was dead. But Gallagher himself had been in the saloon the entire evening, and he was quite certain he would have seen Ripley pass through the room; the man was unmistakable. His waistcoats alone were probably visible from a thousand yards.

It was possible that he could have left the same way Gallagher had just entered, past the bar and through the verandah café and then out along the boat deck and back inside to the foyer and main stair. The weather had been filthy and Ripley would have been wet with sea spray by the time he returned to his card game; unless he had planned the whole thing earlier and left an overcoat somewhere, perhaps in the gentlemen's lavatories behind the bar.

Gallagher walked over to the bar and laid a half crown on the counter. 'Were you on duty Saturday evening?' he asked the bartender.

'Yes, sir.'

'Was Mr Ripley here?'

'Yes, sir. He was playing cards the whole evening.'

'He didn't go out at all?'

'Only to use the head, sir.'

The head, the gentlemen's toilet, was between the smoking room and the café. 'How long was he gone?'

The bartender frowned. 'I couldn't rightly say, sir. Five minutes or so, I suppose.'

Going back into the café, Gallagher checked his watch and then walked briskly outside and along the deck to the foyer, downstairs to the promenade deck and along the corridor to cabin B16. He checked his watch again. Three minutes and twenty-two seconds; say another minute to knock at the door, enter the cabin, shoot Dowrich, drop the fake key, let himself out and lock the door again, and another three and a half minutes to go back up to the smoking room. Eight minutes in total; longer than the bartender's presumed five minutes, but not by much.

He walked back to the purser's bureau where he filled out two more telegram forms, the first addressed to the Toronto Police Service in Canada and the second to Captain Peters in New York. *One more favour, Steve.* 'Hammy,' he asked, 'did you find out when Ripley asked for his spare key?'

'The boys think it was probably issued some time on Saturday afternoon, just after we sailed.'

'It was definitely Ripley who collected it?'

'They assumed it was him, but they couldn't say for sure. No one actually remembered seeing him approach the desk.'

Gallagher nodded. 'I need to interview Ripley this afternoon. Can I use your office?'

'Be my guest, son.' The purser leaned back in his chair. 'You think it's him?'

'No. I think he's a scapegoat. But if I put enough pressure on him, perhaps I can find out what's really going on.'

WEDNESDAY, 5 MAY 1915

3.21 P.M.

LUNCH HAD BEEN another extravagant parade of food: potted shrimps and omelettes, poached eggs and cold salmon, roast chicken, ham, pressed beef, ox tongue and salads followed by cheese and fruit, largely wasted on the people who ate it. Chalfont was so drunk he was barely awake; Ripley spilled egg yolk on his goatee beard, dabbing it away with his napkin. Schurz and Franklin got into another argument about pacifism which ended with the engineer throwing down his napkin and storming out of the room. Corazón López watched him in surprise. 'I have never seen Señor Schurz so agitated.'

'The man is a fool,' Franklin said cuttingly. 'An intellectual poseur, nothing more.'

Maurice the maître d', who had observed the whole scene, bent down beside Gallagher. 'I told you,' he murmured. 'Climbing the walls. I liked it better when they were seasick, and stayed in their cabins.'

Dolly Markland did not join them; she had missed so many meals now that no one even commented on the fact. Juan Arango sat at his usual table, but he had changed places so he could see their own table more clearly. The Lópezes ignored him.

After lunch, Ripley returned to the smoking room, where he sat playing poker and gulping down brandy and soda. Jan Steen was one of the poker players; the others, according to the barman, were an American judge, a Canadian timber merchant and a retired tea planter. Gallagher watched them, nursing a glass of Canada Dry and waiting for his moment. At length, after a long series of heavy bets, Ripley won a large pot and barked with laughter, raking the money towards him. His companions rose to their feet. 'That's enough fun for one day,' the judge said. 'See you tomorrow, Ripley.'

They departed. Steen glanced at Gallagher as he went, nodding in recognition. Gallagher picked up his glass and walked over to sit down opposite Ripley. 'Your luck is in,' he said.

'Damn right it is,' Ripley said. He counted the money,

gloating. He was in a good mood, which was exactly what Gallagher had been hoping for. 'Say, you want a game?'

Gallagher shook his head. 'I'm not a poker player. There's something I'd like to talk to you about, though.'

'Go ahead.'

'Somewhere private. The purser will lend us his office.'

Unsuspecting, Ripley followed Gallagher down to the foyer. Hamilton let them into his office and then stood by the door, arms folded. 'What's this about?' Ripley demanded, some of his good humour evaporating.

'Our mutual acquaintance, James Dowrich,' Gallagher said. 'I'm afraid he's dead.'

Ripley stared at him. 'Dead? You're kidding me. Somebody said he just had a knock on the head.'

Gallagher shook his head. 'A necessary deception, to avoid alarming the other passengers. Dowrich was shot and killed in his own cabin.'

'Jesus! Are you serious?'

'Very serious,' Gallagher said.

Ripley stared at him, the goatee wagging belligerently. 'All right. So how come you know all about it? What's it got to do with you?'

'Captain Turner has given me full authority to look into his death,' said Gallagher. He paused for a moment, still watching Ripley's face. 'I should inform you, Mr Ripley, that I have searched your cabin and confiscated your gun.'

'What? God damn it, you can't take my gun! I need it!'

'The gun had been fired recently. Both barrels. Would you care to explain why?'

Ripley's mouth opened and shut. He waved his hands in the air. 'I was shooting at rats.'

'On board this ship?' asked Hamilton, with an ominous tone in his voice.

'No, back in New York. Can somebody tell me what the hell is going on?'

'Let me tell you a story, Mr Ripley,' Gallagher said. 'It's about a man named Victor Balthazard, a professor of forensic medicine at the Sorbonne. Just before the war, he discovered that you could compare bullets to see if they had been fired from the same gun. Each gun leaves different marks on the bullets, as individual as a fingerprint. When we reach Liverpool, I will hand your gun over to the police laboratory. The technicians well tell us whether the bullets from your gun match those that killed James Dowrich.'

Ripley said nothing. His face was wary, his eyes looking from Gallagher to Hamilton and back again as he digested how much trouble he might be in. 'I didn't shoot him,' he said. 'Hell, I didn't even know he was dead.'

'You told me about your debt, and how Paul Kelly had bought it and Dowrich demanded repayment. You said he threatened you, and he had a gun.'

'So what? I also said I was going to get him the money. Once I paid off the debt we'd have been all square. I had nothing to worry about.'

Hamilton stared at him. 'He threatened you with a gun, and you thought you had nothing to worry about? Does this happen often in your life, Mr Ripley?'

'More than you might think,' Ripley said. 'Look, I told you Dowrich had plenty of enemies. Anyone who wanted to bump that bastard off would have to stand in line.'

Reaching into his pocket, Gallagher placed on the desk the key he had taken from Dowrich's cabin. 'The tag says cabin B16,

Dowrich's cabin. But the key is for B14, your own cabin. How do you explain that?'

Ripley looked blank. 'I don't follow you.'

'Here's what I think happened,' Gallagher said. 'Dowrich demanded the money from you, and you realized you were going to have to pay him. Your first thought was to go to Franklin and ask him for the money. He had helped you out before, so you thought he might do so again. But he turned you down.'

'How do you know about that?'

'You then devised a scheme to blackmail Mrs Markland by exposing her past relationship with Billie Dolan to her husband. However, she also turned you down. Realizing you were cornered, you knew you would have to deal with Dowrich yourself.'

'But I didn't—'

'You collected your spare key from the purser's bureau on Saturday afternoon. You then arranged to meet Dowrich after dinner and went upstairs to play poker. At the appointed hour you excused yourself, slipped out of the smoking room and went down to Dowrich's cabin, where you shot him. You took his key from his pocket and removed the tag, placing it on your spare key, and left this in the cabin.'

'This is just bullshit. I never took any spare key, and even if I did, why in hell would I leave it in Dowrich's cabin?'

'You locked the door with Dowrich's key and went back upstairs, presumably throwing his key overboard, and resumed your game. Later you replaced your gun in your strongbox and went about your business. Concealing the news that Dowrich was dead, you continued to try to blackmail Mrs Markland.'

Surprisingly, Ripley had retained his composure. 'You really think I'd be stupid enough to leave my own key lying around in his cabin, even with a fake tag on it? And don't waste any sympathy on the Markland dame. She's a hard, vicious bitch, and she owes me for a lot of things. I'm just getting my own back.'

'By threatening to destroy her marriage?'

Ripley smiled, baring yellow teeth. 'I don't give a damn about her marriage. It's probably a sham anyway. The one I'm going to tell unless she coughs up the money is Franklin. He's not going to be happy to learn that his precious little Billie-bird used to be Dolly's lover. He doesn't like shop-soiled goods, you see. He likes everything brand new and shiny, mint condition.'

'Why did you lie to me about the gun?'

'I didn't. I never said I didn't own a gun, only that I didn't carry one. Although maybe I should start.'

'Why?'

'Like I said, Dowrich could have been killed by a lot of people. Maybe he was trying to grab the money for himself rather than handing it over to Paul Kelly, and maybe Kelly found out about it and sent someone after him. Maybe that same someone is after me, too.'

'Someone?'

Ripley jabbed a forefinger at him. 'I'll tell you something for free, mister. If you want someone who has connections with the Five Points Gang, look at that fellow Chalfont. *He* knows Paul Kelly, and he used to spend a lot of time at Kelly's saloon.'

'Don't be ridiculous,' said Gallagher. 'Mr Chalfont was the British vice-consul.'

'Sure. The British don't have corruption, do they? The British don't have gangs. They're all pure and clean as snow.'

'You had motive to kill James Dowrich,' Gallagher said. 'You had the opportunity, and we will shortly be able to prove you had the weapon.'

'And until you run that test on the gun, you've got nothing,'

Ripley said. 'Produce a single shred of evidence against me, and I'll put the handcuffs on myself. Until then, I'm free to go. Right?'

Gallagher nodded to Hamilton, who stepped aside and opened the door. 'One more thing,' Gallagher said. 'Not a word about this to anyone. Those are the captain's orders. Understood?'

'Oh, you can rely on me.' Ripley swaggered out of the office, the strut back in his step. Hamilton closed the door behind him.

'Can they really do that with bullets?' the purser asked.

'It's not yet a proven technique, but the early experiments are promising. The police laboratories take photographs and then use stereoscopes to magnify the images.'

'Clever. So, where does this leave us?'

'He didn't kill Dowrich. But I reckon his gun did.'

'What do you mean?'

'We've been right about one thing. Someone tried to frame Ripley for the killing, but that was almost an afterthought, although I don't yet understand why. But Dowrich was killed because he over-reached himself. He was mixed up in Chalfont's schemes somehow, and he also attempted to blackmail Mrs Markland. I wouldn't be at all surprised to hear he tried something similar on Franklin. And, this is a guess, but I reckon he was going to cheat on Kelly and steal the loan repayment for himself.'

'He already had five thousand dollars,' Hamilton observed.

'Yes, but he wanted more. Why, do you suppose?'

'Greed?'

'That's part of it, of course. But his behaviour over the past days and weeks is strange. Grifters are careful, they set up one mark at a time and they don't hurry them. Dowrich seems to have latched on to everyone he knew who had a secret and tried to squeeze them for money all at once. He needed the money for something big. I wonder what?'

'What about the girl?' Hamilton wondered. 'Did he have his hooks into her too?'

'She knew him, certainly. I keep wondering about her, Hammy. She looks like the picture of sweet innocence, but she is also a survivor. Is she capable of killing Dowrich and framing Ripley in order to get even with him?'

'If so, she didn't do a very good job. Ripley was right, that key is a pretty flimsy trick. We were bound to work out how they did it sooner or later.'

Gallagher shook his head. 'The key was planted to lead us to Ripley's cabin, Hammy. It pointed us to the gun, and once we have the test results that will be the really damning piece of evidence. The more I think about it, the more I'm certain that gun is the one that killed Dowrich. There's no other reason for anyone to go to such elaborate lengths to make sure we found it. The only question is, who really pulled the trigger?'

'Mrs Markland? Both Ripley and Dowrich tried to squeeze her.'

'And she refused. It is possible, but I struggle to see why she would be willing to take such a risk. When I asked if she was worried about the threat of exposure, she shrugged it off.'

'Franklin had quarrelled with both of them.'

'He also has an alibi. He was in plain view in the saloon all evening, I saw him myself.'

'That leaves the girl. Billie Dolan. We know how she feels about Ripley, but does she have a motive for killing Dowrich?'

'I don't know.' Gallagher rose to his feet. 'It's time I spoke to her again.'

Someone knocked at the door. Hamilton opened it to admit

one of the stewardesses. She was pale and her hands were shaking. 'What is it?' Hamilton asked.

The woman glanced at Gallagher. 'I'm afraid something terrible has happened, sir.'

'Go on. You can speak freely in front of Mr Gallagher.'

'It's one of the passengers, sir, Miss Dolan. I went into her cabin just now and found her. She's dead.'

16

Earlier in the day, Miss Dolan had asked for tea to be brought to her cabin that afternoon, as she preferred to be alone rather than mingle with the other passengers in the saloon. The stewardess had delivered the tea as instructed; receiving no answer when she knocked, she assumed the lady had gone out and let herself into the cabin. The tea service still sat on the sideboard, china pot and cup, silver milk jug and sugar tongs, sandwiches and cakes neatly arrayed on plates.

Gallagher turned to the stewardess. 'Are you all right?'

She was still shaking, but her chin came up. 'I'm fine, sir. Thank you for asking.'

The cabin stank of blood and burned feathers. Billie Dolan lay on her back on the bed, fully dressed, her arms loose at her side. Her mouth was open and a little trickle of blood ran from one corner, staining the white counterpane. Her eyes stared blankly at the ceiling. A pillow lay across her chest, with a hole in its centre. The hole and the pillowcase around it were black with powder residue.

'Jesus,' Hamilton said softly.

There was a jewellery case on the sideboard too. Gallagher wrapped his handkerchief around his fingers and opened it. Brilliants sparkled in the evening light. 'No sign of robbery,' he said.

The door opened and stoop-shouldered Dr Whiting entered, carrying his bag. He bent over the body, removing the pillow. The underside was a mass of blood, as was the front of the girl's blouse. 'Shot through the heart,' the doctor said. 'She would have died pretty well instantly, I think. Someone knew what they were doing.'

'Was she assaulted?'

'I can't see any bruises on her skin.'

'When was she killed?'

'Not long ago. The blood is not yet fully dry. There is no sign of rigor mortis. At least an hour, two hours possibly, but no more. Why the pillow, do you think?'

'To muffle the sound of the shot.' Gallagher picked up the pillow carefully by one corner. 'The pillow also prevented blood splatter. The killer wouldn't have had blood on his clothes.'

Or her clothes. He stood for a moment, looking down at the beautiful face sunken in death. He would make a detailed search of the cabin, of course, but he doubted if he would find anything. Black anger flooded suddenly through him, anger directed at himself. She had come to him for help, and he had done nothing. He had suspected her of murder when in reality she was the one in danger. He had failed her, in the same way that he had failed Roxanne. He could have – no, *should* have – done more.

This is getting you nowhere.

He cleared the anger from his mind, looking around the cabin. She had wanted to get away from them, she said, away from them all. Schurz, who she thought was following her. Ripley, who had threatened her. Franklin, her supposed protector. He would need to speak to them all, in due course.

'Very well,' he said. 'Doctor, can you please make arrangements to remove the body? Put her in the hospital room along with the other. I'd also like to see your report once you have examined the body. Hammy, will you pass the word to the captain?'

He searched the cabin carefully, taking care not to disturb any fingerprints that the police could later examine. As expected, he found nothing. Returning to the purser's office an hour later, he sent for the stewardess and questioned her again. She knew no more than what she had already told him.

Hamilton came into the office just after the stewardess had gone. 'He wants to see you.'

Turner was waiting in the chartroom again, bowler hat clamped firmly on his head. 'Tell me what you know.'

'Miss Dolan was killed by a single shot, probably from a pistol or revolver, sometime between 1400 and 1500 hours this afternoon.'

'Any idea why?'

'Not yet. We may know more when the doctor has finished his examination.'

'Is this connected to the killing of that other man? Dowrich?'

'It is possible. Dowrich was attempting to extort money from some of the other passengers who also had connections with Miss Dolan. I will need to interview them, including Franklin.'

Turner rubbed the bridge of his nose. 'Do you have any evidence against Franklin?'

'No, sir, but Miss Dolan was his mistress.'

'Franklin is a pacifist lunatic, but he is also an important American citizen and we need American goodwill. Treat him with care.'

Lusitania's previous captain had been dismissed for antagonizing the Americans; Turner had no intention of following in his footsteps. 'Yes, sir,' said Gallagher.

'As for the rest of the passengers, I want this kept secret until we reach Liverpool. Hush this up, and tell Hamilton and the doctor to do the same. Swear Franklin to secrecy if you have to, but keep a lid on things. I'm relying on you, Gallagher.'

Descending to the purser's office, he relayed Turner's orders to Hamilton. 'People will see us moving the body through the corridor,' the purser observed. 'What are we going to tell them?'

'She has appendicitis,' Gallagher said. 'She is being taken to hospital, and can receive no visitors for the rest of the voyage. That should keep the curious at bay. When we reach Queenstown we can remove the body through the cargo hatch.' He sighed, looking down at his hands. 'I must go and tell Franklin.'

WEDNESDAY, 5 MAY 1915
6.22 P.M.

FRANKLIN WAS IN the regal suite on the starboard side, fine rooms with plastered ceilings and wood-panelled walls that were the epitome of modern, understated luxury. A steward showed Gallagher into the parlour where Franklin sat reading through a sheaf of papers. He looked up sharply. 'Gallagher. What can I do for you? I was about to change for dinner.'

'I have some bad news,' Gallagher said.

Franklin raised his eyebrows.

'Your companion, Miss Dolan,' Gallagher said. 'I'm afraid she is dead.'

Slowly, Franklin laid down the papers and rose to his feet. He walked over to the porthole and stood for a moment, his back to Gallagher, looking out at the sunset light on the sea. 'What happened?' he asked.

'She was murdered,' Gallagher said.

Franklin considered this, still gazing out to sea. 'Poor Billie,' he said quietly. 'What an unfortunate end.'

It was a curious thing to say, Gallagher thought, but shock affected people in different ways. 'The captain has asked me to look into this matter. I'm afraid I have some questions to ask you.'

Franklin turned around. 'Are you competent to undertake such an investigation? I should have thought this was a matter for the master-at-arms.'

'Before I took up my present post, I served for some years with the Special Branch of the Metropolitan Police.'

'Ah, of course.' Franklin nodded, as if a mystery had been solved. 'Ask whatever questions you like.'

'When did you last see Miss Dolan?'

'I called on her at about three thirty, I think. I left about ten minutes later.'

That was just after the time window Dr Whiting had suggested. 'Where did you go then?'

'I went on deck to take some air. I needed to clear my head.'

'Had there been some disagreement between you and Miss Dolan?'

'Not a disagreement, no, but the conversation had been somewhat . . . fraught. She was quite emotional. I managed to calm her down, but I was in a somewhat agitated state myself by the end. I needed solitude.'

'Can you tell me why she was emotional? It might have some bearing on why she was killed.'

Franklin sighed. 'It's all that fellow Ripley's fault. He came to see me this afternoon with some sordid tale about Billie's past. I seldom believe a word that comes out of that man's mouth, but in the end I decided to go to Billie and ask for her version of events. It's always best to have the truth, don't you think?'

'Ripley told you she had been Mrs Markland's lover.'

Franklin was silent for a moment. 'Yes,' he said shortly. 'I don't know how you learned this, but I would be obliged if you would keep the matter quiet. I don't want the poor girl's reputation dragged through the mud, especially not now.'

'I take it she admitted as much to you.'

'Yes. It was at this point that she became emotional. She begged for my forgiveness, and of course I gave it to her.'

'Forgiveness? For what?'

'Mostly for deceiving me about her past, I think. It doesn't matter, and I said as much. She became a little calmer then, and I took my leave. Then, as I say, I went out on deck to take in some fresh air. After that I went into the smoking room for a drink, and to think and reflect.'

'Reflect about what? If you don't mind my asking.'

'Well . . .' Franklin looked down at his hands for a moment. 'To be honest, I was deciding what to do about Billie.'

'What do you mean?'

'I'll level with you, Gallagher. A man in my position tends to attract the attention of beautiful women. But all too often, they are unstable. Women tend towards hysteria in any case, as we all know, but the needy ones, like Billie, tend to exhibit this trait in a more pronounced fashion. I had suspected for some time that she was becoming emotionally frail, and this episode confirmed it. This afternoon, I realized that it was time she and I parted company.'

'What were you intending to do?'

'Pension her off, of course. I've done so several times before, and the process has always been most satisfactory.'

Gallagher watched him for a moment. 'Several nights ago, you lectured Schurz about his efficiency methods and how they denied people their dignity as human beings. What would you say about yourself now?'

'Myself?' Franklin looked surprised. 'I don't know what you mean. Billie would have been treated with respect. She would have a house of her own, servants, a pension for life. What more could she want, or expect?'

'Did anyone see you walking on deck, or in the smoking room?'

'There were people around, but I don't recall who any of them were.'

Gallagher nodded. 'Do you carry a gun, Mr Franklin?'

'I do, for personal protection. A man in my situation cannot be too careful.'

'May I see it?'

Franklin reached into his coat pocket and handed over the gun. It was a small single-barrelled derringer, with ivory grips and gold inlay on the barrel; it looked more like a watch fob than a real gun. He broke it open and saw the breech was clean and oiled, free of powder residue. A .41 Short rimfire cartridge rested in the firing chamber.

'Will this be sufficient to deter an assassin?' he asked, handing it back.

Franklin raised his eyebrows. 'Thus far, it has not been necessary to find out. I've been lucky, unlike some of my fellow industrialists. I think of Henry Frick, ambushed and nearly murdered in his own office, or poor Governor Steunenberg, blown up by a bomb at the gate of his home. Jack Morgan was attacked while he was in church, if you can believe it.'

'There is one more thing. Captain Turner is anxious to avoid alarming the passengers. The official line is that Miss Dolan is unwell with suspected appendicitis and has been taken into hospital. Please stick to that story, and do not repeat anything I have told you.'

'Of course.' Franklin's voice and manner were calm. Gallagher gazed at him, frowning a little. 'Do you feel no grief for her?' he asked.

'Grief?' Franklin considered the matter. 'To be honest, no. I don't get emotionally attached to women, Gallagher. They are too volatile. Billie was an ornament, a particularly fine one, and I do feel a pang of remorse for the waste of beauty. But she was always replaceable. It will not take long for me to find another.'

THE DOCTOR'S REPORT was waiting by the time Gallagher returned to the purser's office. 'That was quick,' he said, picking up the typed document.

The corners of Hamilton's mouth turned down. 'Too quick, I reckon. Problem is, the best doctors are all with the services now. Whiting is the best we could get.'

The report was cursory, but in fairness there had not been much for Whiting to find. Billie Dolan had been shot through the heart by a single .41 calibre bullet. The bullet had remained embedded in the body, and Dr Whiting had extracted it and preserved it as evidence. There were no external bruises on the body, nor were there any marks on her hands, or fibres or dried blood beneath her fingernails, meaning she had not put up a struggle. There was no evidence of recent sexual intercourse. Physically she appeared to have been in good health at the time of death, though a full autopsy would be needed to confirm this.

'She knew her killer,' Gallagher said aloud.

'Same calibre bullet as the one that killed Dowrich. But it can't be the same gun. I double-checked, and it's still in the safe. Did you get anything out of Franklin?'

Gallagher grimaced with distaste. 'Very little. Can you pass the word among the stewards? Ask if they saw Franklin at any time this afternoon.'

Hamilton nodded. 'Of course. They'll be busy with the dinner service now, though.'

'It can wait until morning.' Gallagher stared down at the report again, feeling the deck under his feet heave a little. 'What kind of man kills a beautiful young woman?' he asked.

'One who wants to possess her, but can't.'

Gallagher smiled a little. 'You're a good psychologist, Hammy. You and Joe the barber should set up in practice together . . . Billie was intending to leave Franklin. He gave no indication that he knew this, but if he *had* found out, that would give him motive.'

'What about Ripley?'

'He and Billie quarrelled, and according to one of the passengers they threatened each other. But he gave no indication that he wanted her back. He was trying to push her into the arms of Dolly Markland.'

Hamilton raised his eyebrows. Gallagher explained, and the purser sniffed. 'How different is the home life of our own dear queen. Or so you'd imagine, anyway. Does that give Mrs Markland a motive?'

'Possibly. She told me she was leaving her husband, but she said she was going away to be alone.'

'Perhaps Miss Dolan knocked her back.'

'Perhaps.' Gallagher rubbed his eyes. 'God, what a waste,' he said. 'What a terrible, terrible waste.'

Hamilton watched him with sympathy. 'I know what you're thinking, laddie.'

'*When the time comes to enter night's darkness, she will gaze on the face of death like a newborn child, without hatred and without remorse.* At least, I hope she will. She had enough fear and hatred in her life. Perhaps in death she will at last find peace.'

Ocean liners are floating villages; news travels quickly, and nothing remains secret for long. By the time they sat down for dinner that evening, *Lusitania* rising and falling slowly across the long swells, the whispers had already begun. One of the passengers, a Miss Dolan, had been taken into hospital. 'I am sorry to hear it,' Charles Schurz said to Franklin as the soup was served. 'I understand you know the young lady.'

A sincere condolence, or an attempt to stick the knife in? Gallagher wondered. It was always hard to tell with Schurz; he had absolutely no understanding of nuance. Franklin did not even deign to look at him. 'Thank you,' he said.

Dolly Markland was absent from the table, again, but the Lópezes were there. Looking around the dining room, Gallagher could see no sign of Arango; perhaps he was taking the warning seriously and staying out of sight. Steen was on the far side of the room, talking earnestly with a couple of elderly women. 'You must be very concerned for her health,' López said. 'This will be a worrying time for you, señor.'

'Indeed it is. I can only pray for her speedy recovery.'

'Our prayers will be joined to yours, señor.'

Schurz wrinkled his nose, as if the notion of prayer offended him. Of course, Gallagher thought; a man who prided himself on his rationalism, as Schurz did, was probably also an atheist. Ripley slurped his soup from his spoon. Chalfont leaned forward a little. 'Have you seen the young lady since she went into hospital?'

'No,' said Franklin. 'I am told she is heavily sedated and unable to receive visitors.'

'Sedated? Has she had the appendectomy already?'

'No,' Franklin said. 'The sea is up a little tonight, and I believe the doctor is waiting for calmer conditions tomorrow.'

Chalfont's lips twitched a little. 'Then let us hope he has read the weather forecast correctly.'

'Indeed,' Franklin said calmly. He laid down his spoon and stared off into space. All the others watched him; all except Ripley, who was still busy with his soup.

Gallagher said nothing throughout dinner, but afterwards on the way up from the dining room he joined Ripley in the lift. 'What a pity about Miss Dolan,' he said. 'She used to work for you, didn't she?'

Ripley stared at him, goatee beard jutting. 'How did you know that?'

'She told me,' Gallagher said. 'I was chatting with her in the reading room a couple of days ago. I thought she seemed quite melancholy.'

'Yes, she was always a bit moody. I was glad to get rid of her.'

Gallagher raised an eyebrow as the lift came to a stop on the boat deck, and the liftboy pulled the grating aside. 'She has appendicitis, Mr Ripley. You might show a little compassion.'

'It was a long time ago,' Ripley said irritably. 'I'll send her some god-damned flowers, all right? Now, if you'll excuse me, I have a poker school waiting.'

CHALFONT WAS PROPPING up the bar in the smoking room; Franklin was holding court in the opposite corner, a group of admiring men around him. Jan Steen was not one of their number, Franklin saw. In the saloon someone had prevailed upon López to play again; he sat before the piano, his wife standing solemnly beside him turning pages. Schurz sat reading yet another magazine. There was no sign of Dolly Markland.

Restless and still angry with himself, Gallagher went back

down to the promenade deck and walked along the silent corridors listening to the hum of the ventilation fans. The deck rose and fell beneath his feet, more gently than during the early days of the voyage but still perceptibly. Dowrich had been searching for money, anywhere he could find it, including offering to sell information to Gallagher himself. *This will be worth your while, Pat. I mean it.* But why? Why did he need so much money, so badly?

The annotation in the book still annoyed him. *P.G. – play him.* This presumably was the play; sell information about the venal activities of some of the passengers to keep Gallagher occupied and distract him from the real game. Whatever it was. But ironically, Dowrich's murder had become the biggest distraction of all.

He came to Dowrich's cabin and stopped outside the door, thinking. This was the port side of the ship, up near the bow. Schurz's cabin lay diagonally to the left; Ripley's cabin was across the corridor to the right. A side passage led past the ladies' lavatories towards the starboard side.

Schurz had heard two noises just before 10 P.M., almost certainly the gunshots that had killed Dowrich. When he had looked out, there was no one in the corridor. The stewards had seen no one either, except for Dolly Markland asking for a carafe of water. Frowning, Gallagher walked aft towards the steward's pantry. The same man was on duty, the Boer War veteran who had found Dowrich's body.

'Do you recall Saturday evening?' Gallagher asked.

'I am unlikely to forget, sir,' the steward said dryly.

'Someone saw Mrs Markland in the corridor. Was that you?'

'Yes, sir.'

'Tell me what happened.'

'I was checking on my passengers as I said to you. I knocked at Mr Ripley's door and looked in to make sure he was well, but he wasn't in his cabin. Just then the lady approached me and asked if I would take a carafe of water and a glass to her cabin.'

'Did you do so?'

'Of course, sir. I then returned to Mr Ripley's cabin, turned down the bed and resumed my rounds.'

'What time was this?'

'About ten fifteen, sir.'

'And you didn't find Dowrich's body for another forty-five minutes?'

'I have a number of cabins to look after, sir. My routine is to work my way down the right-hand side of the corridor, and then back up the left-hand side. That is when I discovered Mr Dowrich.'

'Which cabin is Mrs Markland's?'

The steward pointed along the corridor. 'It's just there, sir. B70, the parlour suite.'

Gallagher reached into his pocket for a tip, but the steward shook his head. 'There's no need, sir. This is my duty.'

17

GALLAGHER KNOCKED AT the door of the parlour suite, waited for a moment, and knocked again. There was no answer. Taking out his pass key, he opened the door and turned on the electric light. The parlour room was empty, and so was the bedroom beyond.

Searching the cabin did not take long. All of Dolly Markland's possessions were stowed away neatly, her clothes folded precisely, her toiletries arranged in severe rows. Three books lay on the bedside table, *Jane Eyre*, *The Time Machine* by H. G. Wells and an English translation of Dostoevsky's *The Idiot*; none were inscribed, nor did they look like they had been read. A jewellery box contained a small collection of not particularly expensive jewels. There was no sign of a gun. Nor were there any letters, diaries or photographs, not even of her husband, or of Billie Dolan.

This cabin could belong to anyone, he thought. There was absolutely nothing here to show the personality of the woman who occupied it. The clothes, the jewels, the books were like stage props. Dolly Markland might as well not exist.

He closed the cabin door behind him, locked it and went back up to the saloon. López was still at the piano, playing New World music now, *Le printemps* by one of the great virtuosas of the age, Teresa Carreño. Gallagher had heard her play in

Europe, several times; people called her the Valkyrie of the piano. As with Amy Beach, it was Roxanne who had first introduced him to her music. At the end of the piece he drew breath and joined in the applause.

'There it is again,' said Chalfont's voice in his ear.

'There what is?'

'The look in your face. Whenever you listen to fine music, you look like you have been transported to another world.'

'Isn't that what music should do?'

'Perhaps. Of music, as of so many things, I am lamentably ignorant. May I have a word?'

They walked into the deserted reading room, hearing López begin to play a Chopin nocturne; Gallagher could not remember which one. 'What really happened to the delectable Miss Dolan?' Chalfont asked.

'What makes you think I know?'

'Dear boy, if anyone on this ship knows anything, it is you. But even a medical ignoramus like myself knows that when you have appendicitis, it is imperative to operate *immediately*, lest the appendix rupture. If it does, then septicaemia and peritonitis are almost inevitable.'

'Come to the point, Harry.'

'My points are threefold. First, Miss Dolan does not have appendicitis. Second, Franklin knows this. And third, you know he knows it. I could speculate on whether he knows you know he knows, but I haven't had enough whisky for that to make sense.'

Gallagher rang the bell for the steward and ordered two whiskies, thinking about what he should tell Chalfont. The drinks arrived and he signed for them and waited until the steward had gone.

'She came to me on Monday and told me she wanted to

leave the ship at Queenstown.' He gave Chalfont a quick, edited summary of his conversation with Billie Dolan. 'It struck me she was frightened of both Franklin and Ripley. She also thought Schurz was following her, whereas of course it was really you.'

'I give you my word of honour, I would never have harmed a hair on her head. I merely wanted to admire her. She is a beautiful creature.'

'Franklin referred to her as an ornament.'

'An *ornament*? My God, is that all she was to him? That explains why he was so cold at dinner. For a man to describe his mistress as an *ornament* is degrading beyond words.' Chalfont shook his head. 'Even I am disgusted by his behaviour.'

'Your moral code recognizes the existence of other people. Franklin's does not.'

'Do you really think so, dear boy? That may be the nicest thing you have ever said to me. Do you suppose Franklin has a moral code?'

'Everyone has a code of some sort.' He looked at Chalfont. 'We all have principles we live by. But sometimes those principles are malign ones.'

'Indeed.' Chalfont raised his glass. 'And even if we mean well at the beginning, the passage of time corrupts us all. Perhaps that is how men like Franklin become men like Franklin. They don't start off bad, but the years and circumstance change them.'

'Time eats our lives,' Gallagher said, 'and the hidden enemy gnaws at our hearts.'

'There you go, quoting Baudelaire again. Don't tell me you found his poems in the library of the Shanghai Seaman's Mission.'

'Unlikely, as it was run by Scots Presbyterians. A friend gave me a book of his poems.'

'A friend? *Les Fleurs du Mal* is an unusual gift.'

'She was an unusual person.'

'Care to tell me about her?'

Gallagher looked at the whisky swirling in his glass. 'Another time.'

'Dear boy, we are two days from the war zone. There may not be another time.'

Gallagher said nothing. Chalfont sighed. 'Very well. Something has happened to Miss Dolan, but I am not allowed to know what it is. Something fatal?'

Gallagher looked at him.

'I will take that as a yes,' Chalfont said. He sighed again. 'It seems faintly ludicrous when so many are dying on the battlefields in France and Mexico and on the high seas, but I feel her loss. Did you know much about her? Who her family were, where she came from?'

'No. I don't know if anyone did. Women like Billie Dolan are fated to have their stories told by other people. Since you are so damned prescient, you can answer a couple of questions for me. Did you happen to see Franklin walking on the deck at any time this afternoon?'

'I fear not. I was in the smoking room, deeply absorbed in a bottle of whisky.'

'Did you see Ripley?'

'Yes. He was playing poker at the table next to mine, all afternoon.'

'And Schurz?'

'My watchdog? Yes, he was there, seated by the window smoking a cigar and reading *Slide-Rule Quarterly* or some such rubbish. I haven't been very helpful, have I?'

'On the contrary. This has been useful.'

Chalfont held up his empty glass. 'Useful enough for another drink?'

'I'll call the steward,' Gallagher said. 'Keep quiet about this, Harry. Or I really will lock you in your cabin.'

'You may rely on me, dear boy, in this matter if nothing else. Do you know who killed her?'

'I said she was dead. Did I say anyone killed her?'

'You didn't have to.'

Gallagher paused. 'I know who killed both of them,' he said. 'What I don't yet have is proof.'

'LET'S CHANGE THE subject,' Gallagher said after the steward had come and gone. 'You told me you've met Paul Kelly. How well do you know him?'

Chalfont's hand, raising his fresh glass of whisky, was perfectly steady. 'Kelly? Splendid fellow. Bit of a diamond in the rough, you might say, but a real gentleman. I used to go drinking down at the New Brighton Club. Ever been there?'

'No.'

'Splendid establishment. You can get a glass of beer, a plate of spaghetti with clams, and admission to a prize fight, all for a *dollar*! I was wrong, you know. America really does have culture.'

'The Americans also have a word for what you are telling me,' Gallagher said. 'That word is "bullshit". Was Kelly involved in your arms deals?'

'Yes. There were times when his talents and connections came in useful. He is a gangster, of course, but one uses the tools one has to hand. I'm sure you know what I mean.'

'What about the Mexican business? Was Kelly involved in that?'

'Yes.' Chalfont frowned. 'Though I'm not sure he didn't double-cross me a bit there. Remember I said he was a gentleman? Thinking about it, I'm not so sure.'

'What exactly happened? All I know is that a shipment of live shells intended for Villa's army was switched for one with inert fuzes. How did it happen?'

'I understand your confusion, dear boy. It was a complicated plot, which is probably why it went wrong. Let me begin at the beginning. Two consignments of artillery shells were ordered from the Union Metallic Cartridge Company in Bridgeport, Connecticut. One, with the full consent of the US government, was destined for Pancho Villa's army. It would be sent by rail to El Paso where the Mexicans would collect it. The other, ordered in secret by Captain von Rintelen's agents, was destined for government forces. That was all on the QT, because the Americans are backing Villa and the State Department had forbidden arms exports to the Mexican government.'

'That clearly didn't bother the owners of U.M.C. They were happy to sell to both sides at the same time.'

'Of course. Profit is profit, no one cares where it comes from. Rintelen had a man working inside U.M.C. This man discovered the State Department had found out about the secret shipment destined for the Mexican government. There was a hell of a stink, but eventually someone at the State Department had a clever idea. They would go ahead and send the shipment to the Mexican army, but the shells would be sent with inert fuzes. In other words, duds.'

'And Rintelen decided to switch the consignments. The Mexican army gets the live shells, Villa gets the duds.'

'Exactly. Rintelen asked me to handle it, so I went to Kelly. In exchange for a substantial payment, Kelly used his contacts to make the switch. The duds went to El Paso and Villa, the live shells and fuzes went to the government.'

'Who were these contacts?'

'Members of a trade union, the Brotherhood of Railroad Trainmen. Without telling Rintelen, I went back to Kelly and, for an even larger sum of money, asked him to switch the fuzes back again. He assured me it had been done, the live rounds were on their way to Villa, and I was left to bask in the warm glow of my own brilliance. Except I celebrated a bit too soon.'

'Something went wrong. Kelly didn't make the switch.'

'No. Like I said, not such a gentleman after all. Presumably somebody got to him and paid him even more money than I did. The next thing I knew, Villa had been beaten at Celaya and the Bureau of Investigation were raising merry hell and demanding to know what had happened. Someone pointed the finger at me, and you know the rest.'

'This person who paid him even more. Could that have been Dowrich?'

Chalfont sipped his drink. 'The thought has occurred to me. As I said on a previous occasion, it all depends on who Dowrich was really working for; the Germans, the American authorities, or himself.'

'Why didn't you let anyone else know what you were doing? The service has officers in Washington, on the ambassador's staff.'

'It's like I said before, dear boy. I was fishing in very murky waters. I had to make certain Rintelen trusted me. And while I am sure your service is very discreet, I felt I couldn't afford to take the chance. As it turns out, I made the wrong decision. Again.'

'Who were the contacts in Mexico?'

'Major Arango would collect the munitions from the Southern Railway depot in El Paso and see them convoyed across the border to Villa's arsenal at San Luis Potosí. After that the shells would go to General Villa's commander of artillery, a man named Colonel Stellan Skarpö.'

'Skarpö? Doesn't sound very Mexican.'

'A soldier of fortune, I presume.' Chalfont's eyes twinkled. 'The world is full of them, you know.'

'Have you ever met Skarpö? Do you know what he looks like?'

'No. As I said, I had nothing to do with the original contracts. Why do you ask?'

Gallagher weighed the matter for a moment, and came to a decision. 'I think the name is Swedish,' he said. 'And I think Skarpö is on this ship.'

'Ah. Now who has been holding out on whom?' For a moment Chalfont looked remarkably sober. 'Are Arango and Skarpö working together?'

'Probably.'

'Sent by Pancho Villa to discover who was responsible for the dud shells. How ironic that I was actually trying to help them. Am I in danger, do you think?'

'Probably,' Gallagher said again. 'I spoke to Arango and warned him I had his number, and I will do the same to Skarpö. All the same, we might want to think about getting you off the ship at Queenstown, rather than Liverpool, and making sure the two of them don't follow you.'

'An interesting idea. Are your Special Branch colleagues in Ireland equally adept with thumbscrews?'

'More so,' said Gallagher. 'They get more practice. Good. Queenstown it is, then.'

Wednesday, 5 May 1915
10.48 p.m.

Gallagher found Jan Steen in the smoking room talking with the judge and the retired timber dealer. He caught Steen's eye and the latter rose at once, excusing himself to his companions and following Gallagher out onto the boat deck.

The night was calm and clear, the stars glittering with ominous brilliance off the boiling white sea of *Lusitania*'s wake. 'What can I do for you?' Steen asked.

'Let's lay our cards on the table,' Gallagher said. 'I presume I am addressing Colonel Stellan Skarpö, lately commander of artillery with the Northern Division?'

Skarpö nodded. 'How did you work it out?'

'You did a passable imitation of a Dutchman speaking English, but I spent some time in Sweden before the war. Your accent is faint, but recognizable.'

'So much for an English public school education. My father should ask for his money back. Most of what I told you is true, including the fact that I served on General Botha's staff as an intelligence officer during the South African war.'

'What about the fortune in rubber?'

'That, alas, was a falsehood. A fortune of any kind has so far eluded me.' He smiled without warmth. 'I have fought in twelve wars, and been on the losing side every time.'

'Don't take it personally,' Gallagher said. 'What was a public school-educated Swede doing fighting with Pancho Villa?'

Skarpö spread his hands. 'Passing the time,' he said. 'I came to Mexico a couple of years ago to investigate some Aztec ruins near Hidalgo. As well as a soldier I'm also an amateur archaeologist.'

'You mean you're a treasure hunter.'

'If you like. In the profession of archaeology it's a distinction without a difference. Think of Schliemann, or Ludwig Borchardt. To cut a long story short, the site wasn't producing any finds of value, and I got bored. When the revolution started to heat up, I advertised my services. Villa offered to pay more than the government.'

'Is that what you fight for? Money?'

Skarpö smiled a little. 'Soldiering is my trade, and I happen to be quite good at it. But I admit I don't always choose the right causes. What about you? Secret service, I assume?'

There was no point in denying it. 'I presume you want to talk about the artillery shells,' Skarpö said. 'I am willing to help you, but I want some information in turn. I need to know what you know about Charles Schurz.'

Gallagher took his time before replying. 'Why?'

'The intelligence we received in Mexico suggested Señor López and his wife were behind the swap. General Villa sent Major Arango and myself to find them.'

'And to kill them, I assume,' said Gallagher. 'Why didn't you?'

'I had doubts. Where would an elderly Spanish musician and his wife learn how to tamper with shells and fuzes? Some of their communist friends might have known, but I reckoned this operation was planned and carried out in America.'

'That seems reasonable,' Gallagher said, thinking of Chalfont. 'But why do you want to know about Schurz?'

'Major Arango went to see the Lópezes and asked them outright what they knew. They pointed the finger straight at Schurz, but claimed he was acting on the orders of the US government. According to the copy of *Rumbelow's Business Directory* in the ship's reading room, Schurz is indeed a consulting engineer who works with U.M.C., but there is nothing what-ever about him being employed by the American government.'

'He might have been working in secret, of course.'

'Of course. But my ears really pricked up when I heard about his job with your government.'

'How did you hear about that?'

'He told me,' Skarpö said. 'Or rather, he told a group of us sitting in the smoking room. He's mighty proud of himself. Overseeing shell production for the Ministry of Munitions was the greatest engineering job in the world, he said, and he had been chosen for it ahead of all his rivals.'

'Schurz has a keen sense of his own importance, I grant you. But as I told you once before, you should not be concerned by him.'

'Perhaps not, but I think *you* should.'

Gallagher paused. 'When we first met, you suggested Schurz was not all that he seemed to be. Why did you say that?'

'To see how you would react. I really did suggest to him, in my guise as a Dutch steel magnate, that he might come to work for me. He turned me down flat. I offered him more money than the British, a lot more, again to see how *he* would react. I could see he was tempted, but he still turned me down. That was when it occurred to me that he was playing some other game.'

'Out of curiosity, what would you have done if he had accepted your offer?'

'I would have claimed the British put pressure on me and forced me to withdraw it. As indeed they would have done, I suspect, had the offer been genuine. Getting back to Schurz, it was not long after that Franklin told me about the industrial unrest everywhere Schurz introduced his scientific methods.'

'Franklin never loses a chance to denigrate Schurz.'

'True. But on this occasion, could he be right? Could Schurz in fact be an agent provocateur?'

'The Germans are paying him to disrupt the Ministry of Munitions by causing unrest in the shell factories?' That was almost exactly what Franklin had suggested. 'It is possible,' Gallagher said. 'On the other hand, if the Lópezes are to be believed, he tried to send a consignment of dud shells to Germany's allies in Mexico. Hardly the act of a dedicated servant of the Fatherland.'

'There's something else you might want to know,' Skarpö said. 'Schurz has also been sniffing around the forward part of the ship like a dog looking for a lost bone. There's something there that interests him, but there doesn't seem to be any passage down to the lower decks.'

'No. Some of the third-class cabin space has been sealed off and turned into an additional cargo hold.'

'May I ask what you are carrying?'

'Foodstuffs, I am told. I'm sorry, I can't really tell you much more about Schurz. I very much doubt that he is a professional spy; I know what those look like, and so, I am sure, do you. The possibility that the Germans have some hold over him cannot be discounted entirely, but given his recent actions it seems unlikely. The fact that he worked with U.M.C. could be merely coincidence.'

'You could arrest him and interrogate him,' Skarpö suggested.

'He has friends in high places. And if he really is what he says he is, an engineer who can revolutionize the production of artillery shells, he could help us win the war.'

'Those were my guns that failed at Celaya,' Skarpö said. 'The defeat is a stain on my reputation. I have a right to know what happened.'

'Sorry. Right here and right now, my war is more important than yours. Stay clear of Schurz.'

'You're operating on your own, aren't you? Major Arango and I can assist you, if you will trust us.'

'Forgive me, colonel. But why exactly should I trust you?'

'Because we all want the same things, I think. Let us help you.'

'I'll bear it in mind. But remember what I said. Stay away from Schurz, and tell Arango to leave the Lópezes alone, too. They're no threat to you, or to anyone.'

GOING DOWN TO the promenade deck, Gallagher walked aft to cabin B111. The guard outside the door saluted and stood to one side. Gallagher knocked once to signal his intent, unlocked the door and let himself in.

Kreutzer had been lying on the bed, but he sat up as Gallagher entered. Despite the lateness of the hour he was still fully dressed. 'I apologize for disturbing you,' Gallagher said. 'But I need to ask a few more questions.'

'As always, I am at your disposal,' Kreutzer said, his eyes watchful.

'Did Rintelen have an agent working for Union Metallic Cartridge Company?'

'Yes. He was a very useful source of information. We were able to buy several consignments of ammunition destined for Britain and destroy them, as I said before.'

'Do you know his name?'

'I fear not.'

'Was he a company employee, or a consultant brought in from outside?'

'I don't know. But he had full access to company records. Is that all you want to know?'

Gallagher nodded. 'Thank you, Leutnant. Sleep well.'

'One moment, if I may. What is our present position?'

'About five hundred miles west-southwest of Fastnet Rock.'

'Fastnet. I see.' Kreutzer picked up something from the table beside the bed. It was a paper heart, crumpled and a bit travel-stained and decorated with what looked like faded rose petals. Gallagher remembered something he had said earlier in the week. *A girl called Jeni who once gave me a paper heart.*

'It will be interesting to see what awaits us there,' Kreutzer said. 'Will it not?'

18

The Lópezes did not come down for breakfast in the morning. 'I am informed Mrs López is unwell, sir,' said the waiter, when Gallagher enquired. 'Nothing serious, I believe. A touch of mal-de-mer.'

Dolly Markland was absent too, and so was Schurz, which made Gallagher uneasy. He needed to talk to Schurz, to find out what he was searching for in the forward part of the ship, but other more urgent things were crowding through his mind. Looking around the other tables, he saw anxiety in many faces. This evening, *Lusitania* would enter the war zone.

Even Ripley had become infected by the general mood. 'Those advertisements in the New York papers. Vessels flying the British flag are liable to destruction, and all that. Were those real?'

'Of course they were real,' Chalfont said. 'There is a war on, Ripley, or hadn't you heard?'

Ripley ignored him. 'So the Germans could be waiting for us? There could be U-boats out there, wanting to sink us?'

'We shall be perfectly safe,' Franklin said. 'I told you. A naval escort will meet us at Fastnet.'

'Ah, yes,' said Chalfont, draining his coffee cup. 'The protected cruiser. But will it be enough to protect us?'

'I have been assured that it will,' Franklin said calmly.

'The Admiralty are also monitoring German radio transmissions, including communications with U-boats,' Gallagher said. 'If any submarines are detected in our path, a wireless signal will be sent and we can change course. *Lusitania* can outrun any U-boat.'

Ripley looked sceptical. 'We should do what they did on the last voyage. Pretend this is a neutral ship, and get the captain to fly the Stars and Stripes.'

'That would be a violation of the laws of war,' Chalfont pointed out.

'Who gives a damn? All's fair in love and war, right?'

'Mr Chalfont is right,' Franklin said. 'It would cause another diplomatic incident, and for nothing. Our escort will protect us. Hold your nerve, Ripley.'

'There's nothing wrong with my nerves,' Ripley snapped.

Chalfont changed the subject. 'Is there any word about Miss Dolan?'

'I'm afraid it is bad news,' Franklin said calmly. 'She developed complications from the appendicitis, and her condition worsened. She died during the night.'

Gallagher stared at him. Franklin ignored the look. 'I am sorry for your loss,' said Chalfont, irony running in a thin vein through his voice.

'I take your words to be well-meaning, Chalfont,' Franklin said, 'but there is no need for condolences. I had already decided to part company with the young lady. It was time to move on.'

Ripley looked up from his plate, his eyes bright with malice. 'Had you, now? I wonder why?'

'It is none of your business, Ripley.'

'I could make a guess.'

Franklin stared at him for a long moment, his face hard with arrogance and anger. 'Do not presume to threaten me, Ripley. If you try, I will crack you like an egg. Do you understand me?'

Under Franklin's gaze, Ripley seemed to shrink a little. 'Just making conversation,' he said finally.

'Then oblige me by changing the subject. I would be grateful, gentlemen, if you would never mention Miss Dolan in my presence again.'

The rest of the meal passed in silence.

THURSDAY, 6 MAY 1915
9.29 A.M.

THE TELEGRAM FROM the Toronto police arrived shortly after breakfast. Gallagher read it through twice and sat thinking for a long time, before finally rising and going to the purser's bureau. 'I need to borrow your office again, Hammy,' he said. 'And I'd like you there again too, as a witness, if you can spare the time.'

Dolly Markland was at her usual place on deck behind the verandah café, watching the woman painting eggshells a few tables away. An empty coffee cup sat on the table before her. 'Mrs Markland,' Gallagher said quietly. 'I need to speak with you in private.'

She looked up, her face tired and drawn. 'It sounds serious.'

'I'm afraid it is,' he said. 'Would you please come with me?'

In the purser's office he held her chair while she seated herself and then sat down opposite her, taking the telegram out of his pocket. Hamilton stood by the door, his face expressionless. 'I have some difficult questions to ask you,' Gallagher said. 'Would you like one of your own sex present in the room, Mrs Markland? We can send for one of the stewardesses, or a fellow passenger if there is someone you trust.'

'There is no need. Ask what you wish.'

Gallagher nodded. 'First of all, we need to clear up a misconception,' he said. 'You led me to believe, Mrs Markland, that you had been in contact with Dowrich only a few times since you moved to Canada. But that's not true, is it? According to enquiries made by Inspector Craig of the Toronto police, you were in fact sending him money, every month. Would you care to tell me about it?'

'I don't see that it is any of your business,' she said calmly.

'It is if you murdered James Dowrich. And if he was blackmailing you, Mrs Markland – and he was, despite your denial when we last spoke – then you have a strong motive.'

'And how am I supposed to have murdered Dowrich?'

'I know exactly how he was killed. I'll explain later. Tell me about the blackmail.'

She moistened her lips with her tongue, but otherwise she remained perfectly still. 'As I said, Dowrich found out that I had gone to Canada and somehow managed to track me down.'

Gallagher glanced at the telegram. 'He used a private detective agency.'

'How clever of him. You are right, I lied about the blackmail. It was small amounts at first, and I could pay without anyone knowing. Arthur gave me a very generous allowance. But at the beginning of this year the amounts started to increase, from a few hundred dollars to several thousand. I could no longer afford to pay.'

'And that is when you began stealing from your husband. According to the police, you forged a letter in your husband's name, authorizing you to draw on his funds whenever you wished. And his solicitors accepted this letter without question?'

'They did.'

'Which is odd, because when the police asked to see the letter they detected the forgery almost at once. Did you suborn one of the solicitors?'

She said nothing.

'Doubtless that will all come out in time,' Gallagher said. 'The police are considering charges of fraud against yourself, and are also taking steps to contact your husband in France. Presumably you guessed this might happen, which is why you have chosen to leave your husband and help yourself to as much money as you could before you departed.'

She swallowed suddenly. 'That's not how it is. I wanted to stay with Arthur, I swear to God I did. I did everything I could, but it wasn't enough. Now I have to get away, disappear, before I do still more damage. This is the only way.'

'The only way,' Gallagher said, watching her face. 'Was murdering two people the only way you could protect him?'

Dolly Markland stared at him, face white with shock. 'Two people?'

'Yes. Billie Dolan was killed yesterday afternoon.'

She sat silent for a long time, hands clenched in her lap and staring into space. For a moment it seemed like she was physically withdrawing from the room, even though she had not actually moved. Gallagher remembered the copy of *The Time Machine* in her cabin, and had a sudden fancy that she was in such a machine herself, watching the years blur by as time sped past her. Was she going forward, he wondered, or back into her past?

When she finally spoke her voice was so quiet he could barely hear. 'What happened?'

'I was hoping you could tell me,' Gallagher said.

Her hands tugged at each other. 'I would never have harmed Billie. I loved her.'

Hamilton shifted position a little. 'Many people have gone to the hangman with those words on their lips.'

'Believe what you like,' she said, her voice still very quiet. 'I did not kill Billie Dolan.'

Gallagher sighed, studying the telegram. 'Here's what I don't understand,' he said. 'Dowrich was blackmailing you over your relationship with Billie, threatening to tell your husband if you didn't pay him off. But why didn't you tell him to go to hell, as you claimed you did? You're a tough, resourceful woman, Mrs Markland. I'm sure you could have found a way of discrediting Dowrich, or just brazening it out. Why surrender to him?'

She had begun to tremble, but she said nothing. 'And why did the amount suddenly go up?' Gallagher continued. 'You told me he came to see you in New York, just before we sailed. Why?'

'To demand more money.'

'Did he tell you what he wanted the money for?'

'No,' she said. 'Why would he? Why don't you ask some of the other people he was blackmailing? There's Franklin, for a start.'

Both men stared at her. 'How do you know this?' asked Gallagher.

'Dowrich told me as much. He said there would be rich pickings on *Lusitania*, not just me but Ripley and Franklin. And López.'

'López?'

'That's what he said. The name meant nothing at the time. It wasn't until we sat down for dinner on Saturday that I realized who he meant.'

Gallagher shook his head. 'So. You corrupted a solicitor and defrauded your husband of several thousand dollars a month. You paid Dowrich, I assume, through the account at the Brooklyn Trust Company, to which he presumably also had access. Shall I tell you what happened next?'

The trembling had increased. 'Do whatever you like,' she said.

'As you said, Dowrich came to see you at your hotel in New York before we sailed. This time his demands were much higher. You wired your solicitor friend and asked him to get the money ready, the transfer to be made when you sent a second telegram of confirmation, the one I showed you yesterday. This was a backstop, in case your first plan went wrong.'

'Are we getting to the cabin key?' asked Hamilton.

'We are. A small consideration to one of the clerks at Cunard's office in New York allowed you to learn which cabin had been assigned to Dowrich. As part of your plan, you also obtained Ripley's cabin number. Once aboard, you sent a message to Dowrich offering to meet him in his cabin after dinner the day we sailed. Presumably you also tipped to Maurice to ensure you were seated at our table, so you could keep an eye on them both.'

Hamilton nodded. 'We can easily confirm that with Maurice.'

'Yes, Maurice has no shame where these things are concerned. Earlier in the day you approached the purser's bureau and asked for the spare key to Cabin B14, as you had lost your original key. The assistant purser, who was probably very busy, handed over the key without checking the passenger register. B14, of course, is Ripley's cabin. You knew Ripley was upstairs playing poker, so you let yourself into his cabin and stole his gun.

'After dinner, you met Dowrich as previously arranged. Once inside his cabin you shot him, took his cabin key and swapped tags with Ripley's key, which you left in the cabin. You let yourself out and locked the door with Dowrich's key and then slipped into the ladies' lavatory and waited to see if anyone had heard the shots. That was good thinking, because Schurz *had* heard the noise and came out to see what was going on.'

'You can prove none of this,' she said.

'After he had gone you waited until the steward came around to check on the passengers. As he opened Ripley's cabin, you asked for a carafe of water to be sent to your cabin. He went away to the steward's pantry, leaving you enough time to enter the cabin and replace the gun where you found it. You did a nice job of picking the lock on Ripley's strongbox and re-locking it, by the way. I didn't see a single scratch on the keyplate. But I'm guessing you've done this before.

'Finally, you threw Dowrich's key overboard. The deck was wet, and one of your shoes was still damp when you came up to the saloon and engaged me in conversation. I must give you credit, Mrs Markland, you were cool as a cucumber. I never suspected a thing until I realized the keys had been swapped. That led me to believe someone had stolen his gun, too. Was that a genuine attempt to frame Ripley for the murder, or just an attempt to throw us off the scent until the ship reached Liverpool and you could disappear?'

'Why are you so sure it was Ripley's gun?'

'We can run tests on the bullets that killed Dowrich,' he said gently. 'But you already knew that, didn't you, Mrs Markland? That's why you decided to steal the gun.'

'Murdering someone is a desperate act,' said Hamilton. 'Dowrich must have had some powerful hold on you, Mrs Markland, to make you risk the gallows.'

After a long silence, she spoke again. 'You can prove it was Ripley's gun, but you cannot prove I pulled the trigger. Everyone will believe Ripley is a murderer.'

'And why will they believe that?' asked Gallagher.

'Because he killed Billie Dolan,' she said, and then with shattering suddenness she broke. Leaning forward in her chair, she pressed her hands to her face, tears streaming between her fingers as she sobbed over and over in broken-hearted longing for the thing she had wanted most in the world, and now would never have.

To interrupt her grief would have been cruel beyond measure. Gallagher waited until she lowered her hands and then offered her a handkerchief. She wiped her face and blew her nose, and then sat back in her chair staring at him, red-rimmed eyes dull with anguish. Another woman might have apologized for making a scene; Dolly Markland was too far sunk in misery to care.

'I thought I had worked it all out,' she said. 'I thought I was in control of my life and everything would go to order, exactly as I planned. I never dreamed I would see her again, or that I would still feel . . .'

Gallagher continued to wait.

'You wanted to know why I paid Dowrich,' she said. 'I will tell you, but this will be the end for me. You're right, it would have been difficult if the affair with Billie had come to light, but I could have ridden that storm. The truth is far darker.'

'Tell me,' Gallagher said quietly. 'I am not here to pass judgement on you, Mrs Markland.'

A bitter smile crossed her lips. 'Wait until you hear my story. You may think differently then.'

'Tell me,' he repeated.

She rested her hands in her lap. 'I joined the chorus line at Ripley's theatre when I was sixteen years old,' she said. 'I loved everything about it, the crowds, the costumes, the music, the dancing, the chance to show off and be the centre of attention. It was like a drug to me, and I seized on everything that came my way with the enthusiasm of an opium eater. That included the sex.'

Gallagher waited. 'I slept with Ripley a few weeks after I joined the line,' she said. 'I knew he was sleeping with the other girls. I didn't care. I slept with them too, and when Ripley found out he laughed and encouraged me. To me it was all part of the life, part of the excitement. When he decided to call us Ripley's Roses, it was me that suggested we all have tattoos.'

'As a mark of belonging? Like a member of a gang?'

She shook her head. 'Like a mark of ownership, like you brand cattle. I gave myself over to Ripley, I belonged to him. I loved that sense of being owned, and I wanted it to last for ever. The brand was a way of making that permanent.'

'I see,' Gallagher said. He saw the strain in her face, and knew how much this was costing her.

'But of course, it couldn't go on for ever. Like I said, I got too old. So, when I retired I invented a new role for myself. What I told you was true. I recruited and trained new dancers for the line. I didn't tell you the rest.'

'What did you do?'

'I broke them in,' she said quietly. 'Like cattle.'

'MOST WERE VIRGINS when I found them,' she said. 'In fact, I looked specifically for those, because I knew it would please him. I trained them to dance and sing, but I also instructed them about sex. Just talk at first, until they got used to the idea, and then I showed them how by touching myself, and encouraged them to touch me and I did the same to them. Do you need further details?'

'No,' said Gallagher.

'After they had been schooled, Ripley would come in. At first he just watched; he was always there when they were tattooed.

After the first few times, he would join in. A few more sessions, and my work was done. I handed them over to Ripley and went out and looked for new blood.'

'Were these girls willing? Or did you coerce them?'

'Truthfully, Mr Gallagher, I didn't care one way or the other. All that mattered was whether I could bend them to my will, to get them to do what I wanted them to do. Some played along, or pretended to. Others had to be compelled.'

There was a long silence before Gallagher spoke again. 'What happened to these girls?'

'Some got through. They did their four or five years on stage until they got too old, and then they left and we never saw them again. Others broke. Some collapsed mentally, a few attempted suicide. Some tried to run away, but Ripley always sent men to drag them back, and they were taken into his office and beaten. When a girl had particularly offended him, he carried out the beating himself; otherwise it was left to me. I was a female version of Ripley, you see. All that mattered was my own pleasure, and of course, much of that pleasure came from my ability to control them.'

'And then Billie came along.'

'There was something different about Billie. They were all innocent, sweet girls when they arrived, of course, and corrupting them was part of the fun, part of the game. But with Billie, I simply couldn't imagine her being anything other than what she was, pure and gentle and . . . and *good*. I realized that I cared more about her than I did about myself. I wanted *her* to be happy, whereas before I couldn't have given a tuppeny damn whether they were happy or not, so long as I was. Billie changed me.'

She paused, gathering her words. 'She became the centre of my world. I had to have her, I had to possess her. I couldn't bear to think of handing her over to Ripley as I had so many others, and that changed how I felt about Ripley. He was the enemy now, trying to take away what was mine. Finally, I persuaded Billie to run away with me. She would have come, too, not because she loved me, I know that now, but because I could help her escape the fate of the others. But Ripley stopped her.'

The deck beneath their feet moved a little. How little we know about people, Gallagher thought. All too often we see only the bright facades. We never know the shadows that lie underneath; at least, not until it is too late.

As the thought came, she spoke again. 'I know what kind of monster I am,' she said quietly. 'I had plenty of time to reflect on this, in the days and weeks after I left Ripley. I saw myself for what I am, and I understood the pain and suffering I had caused. More than once, I considered throwing myself into the river and ridding the world of my presence. I lacked the courage to do so, of course; bullies like me are never brave. So I stayed in Canada and invented a new life for myself and became, or tried to become, a different person. I thought I had closed the door on the past. But that isn't really possible, is it?'

'When did you realize Billie was on *Lusitania*?'

'I knew before we boarded. Dowrich told me. He also told me she was with Franklin; I think that must have something to do with why he was blackmailing Franklin. I thought it didn't matter, it was all in the past. All the same, I tried to avoid her and I had no intention of speaking to her. And then that bastard Ripley threw her straight at me.'

Gallagher nodded. 'Dowrich was pressing Ripley to pay back the loan he owed to Paul Kelly and his friends, and Ripley thought he could extort the money from you. You already had the money ready to hand, as Ripley may well have known.'

'Probably. I refused, and Ripley sent Billie to beg from me.

She was the bait; if I paid over the money, Ripley would detach her from Franklin and give her back to me. Except that Billie refused to go with me.'

'That must have been very hard,' Gallagher said.

'Hard? It broke me. I had reinvented myself, made a new life for myself, but part of me always remembered those days and nights with Billie and I took comfort and solace from the fact that once upon a time we had loved each other. It was the one bright spark of light in the echoing darkness of my soul. She shattered my hope, Mr Gallagher. I was already living a lie in the present. She told me I had been equally deluded in the past.'

The tears came again, more slowly this time. 'I begged her to come with me, to love me as I loved her. She threw my words back in my face. She didn't just refuse me, there was real . . . anger, venom even, in her voice. I realized she had hated me all along. And then, there was nothing left.'

'And so, you were bitter and heart-broken,' Gallagher said. 'Mr Hamilton is right. Loving someone is no bar to murdering them.'

She shook her head. Her voice was calm but desolate. 'You don't understand, Mr Gallagher. Killing Billie would have been like killing part of myself, and as I said, I don't have enough courage for that. I don't expect you to believe me.'

Gallagher said nothing. 'All I ever wanted to do was protect her and keep her safe,' Dolly said softly. 'To love her, and be loved in return. That was all.' She wiped her eyes again. 'I don't expect you to understand. Men tend not to understand these things, especially when they happen between women.'

Gallagher watched her, still silent. 'What makes you think Ripley killed her?' he asked finally.

'Vengeance,' she said. 'I refused to give him the money, and she refused to follow his orders. He knew killing her was the best way to hurt me.'

'So, why didn't you give him the money? You might have saved her.'

'I have asked myself that question, of course.' She gave a bitter little laugh. 'I hated Ripley and I didn't want to let him win, simple as that. But in doing so, I put my own interests ahead of hers, again. I told her I would die for her. But in the end, I couldn't even do this much. And so, you are right. I am responsible for her death.'

She turned to look at Gallagher again. 'It is time I atoned,' she said, 'for this and for everything I have done in the past. It is not much, but at least it is something. Arrest Ripley, Mr Gallagher, and I will testify against him, no matter what the cost to myself. I will pay any price, I will sacrifice myself utterly, if that is what it takes to see him hang.'

The silence that followed lasted for a long time. 'Very well,' Gallagher said finally. 'You may go.'

Hamilton blinked. Dolly Markland looked startled. 'That's all? Nothing more?'

'As it happens, I do believe you about Billie Dolan. I don't think you intended her to come to harm.'

'Don't be kind to me,' she said. 'I don't deserve it.'

'I am not a judge, Mrs Markland. When we reach Liverpool, I will hand over a dossier of evidence to the police, and you will be required to report to them as well. The Toronto police may also decide to get involved. However, that is up to them.'

She rose to her feet. 'I will do whatever you ask of me,' she said.

Hamilton closed the door behind her. 'Well?' the purser demanded. 'Did she or didn't she?'

Something hit the deck overhead with a hard thud. 'She

killed Dowrich, I have absolutely no doubt about that. He had increased his demands and she decided to take action. However, the case against her is circumstantial and a lot more evidence will be required to make it stand up. The police might even think the evidence really does point to Ripley. As she pointed out, he has motive and his alibi no longer stacks up.'

'And then there's the smoking gun,' Hamilton observed. 'At least there will be, if that test comes back positive. The wrong man could go to the gallows for this.'

'It won't be for the first time, nor the last. On the other hand, does Dolly Markland deserve to hang? I have sympathy for her, Hammy, I really do.'

'Really? What she did to those girls? She said it herself, she was a monster.'

'But even monsters can repent,' Gallagher said, 'and some-times they deserve a second chance. If Dowrich had kept his demands moderate he might have lived, but he pushed her too far. She had no choice but to fight back.'

Hamilton looked sceptical. 'Are you going soft on her?'

'No. But I understand people who are damaged.'

'And the girl? Did Mrs Markland kill her too?'

The noise overhead continued, grating and rasping, and Gallagher looked up in irritation. 'No, of course not. I've been pretty sure all along who it was, but I didn't understand why, until now. Ironically, it was Mrs Markland who gave me the last piece of the puzzle. For Christ's sake, what is that noise?'

Someone pounded on the door. 'Mr Hamilton!' called one of the stewards, his voice full of tension and fear. 'You'd better come quick, sir! One of the lifeboats has broken loose!'

19

Lifeboat Number 2, on the port side of the boat deck, had slipped from its davits and was sliding loose. Even though the boat was built of teak and weighed several tons, the motion of the ship was enough to pitch it back and forth across the wooden deck, tearing up splinters as it did so. By the time Gallagher reached the deck the wreckage of several chairs, the fragments of a coffee pot and the shreds of a woman's shawl lay in its wake.

Two sailors with ropes were trying to harness the lifeboat. Every time they came close, the boat lurched towards them and they had to scramble to safety. A crowd of passengers watched, faces full of alarm.

A single voice rang out, full of command and authority. 'Stand back, everyone! You men! Get those ropes attached to the boat and man the davits. Quickly now!'

It was Edwin Franklin, standing fearlessly in front of the boat and pointing to the two sailors. A young man in a blue uniform ran up alongside him. 'Sir, step back out of the way! At once, if you please!'

Franklin turned on him. 'Who are you? Officer of the deck? Get these people to safety, and then get some more hands up here. Come on, man, jump to it!'

'Sir!' the officer said in outrage. 'I'm in charge here!'

'Don't argue with me,' Franklin instructed. 'Get these people away, I say! Come on, you men, hurry up with those ropes!'

The lifeboat lurched again, crunching into the deckhouse bulkhead and grinding another deck chair to sawdust under its keel. Gallagher climbed onto the rail and stood, balancing against the roll of the ship. 'Throw me the rope!' he called to the nearest seaman. The man hesitated for a moment, then threw the free end of the heavy manila rope. Gallagher caught it in his outstretched hand just as the ship rolled back the other way. A woman screamed. The lifeboat slid across the deck and smashed into the rail just as Gallagher jumped down onto the canvas cover. Grabbing the steel eyebolt protruding from the gunwales, he ran the rope through the lifting eye and jumped onto the davit housing, where he and the seaman attached the free end to the block. More sailors arrived on the run, taking the second rope and running it through another eyebolt to attach it to the second davit. Throwing themselves on the cranks, they winched the boat back into position. Gallagher climbed onto the boat again and picked up another length of rope lying on the cover, studying it for a moment.

Franklin was there, clapping his hands. 'Well done, you men. Well done. All right, everyone,' he said, turning to the other passengers. 'The situation is under control. We can go about our business now.'

'Pompous ass,' murmured the young officer. He turned to Gallagher. 'Thank you, sir. I'd say you've done that before.'

'South China Sea in a typhoon,' Gallagher said. He held up the length of rope. 'Are you reporting to the captain? Do you mind if I come with you?'

'The rope was cut,' he said on the bridge. He held up the length of rope again, showing where the manila fibres had been neatly severed. 'I haven't checked the other davit yet, but I'll wager its rope was cut too. Someone saw the sea was coming up, and set the boat free to do what damage it could.'

High above the blue sea, the bridge seemed like an island in the sky. Looking around, Gallagher noticed extra lookouts posted on the wings, scanning the sea with binoculars. They were not yet in the war zone, but Captain Turner was taking no chances. A navigational chart of the south coast of Ireland had been brought in from the chartroom, and Gallagher saw their course plotted to Fastnet and beyond, past Cape Clear and Galley Head to the Old Head of Kinsale and thence to Queenstown, a little over twenty-four hours away.

Men on the bridge around them had paused to listen. 'Any injuries?' asked the captain.

'None, sir,' said the young officer. 'A few deck chairs are the worse for wear, that's all. It could have been nasty, though.'

'Yes,' Turner said grimly. He looked back at Gallagher. 'Any idea what this is about?'

'Same as the drying room fire, sir. Whoever did this wants to unsettle us and worry the passengers, but most of all they want us to keep looking in the wrong place.'

Turner dismissed the officer, who saluted and departed. The captain nodded to Gallagher. 'This way.'

They walked out onto the port bridge wing, looking down to see the crew securing the rogue lifeboat and sweeping up the debris. Franklin was still there, walking up and down with one hand behind his back. Turner looked at him.

'That man is an idiot. I don't like having him on my ship.'

'I understand, sir. Unfortunately, Cunard doesn't require tests of intelligence before allowing passengers to purchase a ticket.'

'They'd be out of business if they did. All right, Gallagher, what is it?'

'I have a suspect in the Dowrich murder, sir, and I am quite sure who killed the girl. But I need to interview Franklin.'

Turner's eyebrows came together. 'Have you evidence against him?'

'I'm hoping he can help us with that. I'd like you present at the interview if possible. It will show him he is being treated with the respect he thinks he deserves.'

'Very well put. Yes, all right. Make the arrangements through Hamilton. Anything else?'

'Yes, sir. How much is *Lusitania* carrying in ballast?'

There was a moment of silence. 'We're not carrying ballast,' Turner said. 'We're in cargo.'

'So I understand, sir. Mr Hamilton mentioned cheese, I believe. May I ask how much?'

'Twenty-one tons. On top of that, four tons of lard, four tons of butter, eighteen tons of bacon and five tons of canned food. There's some general goods as well. Shoes, cutlery, books, dry goods. Several hundred packets of furs from the Hudson's Bay Company.' Turner sniffed. 'We may be at war, but the fine ladies still need their fox hats.'

Schurz would hardly be interested in butter and furs. 'Is that everything?' Gallagher asked.

Turner stared out over the sea for a moment. 'I have my orders from the board of directors, Gallagher. I accept the cargo manifest that is delivered to me, and sign off on it. I do not ask questions.'

'May I ask about the waybills, sir?'

The waybills were customs declarations, describing the contents of each consignment of cargo, its value, its point of origin and its destination. 'I have taken personal charge of them, with orders to hand them over to the Inspector of Customs at the

Port of Liverpool. They are in a sealed packet, which I have been instructed not to open.'

'You don't know for certain what is in the hold.'

'I know that I have my orders from the board, and the board has its orders from the Admiralty.'

Gallagher nodded. 'Will you give me permission to go down and take a look, once we have interviewed Franklin?'

'Does this concern the safety of the ship?'

'It may,' said Gallagher.

Turner hesitated for a long time. 'Make it so,' he said finally.

THURSDAY, 6 MAY 1915
10.59 A.M.

'MR FRANKLIN,' GALLAGHER said. 'My apologies for disturbing you, sir, but I need a moment of your time.'

Fresh from his heroics with the lifeboat, Franklin was relaxing with a cup of coffee in the verandah café. Around him, other passengers watched him and whispered excitedly behind their hands. He looked up, irritated. 'Really, Gallagher? Can't it wait?'

Gallagher looked at the girl sitting opposite him. He had noticed her before; about nineteen, tall, fair, young, with blue eyes, not dissimilar to Billie Dolan. He wondered how many of Franklin's previous women had looked the same.

Had Roxanne been this young and innocent once? No; Roxanne had been born knowing the world was wrong.

'I'm afraid it's urgent,' Gallagher said. 'The captain is waiting for us in his cabin. He wants your advice on how to proceed once we reach the war zone.'

Franklin's expression changed at once. 'I am happy to be of service. Forgive me, my dear,' he said to the girl. 'Duty calls, I fear.' She gazed back at him with adoring eyes.

Billie was an ornament, nothing more.

They walked forward through the public rooms and down the long panelled corridors past the cabins on the boat deck. Outside, the sea sparkled, sunlight dancing joyous across the waves. People stood or sat silently on deck, watching the horizon. Gallagher knocked at the captain's door. 'Enter,' said a gruff voice.

There were two people in the room; Hamilton the purser, and the captain, seated behind his desk with his bowler hat resting on the polished wood before him. Hamilton closed the door and stood in front of it.

'Good morning, Captain Turner,' Franklin said, sitting down without waiting for an invitation. 'How may I help you?'

Turner did not move. 'Mr Gallagher will ask the questions.'

Franklin looked blank. 'Questions?'

'I am sorry for the deception, Mr Franklin,' Gallagher said. 'But I wanted to ensure we spoke in private. This concerns Miss Dolan.'

'I see,' Franklin said coldly, rising to his feet again. 'And you thought that by dropping the captain's name, you would persuade me to accompany you. Well, I don't take kindly to being duped, Gallagher, and you may rest assured you have not heard the last of this. Now, you will excuse me.'

No one moved. 'Please sit down, sir,' Gallagher said gently. 'This won't take long, I assure you. We think we know who killed Miss Dolan. But we need your help to prove it.'

There was a pause of several seconds, and then Franklin slowly sat down again. 'I would prefer to put this entire affair behind me.'

'And you will, Mr Franklin, as soon as we identify the killer. May I explain where we are at the moment?'

Franklin took a gold cigarette case from his pocket, removed a cigarette, tapped it and put it between his lips. Hamilton stepped forward with a Ronson lighter and lit the cigarette, his face expressionless. Franklin blew out smoke.

'Please proceed,' he said.

'You were seen on deck around the time Miss Dolan was killed.' Gallagher glanced at Hamilton, who nodded. 'Several of the stewards saw you, and confirm your story.'

'I was not aware my story required confirmation,' Franklin said stiffly. 'People tend to accept my word.'

'Of course. I'm just getting the details straight in my own mind. Now, from the beginning, the evidence pointed to the killer being one of two people. The first was Ripley, her former employer. A witness heard them quarrelling violently the night before Miss Dolan was killed.'

Franklin looked disinterested. 'Mr Franklin,' Gallagher said with patience, 'are you aware of any animus between Miss Dolan and Ripley? Do you know why they might have quarrelled?'

'Ripley treated her abominably when she worked for him,' Franklin said. 'As he did with all his chorus girls. When I discovered the conditions in which these poor women worked, I stopped going to the theatre. The entire atmosphere had become repellent to me.'

Gallagher shook his head. 'I understand why Miss Dolan has cause to hate Ripley, but that's looking at the problem from the wrong end. Did Ripley have any reason to kill Miss Dolan? Did he have a motive?'

'Thankfully, I am not privy to what goes on in Ripley's mind. And surely it is your job, Gallagher, to establish motive in this case.'

'Indeed, sir. I am grateful to you for the reminder. The other person in the frame is Mrs Markland. Until recently, I believe you were unaware that she and Miss Dolan had been lovers. Miss Dolan has since explained what happened, and you forgave her.' Gallagher paused. 'I must say that was very generous of you. An ordinary man might have been furious at the deception.'

Franklin smiled briefly. 'As you should know by now, Gallagher, I am not an ordinary man.'

Smoke rose from his cigarette, in a straight line at first, then curling as it met the currents of air before finally dissolving. Turner and Hamilton watched the other two men in silence.

'Were you also aware that Mrs Markland had tried to persuade Miss Dolan to leave you?' Gallagher asked.

'I wasn't, but I am not surprised. As I told you, I had decided to end things with Miss Dolan, so it makes no difference to me.'

'Did you also know Miss Dolan refused to go with her?'

Franklin's eyebrows rose. 'Did she? Well, I must say her loyalty does her credit.'

'But you were still going to turn her off.'

'Of course.'

Gallagher nodded. 'We are pursuing a theory that after Miss Dolan rebuffed Mrs Markland, the latter killed her in a fit of jealous rage.'

Franklin drew on his cigarette and blew out smoke. 'As I said to you, Gallagher, women are emotionally unstable. This proves my point, I think. They cannot contain their emotions the way men do. Have you arrested Mrs Markland?'

'Not yet,' said Gallagher. 'We are still looking for the murder weapon.'

'Perhaps she threw the gun overboard,' Franklin suggested.

'Gun? Did I say she had been shot?'

Franklin's face was full of disdain. 'Really, Gallagher. Credit me with some powers of deduction. Billie was younger and stronger than Mrs Markland. The chance that she could have been overpowered and strangled or stabbed is very small. Shooting is the only method that makes sense.'

Gallagher nodded. 'You are correct, of course. And yes, she *could* have thrown the gun overboard, but it is unlikely. It was a fine afternoon, and many of the other passengers were on deck. I think it much more likely that she stole a gun from someone else and then replaced it. So, first of all we need to identify the weapon.'

Franklin stubbed out his cigarette. Gallagher could almost see the wheels of his mind turning. 'How would you know which gun killed her?' Franklin asked.

'There are tests that can help us. For example, if the bullet had been fired from your gun, we could fire another shot from the same gun and compare the two. If they match, we would know the first bullet also came from your gun. Would you mind if I examined it again, please?'

Franklin's eyes narrowed, but he handed over the derringer. 'And what makes you think the bullet might have come from my gun?'

'Let me offer a hypothesis,' said Gallagher. 'Mrs Markland was angry with Billy, but she was also jealous of you, her lover and protector. Stealing your gun to kill Billie would have been a way of getting back at you. Has this gun been out of your sight at any point in the past few days?'

'No.' Suddenly Franklin raised a finger. 'Ah, wait a moment . . . Yes, now that I think of it, I left it behind when I went to see Billie. She didn't like guns, was quite frightened of them in fact. I always left it in my cabin when I called on her. If Mrs Markland somehow gained access to my cabin . . . yes, yes it is quite possible. Good work, Gallagher. That would never have occurred to me.'

Gallagher looked down at the derringer in his hands. 'How ironic that Miss Dolan was frightened of guns, and yet a gun killed her. That poor young woman. Such a waste, don't you think?'

'Yes, I agree,' Franklin said. 'But . . . there it is.'

Turner looked at him. 'Is that all you have to say about the death of your mistress? *There it is?*'

'What happened is in the past,' Franklin said calmly. 'We cannot change it. Time to move on.'

He spoke as if the interview was coming to an end. Gallagher leaned back in his chair. 'You don't tend to dwell on the past, do you, Mr Franklin?' he asked, his voice conversational. 'For you, it is all about the future, and how you can help to make it and shape it.'

'Other people judge a man by his deeds,' Franklin said. 'I judge him by his potential. And it goes without saying that I judge myself by that same yardstick.'

'So it must be particularly galling for you when the past comes back to bite you. I am referring of course to James Dowrich and his threat to expose your past relationships.'

Franklin looked blank. 'What do you mean?'

'I mean your failed bid to run for the United States Senate, backed by Tammany Hall and money from the New York gangs. Dowrich knew every detail; he had probably helped gather the money. You would have been a real asset to them. There's nothing the Five Points Gang would have liked better than a US senator in their pocket. The sky would have been the limit.'

'Allow me to correct you,' Franklin said coldly. 'My bid for the Senate did not *fail* because I did not run. Once I became aware of the source of the funds Dowrich and his friends were providing, I withdrew from the contest, returned the money and renounced all interest in politics.'

'But you didn't return the money,' Gallagher said. 'You kept it. Miss Dolan told me as much.'

'Miss Dolan had no more financial nous than a mosquito. Quite clearly she did not know what she was talking about.'

Gallagher shook his head. 'Let me paint you a picture, Mr Franklin. Dowrich approached you recently and asked you for money. If you refused, he would make public your connection with the gangs. You would be exposed to the world as a man who profited from prostitution, gambling, extortion and all the other unpleasant ways the gangs make their money. That wouldn't do your saintly image much good, would it?'

Franklin rose to his feet. 'I don't have to listen to this—'

'Sit down,' said Captain Turner.

'Don't give me orders—'

'*Sit down.*'

Bullies are never brave, Dolly Markland had said, and so it proved. Franklin sat, his eyes alive with anger. 'Everything I have just said has been confirmed by the New York Police Department,' Gallagher said. 'They have a file on you, did you know that? Carefully hidden away, of course, but available to those who know where to look. The telegram came in this morning.'

Franklin said nothing. 'You knew Dowrich was a threat,' Gallagher continued, 'and you decided to . . . what was the phrase you used? Squash him. You first tried to pay Ripley to kill him; Miss Dolan overheard you asking Ripley to "get rid" of Dowrich. When Ripley refused, you decided to do the job yourself. You were ready to kill Dowrich, but someone else beat you to it.'

'This is delusional nonsense,' Franklin snapped. 'I have never tried to kill anyone. For God's sake, man, I'm a pacifist!'

'So you keep saying, and yet you were ready to threaten Schurz if he did not leave Billie alone. And you knew Dowrich was dead, of course. *Dowrich is no longer in any position to bother me*, you said. I wonder how you found out? A bribe to one of the hospital attendants, perhaps? We shall find out in due course. Dowrich was dead, but one other person knew the truth.'

Hamilton frowned. 'Doesn't Ripley know as well?'

'I doubt it, or he would have pressed his case much harder when he came to ask Mr Franklin for money. You were able to fob him off with relative ease, weren't you, Mr Franklin? No, the other person who knew the truth was your mistress, Billie Dolan. So long as she was with you, you could control her. But when you learned she was planning to leave, you realized she was a threat to you. And that is when you killed her.'

Franklin stood up again. 'This is utter nonsense. Have you a single shred of proof to back up any of these wild allegations? Of course you don't.'

'I have all the proof I need,' Gallagher said. 'Edwin Peabody Franklin, by the power vested in me by Captain Turner, I am arresting you for the murder of Wilhelmina Dolan on the fifth of May 1915. You will remain under confinement until the ship reaches Liverpool, where you will be handed over to the civil authorities.'

The expression on Franklin's face was sheer, blank amazement. How long had it been since anyone crossed him or stood up to him? Gallagher wondered. Perhaps never.

'You cannot arrest me,' Franklin said, his voice echoing the disbelief in his face.

'He can,' said Captain Turner. 'Hamilton, call the master-at-arms, if you please.'

'I told you!' Franklin said. His voice rose a little. 'When I called on Billie, I didn't have the gun!'

Gallagher stood up. 'Of course you had the bloody gun. You took it with you, pushed her onto the bed, put a pillow over her chest to silence the report and prevent blood splatter, and shot her. You returned to your cabin, cleaned the gun, replaced the empty cartridge, returned it to your pocket and went out on deck to create an alibi.'

Franklin sat in sudden, uncharacteristic silence. 'We'll test the gun when we reach England,' Gallagher said. 'That, plus the fingerprints we will take from her cabin, will be more than enough to convict you.'

From stillness, Franklin exploded into sudden rage. 'Don't you people know who I am? Don't you understand how much trouble I can make for you? Turner, once I have spoken to Cunard's board you will never go to sea again, with this or any other shipping line, is that clear? And Gallagher, I don't know which branch of the service you work for, but when we reach England I shall make one telephone call to the Palace – and one is all I shall need – and you will be a private soldier in the next battalion of replacements, bound for the Western Front.'

'A pacifist, sending a man to his death on the battlefield,' Gallagher said. 'How ironic.'

'Oh, for God's sake! Be reasonable, gentlemen.' Franklin's voice dropped a little, persuading now, almost pleading. 'I am here to make peace, remember? In a few weeks, a month at most, the war will be over. Hundreds of thousands of lives will be saved, perhaps even millions. But if you try to stop me now, more men will die. Believe me, every second of delay means death for someone's loved ones, someone's sons.'

He paused, looking at their faces. 'Set these matters in the balance, gentlemen. The lives of all those young men, so full of promise with everything before them, against that of one silly girl. Which is more important?'

'That is not a choice you are entitled to make,' said Gallagher. 'None of us has the right to set a value on the life of another human being. Billie Dolan also had her whole life in front of her, just like the soldiers. Is her death just a cost to you, like the price of a component for one of your tractors? A price to be paid for bringing peace to Europe?'

'Yes,' said Franklin. 'Her death is a tragedy, but it is a drop in the ocean compared to all the other tragedies unfolding around us. Gentlemen, I beg you. Let me complete my work.'

'You are attempting to make a logical case, if not a moral one,' Gallagher said. 'I might be tempted to listen, were it not for one thing. You can't make peace, and you know it. The slaughter on the Western Front has inflamed passions on both sides. The people don't want peace; they want vengeance for all the men who have died so far. Even if you did speak to the king and the Kaiser, they would not listen.

'But you don't care. This entire exercise is about you, a chance to boost your own ego and increase your public image, so yet more people will bow down to admire you. Franklin the Peacemaker, they will call you, Franklin the Hero. It's what you need, isn't it? It's what you feed on, it's what you live for. And that's why you killed Billie Dolan.'

He knew he should not be speaking like this, but he didn't care. Anger surged through him, and he knew the anger was for Roxanne as well as Billie. 'You didn't give a tinker's damn about Billie as a human being,' he said. 'All that mattered was that she had betrayed you and deceived you. Your pride and your vanity demanded retribution. What did you call her? An ornament. And when she no longer pleased you, you smashed her like glass.'

'She was a stupid little whore who didn't deserve to live,' Franklin said. 'I can't think why I wasted my time with her. But if you think you can prove in a court of law that I killed her, you're making a grave mistake. I will hire the best barristers in England, and I will tear your case to pieces and walk free.'

'I don't doubt it for a moment,' Gallagher said. 'Your kind always do. Mr Hamilton, fetch the master-at-arms, please, and take this man away.'

FRANKLIN LEFT IN silence, the master-at-arms close behind him. Turner had given orders for him to be confined to his cabin, with a guard at the door. 'The passengers will talk, sir,' Hamilton said.

Turner stood up, ramming his bowler hat down on his head. 'Tell them he has gone insane. He has been confined for his own safety. That's probably not too far from the mark. Now if you'll excuse me, gentlemen, I am needed on the bridge.'

He went out, closing the door behind him. Hamilton looked at Gallagher. 'I checked with the stewards like you said. Franklin was on deck between 1400 and 1500, the time Doc Whiting says the girl was shot. He seems to have been there pretty much the entire afternoon.'

'He was creating an alibi, of course, but we can knock holes in it. He only needed a few minutes to kill the girl . . . But he's right. He'll get off, no matter how strong the case against him might be.'

He had seen it before, many times. He believed in justice; still believed in justice, after all this time and tragedy, but he knew how easy it was for justice to be bent inward upon itself. Faith and good intentions were no match for wealth and power. You did your best, and you watched it all go to waste.

I am a painter that a mocking God has condemned to paint

upon darkness. Sometimes, he thought, I really only understand Baudelaire long after I have read him.

'He'll make trouble for you,' Hamilton predicted.

'Probably.'

'All the same, well done, laddie. You've got Franklin, and I'd back you on Mrs Markland for Dowrich's killer, despite your reservations. Two out of two.'

'But there's still the problem of Dowrich. Why was he so desperate for money? And López; God in heaven, what on earth did Dowrich have on López? And I still have to get Chalfont to Liverpool, with the very real possibility that there is another German agent loose on this ship. We're twenty-eight hours from Queenstown, Hammy, forty-eight from Liverpool. Time is running out.'

'What are you going to do?'

'I need to speak to Schurz,' Gallagher said.

20

It took nearly an hour to track Schurz down. Gallagher finally found his quarry in the smoking room reading another of his technical magazines, and this irritated him because he had checked the smoking room fifteen minutes earlier and there had been no sign of the engineer. 'Might I have a word with you, Mr Schurz? In private?'

The smoking room was busy, gentleman passengers enjoying a drink before lunch. Not even the threat of U-boats could put them off their pre-prandial sherry. The two men walked out onto the boat deck and stood looking out over the sea. 'What is it?' Schurz asked.

'I recall you saying that you had worked with the Union Metallic Cartridge Company. May I ask how long you spent with them?'

'Several years, right up until the end of April. When I took up the appointment in London, I handed over the work to one of my associates.'

'To whom did you report at U.M.C.?'

The engineer looked at him. 'Does the Paymaster General pay you to go around prying into other people's business?'

There was an edge to Gallagher's voice. 'Surely by now, Mr Schurz, it must be obvious that I do not work for the Paymaster General.'

'So you are with the police. I knew it.'

'Answer the question, please.'

'I reported to the managing director, Jonathan Buckland,' Schurz said after a moment. 'He is a personal friend of mine.'

'Were you aware that U.M.C. was selling arms to both sides in the Mexican conflict?'

'No. Should I have been?'

'Someone at U.M.C. tampered with a consignment of artillery shells destined for Pancho Villa's forces,' Gallagher said. 'Was that you?'

'Of course not. Why would I do such a thing?'

'Well, one possibility is that the Germans were paying you. Germany supports the Mexican government, not Villa and his rebels.'

'That is outrageous!' Schurz was angry, but there was also fear in his eyes. 'How dare you insinuate that I—'

'The managing director was a friend of yours, you said. You would have known about every consignment of arms that went out, no matter what the destination.'

Schurz stared at him. 'I *could* have known,' he said, controlling himself with a visible effort. 'I could have asked, if I had wanted to. But I didn't.'

'Why not?'

'Because I don't care. I'm not like Franklin, boasting about how his tractors are ploughing up fields all over the world. I'm not interested in who my clients sell to, or what happens to the arms they make. That is nothing to do with me. I am only interested in making their production processes as efficient as possible. That is what I do, Gallagher, and I am very good at it. The rest is of no interest to me.'

'Someone at U.M.C. leaked information about the ship-ments to German agents in New York.'

'Well, it wasn't me.'

The answer had the ring of conviction, but the problem with Schurz was that he always sounded absolutely convinced of what he said, even when it was palpably absurd. Gallagher tried a different angle. 'You are a member of the Deutscher Bund, you speak German fluently, and you have strong connections in the German-speaking business world in America.'

'Oh, Christ, not this again.'

'And it was you who went up to the forward deck and spotted the German spy.'

'I reported him immediately!'

'And claimed you didn't recognize him.' He paused for a moment. 'How well do you know Professor Hugo Münsterberg?'

The change of direction caught Schurz off guard. 'I . . . I know him quite well.'

'How well?'

'I have attended some of his lectures, and we correspond often. He has been kind enough to read some of my papers.'

'Professor Münsterberg is a member of the Deutscher Bund, and one of Kaiser Wilhelm's foremost supporters in America. He has urged President Wilson to stay neutral in the war, and not to supply arms to Britain. Do you share his views, Mr Schurz?'

'I do not. I told you, I am a positivist and a rational man. The only cause that interests me is the science of engineering.'

'Then why associate with Münsterberg?'

'Because he is a brilliant man!' Schurz exclaimed. 'He is one of the foremost pioneers in the field of experimental psychology. His contribution to scientific management has been immense! He has demonstrated how we must select the right people with the correct psychological characteristics, to perform tasks in order to achieve maximum efficiency. Brains are the key to it all, not brawn. Read his book, *Psychology and Industrial Efficiency*, and you will understand.'

'And do you apply his principles in your own work?'

'Of course I do.'

'At Watertown and at U.M.C., there was labour unrest when your methods were introduced. The workers didn't like them at all.'

'Exactly! It wasn't the methods that were wrong, it was the people! That is what I have learned, that we must not only design each task carefully, but also select the right people for the task. That is the only way to true efficiency.'

'Your new employers in the British government. Do they know about your association with Münsterberg?'

Schurz looked blank. 'I don't know. I don't think so. No one asked me.'

'They might not be very happy if they knew,' Gallagher suggested.

He saw the fear in Schurz's face again. 'Then I beg you not to tell them,' he said.

'Why not?'

'Because this is the biggest thing in my career, Gallagher. The chance to set up the Ministry of Munitions, based on scientific methods, is the kind of project I have always dreamed of, all my professional life. When they come to write the history of scientific management, mine will be the first name they mention. This will be a triumph. And then we'll see what men like Franklin have to say about efficiency.'

Dear God, Gallagher thought. 'What about the war?'

'Oh, you'll win, don't worry. All you have to do is adhere to the methods of production I shall design for you. The rules are simple, people only need to follow them. It might take a couple more years, but with your superior industrial capacity, you'll come out on top.'

Gallagher nodded. 'You have spent a lot of time exploring the ship over the past few days. Especially the forward part. May I ask why?'

'Have you been following me?' Schurz demanded.

'No. But other people have noticed you.'

Schurz stared down at the water rushing past the hull. 'Like I said, there are too many mysteries. Something is different about the ship itself. Part of the third-class accommodation has been closed off, with no explanation as to why.'

'It has been converted into cargo space,' Gallagher said.

'Has it? Then why is there no access to that space? And what are we carrying? The ship is riding lower in the water than she should, given that the passenger cabins are only half full. There is something very heavy down in the forward part of the ship.'

'Why should it interest you?' Gallagher asked.

'I'm curious. It is the nature of my profession to be curious about problems we cannot solve. This is an unarmed, civilian ship. Why is it carrying heavy cargo in a time of war?'

Gallagher looked at the engineer for a long time. 'You make great play of being a neutral citizen,' he said. 'But neutrality only covers so much. You're about to go to work for the British government, Mr Schurz. If you want to keep that contract, which matters so much to you, then I advise you to keep out of things that don't concern you. Do you understand me?'

'Yes,' Schurz said unwillingly. 'But you have to admit, it's still curious.'

THURSDAY, 6 MAY 1915
12.31 P.M.

SCHURZ IS RIGHT about one thing, Gallagher thought. It is curious.

'You can get into the new cargo space from the main deck,' Hamilton said. 'The cargo itself is lifted in and out through the forward cargo hatch, just as before. But they put in an emergency companionway on the main deck, just where Number Two funnel comes up. There's a new bulkhead and a locked door with a special lock, to conceal it from the public.'

'And do you have the key to this special lock?'

Hamilton reached into his desk. 'I do. And I suppose you're wanting to go down and take a look. What are you expecting to find, Pat?'

'I don't know,' Gallagher said. 'I have a hunch, that's all.'

'Let's go now, then. It's lunchtime, and the passengers will be stuffing their faces. There will be no one around to interfere.'

They went down the stair into the depths of the ship, the heat from the boilers rising as they descended. At the foot of the stair Hamilton led the way forward down a short passageway which ended in a white painted bulkhead. A heavy door was set into the bulkhead, with a gleaming steel wheel for a handle. Hamilton took a bunch of keys from his pocket. Behind them, someone cleared his throat. 'Mind if I join you?'

Gallagher wheeled around. Colonel Skarpö was standing in the passageway, hands loose at his side. His red face was smiling, but his eyes were watchful. 'What are you doing here?' Gallagher asked sharply.

'Same as you, I reckon. Trying to find out what your friend Schurz was looking for.'

'Does someone want to tell me what is going on?' demanded Hamilton.

'Hammy, this is Colonel Skarpö from General Villa's staff. He wants to know who stole a consignment of artillery shells from Villa's army.'

'So what's he doing down here?'

'I expect we're about to find out,' Gallagher said. He looked at Skarpö. The colonel was a soldier of fortune, but from his own experience, sometimes soldiers of fortune could be on the side of the angels. Skarpö was competent and, by the standards of his profession, honest; and something told Gallagher he was going to need help before this was all over.

'All right. You've come this far, you may as well come the rest of the way. Don't worry, Hammy, I'll be responsible for him.'

Still dubious, Hamilton unlocked the door and spun the wheel to open it. Beyond was a small square compartment with a hatch set into the deck. The hatch opened smoothly on brand-new, well-oiled hinges. The purser pressed a switch and light bulbs crackled into life, lighting the companionway, a plain iron-runged stair leading down to the next deck.

Climbing down the stair, Gallagher found himself in a huge chamber, seventy feet wide and perhaps a hundred and fifty feet long. Formerly this had been part of third-class accommodation, a warren of corridors and cabins; now all the partitions and furnishings had been removed and the space was piled high with cargo. Rows of portholes ran down both sides of the ship, their light partly obstructed by stacks of boxes and bales.

They were just above the waterline now, and they could hear the rush and gurgle of water outside, flowing past the ship's hull. The air smelled of saltwater and coal dust and the rich acrid tang of cheese. 'Twenty-one tons,' said Gallagher.

'Aye.' Hamilton wrinkled his nose. 'Though you'd not know

whether it's for eating, or taking over to France to lob at the Germans. Fair smells like our answer to chlorine gas.'

'What about the perishable goods?'

'There's a refrigerated space further aft.'

Wooden cases were stacked against the bulkhead, bearing the familiar labels of Armour and Swift and H. J. Heinz, producers of tinned meat and vegetables. Gallagher moved on, noting Captain Turner's despised bales of fox furs, crates of books from New York publishers, leather and wire, automobile parts and electrical components. He stopped before a towering stack of flat wooden crates, painted white and bound together with heavy rope. He counted twenty crates, reaching up almost to the deck above. Beyond were more crates, many more, filling the whole forward section of the cabin. All had been painted the same brilliant white and then stencilled in black with the maker's name, DOMINION MACHINE TOOL CO. LTD, NEW YORK.

'What do you reckon these are?' he asked. 'There's a hell of a lot of them.'

Each box had a paper customs label attached to one end. Skarpö squinted at one of these. 'It just says, "machine parts". The port of origin is New York, and the consignee is given as Customs House, Liverpool. Why is there no named receiver?'

Gallagher's scalp had begun to tingle. 'Because the real consignee doesn't want their name to be known. And these boxes have been painted over.' He pointed at the white paint. 'That pigment is a new one, titanium white. It is very useful for over-painting. Light reflects off the surface, and doesn't show what lies beneath.'

He turned to the others. 'Look for something we can use as a solvent. Vinegar will do, if nothing else.'

It was Skarpö who found the crates of medical equipment and in them, some gallon drums of alcohol disinfectant.

Gallagher soaked his handkerchief in alcohol and rubbed at the side of one crate. 'Does anyone have a knife?'

Skarpö handed over a clasp knife, and Gallagher scraped gently at the loosening paint with the blade, as he had seen restorers do when removing layers of paint from a picture. Gradually the paint stripped away until he could see the original wood and the label burned into it:

UNION METALLIC CARTRIDGE COMPANY
BRIDGEPORT, CONNECTICUT

One corner of the customs label was loose. Gallagher dabbed it to loosen the glue and pulled it away. Beneath was another label, a railway transport label this time.

11470
SOUTHERN PACIFIC RAILROAD
DESTINATION: EL PASO, TEXAS

Skarpö drew a sharp breath. 'God damn it!'

'Take a look,' Gallagher said, handing back the knife. Skarpö rammed the blade under the wooden sideboard of the crate, grunting a little with strain as he pried at it. After a moment the nails gave way and the board came loose in his hand. Something heavy and gleaming rolled out and fell onto the deck at Gallagher's feet with a bump.

It was an eighteen-pounder artillery shell.

'Well,' Gallagher said after a moment. 'Colonel, I think we have found your missing munitions.'

Skarpö bent and picked up the shell. The brass casing gleamed in the dull light; the projectile was painted yellow with a red band around it. 'High-explosive round,' he said, letting out his breath. 'My God, we could have done with these at Celaya.'

'Is that live?' demanded Hamilton.

The colonel shook his head, pointing to the empty cavity in the nose of the projectile. 'It hasn't been fuzed. The fuzes are stored separately during transport, to avoid accidents. They'll be in boxes somewhere else in the hold.' He looked around at the stacks of crates. 'There are thousands of rounds here. It must be the entire consignment we ordered.'

He put the shell back in the box and replaced the side, pounding in the nails with the butt of his clasp knife. 'The question is, how did my shells get *here*? And who is responsible?'

'I think I know,' Gallagher said. 'And what's more, I think I have figured out how.'

He walked past the stacks of white crates. One stack caught his eye; the crates were larger, and he saw wisps of straw sticking out of one of them. 'Open one of these, colonel, if you please.'

Skarpö prised open one of the crates. It was stuffed with straw and burlap, wrapped around more shells. Gallagher pulled one out and held it up to the light, and his breath hissed in shock. Unlike the high explosive shells, the warhead of this one was painted green with a stencilled white star on the side.

'Jesus Christ,' he said, and his voice was shaking. He turned on Skarpö. 'Did you know about this?'

'Yes,' Skarpö said quietly.

'What is it?' Hamilton demanded.

'White Star,' Gallagher said. 'These are gas shells.'

He looked at the stack of crates. 'General Villa was going to use them on his own people. And you, Colonel Skarpö, were his commander of artillery.'

'It's war,' Skarpö said. 'You use the weapons you have to hand. Nothing matters but victory.'

Gallagher said nothing. 'And before you come over all holier-than-thou,' the colonel said, 'you might want to note that White Star was invented in a British laboratory. Your own people created this weapon.'

'I know,' Gallagher said finally. 'We are all equally guilty, and we are all going to a hell of our own making.' He put the shell back into its crate and Skarpö replaced the wooden slat. 'We have chaplains with our army in France,' Gallagher said. 'They tell the men that God is watching over them, and will give them victory.'

'Aye, while the German soldiers wear belt buckles inscribed with *Gott mit uns*,' said Hamilton. 'God is on our side.'

'I know. Whose side do you suppose God is really on?'

'God is on the side with the best artillery,' Skarpö said. 'I learned that much at Celaya.'

BEFORE THEY DEPARTED, Gallagher turned to Skarpö again. 'Thank you very much for your help, colonel. I will take over from here.'

'What am I to tell Major Arango?'

'Tell him to stand back. Give him an order, if you like. You outrank him.'

'He is Pancho Villa's nephew. That means he outranks everybody, except Villa. I've controlled him so far, but if he gets wind of this . . .'

'Then don't tell him. Let him continue to think Schurz swapped the consignments, if you like. It will keep him out of trouble. But impress upon him that he is not to harm Schurz, or anyone else. Whatever crimes have been committed, and whoever committed them, we will deal with them.'

'I will make you a deal,' Skarpö said. 'I will do everything you ask, including keeping Arango out of trouble. But I want to be there when you question them. I want to hear the truth for myself.'

'Question whom?' demanded Hamilton.

Gallagher did not answer. 'Your orders were to kill the Lópezes,' he said to Skarpö.

'Yes. But I haven't yet. And I won't, if they tell us the truth. I promise you, that's all I want.'

'Turn out your pockets,' Gallagher said.

Skarpö emptied his pockets. His only weapon was his clasp knife, which Gallagher took. To be on the safe side, he opened the colonel's coat and patted him down. Skarpö stood still, his hands raised. He had clearly been through this procedure before.

'Very well,' Gallagher said, ignoring Hamilton's scowl of disapproval. 'You can come.'

21

'SEÑOR GALLAGHER,' SAID López, bowing a little and ushering them into the cabin. 'We missed you at lunch.'

'I am afraid I was detained on business,' Gallagher said. 'You know Mr Hamilton, of course. Allow me to introduce Colonel Stellan Skarpö of the Northern Division.'

It took López a couple of seconds to recover his poise. 'It is a pleasure,' he said, bowing again. His wife, sitting in an armchair and looking greyer than ever, inclined her head. 'Would you care for refreshments?' she asked. 'I shall ring for the steward.'

Gallagher shook his head. 'We found the munitions,' he said.

López stood stock still. His wife, in the act of reaching for the service bell, paused and withdrew her hand. 'It does not matter now,' she said. 'Our work cannot be undone.'

López smiled a little. 'And your government will be grateful, I think, for the gift of several thousand rounds of eighteen-pounder shell. It will help, perhaps, until your Ministry of Munitions is established.'

'I thought you were opposed to war,' Gallagher said.

'We find war abhorrent,' said Corazón López. 'But we are not dogmatic pacifists like Mr Franklin. We are realists, señor, and we recognize that sometimes war is necessary. That is why we helped to raise the Red Battalions.'

'Which were certainly effective,' Skarpö said ironically.

'I am glad to hear it,' she said. 'I would hate to think of all that money going to waste.' She looked at Gallagher. 'How did you work it out?'

'Railways,' Gallagher said. 'Your father worked on the railways, señora, and I suspect he had friends in other railway unions as well, contacts he passed on to you and your husband. You helped the railway workers organize in Mexico, and I assume your contacts in America included unions such as the Brotherhood of Railroad Trainmen. They struck last year against the Southern Pacific Railroad. And Southern Pacific runs to El Paso, where the munitions were bound.'

'We supported the Brotherhood during the strike and sent them money,' López said quietly. 'They owed us a favour.'

'How did you learn about the shells in the first place?'

'From Colonel Kloss. He offered support for the Red Battalions, arms and ammunition, in exchange for our help switching the two. We agreed.'

Skarpö's hands clenched at his sides, but he said nothing. 'Why New York?' Gallagher asked. 'Why not send the shells to the Mexican army as Colonel Kloss asked?'

'We did not like Colonel Kloss,' Corazón López said. 'We knew that once the rebels had been defeated, he planned to force Mexico into a war with America, a move that would have been disastrous for the country. We had no desire or need to please the Germans.'

'From the newspapers, we knew about the shortages of munitions in Britain,' said her husband. 'A German victory would be a catastrophe for the working people of Europe. Your government is objectionable, but we can tolerate it. We have no desire to see Europe subjected to the tyranny of the Kaiser. So, we asked the Brotherhood to use their connections in New York to smuggle the shells onto a ship bound for Britain.'

'What did Colonel Kloss say when his shells did not arrive?'
Gallagher asked.

'We do not know. We decided not to stay and find out. Word
had reached us from Spain that pardons were being issued for
those who participated in the Tragic Week. It was time to go
home.'

'And so, you came to New York and booked passage on the
Lusitania. When did James Dowrich first approach you?'

The couple looked at each other. 'The day before we sailed,'
López said finally.

'Did he demand money from you?'

'No,' said López. 'He wanted the shells.'

Gallagher closed his eyes for a moment. The pieces were
beginning to fall into place, but this brought no relief; instead,
he felt rather sick. 'Tell me exactly what he said.'

'The Brotherhood, like many trades unions, also has links
to the criminal underworld. This is not a good thing, but it is
to be expected. Both are in opposition to the authorities, and
sometimes they make common cause.'

'I understand. Go on.'

'Dowrich had heard rumours in the underworld that we
had stolen the shells. He thought we had done so only for our
benefit, to enrich ourselves. He offered to buy the consignment
from us for a vast price, many thousands of dollars. We refused.'

'We asked him, if he wanted shells so badly, why did he not
go to the arms makers and order them directly,' said Corazón.
'He admitted then that he only wanted the White Stars, the gas
shells. We had never heard of White Star, and certainly we did
not know there were gas shells in the consignment.'

'We were horrified!' exclaimed López.

His wife did not look particularly horrified, Gallagher
thought. 'We explained we no longer knew where the shells

were,' said Corazón, 'only that they were on a ship bound for England. Señor Dowrich grew angry then. He thought we were bluffing, and demanded we tell him where the shells were. He threatened to tell the Germans what we had done, and said they would send men after us to kill us.'

'We bargained for our lives,' López said. 'We asked for time, and said we would try to track down the shells. But we realized we had to do something to save ourselves.' He paused for a moment. 'Señor Gallagher, I beg you to tell me the truth. What happened to Señor Dowrich? Is he dead?'

'Yes,' said Gallagher.

The couple looked at each other again. 'Then I fear we must make our confession,' López said finally. 'We killed him.'

Gallagher paused for a moment. 'How?' he asked, his voice gentle.

'I suffer from asthma,' said Corazón. 'I have been prescribed a compound of arsenic for treatment. At dinner the first night, I put arsenic into my own wine glass, then switched glasses with Señor Dowrich. He was too busy concentrating on my husband to notice. I was only a foolish, frail old woman, you see, not worthy of attention. Within a few minutes he had drunk the entire glass.'

'I saw you switch the glasses and thought it was a harmless mistake,' Gallagher said. 'I didn't see you put the poison in.'

'You prove my point,' she said.

'Why are you telling me this now?'

'Because we have committed a mortal sin,' López said quietly. 'We wish to atone for the crimes we have committed in this life, before we enter the next world. We are prepared to accept whatever punishment awaits us.'

Gallagher's lips twitched. 'Then you can rest easy, señor. You weren't the only ones out to kill Dowrich that night. You may have poisoned him, but someone else shot him before the poison had time to work.'

'Shot him?' López asked incredulously.

'Twice in the chest. The wounds were fatal.'

'Who did this?' López asked after a moment.

'We have a suspect. Tell me, was it part of your plan to travel on the same ship as the munitions?'

They stared at him. 'The shells are here?' López said, still stunned. 'On the *Lusitania*?'

'Four decks below us,' said Gallagher.

There was a little silence. 'How ironic,' murmured López.

'You really did not know?'

'We asked the Brotherhood to put the munitions on a ship, any ship,' Corazón said with asperity. 'We did not specify which one. This has nothing to do with us.'

'The fact remains, however, that this ship is carrying contraband, in violation of the laws of war. If the Germans have discovered what you did, they would be within their rights to sink the ship without warning. Señor, señora, not only have you broken American and international laws, you have also endangered this ship and the lives of everyone on board.'

'And you sacrificed thousands of good men at Celaya,' Skarpö said.

López nodded slowly. 'We regret their loss,' he said. 'We grieve for them and their families. But tell me, colonel. If you were in our position, would you not have done the same?'

Skarpö was silent. 'As for you, Mr Gallagher,' López said, 'I suppose it is no good pleading that we acted in the best interests of your country? To help it win the war?'

'That remains to be seen,' Gallagher said. 'I could place you under arrest and order your confinement right now.'

'I beg you not to. My wife is not well, and she needs fresh air.'

After a long moment, Gallagher nodded. 'You are at liberty until we reach Liverpool. Once there, I will arrest you and hand you over to the police. Do not try to leave the ship when we call at Queenstown. The gangways will be watched.'

'We are too old and tired to attempt escape,' López said. 'We are in your hands, señor.'

OUTSIDE IN THE passageway, Gallagher looked at Skarpö. 'Satisfied?'

'Do I have a choice?' the colonel asked.

'The Lópezes are small fry, colonel. Rintelen and his gang in New York, Kloss in Mexico; they're the real architects of all this. My guess is that Rintelen also knew about the White Star shells and wanted to get his hands on them.'

'López said they didn't know about the gas shells. Do you believe him?'

'It's one of the few things they said that I do believe. They're not specialists in munitions. But equally, I suspect that even if they had known, it wouldn't have changed their minds.'

'I don't know what in hell I'm going to tell the general,' Skarpö said.

'Tell him the Germans are to blame. And suggest to him that the Germans are only in Mexico because President Carranza needs support against the rebels. If General Villa makes peace with the government, they could combine forces and throw the Germans out. That would be fitting revenge, I think.'

'It sounds logical,' Skarpö said. 'Unfortunately, General Villa is not a logical man.'

'Then perhaps you need a new boss. Twelve wars, you said, and all on the losing side.'

Skarpö smiled slightly. 'Don't remind me. Thank you, Mr Gallagher.'

The colonel walked away. Gallagher looked at Hamilton. 'Yes, Hammy. I really do know what I'm doing.'

'Aye,' Hamilton said. 'There's a first time for everything. Do you think they really tried to poison Dowrich?'

'They're certainly capable of it. We'll get a full report from the coroner, of course.'

'And the old boy didn't confess because he was worried about his immortal soul,' said Hamilton.

'A communist who believes in heaven and hell? Pull the other one. He told me to distract me, to drag me back to focusing on Dowrich's death rather than the shells. Except it was too late. Did you see Señora López's eyes when I told them we had found the shells? Dismay, anger, hatred even. They knew the damned shells were here, and I wouldn't put it past them to have lugged them on board and stowed them themselves.'

Hamilton clapped him on the shoulder. 'Youth and enthusiasm will always be defeated by old age and guile,' he said. 'Don't take it personally, laddie. I'm going to check on Franklin, to make sure he isn't giving us any trouble. Will you tell the captain?'

'Yes. I don't think he is going to be very pleased.'

INSIDE THE CABIN, López looked at his wife. 'This changes everything,' he said.

'No,' she said, and the strength of her voice belied her pallor. 'This changes nothing. We do what we must, in order to survive. This is not our conflict. Whatever happens, it is no concern of ours.'

'I wish we had never become involved in this business.'

'It is too late for that now,' she said. 'Things are bad, Esteban, very bad.'

'Yes,' López said finally. 'And if we are not careful, we shall make them worse.'

GALLAGHER FOUND DR Whiting in his surgery, cleaning a bowl of medical instruments in soap and hot water. 'Is there any chance Dowrich could have been poisoned?' he asked.

Whiting blinked in surprised. 'What a peculiar question. He was shot, you saw that.'

'And that was definitely the cause of death?' Gallagher asked.

'I am certain of it.'

'Yes.' Gallagher was not a doctor, but he had seen enough gunshot deaths to know how Dowrich had died. 'However, I believe he may have also ingested arsenic not long before he died.'

'If so, I saw no sign of it. Of course, when he was shot the blood stopped circulating, so the poison may not have fully reached his vital organs. A full autopsy might find traces of arsenic, but that will have to wait until we reach Liverpool.'

'Can you arrange for an autopsy, and send me the full report?'

'Of course,' the doctor said. 'By the way, the captain wants to see you. He is on the bridge.'

'Tell him I am on my way.'

TURNER WAS ON the bridge wing, resplendent in blue and gold uniform with his bowler hat clamped firmly on his head, staring forward at the pale line of the horizon. Gallagher drew a deep breath. 'We're carrying munitions, sir,' he said. 'Eighteen-pounder artillery shells smuggled on board in the guise of machine tool parts. At least five thousand shells, probably more, and some of them are gas shells.'

'I know,' Turner said grimly. 'After you left, I disobeyed orders and opened the cargo manifests.'

Gallagher stared at him. 'The shells are listed on the manifests?'

'Yes. They are disguised as machine parts to conceal them from the eyes of German agents. They must have passed through customs, which means the American government knows all about them.'

'Not necessarily,' Gallagher said. 'Customs officers can be bribed. But if the shells are listed on the official manifests, that suggests our own government *does* know about them, and is waiting for them.'

'Contraband munitions on a civilian liner,' Turner said grimly. 'Putting the lives of her passengers and crew at risk. By God, I won't stand for this. The board of Cunard shall hear of this.'

'It is entirely possible they already know,' Gallagher said. 'And despite the disguise, it seems likely that the Germans know too. I don't think they will let those munitions land at Liverpool.'

'Will they try to sink the ship?'

'Possibly. They might also try to seize the munitions, sending a cruiser rather than a U-boat and threatening to sink us unless we heave to and offload the shells. Several German commerce raiders are still active in the Atlantic.'

'I know. We encountered one last year. Very well, Gallagher. At least now we know what we are up against.'

'Yes, sir.'

'Then stay alert. Right now, it's about all we can do.'

THURSDAY, 6 MAY 1915
3.02 P.M.

KREUTZER LOOKED UP when Gallagher let himself into the cabin. 'What is our position?' he asked. 'We must be getting close.'

'About two hundred miles from Fastnet,' Gallagher said. 'We'll reach Queenstown tomorrow, just after lunch.' He looked around the cabin. 'Thinking of trying to escape?'

'No. I am resigned to my fate, whatever it is.' He looked down at his hands. 'I keep thinking about my friends who died on the *Scharnhorst*. I am not a brave man, Mr Gallagher, nor am I a patriotic one. Should I feel ashamed of my weaknesses, do you think?'

'Patriotism is a highly overrated virtue. And only a psychopath doesn't know fear, Leutnant. It's how you deal with it that matters.'

Roxanne had said that to him. They had been discussing stage fright, from which she had suffered for most of her career, although very few people knew of it. He was one of the few in whom she had confided. He still felt honoured by this, that she trusted him enough to show her weakness. If only she had trusted him a little more.

He tore his mind away from Roxanne. 'When we last spoke, you confirmed that Rintelen has an agent at the Union Metallic Cartridge Company. This man is the key to everything. He knows about Chalfont, he knows about the arms shipments to Mexico, and he can help us unravel Rintelen's network. Are you certain you don't know who he is?'

Kreutzer shook his head. 'I am sorry. If I did know, I would tell you,' he added.

'Did Rintelen deal with anyone else at U.M.C., apart from this man?'

'I don't think so.'

'And you said also that this man had access to all the company's records. Who in the company might be in such a position?'

Kreutzer thought. 'The works accountant should know, of course. And there would be a dispatcher who sent shipments out by wagon or by rail; he would know the destination of each official consignment. But secret sales might well be off the books, in which case neither man would know about them.'

'Is that common practice?'

'Very much so. Arms manufacturers and arms dealers don't always want the world to know what they are selling, or who they are selling it to. The one person who would know everything is the managing director.'

I reported to the managing director, Schurz had said. *He is a personal friend of mine.* He could ask Schurz whether Buckland had been making off-book sales, but like many highly intelligent men Schurz could also be extraordinarily stupid, including stupid enough to fire off a telegram to Buckland warning him that the police were asking questions. 'Thank you,' he said. 'Incidentally, did you mean what you said about patriotism? You have no love for the Fatherland?'

'The Fatherland is a theoretical concept invented by the greedy to hoodwink the gullible. I believe in things I can see and feel and touch.'

'Would you consider coming to work for us?'

'You mean, spying on my own people for the British?' Kreutzer considered this. 'I am not sure I could go that far. I do not love my country, but it would not feel right to betray my friends.'

'Not active spying. But we could use your knowledge and

understanding of how the Nachrichten-Abteilung works, and how men like Rintelen run their networks. Helping us put Rintelen out of business would be a start. In exchange, we will pay you well and offer you a safe place when the war is over.'

'Can you help me find Jeni?'

The question caught him by surprise. 'Possibly,' Gallagher said after a moment. 'I make no promises.'

'Bring me word of Jeni, let me know she is safe and well, and send her a message that I will wait for her. Bring me proof that the message has been delivered, and I will work for you.'

Gallagher studied the other man. This is not a new decision, he thought. The voyage, the enforced solitude, the belief that he had been deliberately betrayed, all had worked on Kreutzer's mind. He had made his decision some time ago.

'I'll do what I can,' Gallagher said.

Thursday, 6 May 1915
3.15 p.m.

Going forward, Gallagher stopped at the purser's office and asked for a telegram form. 'How is Franklin?' he asked, filling out the form.

'Kicking up a stink,' Hamilton said. 'We've had to disconnect his telephone because he kept calling the exchange every two minutes, demanding to be put through to the captain. He also wants to see you, by the way.'

'I have better things to do than listen to rants from Franklin.' Gallagher handed over the form. 'Can you ask the Marconi office to get this off to New York? It's urgent.'

'I'll pass it on immediately.'

*

DOLLY MARKLAND INTERCEPTED him at the top of the stairs on the boat deck. 'When are you going to arrest Ripley?' she demanded.

Gallagher looked around, but there was no one within earshot. Most of the first-class passengers were in the saloon having tea; a quiet hum of conversation floated through the door. 'Ripley is not a suspect in Miss Dolan's death,' he said. 'We have identified the culprit, and he will be taken into custody when we reach Liverpool.'

'Ripley is not a suspect?' She did not appear to have heard anything else. 'What are you talking about? He killed her, Mr Gallagher!'

'Keep your voice down,' Gallagher commanded. 'I am sorry, Mrs Markland, but Ripley didn't do it.'

Her eyes were full of anger, but this time she kept her voice low. 'You are covering up for him. Why?'

'I'm not. I know how painful this is for you, Mrs Markland, but facts are facts. Ripley is a reprehensible human being, but he did not kill Miss Dolan.'

The anger faded a little, replaced by sorrow and disappointment. 'I thought I could trust you,' she said. 'I thought you believed me.'

'I do.'

'Then trust me about Ripley. I'm right, I know I am.'

Gallagher shook his head. 'I'm sorry, Mrs Markland.' He looked at the lines etched in her face. 'You need some sleep. I strongly advise you to go to your cabin and rest.'

'Rest,' she said pathetically. 'How can I rest? If someone you loved had been murdered, would you rest?'

'No,' he said softly. 'But mine is not an example you should aspire to. I beg you, Mrs Markland, go and rest.'

Silently, she turned away. Gallagher watched her go, his

concern rising. Turning, he walked into the reading room and picked up the telephone receiver and mouthpiece that stood on a table just inside the door. When the operator answered he asked for the doctor's office. Whiting answered almost at once.

'Doctor, it's Gallagher. One of the first-class passengers, Mrs Markland, is in some distress. I think she needs your attention. Can you give her something to keep her calm until we reach Liverpool?'

UP ON THE boat deck, the stewards were serving afternoon tea in the saloon. A young girl was playing the piano, rather well. 'Usually I love being at sea,' said a woman in a teal blue gown, a rope of pearls around her neck. 'It is so wonderfully tranquil, do you not think? It's such a pity the war has to spoil everything.'

Dolly Markland found an empty place and sat down opposite two middle-aged women who were drinking tea and eating sandwiches and slices of Victoria sponge. A waiter offered her a cup of tea and she accepted, but for some reason the tea tasted bitter as acid in her mouth. It was all she could do to swallow it. Outside, the sea was a brilliant sapphire blue, the colour of Billie's eyes.

The Victoria sponge stood on a silver stand, the sandwiches cut in quarters arranged neatly at its base on china plates. A knife lay on the stand next to the sponge. She studied it. The hilt was twisted silver in a swirling pattern; the blade was broad and ornate, serrated on one edge and tapering to a long point. Fascinated, almost trance-like, she leaned over and picked up the knife. The point was surprisingly sharp, sharp enough to prick her finger. She looked around. No one was watching her; the two women were engrossed in their conversation. She slipped the knife into her reticule, took another sip of bitter tea, rose and left the room.

22

CHALFONT WAS ENSCONCED in his favourite position in the smoking room, leaning on the bar with a glass of whisky in his hand. Gallagher approached him slowly, trying to work out how drunk he was. The older man turned and saw him. 'My dear fellow. Do join me.'

Gallagher asked the barman for a Canada Dry. Chalfont wrinkled his nose. 'Why on earth are you drinking that muck? Have a whisky, for God's sake.'

'We are approaching the war zone,' Gallagher said. 'I intend to stay sober.'

'Really? I can't think of a better reason for staying as drunk as possible. I gather our friend Ripley and some of the other passengers have planned an ambush for the captain tonight.'

'Oh?'

'There is to be another musical soirée. Señor López has kindly volunteered to play, and the captain has deigned to put in an appearance. Ripley and the others will meet him and demand he hoists the American flag.'

Gallagher waited until the barman moved away. 'I need a word with you, Harry.'

'My dear fellow, how splendid. I do so enjoy our little chats. What's on your mind?'

'I am starting to become annoyed,' Gallagher said. 'Every

time you claim to have told me everything, something new comes to light.'

Chalfont considered this. 'I don't think I have ever claimed to tell you *everything*. Don't you know the motto of the British Foreign Service? "The truth, nothing but the truth, but never the whole truth."'

'Why not?'

'My dear fellow, if I told you everything at once, where would the mystery be? Think of me as Scheherazade, spinning marvellous stories that keep you gripped and entertained.'

'I'd rather not,' Gallagher said. 'Let's start with the Union Metallic Cartridge Company. How many consignments did you order from them?'

'Six in all.'

'How many did you hand over to Rintelen?'

'Two. The rest I shipped to Britain, as I told you.'

'We'll need the names of the ships you used.'

Chalfont's eyelids flickered. 'You shall have them. In due course.'

Gallagher regarded the other man. 'You're still holding out on me, Harry.'

'Of course I am, dear boy. In this case, I suspect the information you want from me is my best bargaining chip. It is the one thing that will keep me from facing a firing squad.'

Gallagher looked irritated. 'What makes you think we're going to shoot you? You've been cooperative, you've given me a great deal of information already. We'll pump you dry, yes, but you've nothing to fear.'

'Really? I can't help thinking they're going to shoot me anyway. You know. *Pour encourager les autres.*'

'What makes you say that?'

'Things are getting hysterical, dear boy. The Germans are no

longer *an* enemy, they're *the* enemy, the filthy Huns, the bayo-
netters of Belgian babies. Anyone who associates with them, no
matter how honourable and patriotic their motives, is tainted.
Isn't that so?'

'Not necessarily,' said Gallagher, thinking of Kreutzer.
'There is another way. You said no one is willing to corroborate
your story. But there is one person who might be able to do so.
Jonathan Buckland, the managing director of Union Metallic
Cartridge Company.'

'Ah.' Chalfont watched him with hooded eyes. 'You know
about him. Have you by any chance been using that Marconi
contraption again?'

'I've known about him for several days. I have a very helpful
contact in the New York City police.'

Chalfont finished his drink and signalled for another. 'Are
you accusing Jonny Buckland of being a German agent?'

'No. You and Kreutzer both believe Rintelen had an agent
inside U.M.C., but I doubt it. I think Buckland was duped into
giving out confidential information and taking secret contracts
on the quiet, without realizing he was dealing with foreign
agents. He is already in trouble over the Mexican affair, and if
I tell my friends in New York that he is involved in shipping
contraband, they'll pass the word to the Bureau of Investigation,
who will arrest him and interrogate him. He'll tell the truth, to
save himself and his business.'

'And you want to know the names of the ships I used as evidence to help you arrest Buckland.'

'The names are evidence in your favour too, of course,' Gallagher pointed out.

The drink came and Chalfont raised his glass and sank
about half of the whisky. 'Why don't you ask Kreutzer about
Buckland?'

'I already have. He made a guess, but he doesn't know any-thing for certain. However, you do.'

'Ah.' Chalfont smiled. 'Kreutzer *is* on this ship.'

'You knew he was. That's why you were wandering around the promenade deck pretending to be blind drunk. You were looking for his cabin.'

'Yes, well. That may have been a bit misguided of me. I was hoping to talk to him, and perhaps persuade him to be a witness for my defence. At the moment, I need all the friends I can get.'

'Then you're in luck. We arrested him shortly after he boarded the ship. I have persuaded him to change sides, and work for us.'

There was a long pause while Chalfont swirled the whisky in his glass, watching the liquid glow in the afternoon sunlight. 'Have you,' he said slowly. 'Have you now. That is interesting. Very interesting indeed.'

'Answer me another question. When you met Dowrich at the Deutscher Bund, who made the first move? Did you invite him? Or did he call on you?'

'As it happens, he approached me. I welcomed him with open arms, of course, because I knew he could be helpful. But he initiated the conversation.'

'Do you know why?'

'He knew there was a game on, and he wanted in on it. I was happy to oblige him.'

'During the conversation, did he mention White Star?'

'Ah,' Chalfont said slowly. 'Now I see where this is going. Yes, he did. He wanted to buy some White Star shells.'

'Why didn't he just go to the manufacturer?'

'Because the US government won't grant an export licence for gas shells. They allow firms to export HE and shrapnel, but not gas. They are happy, it seems, to allow people to be blown to kingdom come with trinitrotoluene, but squeamish about having them cough their lungs out with phosgene. Go figure.'

'Earlier, you said Rintelen was desperate to get his hands on some gas shells. Could Dowrich have been working with him?'

'As I have said before, dear boy. It depends whose side Dowrich was really on.'

'Stop prevaricating, Harry. I think you knew there were gas shells in the shipment to Pancho Villa's men, and I think Dowrich knew too. He wanted you to divert those shells to him. Am I correct?'

'Yes,' Chalfont said finally.

'Then I know the answer,' Gallagher said. 'Dowrich wasn't working for the American government, but very probably he was in contact with Rintelen. He knew Rintelen needed shells and was prepared to supply him. First, he needed to buy the shells himself.'

'So you think Dowrich was a German agent.'

Gallagher shook his head. 'He regarded the Germans as potential customers, that's all. He was freelance, out for profit for himself.'

'Why do you say so?'

'Have you ever read a book called *A Connecticut Yankee in King Arthur's Court*? An arms manufacturer travels back in time and uses his skills to build weapons which allow him to dominate Arthur's kingdom. He eventually triggers a war that destroys Camelot and its entire society, and in the process gathers wealth for himself. Dowrich took his inspiration from that.'

'He was going to set himself up as an arms dealer,' Chalfont said slowly.

'The gas shells were the first step. Sell those to the highest bidder, Rintelen or whoever put up the cash, and reinvest the profits, like a good little capitalist. That's how Basil Zaharoff made his millions, after all. I suspect Dowrich intended to follow in his footsteps.'

'Then his killer, whoever it was, did the world a good service.'

'I am beginning to think so,' said Gallagher. 'Tell me the names of the ships, Harry, and tell me about your own relationship with Buckland.'

'I certainly will, dear boy. Just as soon as we reach Britain and I am assured of my safety.'

'I'm not happy about this, Harry.'

'Be patient, dear boy. It's only one more day.'

THURSDAY, 6 MAY 1915
6.32 P.M.

CHALFONT WAS PLAYING games, that much was obvious, but the stakes in this game were high. Underneath the banter, Chalfont was deadly serious. He had been correct to suggest that the authorities might well decide to wring him dry and then execute him; the same was true of Kreutzer. The German's offer to turn his coat should save his life, but Chalfont was still resisting. The full confession that might save him from the firing squad or the hangman would not come. Gallagher wondered why.

It was nearly time to change for dinner. He started towards his cabin, but remembered with a flash of irritation that Franklin wanted to see him. Going down to the promenade deck, he walked forward to the royal suite where an armed sailor stood guard outside the door. The man appeared ill at ease, and his uniform was wrinkled and his boots needed polishing. Like Hamilton said, the best crew had gone.

'Has he given you any trouble?' Gallagher asked.

'He's been quieter of recent, sir.'

Gallagher still had the pass key. He knocked, then opened the door and went in. Franklin was waiting for him in the parlour room of the suite, hands clenched at his side. 'How long do you intend to keep me confined here?'

'As I said, until we reach Liverpool. Then I will hand you over to the police.'

'This is intolerable. An outrage.'

Like Mrs Markland, Franklin had changed. His face seemed to be collapsing on itself and there was a nervous tic at the corner of one eye. His old arrogance was still visible but it was eroding fast. He reminded Gallagher of an addict deprived of his injection.

'I demand to be released,' Franklin said.

Gallagher shook his head.

The other man's face flushed with sudden anger. 'Damn it, Gallagher, I have work to do! Vital, important work! The fate of nations hangs in the balance! You must let me out of here!'

'I cannot do that.'

As swiftly as it had come, the anger vanished. A note came into Franklin's voice that Gallagher had not heard before, and after a moment he realized it was self-pity. 'Why not, for God's sake? I've done nothing wrong, nothing! Billie's death wasn't my fault. Please, just let me out.'

'Whose fault was it, then?'

'Theirs! All of them, Ripley, Markland, all the ones who mistreated her and abused her, they're the ones! I was good to that girl, Gallagher, I gave her everything, a home, security, fine clothes, jewels. I always treated her well.' His hand clawed suddenly at his face. 'In the name of God, let me out of here!'

Gallagher waited for a moment before replying. 'Are you uncomfortable, Mr Franklin?'

From self-pity, Franklin had moved to desperation. 'This is horrible. I feel like I'm in prison.'

'Then you don't know very much about prisons. At present you have four spacious rooms plus a bathroom. In Walton Gaol you'll be slopping out in a single cell with five other men. Enjoy it while you can.'

Franklin had begun to shiver. 'What happens if the ship is torpedoed? I'll never be able to get out. I'll die here like a rat in a trap.'

Gallagher hesitated. Just for a moment, he felt a flash of sympathy. Franklin was clearly suffering from acute claustrophobia. But he had also shot a young woman and watched her die, and then gone for a walk on deck before having a drink in the smoking room. 'I can offer you anything else you might need, within reason, but I will not allow you to leave this suite. If you attempt to do so, the guard outside has orders to prevent you.'

'What do you want?' Franklin asked. The shivering had increased. 'I'll give you anything you want, any amount of money you care to name. Thousands, tens of thousands. Millions. Just get me out of here.'

Gallagher considered this. 'Anything I want?' he said. 'Very well. Give me your confession.'

'My *what?*'

'Write a statement detailing how and why you killed Billie Dolan, and sign it. You can do it now. I'll wait.'

Franklin stared at him, breathing deeply. Gallagher shrugged and turned towards the door. 'No,' said Franklin in a voice full of panic. 'Wait. I'll do it.'

Gallagher stood while Franklin wrote out his confession on the *Lusitania*'s headed notepaper. Taking the sheet of paper, he read through it quickly. All the details were there, including confirmation that the weapon was Franklin's own derringer. At the end he had written:

I consider myself to be fully justified. I have important work that will not wait. The destiny of nations hangs upon my efforts, and mine alone.

That self-righteousness, still shining through even amid the panic and claustrophobia, stiffened Gallagher's resolve. 'Excellent,' he said. 'Most satisfactory.' He tucked the confession into his coat pocket along with Kreutzer's will. 'I will bid you good evening, Mr Franklin.'

He had his hand on the doorknob before Franklin realized what had happened. 'Are you letting me go?'

'Of course not. You are a confessed murderer.'

'God damn you! You gave me your word!'

Gallagher closed the door behind him and locked it, listening to Franklin pounding his fists on the other side and screaming abuse at him. He turned to the guard, and there was iron in his voice. 'Whatever he does, whatever he says, do not let him out.'

THURSDAY, 6 MAY 1915
9.42 P.M.

THEY ROSE FROM dinner after the ices and made their way upstairs. Corazón López lingered a little, picking up the empty bottle of burgundy that Ripley had ordered and examining the label. Out of the corner of his eye, Gallagher saw her wrap the bottle in her mantilla and carry it away. He turned to see Maurice watching her too, his dark eyes sharp with enquiry.

'Customers often steal full bottles of wine,' the maître d'
said. 'Rarely do they trouble to take empty ones.'

'I'm sure she has her reasons.'

'Of course. Passengers always have their reasons. Enjoy the
rest of your evening, if possible.'

'Do you not like music, Maurice?'

'French music, yes. Spanish music is all the same. Plink.
Plonk. Plinky-plinky-plinky plonk. I shall read an improving
book instead.'

The musical soiree had been Hamilton's idea, to take the
passengers' minds off their situation. Earlier at dinner, a whisper had run around the big domed dining room, and every head
had turned to listen to it. *In a few hours we will enter the war zone.*

The purser, coming around to each table, had been noncha-
lant. 'We're already travelling faster than any U-boat, and we're
not even at full speed yet. And the captain has just received a
cable from the Admiralty. HMS *Juno* will be waiting for us at
Fastnet.'

'I still think we need a squadron of destroyers,' Chalfont had
said. He had looked around the table. 'I see we are without Mrs
Markland's company again, and Mr Franklin. Our numbers are
being whittled away, one by one.'

'Is it really true about Franklin?' Ripley had asked. 'He's
gone off his nut?'

Schurz sniffed. 'He always was a bit mad, if you ask me.'

Corazón López had looked severe. 'You are unkind, señores.
The responsibilities of power are a heavy burden. If poor Mr
Franklin is no longer able to bear the weight, then he deserves
our pity and sympathies. I for one pray that he will recover
soon.'

'Amen,' Chalfont had said, his eyes twinkling.

Now, they sat or stood in the saloon, applauding lightly as

López once again took his seat at the piano and his wife, dressed in black like himself, stood ready to turn the pages. The windows were sealed off by heavy drapes to prevent light showing outside the ship. 'This is the *Aires Nacionales Mexicanos*, by the Mexican composer Ricardo Castro,' López said. 'Señora López and I are returning to our homeland after many years. But a little part of our heart will always remain in Mexico, and whenever we hear this music, we will remember.'

The music began to flow, notes rippling from the piano and hanging in the air for a moment before they faded. Gallagher looked around the room. Skarpö was standing by the window, chin in hand, his face expressionless. The young man, Arango, was lost in wonder. He needs to get out of it all, Gallagher thought. A man who is enraptured by music and who marvels at the cavorting of whales is not hardened enough to be a soldier or a spy. Pray God he never becomes either.

Pray God none of us ever do. Pray God that future generations will learn to lay down their arms and look in wonder at the world around them, and listen to the music. But he knew that would never happen.

Listening, he lost track of time. He roused a little when the music ended, and joined in the applause as López rose from his seat and bowed. Heads turned and there was a little stir as Captain Turner walked into the room. Men bowed and women dipped in curtsey; he waved them down.

'My lords, ladies and gentlemen, I will not interrupt you for long,' the captain said. 'Urgent matters compel me to return to the bridge as soon as possible. But I need your attention for a moment.'

Silence fell in the big room. 'As you know, we have now entered the war zone,' Turner continued. 'All windows and portholes must be kept closed at night, and curtains pulled across them to prevent us showing a light. The ship's running lights have been turned off and it will be very dark on deck. I do not advise you to go outside until morning.'

'Will we be safe, Captain?' asked a woman, her voice full of alarm. Others joined in. Turner held up one hand.

'My crew are in the highest possible state of alert. In the morning we shall make rendezvous with HMS *Juno*, who will escort us during the remainder of the voyage. *Juno* carries nearly thirty quick-firing guns, any one of which can blow a submarine out of the water, and she has three torpedo tubes of her own. She is more than a match for any enemy we may encounter.'

There was a scattering of applause. Chalfont winked at Gallagher. 'In the meantime,' the captain said, 'I must ask all of you to remain vigilant. When you retire tonight, make certain you have warm clothes ready to hand. If the emergency signal sounds, dress as quickly as possible and proceed to the lifeboats, leaving your possessions behind. It is important you proceed in an orderly fashion. There are more than enough lifeboats for all the passengers and crew, and no one will be left behind. In the event that you are asked to embark in the lifeboats, follow the orders of my officers. But we can trust in God and the Royal Navy to see us safely home.'

More applause, this time with Ripley's voice cutting across it. 'There's another way to make sure we are safe, Captain. Order the American flag to be flown at the masthead. The Germans will never dare attack a neutral ship.'

In the room there were murmurs of agreement, but there was anger too. 'It is against international conventions!' one man said, outraged.

'International conventions won't do us much good if we're sunk,' Ripley said. 'There's more than a hundred American citizens on board, captain. On behalf of them all, for their protection, I demand you fly the Stars and Stripes.'

Others were nodding. 'There are citizens of sixteen neutral countries on board the *Lusitania*,' Captain Turner said. 'Are you suggesting I should fly the flags of all of them?'

Ripley waved his hands. 'If it gets us safe to Liverpool, why the hell not?'

'I agree,' said another voice, and more joined in. Charles Schurz was one of them. Gallagher wondered what had happened to undermine the engineer's faith in cruiser rules and the laws of war. Turner took a pace forward and the voices stopped.

'Enough,' he said. 'This is a British ship, and she will sail under a British flag. That is my final word on the subject.'

He turned and strode out of the room, followed by a babble of voices. People gathered in groups, talking in tones ranging from earnest debate to near panic. Some supported the captain. Others, coalescing around Ripley, argued for marching up to the bridge and demanding the captain obey their wishes. Gallagher stepped swiftly into this group.

'Don't be bloody stupid. There are armed sailors on the gangways to the bridge, you will never get near it. As for you, Ripley, neutral citizen or not, what you are suggesting is tantamount to mutiny. And the penalty for mutiny, you will remember, is death.'

Ripley fell silent. The others subsided too, muttering. Gallagher walked back to the piano. 'I advise you to play something cheerful, señor.'

'I was thinking the same,' said López. After a moment a triumphant skirl of notes began dancing around the room, a Paganini caprice. The atmosphere relaxed a little. Colonel Skarpö moved up alongside Gallagher. 'You sure know how to handle men. Maybe we should go into business together.'

'As mercenaries? No, thank you. I have done all the fighting I ever intend to do.'

Skarpö nodded towards Arango. 'I spoke to my young compañero. He remains convinced Schurz is the one who sabotaged our ammunition. Have you learned any more?'

'I have narrowed down the possibilities. Keep Major Arango in line. When we get to Liverpool, I will tell you who the German spy is, and you can take the name back to your general.'

'That is the best you can give me?'

'If you wish, I will write you a testimonial to give to General Villa, telling him you carried out your duties faithfully and well.'

There was a moment of silence. 'I see you do not know much about General Villa,' Skarpö said. 'He wipes his arse on testimonials . . . I'm also beginning to think that going back to Mexico may not be the best idea right now.'

'Where would you go instead?'

'I have a few ideas. There are some handy little wars going on in other parts of the world, places where a man might make a decent profit. The offer of partnership remains open, by the way.'

Gallagher smiled. 'Thanks, but no thanks.'

'If you ever change your mind, come and find me. It's been a real pleasure to meet you, Mr Gallagher.'

'Likewise.' The big man bowed and walked away. Gallagher watched him go, his eyes thoughtful, and then he turned back to listen to the music.

23

DAWN FOUND DOLLY Markland on deck after a sleepless night.
Dr Whiting had visited her cabin and given her two pills and
watched her take them with water. After he left, she spat them
out from under her tongue and spent the rest of the night
trying to work out a plan for killing Ripley. She had only one
weapon, the knife she had stolen yesterday. She formed a hundred schemes of murder in her mind, running over each and
discarding it.

The sun rose clear and golden, shining off a sea of rippled
glass. The white water of *Lusitania*'s wake sparkled, rainbows
dancing in the spray as the big ship steamed onward. Gulls rose
and fell on the currents of air. She watched the morning, and
the beauty of the scene tore at her like barbed wire, racking her
with pain. After a while she began to cry. Her sorrow was not
for Billie; it was for herself, for everything she had done since
the beginning, for all the hurt and pain and misery she had
caused and could never put right.

Billie had been her chance of redemption, and now that
chance was gone. She stood alone, clutching the rail while tears
of selfish grief fell onto her coat, and far ahead the pale spike of
a lighthouse rose above the horizon.

Friday, 7 May 1915
6.52 a.m.

Gallagher stepped out on deck. Some of the other passengers were there too, whispering in little groups or just watching in silence. The sky was vivid blue, the colour so strong it almost made his eyes hurt. Glorious sunlight poured across the sea. A light wind ruffled against his cheek. He remembered, as he remembered almost every day, the two lines Roxanne had underlined in *Les Fleurs du Mal*.

> *Like a ship waking in the morning wind*
> *My dreaming soul sets sail for a distant sky*

Fastnet was close by, a dark wedge of rock with the sea foaming around its cliffs and the white pillar of the lighthouse. From the heights of the promenade deck they could see the dark rocks of Cape Clear in the distance and beyond it, low on the horizon, the Irish mainland.

There was no sign of any escorting warship. *Lusitania* was alone on the sea.

Gallagher turned his head and saw Hamilton beside him. 'Where is HMS *Juno*?'

'She isn't coming,' the purser said.

Gallagher stared at him. '*What?*'

'A telegram came through from Haulbowline a few minutes ago. *Juno* has been ordered back to port.'

Haulbowline was the Royal Navy station at Queenstown. 'We have been instructed to proceed independently at full speed,' Hamilton said. He pulled out his watch. 'We're only eight hours from Queenstown. Perhaps it won't matter.'

The big ship shivered as she began to pick up speed. 'A lot can happen in eight hours,' Gallagher said.

'Aye. But for all his quirks, Bowler Bill is a damn fine sailor. If anyone can get us through, he can.' Hamilton hesitated. 'He wants to see you on the bridge.'

BY THE TIME Gallagher reached the bridge, *Lusitania* was plunging forward at full speed, her mighty hull quivering with power, sheets of spray flying up from the bow as she knifed through the water. Even with one engine room shut down she was still travelling at twenty-one knots; Fastnet was already sliding away astern.

Captain Turner and Gallagher faced each other in the chart-room. 'You've heard *Juno* isn't coming,' the captain said. His voice was dark with anger. 'The bloody bastards. How dare they do this? How dare they do this to *my ship*?'

Gallagher paused. 'Who do you mean by *they*, sir?' He knew the answer, but he wanted to know how much Turner knew.

'I mean the Admiralty.' Turner's face was grim. '*Juno* has been withdrawn because they are inviting an attack. You were right, the Germans know about the munitions. That's why they put those damned reports in the New York papers, to warn off the passengers. But if *Lusitania* is attacked and any of our American passengers are hurt or killed, public opinion in America will force President Wilson to declare war.'

'Which is what the Admiralty and the politicians want,' Gallagher said quietly. 'The Germans want the shells; our people know they want them, and are inviting them to come and get them.'

'Exactly. This is a tiger hunt, Gallagher, and we're the tethered goat, staked out as bait. What about Chalfont? Is he a danger?'

'I still don't know for certain. To be on the safe side, I shall lock him in his cabin after breakfast. Kreutzer is already safely confined, of course, with a guard on his door.'

'Put a guard on Chalfont too. I don't want either of them getting loose.'

'Yes, sir.' Gallagher hesitated. 'What about Schurz?'

'Have you any evidence against him?'

'There's something not right about him, sir. But I can't say anything definite.'

'I have received fresh orders about Schurz. His friends in London have made it clear we are not to investigate him or interfere with him in any way. His work is vital to the war effort. If we disobey it could spell trouble, for me and for you.'

Someone had sent orders from London concerning Schurz. Why? Gallagher wondered. Had Schurz himself been sending messages? 'What are your intentions, sir?'

'Run straight through to Queenstown at top speed, and hope we can leave the hunters behind us. I have insisted that Haulbowline pass on any reports of submarine contacts so we can take evasive action. Once we are in harbour, I shall refuse to sail again until a full escort has been provided.' Turner reached up and pulled the bowler hat down hard on his head, his face grimmer than ever. 'Think they can sacrifice my ship, do they? I'll teach those bastards a lesson.'

FRIDAY, 7 MAY 1915
7.47 A.M.
SEVEN HOURS FROM QUEENSTOWN

RIPLEY WAS EATING devilled kidneys, cooked rare; blood leaked from the meat and pooled pink amid the poisonous yellow of the mustard sauce. 'What happened to this escort we were promised?' he asked, chewing with his mouth open. 'This protected cruiser?'

'She isn't coming,' Gallagher said. There was no point in denying it, not now. 'Her orders have changed.'

'Changed to what?' asked Schurz, his voice sharp with surprise.

'I don't know,' Gallagher said. 'However, the Royal Navy will pass on any reports of submarine activity. If we are warned in time, we can steer away from them.'

'How does the navy know where the submarines are?' asked López.

'Sometimes they are spotted on the surface, recharging their batteries. The Admiralty can also intercept the radio signals between U-boats and their base in Germany, and triangulate to estimate the enemy's position.'

Chalfont nodded. 'Very clever, those Admiralty chaps.'

'I don't care how clever they are,' Ripley said. 'We should run up the Stars and Stripes. It's the only way we're gonna be safe.'

'You heard the captain,' said Chalfont. 'He won't do it, old boy. It's his ship, and that's the end of it.'

'Why not, for God's sake? It's only for a few hours, until we get to Queenstown. Who's going to get hurt? Who's even going to know?'

'All the other passengers will know,' said Dolly Markland. To Gallagher's surprise she had joined them; she sat gaunt and red-eyed, drinking cup after cup of black coffee, her hand resting on her reticule. She looked fractionally better, Gallagher thought. She had pinned her hair up and something, perhaps the coffee, had put a little colour in her cheeks.

'To hell with them,' said Ripley, slicing open another kidney. 'It's for their own safety. After breakfast, I'm going to talk to the captain again. This time, he'll listen.'

The hull around them shivered with power. 'The last captain who tried a ruse like that was dismissed from his post,' Chalfont said. 'Captain Turner won't want to go the same way.'

'Jesus Christ,' said Ripley. 'It's only for a few god-damned hours.'

'Señor, please mind your language,' López said quietly. 'There are ladies present.'

Silence fell. Schurz glanced uneasily around the half-empty dining room, as if he was looking for someone. Gallagher followed his gaze. Colonel Skarpö sat on the far side of the room, talking to an elderly woman and a clergyman. There was no sign of young Major Arango. At the table, Chalfont tucked into his bacon and eggs, eating with an unusually hearty appetite. Dolly Markland watched Ripley, her face expressionless. Ripley continued eating, ignoring her and muttering under his breath. The Lópezes sat quietly, food untouched in front of them.

'I strongly advise you all to relax,' Chalfont said. 'What will happen, will happen, and there is nothing you or I can do about it.'

López smiled slightly. 'Your fatalism is admirable.'

'Oh, I'm not a fatalist, señor. I believe very strongly that we can make our own destiny, if we try hard enough.' Chalfont glanced sideways at Gallagher. 'Our friend here, the student of Baudelaire, will tell you. Evil comes without effort, the natural product of fate. Good is only produced through the workings of art.'

Dolly Markland sipped her coffee. 'I agree,' she said.

'So do I,' said López. 'But sometimes, fate knocks at the door. Then, we have no choice but to let it in.'

Chalfont laughed. 'Bravo, señor. A good answer. But I wonder if you are always right. Take my own case, for example.

Fate will knock at my door when we reach our destination. But, will I be there to answer it? I'm not sure.'

'This is all very well,' Ripley said sharply. 'But can I remind you all that we are in the war zone, unescorted, and at any moment a U-boat could put a torpedo into our hull? What happens then?'

'There really is nothing to fear,' Schurz said. 'Even if this ship is torpedoed, given her size I have calculated that she will take at least three hours to sink. We shall have ample time to abandon ship, and the coast of Ireland is only a few miles away.'

'Mr Schurz is right,' Chalfont said. 'And also, *Lusitania* is now travelling at top speed. Hitting it with a torpedo won't be easy. There is every chance we will reach Queenstown safely.'

He inclined his head towards López. 'Unless, of course, fate decides to knock at the door.'

As THEY LEFT the dining room, Gallagher caught Chalfont's arm. 'Are you by any chance thinking of doing a runner, Harry?'

'What? Oh, you mean the bit about whether I will be there to answer the door? I must admit, dear boy, the thought has crossed my mind. Slip ashore at Queenstown before anyone notices and then head for the hills. However, I have decided against it.'

'Have you? Why?'

'Dear boy, look at me. I'm a beaten-up old drunk. If I tried to run from pursuit, I wouldn't get a hundred yards without coughing my guts out. No, I have no choice but to stay here and take my lumps.'

Gallagher surveyed him. 'You are nowhere near as old and tired as you pretend to be. If you laid off the booze for a while, you'd be as fit as me.'

Chalfont smiled. 'That's not enough to make me take the pledge, I fear. Have you come to lock me in my cabin?'

'Yes.'

'Very sensible of you. Don't want me absconding at the last minute, or doing anything else to evade the course of justice. Do you want to confiscate my razor and other sharp objects, or are you prepared to accept my word that I won't do away with myself?'

'I think if you wanted to kill yourself, Harry, you'd have done so long before now.'

'Yes,' Chalfont said, and for a moment he sounded almost serious. 'Yes, I expect you are right.'

A BANK OF fog had arisen while they were at breakfast, thick and swirling around the ship. *Lusitania* pressed on through the oily dark water, siren booming in the glutinous air. Dolly Markland stood, resting her arms on the rail and gazing out at the fog. At first she seemed not to notice Gallagher standing beside her, and only slowly did she turn her head.

'Why are you so certain Ripley didn't kill her?' she asked.

He knew he shouldn't discuss details with her, but he could also see the uncertainty eating away at her mind. 'He has a solid alibi. He was in the smoking room the entire afternoon. I can assure you that the British and American police will be checking to see what crimes Ripley *has* committed. But he is innocent of Billie Dolan's murder.'

'Then who did kill her?'

'I'm sorry, Mrs Markland, but I can't tell you that.'

She did not answer.

'I wanted to speak to you about another matter,' Gallagher said. 'I have a deal to offer you.'

'I am not interested in deals, Mr Gallagher.'

'You should be interested in this one. Tell me truly whether you shot James Dowrich, yes or no. In exchange, I will destroy the report I had written, and I will make no mention of your involvement to the police. I will also quash any charges of fraud that may be laid against you. You will be free to go.'

Two spots of sudden colour appeared in her pale cheeks. 'Why would you do this?'

'Because if I have learned one thing in life, it is that everyone deserves a second chance.'

'I had my second chance, with Arthur. I'm running out of lives, Mr Gallagher.'

'Someone I cared about very deeply decided she was tired of fighting, and accepted her fate. I don't want to see you make the same mistake.'

She considered this, and he thought she understood. 'Very well,' she said finally. 'It happened just as you said. I stole Ripley's gun, I switched the keys and I shot Dowrich and replaced the gun. Framing Ripley for the murder added a touch of poetic justice, I thought.'

'As it happens, an entire parade of people were trying to kill Dowrich. You just happened to be successful. Dowrich was involved in much more than just blackmail, Mrs Markland. He was a traitor who was preparing to sell armaments to our enemies.'

'What has this got to do with me?'

'We need to keep our investigation secret until we can discover in more detail what Dowrich was doing and who else was involved. If you are arrested and put on trial, the case becomes public. There is a real danger that details could leak out, and that would put the enemy on their guard. Letting you walk free is in the interests of the greater good.'

'And if I should choose to tell the world what you have just told me?'

'Everything I have just said is covered under the Official Secrets Act. Violation of the act is a capital offence.' He paused for a moment, watching her face. 'Go far away, Mrs Markland. Find some place where you can be alone, as you said. Try to forget all of this ever happened.'

'How can I forget Billie?'

'You cannot, and I would not expect you too. But when you think of her, try to remember her life, not her death. Find some meaning in her existence. It may help you to come to terms with your own.'

She said nothing. Quietly, Gallagher turned and walked away.

FRIDAY, 7 MAY 1915
9.10 A.M.
SIX HOURS FROM QUEENSTOWN

GALLAGHER RETURNED TO the foyer and went to the purser's office, where he found Hamilton sitting behind a desk awash with paperwork, preparing for the landing at Queenstown. 'It's bloody thick out there,' he said.

'Aye,' said the purser. 'God grant it remains so. While the fog is down, we're hidden from enemy periscopes.'

'True enough. Hammy, can you tell me if Schurz has sent any telegrams in the past few days?'

'Give me a minute.' Hamilton pulled a manila file full of buff telegram forms out of his desk and began leafing through them. 'Here we are,' he said. 'Addressed to Colonel James Carmichael at the War Office, whoever he may be.' His eyebrows rose. 'You're not going to like this,' he said, handing over the form.

Gallagher knew who Colonel Carmichael was; he was an engineer and secretary of the Armaments Committee, the body that was helping to establish the Ministry of Munitions. The telegram was long and rambling, complaining of surveillance and harassment by the captain and crew and particularly by a passenger calling himself Gallagher. It ended with an appeal to Carmichael to use his influence to make this stop.

'He's appealing to the War Office, in hopes that someone there will have more clout than your bosses,' Hamilton said.

'He may be right. Hammy, do you know if the captain has received any personal telegrams? From the War Office or anywhere else?'

'I only see telegrams to and from the passengers. Any messages for the officers are private.'

'But the Marconi operators see them, don't they? Ask them on my behalf. Tell them there's a bottle of rum in it.'

'If Bowler Bill finds out you've been intercepting his correspondence, he'll keelhaul you,' Hamilton warned.

The siren boomed again, echoing in the fog. 'Bowler Bill has other things on his mind.'

Hamilton picked up the telephone mouthpiece and receiver and asked the switchboard to patch him through to the Marconi room. He spoke briefly, waited and listened. 'Telegram for the captain came in late last night, from the War Office,' he said, replacing the receiver in its cradle. 'The text was in code, so they don't know what it says. But the sender's name was in plain English. Colonel James Carmichael.'

'Schurz is trying to get me off his back,' Gallagher said slowly. 'Why? If he is who he claims he is, I am no threat to him.'

The telephone rang and Hamilton picked up the receiver again. 'Yes?'

A voice squawked anxiously in the receiver. 'Inform the captain,' Hamilton snapped. 'And tell the chief to send an electrical fitter, right away.'

'What is it?' Gallagher asked.

'The electric supply to the telegraph has just this moment been cut again. They still have the telephone, but Marconi is dead as a doornail. Do you suppose it really is rats this time?'

'Rats?' said Gallagher. 'We're in the middle of the war zone without an escort, very likely with German U-boats waiting for us. If Haulbowline does receive word of submarine activity, they have no way of warning us. We're sailing into danger, Hammy, and we're sailing blind.'

IN THE FOYER on the boat deck, Gallagher opened the mahogany cabinet and stepped sharply back. The paint at the back of the cabinet had bubbled and in places hung down in strips. The recently repaired aluminium wires had been stripped away from floor to ceiling, and what remained of the braided cloth insulation was smouldering. A harsh acrid smell drifted in the air.

'What in God's name?' said Hamilton.

Two passengers, a young couple with the look of newlyweds about them, had stopped, wrinkling their noses at the smell. 'There is nothing to worry about,' Gallagher told them gently. 'A small problem with the electrical wiring.'

'Is the ship safe?' the young man asked anxiously.

'Of course. This will soon be repaired.'

Looking apprehensive, they continued on their way into the saloon. Hamilton turned to Gallagher. 'Acid,' he said. 'They've burned the bloody wires away with acid.'

'Yes. If rats did this, then they're carrying Nachrichten-Abteilung identity papers. Why hasn't the telephone been affected?'

'It runs through a different conduit to the exchange,' Hamilton reminded him. 'Where did they get the acid?'

'Your staff use oil of vitriol to clean the drains, am I right? If you were to do an inventory, I suspect you'll find you are missing a salt cellar and a tin of cleaning fluid. Mix oil of vitriol with table salt, and you have hydrochloric acid. Someone probably made this in their cabin, perhaps using an empty bottle, and poured it on the wires.'

The electrical fitter, a small man in blue uniform carrying a box of tools, arrived and peered into the cabinet. 'How long to mend this?' Hamilton asked.

The man sniffed, smelling the acid. 'We'll need to wipe everything down with an alkaline solution, sir, otherwise the wires will just corrode away again. Then we'll have to replace and test the wires and insulate everything. Four or five hours, maybe more.'

'Do your best.' Hamilton turned to Gallagher. 'It can't have happened more than a few minutes ago. Between the first and second telephone calls.'

'So the saboteur has not gone far. Hammy, ask the deck stewards if they have seen anything. Someone throwing an object into the water, for example.'

Hamilton went out on deck. Gallagher walked through into the saloon. Through the tall windows he could see people lining the rails between the lifeboats, peering into the fog. Some had brought out field glasses and were studying the water, presumably looking for U-boats. Amateur lookouts, Gallagher thought. Well, good luck to them; if they do spot something, they may yet save us.

He looked around the big room. Only a few people were here. The couple he had seen earlier were seated at the piano playing 'Chopsticks' as a duet, both clearly trying to use the music as a distraction. Colonel Skarpö sat with his back to the window, a copy of last Saturday's *New York Times* in his hand. Glancing at him, Gallagher saw that his eyes were not focused on the page. His absolute stillness reminded Gallagher of a tiger waiting to spring.

This is a tiger hunt . . . Gallagher walked over to him. 'Where is your friend Major Arango?'

Skarpö looked up. 'I don't know. I haven't seen him for a while.'

'Your orders from General Villa were to find out who was responsible for the disaster at Celaya, and kill them. Did that only mean the Lópezes?'

Skarpö glanced at the Lópezes, sitting together in a corner of the room. 'No. Anyone who might have been involved.'

'I watched you when López described what happened to the shells. You knew part of the story already, didn't you? Or you guessed it.'

'When I found out the shells hadn't been sent to Mexico, I suspected they might have gone back to New York,' Skarpö said. 'I did a little digging when we arrived there. I discovered Schurz's connections with U.M.C. and I thought he might have been involved, but then I discovered the Five Points Gang had probably helped smuggle the munitions aboard a ship. They have connections with the unions.'

'They have tentacles everywhere,' Gallagher agreed. 'Did you know the shells were on *Lusitania*?'

'No. I was as shocked as you when we found them.' Skarpö nodded towards the corner of the room. 'Have you noticed how still the old couple are?'

The Lópezes sat in a corner of the room, facing each other. López was staring at the floor, hunched over a little as if he was feeling unwell. His wife sat with her hands in her lap, watching him quietly. Her hair seemed to be more grey than Gallagher remembered, but that might have been a trick of the light reflecting through the fog. A sudden suspicion formed in his mind. He turned away from Skarpö and walked towards them.

'There she is!' Ripley stormed into the saloon, red-faced and panting, flinging out one arm and pointing at Señora López. 'You! What the god-damned hell were you doing?'

The couple at the piano stopped playing and watched, open-mouthed. Skarpö laid down his newspaper and rose to his feet.

'Please, señor,' murmured López. 'Your language.'

'You threw something overboard,' Ripley said. 'I was down on the promenade deck, and I saw you. What was it? A bottle?'

'Yes,' Corazón López said calmly. 'I wrote a message in a bottle and threw it into the sea. It is an amusement, Señor Ripley. One day the bottle will wash up on shore, perhaps in a faraway land, and someone will read the message and write to me. Then I will know how far my bottle has travelled.'

'Faraway land? Like hell! You were sending a message to the U-boats, weren't you? You were telling them where to find us!'

'Don't be absurd,' Corazón said curtly. Her face was greyer than ever. 'You do not know what you are talking about.'

Ripley's fists clenched. 'You god-damned German spy.' He started towards her and then stopped, wincing in pain as Gallagher's hand closed on his arm like a vice. 'Once again,' Gallagher said. 'Mind your language in front of the ladies.'

Dolly Markland came into the room and stood, watching. Ripley spun around, confronting Gallagher. 'Are you going to do something about this?'

'Yes,' Gallagher said. Still gripping Ripley's arm, he walked the other man to the door and pushed him out into the foyer. 'Stay away from Mr and Mrs López,' he said. 'And if I hear you making wild accusations again, I will inform the master-at-arms and have you arrested.'

Ripley glared at him, quivering. 'On whose authority?'

'The captain's,' said Gallagher, giving him a shove. 'Get lost.'

Turning his back on Ripley, he returned to the Lópezes. 'Thank you, señor,' said Corazón.

'Don't thank me just yet,' Gallagher said. 'I saw you take the bottle from the dinner table last night. Did you steal the salt cellar then as well? Or later?'

López looked up, and Gallagher saw the blisters and raw burns on his fingers. 'That must be painful,' he said quietly.

The other man made an effort to smile. 'It will be some time before I play the piano again.'

'Hydrochloric acid can be dangerous to handle, if you don't know what you are doing.'

'So I have discovered. I splashed only a little on my hands, but it was enough. That is why I asked Corazón to dispose of the bottle.'

'I presume you were responsible for the earlier incident as well? The rat droppings were a mistake, by the way. A little too obvious.'

'My talent is for music, not for this. On both occasions, my wife acted as lookout while I slipped into the cabinet and disabled the wires, and knocked on the door when the coast was clear and I could come out.'

'You could easily have been caught. Why take the risk, why now?'

'A Faustian bargain,' López said. 'We left Mexico thinking that the secret of our involvement in the munitions swap was safe. Unfortunately, Captain von Rintelen in New York somehow learned the truth. His agents visited us and made a simple proposition. We would agree to disable the Marconi system on two occasions, one on Sunday evening and the other today, as the ship approached Queenstown. In return, he would keep our secret from General Villa's men. If we failed, he would inform Villa's agents.'

'You claimed you sent the munitions to us because you were sympathetic to our cause. Now, you have put this ship in even greater danger.'

'We did what we had to do,' said Corazón López. 'We would prefer you to win this war, but if you fail to do so it will only be a temporary setback to our cause. One day the workers will rise and seize control of the means of production, and on that day all wars will end and the era of universal peace will begin.'

'You sound like Franklin,' Gallagher said.

Her dark eyes snapped a little. 'Do not compare me to a capitalist.'

'Go to your cabin,' Gallagher said. 'I will send Dr Whiting to see to your injuries, señor. Then I advise you to pack. I said earlier that you would be arrested at Liverpool, but I won't risk keeping you on board for that long. In a few hours we will reach Queenstown, and there you will be taken off the ship.'

'What will happen to us then?' López asked.

'It depends to a large extent on how you answer my next question,' Gallagher said. 'If you tell me the truth, I can ensure you receive clemency. If not, then I cannot answer for the consequences.'

They waited, watching him with dark unblinking eyes. 'Two German agents boarded this ship,' Gallagher said. 'We arrested one on the first day. The other is still at large. Tell me who he is.'

'We will tell you nothing,' Corazón said fiercely.

López raised a raw, blistered hand and laid it on her arm. 'No, mi querida. We are involved in this. There is no going back.'

He turned to look at Gallagher again. 'Surely by now you must have realized,' he said. 'Surely you must know it is Señor Schurz.'

24

'I WAS WRONG,' Skarpö said. 'I should have let Major Arango kill them.'

Gallagher turned on him. 'Stay away from them, and keep Arango away from them too. They are my business, not yours.'

'I'm not sure I agree with you. But the Lópezes are not the most important thing at the moment. You need me to help you find Schurz.'

Gallagher hesitated for a moment. The master-at-arms had only a handful of men, and three were already occupied with guarding Franklin, Kreutzer and Chalfont. 'All right,' he said. 'Come with me.'

Swiftly they toured the public spaces of the ship, the smoking room and reading room and café, and walked around the long promenades. The fog began to clear and they saw the green hills of Ireland again through hazy trails of vapour, Toe Head on the port beam with Glandore Bay opening up beyond. There was no sign of Schurz, nor did he answer to a knock at his cabin door. The alarm bells in Gallagher's mind were ringing louder than ever.

Hamilton found them down on the shelter deck, searching still. 'What's going on, Pat?'

'We need to find Schurz, right away. Can you call the master-at-arms, Hammy?'

Hamilton ran towards the nearest telephone. Gallagher turned to Skarpö. 'Do you have a gun?'

'In my cabin. Do you trust me with it?'

'I don't have a choice,' Gallagher said, starting towards the stairs. 'You're right. I need your help.'

THE KEY WAS exactly where they had said it would be, in the cistern of one of the water closets in the gentlemen's room on the main deck. Schurz set down the black leather bag he was carrying and pulled out the key, drying it off with his handkerchief and putting it into his pocket. Opening the bag, he went through its contents again. It contained the tools of his trade: a slide rule and stopwatches and notebooks, along with some more obscure equipment, including a pry bar, nail puller, pliers, a small hammer and, most unusual of all, a box of blasting caps. He had checked half a dozen times already, but a good engineer always makes sure of his tools. Satisfied, he closed the bag and departed, pulling on a pair of leather gloves as he went.

He had spent the last several days trying to discover where the munitions were stored, without success. Yesterday morning he had chanced his arm and aroused Gallagher's suspicions about the cargo, and Gallagher not unnaturally had gone to look for himself. It was a simple matter to follow Gallagher and the purser and the big man, Colonel Skarpö, and see where they went. Then all he had to do was wait, and retrieve the key when he was ready.

Everything had worked exactly as he planned it, thus proving the clear superiority of the rational mind. That did not explain why sweat kept breaking out on his forehead. Slowly he walked down the passageway until he stood before the door the purser had unlocked yesterday. He stopped, listening for any signs he was being followed. There were none. He clenched his fists suddenly, closing his eyes while he fought back the nervous convulsions that threatened to overwhelm him. The risks he was running were horrendous, but so was the price of failure; death on one hand, or professional suicide and the loss of everything he had worked for on the other.

He took the key from his pocket. His fingers were trembling, and he had to use both hands to guide it into the keyhole. Unlocking the door, he turned the wheel. The door opened with smooth, oiled ease, revealing the hatch set into the floor. Drawing a deep breath, Schurz closed the door behind him and locked it, then lifted the hatch and climbed down the steel ladder into the cargo space.

Friday, 7 May 1915
11.16 a.m.
Four hours from Queenstown

Kreutzer had known for some time that they had posted a guard outside his door. The man said nothing, but he could hear the occasional shifting of feet. Fair enough, Kreutzer thought. Gallagher has begun to trust me, a little, but he is taking no chances. In his position, I would do the same.

Now, in the windowless box of his cabin, he could hear different noises, doors opening and closing, voices calling too far away for the words to be audible. He listened for a while but could make nothing of it. Finally he knocked on the door. 'Are you there?' he asked the guard.

There was no answer, but he heard the feet shifting again. 'I can hear things,' he said. 'What is happening?'

After a long moment the guard answered. 'They're searching the ship,' he said.

'Searching? For what?'

'Nobody told me,' said the guard. From his tone, Kreutzer could tell the man was curious too, and faintly resentful at not being able to leave his post and find out. He sat down, staring at the door and thinking. If Gallagher was searching the ship – and *they* in this context almost certainly meant Gallagher – it must mean only one thing; there was another German agent on board.

He sat up a little. That meant he had been right all along; he had been deliberately exposed, set up by Rintelen to fail, so the real agent could succeed.

Rising swiftly, he knocked at the door again. 'Open up, please. I need to get out of here.'

'My orders are to keep you locked up tight,' said the guard. 'Who are you, anyway? Some sort of stowaway?'

'Something like that,' Kreutzer said. 'If you won't let me out, will you at least send a message? I need to speak to one of the first-class passengers, Mr Gallagher.'

'What about?'

'I can't tell you. Please, just tell him it is urgent. I need to see him as soon as possible.'

'All right,' the guard said finally. 'Next time I see one of the stewards, I'll pass the word. Does that satisfy you?'

'Thank you.' Slowly, Kreutzer sat down again. He felt helpless, but there was nothing more he could do. Opening his wallet, he took out the paper heart Jeni had given him. The paper was wrinkled and faded, but to his eyes it was as fresh and white as it had been when it was new. He sat holding it in his hands, staring at it, trying to feel some connection to her. But all he could feel was emptiness.

*

Gallagher met Hamilton in the foyer. 'Any luck?' the purser asked.

Gallagher shook his head. 'We've gone through first class with a toothcomb. Colonel Skarpö and the master-at-arms are looking through third class now. You?'

'I've checked all of the second-class cabins. No one has seen him. It wasn't really much of a hope.'

'That leaves the cargo space.' Up on the boat deck people were talking loudly, arguing about something by the sound of it. Gallagher thought he recognized Ripley's voice.

'He couldn't get in there without a key,' Hamilton objected.

'Maybe. We need to check all the same. We'll wait for Skarpö and the master-at-arms. Then we'll go down and take a look.'

They waited, listening to the voices. Gallagher heard references to a flag, and realized the people upstairs were talking about Ripley's favourite theme, whether the ship should be flying the American flag and pretending to be neutral. It was understandable, of course. People frightened of death are never going to be much interested in the laws of war . . . My God, he thought, I'm actually feeling sympathy for Ripley.

He looked outside. The last vestiges of fog had vanished. Glandore Bay was falling away astern now and Galley Head was on the port beam, another lighthouse jutting into the cloudless blue sky. There was not far to go now; beyond Galley Head lay Clonakilty Bay, then Seven Heads and the long promontory of the Old Head of Kinsale. At Kinsale they would pick up the pilot, and from there they would be able to see the Daunt Rock lightship, beyond which lay Queenstown and safety.

Skarpö and the master-at-arms returned, followed by two of the latter's men. All three seamen wore sidearms. Beneath his coat Skarpö had a Smith & Wesson revolver in a holster attached to a gun belt, worn low on his hip like a professional gunfighter. Gallagher's own Webley was a comforting weight in his coat pocket.

'No sign of him, sir,' said the master-at-arms. 'We've searched the baggage room as well.'

Gallagher nodded. 'We think he may be trying to get at the cargo.'

They hurried down the long stair. All was quiet; most of the passengers were out on deck now, staring at the sea, and the rest were up in the saloon arguing with Ripley. Reaching the main deck they walked forward, feeling the ship roll again in the swirling currents off the Irish coast. Hamilton tried the door.

'Still locked,' he said, reaching for his keys.

'Good,' said Gallagher. 'When we leave, we'll put a guard on the door.'

'I'm very short of men,' protested the master-at-arms. 'What is so important in the cargo hold?'

'Just do it,' Gallagher said grimly, pulling his revolver from his pocket.

The door opened, and he walked into the little compartment and lifted the hatch. Hamilton flicked the switch and electric lights blinked and crackled into life. The scene was exactly as they had left it, the stacked boxes and bales and crates rising almost to the ceiling. 'Spread out,' Gallagher said. 'Search the room, every nook and cranny. Look for signs of damage to any of the larger crates, anything a man could hide in.'

Slowly they moved through the room, weapons at the ready, passing the bales of furs and the wooden crates of tinned meat and books and spools of wire. The towering stacks of boxes containing the shells stood as before, untouched. Gallagher hoped the master-at-arms and his men did not enquire what was inside them.

Near the rear of the compartment he found another stack of

smaller, flat white boxes, also bearing the label of the Dominion Machine Tool Company. He stopped and picked one up. 'These are the fuzes,' Skarpö said quietly. The master-at-arms and his men were too far away to hear.

'Have they been tampered with, do you think?'

Skarpö holstered his revolver and peered at the boxes. 'All the seals are intact, at least so far as I can see.'

Hamilton came up alongside them. 'Nothing has been disturbed, Pat. There's no sign that he's been here.'

'So where the hell is he?' asked Gallagher.

Hamilton looked dubious. 'There's the crew's quarters, of course, and the cold storage and the mail room. And the engine room and the coal bunkers. But I really don't see how he could get in there.'

'He might be hiding in one of the lifeboats,' Skarpö suggested.

The lifeboats had been made ready that morning, the crew prepared to launch them at a moment's notice, but each boat still had its canvas cover; they would make useful places to hide. 'You and I will check those,' Gallagher said. 'Hammy, ask the master-at-arms to start searching the crew's quarters and the rest of the stores. And remind him I want a guard on the door into this cargo space, night and day, until we reach Liverpool.'

THEY DEPARTED, CLOSING the hatch, switching off the lights and locking the door behind them. Their footsteps receded along the passageway overhead. From outside came the rush of water past the hull, the deep throbbing of engines and turbines a couple of decks below. In the room itself, all was silent.

Perhaps fifteen minutes later, something moved on top of one of the stacks. A man's head appeared, looking around cautiously in the dim light coming through the portholes. He waited for several minutes until he was sure that he was alone. Finally satisfied, Charles Schurz dropped his bag onto the deck and climbed down after it, feet groping for toeholds on a stack of crates. He paused again, listening; he had heard Gallagher give orders to put a guard on the door, and he waited to see if the man had heard a noise, but the beat of the engines masked any sound he had made.

Picking up his bag, he turned to the wooden cases labelled as machine tool parts. Using his prybar and nail puller, he removed the side of one of the crates and pulled out an eighteen-pounder shell and set it carefully on the deck. The yellow paint and red band told him this was a high explosive projectile filled with trinitrotoluene. If these shells reached the battlefield, they could cause thousands of German casualties.

Heat from the boilers was pouring up through the deck below. Schurz wiped the sweat from his face. Moving swiftly through the room he found the boxes of fuzes, broke the seal on one and opened it. Inside, resting in wooden racks, were the fuzes, small steel mushrooms each with a screw thread on the stalk. Carrying them back to the boxes of shells, he knelt down beside the first shell and inserted a fuze into the nose of the projectile. A few gentle turns and the fuze was in place. The shell was now live.

He wiped his face again. The plan had seemed simple when he first worked it out. Now, he was not so sure.

Calm down, he told himself. We're still several hours from Queenstown. There is plenty of time to do what needs to be done, and then get clear. He would have to get past the guard at the door to make his escape, an unforeseen obstacle, but he would deal with that when the time came. Methodically, concentrating on his task despite his fears, Charles Schurz set to work; so absorbed in handling the delicate fuzes and high explosive shells that he never noticed the shadowy figure watching him silently from the far side of the room.

Friday, 7 May 1915
12.05 P.M.
Three hours from Queenstown

Inside his stateroom, Edwin Franklin knocked gently on the locked door. 'Guard! Are you there?'

'Yes, sir,' said a voice from the passageway.

'Look, I'm sorry if I was rude to you yesterday.' With an effort, Franklin kept his voice calm and quiet, even placatory. 'I wasn't feeling well, you see. I wasn't myself.'

'That's all right, sir. I understand.'

'Good. Glad to hear it.'

There was a moment of silence. Franklin cleared his throat. 'I've a bit of a problem in here. There's no hot water in the bathroom, and I really would like a wash.'

'I'm sorry to hear it, sir. I'll report it to the stewards.'

'I'd be obliged if you would. Thank you.'

Prisoner though he was, as a passenger in the regal suite he was still entitled to top-class service. A steward arrived less than a minute later, unlocking the door and bowing as he entered. 'I'll take a look, sir, if I may. If I cannot rectify the fault, I'll call the plumber.'

'Very well. Carry on.'

The steward turned towards the bathroom. As he did so, Franklin hit him across the back of the neck with a lead crystal decanter and the man collapsed without a sound. Franklin reached into his pocket and took his keys and hurried to the outer door of the suite, which was still unlocked.

'Guard! Come quickly! The steward has had an accident! Quickly, man, he is bleeding all over the place!'

The guard stepped into the suite. Franklin grabbed him by the arm and threw him bodily across the room, then stepped out into the passageway, slammed the door behind him and locked it. He stood for a moment, breathing hard. These people – these pygmies, these ants – would not stop him. Destiny awaited him. In a few days' time he would sit down with King George and his ministers and point out to them the futility of the war. He could almost see the looks on their faces, the remorse and hangdog shame as they were confronted by the evidence of their own stupidity, and with one voice they would beg him to bring about peace. Then, a fast train, a boat to the continent, another special train racing through the night into the heart of Germany, and he would face the Kaiser and his generals and bring them to heel. The guns would fall silent, and peace would rule.

But first, he had to get ashore. He thought for a moment of the pleasure he would take in crushing Captain Turner and Gallagher – oh, Gallagher, he would enjoy twisting the knife in that one's guts – but that could wait. He started along the passageway towards the main stair, his mind spinning like a kaleidoscope, broken fractals sliding in and out of his mental focus. Get ashore, get ashore. Yes, that was it. Find Turner, demand he be taken to Queenstown and put ashore. From there, he would send a telegram to Buckingham Palace announcing his arrival. All would be laid on from there: the boats, the trains, the fast cars, the escorts. He might inform the newspapers too, so they could publish the news. Crowds would turn out along the route, waving and cheering the man who had come to save them.

In the foyer he paused for a moment, hearing voices raised on the boat deck above. He walked out on deck, looking around for the escorting cruiser. There was no sign of it. That was irritating, because he had been promised that the cruiser would be there. Something was wrong. But never mind, he was here now. He would sort things out.

He strode up the stairs, quickly, decisively. In the saloon, Ripley was standing on top of the piano, balancing precariously against the roll of the ship and shouting. Twenty or thirty people were gathered around him, some listening anxiously, others shouting back at him. The Markland woman was there too, standing behind Ripley and staring up at him, one hand tucked into her reticule. Franklin dismissed her from his thoughts and concentrated on what Ripley was saying.

'For the hundredth time, we have no choice! We must fly a neutral flag! It doesn't have to be the American flag, hell, I don't care; fly the flag of Brazil, or Siam, or the Emperor of Ethiopia, it doesn't matter!'

An elderly man waved a cane in the air. 'You're starting at shadows, man. In a few hours we'll be safe at Queenstown.'

'Safe?' demanded Ripley. 'We still have another day's run to Liverpool, or had you forgotten that? For God's sake, you people, see reason! Neutrality means safety, it's as simple as that!'

Franklin stepped forward. 'Where is the cruiser?' he demanded. 'Where is *Juno*?'

'It never arrived,' said someone.

'Ah.' Heads would roll for this, but later. Now was the time for action. 'It is absolutely essential that *Lusitania* reaches its destination safely. I have urgent business that will not wait.'

Heads turned to look at him. 'Sir,' someone said hesitantly. 'We were told you were unwell.'

'Unwell? I have never been in finer health. Ladies, gentlemen, you must not fear. I took charge when the lifeboat broke loose, and I am here to do so again. Trust in me, and I will see you all safely home.'

They listened in silence, spellbound, he knew, by the power and authority in his voice. The king and the Kaiser would listen in exactly the same way. 'Mr Ripley is quite correct. As the escort has failed to materialize, it is up to us to ensure our own safety. We shall demand that the captain fly a neutral flag. If he refuses . . .'

Franklin looked around the room, holding their attention. 'If he refuses, I will depose Captain Turner and take command myself. Are you with me?'

A few voices raised in protest – there were always a few, the blind who could not see – but most roared approval. A woman screamed, whether from fear or excitement was hard to tell. Satisfied that he was in control, Franklin turned and walked back into the foyer. The others followed him.

THERE WERE TWENTY-TWO fixed lifeboats in davits, eleven on each side of the boat deck, plus about thirty collapsible boats in lockers. 'You take the starboard side, I'll take port,' Gallagher said to Skarpö.

The colonel nodded. People lined the rail in silence, staring out over the sea with anxious faces. The sun was bright and warm. Ignoring the curious looks he received, Gallagher untied the lashings and peeled back the covers on the first lifeboat, and looked inside. It was empty; he pulled the cover across and moved on to the next, and the next. He found nothing. All the while *Lusitania* continued her race towards Queenstown, and the alarm bells kept ringing in his mind.

He searched the last boat and then turned to the lockers, hearing raised voices in the saloon. Skarpö rejoined him. 'Nothing.'

'Where the hell is he?' demanded Gallagher.

'Maybe the others will have more luck.'

'Maybe.' One of the stewards was there, saluting. 'What is it?' Gallagher asked.

'Begging your pardon, sir, but we've been looking all over for you. The gentleman in Nelson. He wants to talk to you?'

'What about?'

'He didn't say, sir.'

The shouting in the saloon had increased sharply in volume. 'Whatever it is, it will have to wait,' Gallagher said irritably. Swearing under his breath, he ran forward, Skarpö following him. The other passengers watched them nervously.

Three men stood in the foyer with their backs to the stair, guns in their hands: Hamilton, the master-at-arms and one of his mates. Facing them were a crowd of passengers, Franklin and Ripley to the fore. 'What is this?' Gallagher demanded.

'Looks like mutiny, Pat,' the purser said, his voice taut.

'I have asked to speak to the captain,' Franklin said calmly. 'He has refused to see me.'

'How the hell did you get out of your cabin?'

'Mr Gallagher, please. Did you really think you could hold me for long? There is no cage built that can contain me. As the captain is refusing to carry out his duty, I am taking command. Gentlemen, lower your weapons and stand aside.'

'Franklin, you are under arrest,' Gallagher said. 'Master-at-arms, do your duty.'

Other passengers crowded forward. Ripley stood in front of Franklin, arms folded. 'If you arrest him, you'll have to arrest all of us. I suppose you're going to tell us again that the penalty for mutiny is death.'

'It is,' said Gallagher, pulling his gun from his pocket. A woman screamed again. 'And because we are at sea, in a time of

343

war, there is no need for a trial, witnesses or evidence. I have the authority to stand you against that wall *right now*, Ripley, and shoot you in the head. Do you understand me?'

Silence fell. Gallagher turned to Hamilton. 'Did you find him?'

'No.'

'God damn it. He must be somewhere. All right, get rid of this rabble and we'll keep looking.' He looked back at the passengers, some frightened, some determined, all desperate. 'You have ten seconds to stand down,' he said. 'After that I will start making arrests, and anyone who resists will be shot.'

'You have no authority here,' Franklin said, his voice still calm. 'And you only have four men.'

'Five,' said Skarpö, the Smith & Wesson level in his hand.

'Five, then. What are you going to do against all of us? You face the might of the people, Gallagher. Their will has spoken, and I am their chosen instrument. It is you who will stand down.'

A hand plucked at Gallagher's sleeve. It was another steward, his face as white as his uniform coat. 'Sir,' the man said desperately, 'something has happened.'

'What is it?' Gallagher snapped.

'The guard outside Mr Chalfont's cabin, sir. He's dead.'

25

THE GUARD LAY on his back in the middle of the passageway. He had been shot in the face at close range through the keyhole of the door, and parts of the doorplate were embedded in his skin. The blood on the floor around his head was still shining and fresh. 'Did anyone hear the shot?' Gallagher asked the steward.

'I heard a couple of bangs, sir, but I thought it was just Big Lucy. We were going through the currents off Seven Heads at the time, and she was moving around a bit.'

Even a ship as big as the *Lusitania* was subject to currents, and sometimes the hull would shudder and shake, especially when moving at high speed. Two shots had been fired, one to kill the guard and one to smash the lock; the bullet from the latter was embedded in the bulkhead on the far side of the passageway. Gallagher pushed the door open and walked inside. The cabin was empty.

'God damn it,' Gallagher said, and he turned and ran down the passageway and up the stairs to the boat deck. Hamilton and the master-at-arms had somehow herded the group of mutinous passengers back into the saloon; others, coming in from the deck and going down to lunch, looked more apprehensive than

345

ever. The grey cliffs of the Old Head of Kinsale loomed on the horizon. They were almost home.

Hamilton came over to Gallagher. 'What happened?'

'Chalfont shot him through the keyhole, and then broke out of his cabin.'

Hamilton stared. 'Where did he get a gun? We searched his baggage.'

'Presumably someone hid it in his cabin before we sailed.'

The purser swore under his breath. 'We can't search for him as well as Schurz, and keep Captain Teach and his friends under control.'

Franklin had begun haranguing the other passengers about world peace. Dolly Markland sat with her head bowed, staring at the floor. Gallagher barely noticed her. 'We don't have to search,' he said. 'I know where he's going. The cargo hold.'

'I'll come with you.'

'No, stay here and keep a lid on things. I'll take Skarpö.' Hamilton was solid and utterly reliable, but Skarpö was a fighting man. 'Give me your key, Hammy.'

The purser handed it over, his face sombre. 'Be careful, Pat.'

'I think it might be a bit late for that.' Gallagher turned to Skarpö. 'Let's go.'

They hurried downstairs, pushing past more startled passengers on their way to lunch. Deep within the ship something coughed, once, then twice more, vibrations felt rather than heard: gunshots, the sound muffled by the intervening decks and bulkheads.

'Jesus,' Gallagher said softly. 'We're too late.'

Reaching the main deck, they ran down the passageway. The sailor left on guard had vanished, but there was a smear of fresh blood on the floor. The door to the cargo space was locked. Motioning for silence, Gallagher inserted his key into the lock and turned it slowly, spinning the wheel to open the door as silently as possible. Inside, the body of the sailor lay beside the open hatch, shot through the chest; his body had been dragged here to keep it out of sight of anyone who might come down the passageway. From the big room below came the voice of Charles Schurz, taut with pain.

'Who sent you? Who are you working for, Chalfont?'

Schurz wiped his forehead for the umpteenth time, drying his hands on his trousers. He laid the last fuzed shell back in its crate and stacked the crate on top of the other five he had already fuzed, lying against the outer hull of the ship beneath one of the salt-streaked portholes. The six crates contained a total of twenty-four eighteen-pounder shells. Detonated simultaneously, they would blow a very satisfactory hole in the *Lusitania*'s hull.

Next, he needed to build a detonator, one that would allow him time to get out of the room before the explosion took place. He had been thinking of building a mechanical clockwork detonator, but the cases of automobile parts had given him another idea. Among other things they contained magnetos, giving him an electricity supply, and copper wire which would generate a stronger, hotter current than aluminium. The electrical current would detonate the blasting caps, which would in turn explode the shells. He could use his stopwatch as a timer; if he set it for five minutes, that would give him plenty of time to get away. There was the problem of the guard, of course, but he thought he could probably come up with a convincing lie to get past him.

He had just finished the detonator, connecting the last wires to the magneto and setting it carefully on top of the crates of shells, when someone stepped out of the shadows behind him. 'Raise your hands in the air,' the man said. 'Turn around slowly.'

The fear was like an electric shock. For a moment Schurz could not move at all. When he did raise his hands, they felt like they were made of lead. Dry-mouthed, he turned around. A man stood facing him, young, dark-haired with a moustache, a revolver in his hand. Schurz recognized him as one of the other passengers.

'You do not know me,' the man said.

Staring hypnotically at the gun, Schurz found his voice. 'How did you get in?'

'When Gallagher and his men searched this place, I followed them in. I hid, the same as you did, and waited until they had gone.'

'Who are you?'

'My name is Major Juan Arango and I am on the staff of General Villa. You are the man who stole our ammunition and condemned us to defeat. Thousands of our compañeros died because of you.'

'I don't know what you're talking about,' Schurz said. He could not tear his eyes away from the gun.

'You deny it? You are a coward as well as a murderer.' With a gasp of terror, Schurz saw his finger tighten on the trigger. 'I shall take much pleasure in killing you.'

'No!' Schurz said, his voice rising. 'Don't shoot! If you hit one of those shells, you'll blow us all to hell!'

It was an act of pure desperation, anything to buy himself a little more time so that something might happen, someone might come to his rescue. But after a moment Arango nodded and motioned with the gun. 'This way. You go first. Keep your hands raised.'

They walked back to the foot of the steel ladder leading up to the main deck. 'I heard about what happened in Mexico,' Schurz said. 'But it was nothing to do with me. I swear.'

'You are lying,' Arango said.

'Please! I can help you. I know the company well, their managing director is a friend. I can send some telegrams, make enquiries. We can work together to find out—'

The crash of the gun was fearfully loud. Schurz felt a sharp, agonizing blow like someone driving a chisel into his lower back. His legs went numb at once and he fell heavily to the deck. Crying out with pain, he struggled up onto his side, trying to drag his dead legs after him. The air was full of cordite fumes and the stink of blood, choking in his nostrils. Arango walked around him, turning to stand with his back to the stair, facing the wounded man. He raised the revolver again.

'Tell me the truth,' he said. 'Everything. Then I will give you a merciful death.'

Pain shot up from Schurz's waist to his head, stabbing like bolts of electricity. His legs felt like they had been disconnected from his body. 'Please,' he gasped. 'Get help.'

'The truth,' Arango repeated.

'What . . . what do you want to know?'

'Were the old couple involved? Did they help you switch the consignments?'

'What old couple? Do you mean the Lópezes? How should I know? Oh, Christ, please help me!'

Arango's eyes narrowed. 'Where did the other shells go? Did you send them to the government?'

'Oh, God,' Schurz begged, weeping with pain. 'I don't know, I don't know! All I know is that the managing director told me the shipment had been held up. He thought it was someone in the New York underworld. That is all I know!'

From overhead came the hard sound of a heavy revolver being fired, followed by the softer thud of something hitting the deck. Arango wheeled around, gun pointed at the hatch. 'What is that? Who's there?'

'Help!' Schurz screamed at the top of his voice. 'Help me!'

Arango turned on him again. 'I will finish you first,' he hissed, and he pointed the revolver at Schurz's belly and began to squeeze the trigger, just as someone came down through the hatch and shot him twice in the back. Arango fell onto his face, the revolver sliding out of his fingers. He tried once to pull himself up, then collapsed and slumped lifeless on the deck.

HARRY CHALFONT CLIMBED down the ladder and walked forward through a haze of smoke, standing and looking down at Schurz.

'Well, well,' he said. 'This is a pretty mess you've got yourself into, Charlie boy. Good thing I'm here to clean it up.'

'Jesus, I think I'm paralysed,' Schurz gasped. 'Send for a doctor, for the love of God.'

'All in good time.' Still holding his revolver, Chalfont picked up Arango's gun and put it in his pocket, then walked across the big room, looking around in the dim light from the portholes. He returned a moment later. 'That Heath Robinson contraption you've built. Will it work?'

'Yes,' Schurz said faintly. The pain was threatening to overwhelm him but even worse was his growing fear of paralysis. How could he do his work from a wheelchair, or lying in bed? His reputation, his life's work were slipping away from him. He looked up at the other man. The light etched Chalfont's face in hard planes and deep shadowy lines; his eyes were dark.

'Who sent you?' Schurz asked. 'Who are you working for, Chalfont?'

'Captain von Rintelen sent me, of course,' Chalfont said. 'I've been working for him all along.'

'I know,' said Gallagher's voice behind him. 'Drop the gun, Harry. The game is over.'

There was a long second of silence and then Chalfont spun on his heel, the revolver in his hand pointed at Gallagher. 'Well, dear boy,' he said conversationally. 'This is all a bit awkward, isn't it?'

Walking forward from the foot of the ladder, Gallagher held out his hands, showing they were empty. His Webley was still in his pocket. Skarpö came down the ladder behind him, gave Arango's body a long look and stood still, watching.

'It needn't be awkward at all,' Gallagher said. 'All you have to do is put the gun down and come with us. I'll arrange for medical attention for Mr Schurz.'

'That seems unlikely,' said Chalfont. 'On top of my other crimes, I've now killed three people.'

'You have,' Gallagher acknowledged. 'But no one else needs to die. Not if you come along quietly.'

'You seem to forget that I'm the one with the gun.' Chalfont waved the revolver. It was an old model, Gallagher saw, a Colt Single Action Army, almost identical to the one he had found in Dowrich's cabin.

'I'm deeply disappointed,' Chalfont went on. 'All those cosy little chats we had. I was quite convinced you had believed everything I told you, and was ready to swear on a stack of Bibles that I was a true British patriot.'

'Those were my orders,' Gallagher said. 'Give you enough rope and see if you would hang yourself.' He glanced at Arango's body. 'Which you have now done.'

'Ah, to hell with it.' Chalfont lowered the gun. 'So you knew all along I was Rintelen's man.'

'I guessed it,' Gallagher said. Schurz was whimpering with pain. 'I didn't know for sure, until now. You never arranged for any shipments of munitions to Britain, and you never paid Paul Kelly for anything, except possibly a plate of spaghetti and admission to a prize fight.'

'No,' said Chalfont.

'Buckland, the managing director of U.M.C., told you about the American government's plan to send dud shells to the Mexican army. You told Rintelen, and he passed the word to Colonel Kloss. Subsequently, you found out that the munitions the Lópezes had stolen had been sent back to New York and smuggled on board the *Lusitania*. The trainmen's union worked with Kelly to get the shells through customs, and Kelly told you.'

'It's good to have friends in low places,' Chalfont said.

'Knowing you were under suspicion and were being sent home, you and Rintelen devised a different plot. He put a dummy on board ship, Leutnant Kreutzer. Once Kreutzer had been arrested, we would think the plot had been foiled and the real agent could set to work undisturbed. Which is where you come in, Mr Schurz. What was your plan? To destroy the munitions?'

'Only some of them,' Schurz gasped. 'I was told to blow a hole in the side of the ship . . . just as she arrived at Queenstown. Everyone would see that the British were carrying arms on the ship. Putting American lives at risk . . . ah, Jesus, the pain . . . would anger the American government. They would stop exporting arms to Britain.'

'I see. Your aim was only to embarrass us.'

'Yes. No one was to be hurt.'

'You're a true humanitarian. Why do this? You have also taken a prominent post with the British government. Why risk losing that?'

In the wan light, Schurz was pale with loss of blood. It was hard to tell how badly he was injured. 'No choice,' he said, controlling his voice with an effort. 'Rintelen knew about my appointment. I didn't trouble to keep it a secret . . .' He winced as a fresh spasm of pain shook his body. 'He blackmailed me. He threatened to tell the British about my German connections, with people like Professor Münsterberg. The connections were harmless, but the British wouldn't think so. They would cancel my appointment.'

'And when the history of scientific management was written, your name would no longer be first on the list,' Gallagher said savagely. 'Did it not strike you as ironic, Schurz? Working for a German agent, in order to secure a position working for the British to make munitions to be used against Germany? Have you no moral compass at all?'

'I told you, I am neutral. I don't take up causes, I don't join sides. I just did what I was told to do.'

'So the answer to my question is *no*,' Gallagher said. He turned on Chalfont. 'And you? What did it take to make you betray your country?'

'Betray my country? Jesus Christ. Just when I was beginning to think you are an intelligent man, you come out with rubbish like that. I have no country, Gallagher. I didn't join the Foreign Service to serve king and country, I joined to have a damned good time. And for many years, that is exactly what I did.'

'And then your wife died,' Gallagher said. He took a step closer to Chalfont. 'The fun stopped then, didn't it?'

Suddenly furious, Chalfont raised the gun again. Skarpö tensed and Gallagher motioned with his hand, telling him to stand fast. 'Don't try to psychoanalyse me, you bastard,' Chalfont said. 'I did what I did because I wanted to do it. I like Rintelen. I like Paul Kelly and his sordid saloon. I've had enough of boiled shirts like Sir Courtenay Bennett. I played the game because I enjoyed it.'

Gallagher took another casual step forward. 'But now your cover is blown. What do you intend to do next?'

'Isn't it obvious? Kill all of you so there are no witnesses – that includes you, Schurz, old boy, sorry about that – and then detonate that infernal device he has cooked up. After that, I'll slip ashore and disappear. By the time anyone gets around to looking for me, I'll be long gone.'

Gallagher snapped his fingers. 'Now I understand,' he said. 'The problem I've had all along was that I couldn't work out why you were here.' Slowly he inched forward towards Chalfont, who was standing with his back to a stack of wooden crates; tinned vegetables, he saw. 'Your purpose was to make sure Schurz set off his bomb, and finish the job if he failed. But you were also here to kill Schurz. He was not to leave this ship alive.'

'Of course not. As soon as Rintelen learned about his contract with the British, he decided to kill him. You see, you're too good at your job, Charlie boy. You really could win the war for the other side. And the Germans can't allow that to happen.'

'And Dowrich?' asked Gallagher. 'Was he part of the scheme too?'

'You got it right about Dowrich, although it took you long enough. He'd had enough of being other people's pawn, he said, and he wanted to become a king. He planned to set up as an arms dealer, supplying anyone who could pay him, whatever side they were on. Once I had finished with Rintelen's business, I intended to join him.'

'Was that the offer he made when you met at the Deutscher Bund?'

'Of course. We'd have worked well together. With his contacts and my nous, we'd have made . . . what is the word? A killing.'

'One more question,' Gallagher said. 'Just to satisfy my curiosity.' He was only a few feet from Chalfont now. 'How did you persuade the guard to look through the keyhole?'

'It was laughably simple. I engaged him in conversation; I can be quite charming, you know. We started talking about women, the ones we'd had and the ones we'd lost, you know, man of the world stuff. After a while, I offered to show him a photograph of the most beautiful woman I had ever seen. He couldn't open the door, so I said I would hold it up to the keyhole. He bent down to look, and . . . boom.'

'Very clever,' Gallagher said.

'It was, wasn't it? You will find, on the whole, that I have been much cleverer than you all along. But I did enjoy our little chats.' He raised the revolver, pointing it at Gallagher's head. 'And now, behold the bloody weapon of destruction,' he said, and he smiled. 'Farewell, dear boy.'

Gallagher did not move but Skarpö's hand was a blur of motion, and there was a gun in Skarpö's hand and the gun boomed and roared in the echoing room. A red hole appeared in the middle of Chalfont's forehead and he crashed back against the crates behind him. He hung there for a moment before sliding slowly to the floor, where he lay still. Gallagher looked at the gory mess on the crates, and a line from Baudelaire rose in his mind.

Death, hovering like a new sun, will make blossom the flowers of their brains.

26

THE TORPEDO STRUCK *Lusitania* on the starboard side just below the bridge, the sound of the explosion reverberating through the hull like the beat of a giant drum. The force of the blast knocked Gallagher and Skarpö off their feet. Another sound followed, a deep roar like a waterfall as the sea poured into the ruptured hull. They were still prone on the deck when another blast, much louder and closer to hand, stunning in its force, filled the compartment with flames and smoke, knocking the stacks of wooden crates apart and filling the air with flying splinters.

By the time Gallagher crawled across the deck to Chalfont's body the ship had already begun to list to starboard, the deck tilting beneath them. Skarpö sat up groggily, shaking his head and wiping blood from a gash on his cheek. 'What the hell was that?'

'The first was a torpedo,' Gallagher said, going through Chalfont's pockets. He found a waterproof wallet and stuffed it inside his own coat. His head was still ringing from the explosions. Smoke drifted through the cargo space and he could hear the crackle of fire. The crates of cargo were shifting as the deck began to tilt.

'The second, I suspect, was Schurz's bomb, set off by the

356

force of the blast. If we list any further to starboard, more water is going to come pouring in through the hole the bomb made. And we're five decks below the lifeboats.'

Even as he finished speaking the ship gave a sudden lurch, the angle of her deck increasing sharply. Water thundered into the compartment, accompanied by a cloud of steam. Bizarrely, the steam smelled like freshly cut grass. '*Christ!*' Gallagher shouted. '*Gas!* Cover your face and get out of here, *now!*'

'Don't leave me!' Schurz screamed. 'Don't leave me here!'

The smell of gas increased. The stacks of wooden crates were falling like dominos now, splitting open and dropping their cargo into the water that surged towards them. Holding one sleeve over his mouth, Gallagher staggered to his feet and grabbed Schurz by one arm; Skarpö took the other, and together they dragged the wounded man towards the ladder and up it, the vengeful sea already washing at their feet. Slamming the hatch shut, they dragged Schurz through the door and Gallagher spun the wheel to close it. 'Will that door keep the sea out?' Skarpö asked.

'No.' Gallagher coughed, feeling the pain in his chest. Water was already leaking under the door. The angle of the deck had become so acute that standing upright was difficult. Something went *whump*, the bulkheads around them vibrating with pressure, and the lights flickered and dimmed. 'Boiler explosion,' Gallagher said, coughing again. 'She's going fast.'

Water was pouring in around the door now. 'Get me out of here,' Schurz moaned. 'For the love of God, find me a doctor.'

'We'll never get out if we have to drag this carrion with us,' Skarpö said.

'We can't leave him to drown,' said Gallagher.

'There's an easy answer to that.' Skarpö drew his revolver and rested the barrel on Schurz's forehead. Schurz screamed with fear, once, and Skarpö pulled the trigger.

Torpedo hit + 2 minutes

Up in the saloon the deck began to tilt sharply, people stumbling and falling. To port the windows lifted towards the sky; to starboard they inclined towards the deadly blue water below. 'The lifeboats!' Ripley shouted. 'Everyone into the lifeboats! Come on!'

Overhead, *Lusitania*'s siren was blaring the signal to abandon ship. Hamilton ran out on deck, shouting orders to his stewards to hand out lifejackets. Two of the ship's deck officers were there too, ordering the crew to make the boats ready; passengers were already scrambling into some of them. Other sailors were pulling the collapsible boats out of their lockers and making them ready to launch.

Ripley shouldered his way towards the nearest boat. 'I say,' someone said. 'Women and children first, old boy.'

'Damn that! There's plenty of room for everyone.' Without waiting to put on a lifejacket, Ripley climbed into the nearest boat and sat down on a wooden bench. Others followed. Dolly Markland forced her way through the crowd and climbed in too, taking a place not far from Ripley. The shock of the explosion had barely affected her; nothing could pierce the numb armour of her mind. Her world had shrunk to the point where she could only think about one thing, the knife still resting in her reticule.

The officers shouted orders. Sailors sprang to the davits, winching the boat out over the rail until it dangled above the water, suspended by ropes. 'Lower away!' someone shouted, and the boat lurched, the bow suddenly pointing down. A woman screamed; people grabbed at the benches and thwarts for support. 'For Christ's sake!' Ripley yelled. 'What's going on?'

'The falls have jammed.' The rope attached to the stern of the boat had caught in the crank and was refusing to turn. Men laboured at the crank, struggling to clear the shreds of hemp caught in the wheel, and then the rope parted and the boat upended, spilling its screaming human cargo into the sea eighty feet below. Some died when they hit the water. Some, the sensible few who had put on lifejackets before they boarded, managed to stay afloat. The remainder, floundering in the water, had just enough time to see *Lusitania*'s hull surging past them before they began to drown.

TORPEDO HIT + 5 MINUTES

THE SHIP WAS still moving, turning away to port as Captain Turner attempted to reach the Irish shore and put her aground before she sank. Her speed was falling away as water flooded through the engine compartment and snuffed out her boilers one by one. Behind her in the water was a trail of debris and struggling people screaming and crying out for help. Only a few lifeboats had been launched successfully; more had overturned in their davits or capsized in the water. People still milled around on the steeply sloping deck, grasping at the railings for support, calling out for friends or loved ones.

On the port side of the boat deck, Franklin forced his way through the crowd and confronted one of the young deck officers. 'Launch this lifeboat at once,' he demanded, pointing to a boat crowded with people, still resting in its davits.

'Sir, we can't do it. The list is too severe. The ropes are jamming in the davits.'

'Then cut the ropes. We'll hoist the boat out manually. Go on, man, do it now! People are in danger here!'

The officer stared at him. 'Sir, that boat weighs several tons, never mind the people in it! We can't possibly shift it!'

It was always the same; puny minds who could not see what was possible, who lacked the intellect and will to shape events and move forward. When it happened, there was only one thing to do. 'Get out of the way!' Franklin snapped. 'I'm taking charge here. You men,' he said, turning to the sailors at the davits, 'cut those ropes. Do it now!'

'No!' the officer shouted. 'For Christ's sake!'

Franklin turned on him. 'You are no longer in command! I give the orders now. Cut the ropes! It's the only chance we have of saving this boat!'

The sailors hesitated. 'I am your commander now,' Franklin told them. 'Serve me faithfully and I will reward you for good service.' He gestured towards the passengers in the boat, watching in fearful fascination. One of them was the young woman whom he had talked to in the saloon, the one he had considered as a replacement for the worthless Billie Dolan. He smiled at her, telling her with his eyes that she would be safe and that she would owe her life to him.

He took a step forward until he was standing just in front of the boat. 'Now, cut the ropes,' he said.

'No!' the officer shouted, but it was too late. Released from its davits, the boat hit the deck and began to slide down the sloping planks, picking up speed. Everyone screamed. Franklin stood still, watching the boat come towards him in stunned disbelief. This was not supposed to happen; this couldn't be happening. His mouth opened in a shout of anger, just before the boat ran over the top of him and crashed its way forward, skidding on the polished teak deckboards and knocking people aside, leaving a long red smear across the deck where Franklin had been.

Torpedo hit + 8 minutes

The foyer of the saloon deck was jammed with frightened people trying to force their way upstairs. Many of the passengers had been at lunch when the torpedo struck and now hundreds of people were trying to climb up from the dining room to the deck. Gallagher could hear the sea roaring through the ship, the bow dragging down even as she continued to heel over to starboard. People were getting into the lifts and he shouted at them to stop, but it was too late.

The lifts began to rise, and went perhaps half a deck before the power went out. The water must have reached the dynamo. The foyer was plunged into gloom, the only light coming from the side windows and the skylight four decks above. 'Into the dining room!' Gallagher shouted. He coughed again, the gas still burning in his chest. 'Follow me, come on!'

The people in the lifts were shouting for help, but it was too late; with the power out, there was no way of bringing the lifts back down or opening the doors. Save what you can, Gallagher thought. He ran into the dining room, scrambling up the sloping deck through a litter of broken china and glass and cutlery, slipping on spilled food, clutching at tables and chairs for support; thankfully, these were bolted to the floor and could not move. Other people followed; he could hear Skarpö behind him, urging them on.

Pushing open the doors into the galley he had to dodge a

litter of pots and pans that came surging out, some of them still hot and sizzling. Ovens had fallen open, spilling roasts out onto the floor; firebox doors had opened too and the floor was dangerous with glowing coals. The kitchen staff were fleeing through the pantries and up the stairs leading to the shelter deck. Maurice the maître d' was there, making sure his staff got away, and Gallagher shouted at him to guide the passengers. Some of the stewards turned back to help. Gallagher himself stood braced in the kitchen doorway, grabbing men and women by the arms and pulling them through, heaving them up the sloping deck through the kitchen towards safety. From below he could hear the thunder of water, the screech of rending bulkheads, the thump of another boiler exploding.

Water roared into the foyer. The cries of help from the lifts were cut off abruptly. The final passengers came half running, half crawling up the deck, Skarpö last of all. 'The rest have got away up the stairs. I reckon most of the bow is underwater by now.'

Gallagher coughed, feeling the gas still in his lungs. 'Nothing more we can do here,' he said. 'Let's go.'

Torpedo hit + 9 minutes

The shock of hitting the sea had knocked the air out of Dolly Markland's lungs. Her mouth and nose filled with water, and she thought she was going to drown. Desperate instinct drove her to fight back and she broke surface, coughing, gagging and spitting out water, looking wildly around for something to cling to. She was vaguely aware of other people struggling in the water around her, and then something bumped into her; one of the lifeboat's wooden benches, which had fallen out when the boat overturned in the davits.

The water was bitterly cold, biting into her bones. She clutched at the bench, gasping and hauling herself up onto it and looking around. *Lusitania* had come to a halt perhaps a quarter of a mile away, her bow completely submerged and her stern lifted so far that her bronze propellers were out of the water, gleaming in the sunlight. Smoke and steam belched from her funnels. A couple of lifeboats were moving through the wreckage, pulling people from the water. She kicked out, cursing at the skirts that tangled around her legs, pushing the bench towards the nearest lifeboat.

People floated in the water beside her, some not moving, others struggling to swim. A hand clutched at the bench, a man struggling to pull himself onto it. She screamed at him, hitting him back-handed to drive him away, but he clung on. She hit him again and this time he raised his head. She saw the drooping waxed moustache, the goatee beard dripping with seawater, and with a sudden thrill she knew who it was. She fumbled underwater with the catch of her reticule. This was it. Her moment had arrived.

It took Ripley a moment to recognize her. 'You,' he said, his voice half-strangled. 'God damn it. Why are you still alive?'

'So I can kill you,' Dolly Markland said harshly, tearing open her reticule. Pulling out the knife, she raised it over her head, lunging across the bench and stabbing at his face. The long, tapering point just missed Ripley's eye and cut a bloody furrow across his face from eye socket to ear. Ripley shouted with pain, grabbing at her arm and missing. She raised her arm to strike again and he punched her hard in the face, knocking her back off the bench into the water. She had just time to draw breath before the water closed over her head and then she lunged forward again, stabbing underwater at Ripley's legs and groin. He shouted again as the knife bit deep into his thigh, and reached underwater and grabbed Dolly's hair, wrapping it around his hands and pulling her down, keeping her under. He saw the trail of bubbles as the air escaped her lungs but she kept on stabbing and when he looked down he saw a dark cloud in the water around him. Christ, he thought, that's blood. The bitch has nicked an artery.

He tried to pull himself up onto the bench, but he could not cling on. The cloud of blood spread, surrounding his body. The cries of others in the water began to grow faint. The sun darkened; he could still see *Lusitania*, her stern lifting higher in the air, but her outline was growing dim. He made one last desperate attempt to cling onto the bench, but his strength failed him and he slipped back into the water. He was aware that Dolly had resurfaced and was watching him, but there was nothing he could do about it. Floating on his back, he struggled to draw breath, but the water closed over his head.

Spitting out bloody seawater, Dolly Markland dropped her knife and clutched at the bench again. The icy water still gnawed at her, sapping her strength. Adrenaline had given her the power to kill Ripley, but now that was fading. She clung desperately to the bench, her nails digging into the wet wood as it bobbed on the water, and then a larger wave slapped her in the face and knocked her backwards. She thrashed around desperately, trying to reach the bench again, but all her hands found was Ripley's body floating in the water. After a while there seemed no point in trying. She lay still, letting the sea take her, and her hair fanned out in the water around her like a shroud.

Torpedo hit + 11 minutes

THE HULL SHUDDERED from stem to stern, steel plates groaning with strain. 'Jesus,' Skarpö said sharply. 'Another torpedo?'

'At a guess, the bow hitting the seabed,' Gallagher said. He coughed. 'The water here is only about fifty fathoms.' *Lusitania* was going down, even more quickly than he had thought she would; the torpedo hit plus the hole from Schurz's bomb had opened her wide to the sea, and boiler explosions had probably caused more rents. Thousands of tons of seawater were dragging her inexorably to the bottom.

They were on the shelter deck, just outside the hospital. Some of the cooks and stewards were outside, ushering the last of the frightened passengers up the outside ladders towards the boat deck. Gallagher coughed again and turned to Skarpö. 'Go after them. Save yourself.'

'Where are you going?'

'There's something I have to do.' Kreutzer was imprisoned almost directly above, and he owed it to Kreutzer to try to save his life. The ship was heeling over more sharply than ever; outside, the starboard rail was underwater and Skarpö had to scramble up a near vertical deck to reach the port side and climb towards safety. Behind Gallagher was the women's hospital. He stared at it for a moment, thinking of Billie Dolan lying where Roxanne's body had once lain, and then the water came for him, surging in a wall of hideous debris, broken furniture, coats, books, children's toys, sucking around his knees as he climbed after Skarpö.

Reaching the promenade deck, he stumbled aft along the steeply canted deck towards the after end of the deckhouse. There was a pantry here, next to the barbershop; to his horror, the shop was already half underwater. A short passageway led to Kreutzer's cabin. Stumbling inside, Gallagher found the deck running with sewage from water closets backing up as the sea flooded the pipes. It was fifty feet to Kreutzer's cabin. There was no sign of the sentry; understandably, he had decided to save himself. He could hear Kreutzer banging on the door, calling for help, and he ran crabwise towards the cabin with one foot on the deck and one on the canted bulkhead, but halfway there the sea came rolling aft like a cold wall, sweeping him up and throwing him back out onto the deck.

Torpedo hit + 12 minutes

KREUTZER STOPPED POUNDING on the door. The guard was gone; there was no one to hear him. He looked slowly around the room. This is where my life ends, he thought. He wondered if it had been like this for his friends who died on the *Scharnhorst*. Had they too been trapped below decks, hemmed in with no choice but to let the water rise around them?

The roar of the onrushing sea reverberated in the hull. He sat down on the edge of the angled bed, perching on the edge of the frame, and opened his wallet and took out the faded paper heart. Jeni would never know how he died; would probably never even know for certain that he was dead. Water began pouring in under the door, flooding the room. He closed his eyes and saw again that morning in the fields below the mountains, heard the cowbells and smelled the flowers in the warm, mild sun. He heard his friends laughing and dancing, and saw Jeni's face, her hands touching his, pressing the little heart to his lips, and just before he died he felt her kiss soft as a rose petal on his cheek.

TORPEDO HIT + 15 MINUTES

THE BIG SHIP was listing at nearly ninety degrees now, her deck vertical to the water, and only the stern portion was visible. Around and behind her lay a horrifying flotsam of debris, swamped and overturned lifeboats, empty lifejackets, deck furniture, bodies of men and women, some struggling, others already floating face down. There were only a few minutes left until *Lusitania* disappeared. Gallagher took off his boots and coat, throwing them away; the Webley was still in his coat pocket, but it was of no use to him now.

Sliding down the deck into the water, he began to swim away from the ship. Almost immediately the cold began to bite into his bones. He could hear the desperate cries of people in the water and wondered how many of them, even those with lifejackets, could survive long in this cold. Something else was in the water around him, and he heard squeaks of fear and realized it was rats, swimming and struggling desperately to keep their pink noses out of the water, eyes bright with terror.

A strong current rushed around Gallagher, pulling him and the rats back towards the ship. Looking over his shoulder, he saw what had happened; the rim of one of the huge funnels had dipped beneath the water and the sea was pouring into it, dragging him towards it. The rats sensed what was happening and their squeals of fear increased. Desperately, Gallagher lunged through the water, but the current was too strong and it sucked him under. He could hear the water pounding in his ears as it roared into the ship and then he was inside the funnel, being pulled down and down, a drowning rat hitting him in the face before it whirled away, daylight vanishing to a small point above him as he was dragged into the heart of the ship. His lungs were burning again, his mouth and nose full of water, and he started to choke. In his oxygen-starved brain a hallucination formed, Roxanne reciting, in a voice dark with death:

> *Who has not held a skeleton in his arms?*
> *Who has not fed upon things from the tomb?*

From below, another deep *whump* of a boiler exploding, and then a wave of black water washed upwards, flinging him back up the funnel and spitting him out into the sea. Shocked and winded, he could only tread water for a moment, wiping the water and liquid tar from his eyes and nose and trying to breathe.

When he opened his eyes he could see sunlight. Sucking air into his starved, burned lungs, he turned and began to swim. Bodies bumped around him like floating logs, most of them face down now but even so he recognized some; one was Dr Whiting. He was cold and exhausted, and he knew the Irish coast and safety were miles away. After a while, he stopped swimming and closed his eyes.

Torpedo hit + 18 minutes

'There she goes,' Hamilton said softly. 'Farewell, Lucy.'

Around him in the lifeboat, the men rested on their oars and they and the passengers, some shivering and wet, watched in fearful fascination as *Lusitania*'s stern slid under the water. The sea boiled for a few moments as the last air escaped from the hull, and then slowly grew calm. Hamilton drew the back of his sleeve across his eyes. He was not alone; many of the passengers were weeping and Joe the barber, manning the stroke oar, had tears on his face.

Hamilton put his hand to the tiller, nodding to the oarsmen. 'All right, lads. There might still be a few out there.'

Slowly they rowed through the field of wreckage and bodies, looking for anyone who was still alive. A few other lifeboats moved in the middle distance, on the same errand. Of the twenty-two lifeboats the ship carried, only six had been launched.

Overhead, the sun blazed down, mocking them with its brightness. Hamilton thought briefly about the U-boat that had fired the torpedo, and wondered where it was now. Some of the passengers said they had seen the submarine rise to the surface, its crew watching for a few moments while the ship sank, and then it had dived again.

López, on watch in the bow, pointed suddenly. 'There is one. I saw him moving.'

Joe was sceptical. 'No lifejacket. He'll be gone by now.'

'I tell you, I saw him moving,' López insisted.

Hamilton turned the tiller. A moment later the boat closed in on the body, and Corazón López leaned over the gunwale and pulled the man's head back. Despite the black stains on his clothing and skin, she recognized him. Her breath hissed in shock. 'It is Señor Gallagher!'

'Bring him inboard,' said Hamilton. Strong hands pulled the body from the sea and laid it across the thwarts. Fascinated, frightened faces looked down. 'Place him on his side,' Corazón said. 'Leave this to me, I know what I am doing.'

They turned the body. With surprising strength, her breath wheezing a little, she pressed the water out of his chest and throat. After a moment, Gallagher coughed and his eyes fluttered open. He looked up at the woman kneeling over him, silhouetted against the sun, and slowly mustered the strength to speak.

'Whoever my guardian angel is, I didn't expect it to be you,' he said.

She smiled a little, her face colourless and her voice gasping with the effort she had just expended. 'In tragedy, there are no sides. We do what we can, to help each other survive.'

Gallagher said nothing more. All was silent apart from the splash of oars and creak of oarlocks. The lifeboat continued her slow, patient search, the May sun beating down, and all around them the bodies spread out like a carpet, locked in their last embrace against the cold, unforgiving bosom of the sea.

An hour later, the first rescue boats began to arrive.

27

'Good to see you again,' said Colonel Skarpö. 'I only just heard you were still alive. Is that coffee?'

They were in the dining room of the Queen's Hotel in Queenstown. Gallagher, clad in dry clothes and wrapped in a thick wool blanket, was sitting at a table near the fire. He gestured to the silent waiter standing at one end of the room and pointed to the coffee pot. 'How did you get away?' he asked.

'We tried to launch one of those collapsible lifeboats. It collapsed as soon as we got it into the water, so I guessed it lived up to its name. We managed to cling on until a fishing trawler picked us up a couple of hours later. At least, most of us did.' The coffee arrived and Skarpö stirred sugar into it. 'What about you? You look like hell.'

'I feel like Jonah, ejected from the belly of the whale,' Gallagher said. He did not elaborate. He did not particularly want to talk to Skarpö, but it was clear that Skarpö wanted to talk to him, and it was not hard to guess what about.

The dining room door opened and Hamilton came in, his broad face full of relief. 'Good to see you up and about, Pat. I have to say, when we dragged you aboard, I didn't give much for your chances.'

'The devil looks after his own,' said Skarpö.

Gallagher ignored him. 'How bad is it, Hammy?'

'About as bad as it can be,' Hamilton said quietly, and his eyes reflected the horrors he had seen that day. 'We think about seven hundred survived, passengers and crew. We haven't counted everyone yet, of course. They're scattered all over the place, hospitals, hotels, private houses. We won't know the true figure until tomorrow.'

There was a long silence. Gallagher stared at the table, feeling sick. 'That means over a thousand dead,' he said. 'Eleven hundred, maybe twelve hundred. Jesus Christ, Hammy.'

'I know,' the purser said. 'It's the *Titanic* all over again.'

The silence resumed. 'Did Maurice make it?' Gallagher asked finally.

'I don't know. Like I said, I haven't seen a full list of survivors, but . . .'

'The captain?'

'He climbed up on top of the wheelhouse, planning to stay aboard, but a wave washed him off. He's over on Haulbowline, making his report to the naval commandant. Poor bastard. The press will blame him for the disaster, of course. They always pick on the captain.'

'What about Franklin? Or Ripley, or Mrs Markland?'

'Franklin was killed in an accident on board ship. The bodies of the other two were recovered from the water.' Hamilton looked quietly at Gallagher. 'What happened, Pat? We heard two explosions. The torpedo, and another.'

'It was a bomb,' Gallagher said. 'Believe it or not, they weren't trying to sink the ship, although in the end the damage they did made her sink a hell of a lot faster.'

'They? You mean Schurz, or Chalfont?'

'Both, as it turns out. They were both working for Rintelen. Kreutzer was a sacrifice, made to cover their tracks.'

He had not been able to save Kreutzer and that hurt, perhaps more than anything else. He thought about the paper heart. 'I don't understand,' Skarpö said. 'If they didn't intend to sink the ship, why the torpedo?'

'I have two theories,' Gallagher said, 'either of which could be true. The first is that Rintelen came up with this bomb plot to expose the transport of contraband munitions and embarrass the British government, but his superiors overruled him and decided to sink the ship instead. The second is that Rintelen's plot was approved, but some glory-hungry U-boat captain decided to ignore his orders, or never received them in the first place. He saw a fat target and pulled the trigger.'

'Unless we find the U-boat captain, we'll never know,' said Skarpö.

'No. Hammy, do you know where the Lópezes are?'

'They're here at the hotel.'

'Would you ask them to attend on me, please? Make it clear it is a request, not an order. I would go and see them, but I'm not sure I can walk yet.'

Despite the fire and the blankets he was shivering, weak as a kitten. Skarpö had been in the water longer than himself and seemed unharmed. *I must not be as strong as I think I am*, Gallagher thought tiredly.

Hamilton ushered the Lópezes into the room a few moments later. Both were in dressing gowns and looked as exhausted as himself. 'Please, sit down,' Gallagher said. 'My apologies for disturbing you. I hope we did not wake you.'

'It will be a long time before I am able to sleep,' López said bleakly.

'I have two things to say,' Gallagher said. 'First, I understand it was you, señor, who saw my body in the sea, and of course it was you, señora, who pumped the water out of me. I would like to express my thanks to you both.'

López bowed his head. 'I would do the same for anyone,' said his wife. 'As I said, in tragedy, we are united.'

'And yet, you caused the tragedy,' Gallagher said.

The couple sat silent. 'Soon after we landed,' Gallagher said, 'I sent a message to the commandant on Haulbowline, asking if any U-boat warnings had been transmitted. In fact, a U-boat was spotted and a warning was sent out to all shipping. We never received that warning, because you had cut the power to the Marconi room.'

There was a long moment of silence, broken only by the ticking of a clock in the hall outside. 'Twelve hundred people died this afternoon,' Gallagher said. 'Men, women, children. Don't their deaths weigh on your conscience?'

'Of course they do,' exclaimed López. 'Do you not think we are aware of this? Do you not know this is why I cannot sleep? Every time I close my eyes, I see the corpses floating in the water and I know I am responsible for their deaths. That knowledge will never leave me.'

'But why did they have to die, Señor Gallagher?' demanded Corazón. 'Why was that U-boat there in the first place? We burned through the wires, but we did not start the war. We are not responsible for the greed and violence of the capitalist empires who began this conflict for their own selfish ends. Twelve hundred died today, you say. Hundreds of thousands have died already; twenty thousand at Neuve-Chapelle alone. Many more will die before all is done. Are we responsible for them? No, señor. The lords and masters in London and Berlin; *they* are the ones who should examine their consciences.'

'Very eloquent,' Gallagher said. 'But I doubt if it will stand up as a defence in court.'

Silence fell again. 'You are Spanish,' Skarpö said. 'You are neutral. Why get involved?'

'No one is neutral,' said Corazón. 'This war is part of the greater dialectic, the struggle between capital and labour. We are all part of that conflict, on one side or another. There are no bystanders now.'

'You knew the U-boats were waiting,' Gallagher said.

'Of course. It was obvious. We knew too that the Germans had made a grave blunder. By sinking this ship and killing neutral Americans, they would anger public opinion in America and put pressure on the American government to intervene.'

'We thought we were helping to bring the war to a swift conclusion,' López said. 'At the moment, all is stalemate. The conflict could grind on for years. But if America intervenes, the might of her industry and her vast reserves of manpower will turn the tide. The war could be over in a few months. Thousands of lives would be saved, perhaps millions.'

'And when the war is over and the working people of the world are no longer fighting each other, we can unite them,' said his wife. 'Worldwide revolution will bring the new age, and hope for humanity.'

'And *Lusitania* was the sacrifice,' Hamilton said. There was no anger in his voice, only a kind of weary sorrow.

'Yes,' said Corazón López. '*Lusitania* was the sacrifice.'

Silence fell again. 'What will happen now?' asked López.

'That rather depends on you,' said Gallagher.

They looked at him. 'What exactly do you mean?' asked Corazón, a little waspishly.

'I need to make a report to my superiors in London, but there may be some delay in getting the report through. I doubt if London will read it until the day after tomorrow, perhaps even longer. That gives you time to get beyond the reach of

British law, and continue your journey to Spain. I advise you to take full advantage of the delay.'

They stared at him. 'You will not hinder us?' López asked.

'No.'

López nodded slowly. 'You are more generous than we deserve, I think.' His wife compressed her lips, but said nothing. López watched Gallagher for a moment. 'Who are you, really?' he asked.

'You know I can't tell you that,' Gallagher said.

The couple rose to their feet and departed in silence. Skarpö looked incredulous. 'That's it? You're not going to arrest them?'

'I wasn't exactly truthful,' Gallagher said. 'A submarine warning was sent out, but it contained a report of activity off Cape Clear, which we had already passed. Therefore, they were not directly responsible for the sinking.'

'They committed an act of sabotage in time of war,' Skarpö said. 'That alone is enough to hang them.'

'But if we kill López, we also kill his music. As for his wife; well, you are a hard man, colonel. But could you bring yourself to hang an elderly woman with a weak heart, who will probably die soon anyway?'

'General Villa would,' said Skarpö. 'But then, I am increasingly glad I am no longer in General Villa's service. Your point is taken.'

Hamilton cleared his throat. 'There is also another problem,' he said.

'Yes. The reasoning the Lópezes used, that sinking the *Lusitania* might drag America into the war, is also popular in some quarters of our own government, especially the navy. The First Lord of the Admiralty is known to have expressed a very similar view, as have several other politicians. So, prosecuting the

Lópezes for something that the government secretly hoped would happen might be tricky, to say the least. My superiors will agree, I think.'

Hamilton looked at his hands for a moment. 'Eight years I served on Big Lucy,' he said softly. 'Two hundred and two voyages she made, and I was there for all but a few of them. She was my home, and her crew and passengers were my family. Now, they're all gone . . . I'm starting to think the old girl might be right. We're all bloody pawns, being sacrificed.'

'As an officer in the secret service, I shall pretend I didn't hear that,' Gallagher said tiredly. 'Will you do me a favour, Hammy? Do what you can to smooth the path for them. Get them as far away from Britain as soon as possible.'

Hamilton nodded. 'I'll contact the port office in the morning. Leave it with me.'

He departed. Gallagher looked at Skarpö. 'Was there something you wanted, colonel?'

'I thought we might need to clear the air,' Skarpö said.

'Very well, if you insist. My orders were to bring Chalfont back to Britain, alive for further questioning. It would have been very useful also to interrogate Schurz. Thanks to you, that is no longer possible.'

'Schurz was holding us back. If we had tried to bring him with us, we would all be dead. I gave him a merciful way out. As for Chalfont, I shot him to save your life.'

'He wouldn't have shot me,' Gallagher said.

'He was about to squeeze the trigger.'

'He was. But he was also out of ammunition. He had used five rounds already, two to kill the guard and break out of his cabin, one to shoot the sentry outside the door, and two to kill Major Arango.'

'Revolvers have six shots.'

377

'Did you not notice the gun? It was a Colt Single Action Army, the kind cowboys wear. Gangsters like them too, because they're plentiful and cheap. They also don't have safety catches, so you can't leave a round in the chamber under the hammer. They're never loaded with more than five shots.'

'He also had Juan Arango's gun.'

'Yes, in his coat pocket. I moved closer so I could knock him down and disarm him before he could use it.'

'All right,' Skarpö said after a moment.

'In fairness to you, Chalfont had also killed your comrade. I can understand the need for revenge. It would have been better, however, to keep him alive so he could face justice for his crimes.'

'That isn't why I shot Chalfont,' Skarpö said. 'But, you are right. I killed two men.'

Reaching inside his coat, he pulled out the Smith & Wesson and laid it, newly oiled and gleaming, on the white tablecloth in front of Gallagher. 'I am in your hands,' he said.

Gallagher watched him thoughtfully. 'Suppose I don't arrest you,' he said. 'What would you do then? Where would you go?'

'As it happens, I've been giving this some thought. I spoke to one of your navy officers after we came ashore, and he gave me a letter of introduction to the general officer commanding in Cork. I'm a pretty fine gunner, when I have shells that actually explode, and if they give me a battery to command in France, I reckon I could make a difference.'

'Don't tell me. You're a convert to our noble cause. You want to avenge the Belgian babies.'

'I'm more pragmatic than that, I hope. Like I told you, I have fought in twelve wars and was on the losing side in all of them.'

'And you think the thirteenth will be different?'

Skarpö smiled a little. 'Lucky for some,' he said. 'To answer the question, yes, I think you will win and I'd like to know how it feels to be on the winning side. And maybe too, I'd like to pay them back for all those who died today. But like I said, it's up to you. I made a mess of your mission, and now you'll never get the information you need about Rintelen and his spy ring. I am at fault, and I will take my punishment.'

Slowly, Gallagher lifted his hand. His limbs still felt like they were made of ice, but he summoned the strength to push the revolver back across the table to Skarpö. 'You are remarkably quick to change allegiances,' he said.

'I give you my word on this one,' Skarpö said. 'If I join up with your army, I will see this through to the end.'

'And Major Arango? He died for nothing?'

'Yes, as it turned out. I liked Juan, he was a good soldier, but he was too innocent for the games we play. I'll see word gets back to General Villa that his nephew died on the *Lusitania*. He doesn't need to know the rest.'

Skarpö holstered the gun and rose to his feet. 'I said that we'd make a good partnership. I meant it. If I get a post, come and join me.'

Gallagher gestured towards the door. 'Go,' he said.

Skarpö smiled and walked out of the room, closing the door gently behind him. After a moment Gallagher reached into his pocket and pulled out the canvas wallet he had taken from Chalfont. The waterproofing had held good and the papers inside were intact. He unfolded them and smoothed them out. Most were in code; he didn't recognize the sequences but the service could doubtless decode them. The last sheet was a letter in plain language, written on headed Board of Admiralty paper.

To the director of the secret service,

Know that the bearer of this letter is protected, and is acting upon my full authority. You are charged to give him whatever aid and assistance is required. This entire matter is to be considered most secret, and the bearer has been instructed to show this letter only to you. You may not disclose any details even to your closest subordinates and all written records are to be destroyed immediately, including this letter. The outcome of the war and the fate of nations are at stake.

There was no signature, but Gallagher recognized the handwriting. He had seen it before; it belonged to a holder of high office in the British government.

We're all bloody pawns, Hamilton had said. He sat for a while, holding the letter and staring into the rustling flames, watching the patterns of light dance and weave together. Like Hamilton, he had lost something that day. *Lusitania* had been his connection to the past, his connection to Roxanne, and now that the ship was gone he felt her loss more keenly and painfully than ever.

No, he thought quietly. My loss is nothing compared to the twelve hundred tragedies today. He would never know, now, where Dowrich had intended to sell the gas shells, or why Schurz believed that science was above morality, or how Dolly Markland had died. Nor did it greatly matter. None of these things were important now, not in the face of the greater tragedy that had engulfed them all.

He thought of Kreutzer, and felt a flash of pain. I failed him too, he thought, just as I failed all the others. Twelve hundred souls . . . and yet I feel his loss more keenly than the others. One day I must go to Thüringen, and find a girl called Jeni.

He looked down at the letter in his hand. Chalfont knew – he must have known – that he was pulling the trigger on an empty chamber, just as he must have known that Gallagher would jump him before he could draw his other gun. That meant he was expecting to be arrested and taken into custody, only he had not reckoned on Skarpö's speed with a gun . . . Presumably, once he had been taken ashore he would have demanded to speak to C, the head of the secret service, and when C arrived Chalfont would have handed over the letter and walked away a free man. But why had he claimed to be a German agent in the first place? Was he working for both sides? What game had he really been playing?

One person knew the answers to these questions; the man who had written the letter. One day I shall confront him, Gallagher thought, and demand the truth. The twelve hundred who had died on *Lusitania* deserved that much, at least.

One day, yes. One day when I am strong again.

What are you frightened of? he had once asked Roxanne, and she had replied, *Life*.

> *Like a ship waking in the morning wind*
> *My dreaming soul sets sail for a distant sky . . .*

Historical Note

WHEN THE LINER RMS *Lusitania* was launched in 1906, she was the largest and most luxurious ship afloat. Four steam turbines powered by twenty-five boilers meant she could reach speeds of over 26 knots, far faster than most warships, and for a time she held the coveted Blue Riband award for the fastest Atlantic crossing. Her first-class cabins and public spaces, designed by some of the leading architects and designers of the day, were the last word in comfort and convenience. Even after the launch of larger ships such as the ill-fated *Titanic*, which sank in 1912, *Lusitania* remained one of the most popular and best-known of the transatlantic liners.

Unknown to most people, *Lusitania* had been built to specifications laid down by the Board of Admiralty, which also helped fund the construction cost and paid the owners, Cunard Lines, an operating subsidy. In return, in time of war the Admiralty would requisition the ship and turn it into an armed merchant cruiser, protecting British shipping.

When war with Germany broke out in 1914, the Admiralty changed their minds. *Lusitania* continued in service as a liner, carrying passengers to and from the United States (which was still neutral at this point). Some of her third-class passenger cabins were converted to cargo space so she could transport badly needed supplies to Britain. The German government gave warning that the ship would be sunk if she sailed into the 'war zone' around the British Isles. In private, the British authorities had mixed feelings, knowing that *Lusitania*'s passengers were at risk, but aware too that if she sank and American passengers were killed, this might be enough to drag the United States into the war against Germany.

Arriving off the south-east coast of Ireland on 7 May 1915, *Lusitania*'s captain expected to be met by a Royal Navy escort, the cruiser HMS *Juno*. But there was no sign of the cruiser; a few hours earlier, the Admiralty had ordered her back to port. Radio signals warning of U-boat activity in the area also failed to reach *Lusitania*. A few hours later, she was hit by a single torpedo from the submarine *U-20* and sank in eighteen minutes with terrible loss of life. Passengers reported hearing a second, more violent explosion shortly after the torpedo struck; the captain of the *U-20*, watching through his periscope, also noted the second explosion. No satisfactory explanation of the cause of this explosion has been found.

IN EARLY 1915, the British army on the Western Front suffered from a severe shortage of artillery shells. Until the establishment of the Ministry of Munitions later that year, the British were forced to rely on imports of shells from the USA. The Germans were aware of this and their chief agent in New York, Captain Franz von Rintelen of German naval intelligence, attempted to intercept shipments of American shells. Sometimes he was successful.

German agents also tried to persuade the government of Mexico to declare war on the USA, offering money and promises of support. They reasoned that if America was dragged into a war with its southern neighbour, the conflict would consume munitions and other supplies that might otherwise have gone to the Western Front. This was not an unrealistic hope; relations between the USA and Mexico were already poor, and American troops had briefly invaded Mexico the previous year. Worried about the rapid rise of German influence in Mexico, the US government now began to support a Mexican rebel army, the Northern Division, led by the charismatic general Pancho Villa.

Early in 1915, Villa's men pushed government forces out of the capital, Mexico City, but popular resistance forced him to withdraw. A few months later, aided by volunteer forces known as the Red Battalions, government troops inflicted a heavy defeat on the Northern Division at the Battle of Celaya. Villa had recently received a consignment of artillery shells from the USA, but during the battle these shells failed to explode. The reason for this failure has never been explained.

Acknowledgements

Thanks first of all to Heather Adams and Mike Bryan, who first saw the potential of this book, and our agent Jon Wood who helped us set the right tone for the story. Jon has been a wonderful source of support throughout the entire process of writing and delivering this book.

We could not have asked for a better team at Pan Macmillan, starting with Alex Saunders whose enthusiasm for the book has been another great source of support. Rebecca Needes oversaw project management, and has been marvellously tolerant of our views on punctuation. Fraser Crichton did a great job of copy-editing, and Lorraine Green was the highly professional and meticulous proofreader. Hemesh Alles came up with an excellent deck plan for the relevant decks of the *Lusitania*, and Kieryn Tyler and James Weston Lewis came up with a visually striking cover which had us excited right from the beginning.

Family and friends have as always been loving and support-ive, especially in the dark final days. Last of all, we want to thank the medical teams and staff at North Devon Hospital, Royal Devon and Exeter Hospital, Holsworthy Community Hospital, North Devon Hospice and, especially, Blake House Surgery. You gave us kindness, compassion and unstinting care right up until the final hours of Marilyn's life, and no praise is too high for you. Thank you.

R. L. GRAHAM is a husband-and-wife team of historians and writers with a broad range of interests in many periods of history, including the belle époque and the tumultuous years leading up to the First World War and the post-war re-ordering of the world. They are very much drawn to the shadowy world of crime, espionage and political intrigue. They are particularly fascinated by historical mysteries: things which have happened but have no apparent explanation. Originally from Canada, they now live in a small village in Devon.

Marilyn Livingstone, one half of R. L. Graham, was diagnosed with pancreatic cancer while this book was being written. She passed away in September 2023.